'I cannot remember when   completely in charge of h   that promising books beco   machinery of their plots or limp gestures at meaningfulness, but Wright tackles his subject with great ease and flair, and his story, within its own clearly defined limits, is almost faultless.' Jake Michie, Sunday Telegraph.

GLOVER WRIGHT

Eighth Day

PAN BOOKS

IN ASSOCIATION WITH MACMILLAN LONDON

First published 1991 by Macmillan London Limited
This edition first published 1992 by Pan Books Limited
Cavaye Place, London SW10 9PG
in association with Macmillan London Limited
1 3 5 7 9 8 6 4 2

© Geoffrey Glover Wright 1991

ISBN 0 330 32398 9

Phototypeset by Intype, London
Printed and bound in Great Britain by
Clays Ltd, St Ives plc

For Karin, with love

ACKNOWLEDGEMENTS

My warm thanks for their time, generous help and advice goes to Jenny Hope, medical correspondent for the *Daily Mail*; George Hollingberry, former chief crime reporter for the *Sun*; Hugh Dykes, member of parliament, Ruth Patterson of the BBC; Nigel Glover-Wright for his usual, ongoing, role; Jenny Lynsey for her particular, specialist, knowledge; Chips and Sally Barber whose delightful, informative yet witty books on Dartmoor, published by Obelisk Publications, should not be missed by anyone planning on visiting the region; Barbara Sowden who was there at the outset and provided much of the essential atmosphere; and most especially, Deryck Laming PhD, DIC, FGS, MIGeol, who 'walked the course, braved the dogs' and returned to give me the benefit of his professional expertise – which within the constraints of the story I've attempted to heed.

... Of dire chimeras and enchanted isles
And rifted rocks whose entrance leads to Hell, –
For such there be ...

John Milton

PROLOGUE

Germany 1945

They moved like shadows and killed in silence, the garrotte and blade their chosen weapons, striking in darkness near the heart of the enemy whilst invasion forces launched their attack on his armoured flanks.

'What'll we find when we get in there?' murmured their young commander, his blackened face close to the civilian beside him.

'Horror,' came the taut reply. 'And knowledge. Years of research. They've had the time, the freedom, and the means.'

'So your ends justify their means?'

'I'm not here to judge – just to appropriate.'

'Will it be worth the human cost?'

A black-clad figure emerged from the darkness and slumped before them, rank vomit on his breath and staining his tunic. 'Secured,' he gasped, turned away and retched drily.

The civilian turned to the commander. 'You signed away your right of protest. Officially, you, your men, I, were never here. What we take out never existed. Neither history nor the British government will ever record any of it. Forget it all.'

'And what about the future?'

'The future is why we're here,' said the civilian and started forward.

Their presence was a feeling thing. Watching them was all mind. She, the part of her which was female, shrieked at her eyes to open, wanting sight, desperate for hope, thrilling at their English voices, raging in the madness which lay in the black reaches between the bright stars of controlled consciousness which were her points of existence.

They were close now, two of them, close enough for their breath to be on her face – thought she felt nothing.

She slipped back into the darkness and they were gone. They now. They present. Not they future. She saw forward as she always did. No. Not always. Since her eyes had closed out the nightmare beyond. However many eternities ago that had been. She saw them older, raging silently, as she did, against the horror. Her hope shrivelled and she slipped deeper into the pit. She felt the torture of one of them, his sickened mind lurching unwillingly onwards, pushing back the edges of insanity. She smelt oil, felt heat building deep in black tunnels taking for ever to blossom yellow, orange, and scarlet into searing pain.

She screamed for him and her eyelids snapped open, two doomed faces confronting her, very close, disgust and horror plain, their eyes wishing her dead. No! she shrieked and clawed at them but her hands, her arms, her body were promises her mind, stranded half-way between madness and immortality, could not keep.

One of the men drew back in horror. 'That's not possible!'

The other moved closer. 'They've made it possible.'

Then she knew.

Saw it all.

What she had been.

What had been done to her.

What was to come. For her and for those like her who would follow.

She screamed with her eyes.

They had left her those.

The nightmare was real.

Kill me, she begged.

ONE

Today

He lay naked, his white body slick with something that was not that morning's dew, curled under low broad leaves like a sleeping animal.

To Eleanor Hale, at first blurred sight, he appeared to be wet polythene tossed into her kitchen garden by some itinerant whom she had, unusually, failed to make welcome at her wicket gate. She put on her spectacles.

Had she not once – too long ago, as she would put it – been something of a war-time heroine at the bloody end of a British Army ambulance, she might have reacted quite differently; naked men, though she had not seen one in the flesh since she'd been widowed years earlier, held no mystery or embarrassment for her, and as now, despite the remote location of her property, no terror at all. She prodded him gently awake with her stick.

He sat up groggily, his pale eyes bewildered.

'You appear to have lost your clothes,' she said, with vowels which left no doubt as to her breeding. She noticed the gel smeared over his body. 'Stag night, I suppose? I'm afraid your bride is going to be livid – you're miles away from the nearest church. Oh dear, your poor feet! Wait there.'

She found an old raincoat in her greenhouse and held it out for him, averting her eyes discreetly as, with strangely uncertain movements, he pulled the coat on.

'My late husband's. Grubby, but it will do for the moment. Aren't you cold?' she enquired, held by the strange translucence of his skin; white and blue-veined, like marble. Or – unforgettable war-time memories reached her

3

– like a corpse. 'It isn't exactly the middle of summer, is it?' she added, suppressing a small involuntary shudder.

'When is it, please?' he asked, his voice faltering and husky.

That's drink, she thought, or exposure. Probably both. 'I think you'd better come along inside. A good breakfast will soon sort out the inner man. Then you'd better get on my telephone and sort out the rest of your life. What do you like?'

'I'm hungry,' he said, following. 'You're not my mother?'

She halted, old fears, old conflicts, stirring again. No, she told herself. *No.* 'I'm afraid not,' she said gently, not turning to face him. 'But I'm sure I can cook you a breakfast that you'll really enjoy. Come along inside.'

They were in the kitchen. She pulled out one of the chairs from beneath her refectory table and moved away.

'We'll start you off with a hot drink. Coffee? Then something cooked? Eggs and bacon with all the extras as my late husband used to say. There isn't a man born who doesn't go for a good cooked breakfast – I mean an Englishman naturally. I'm not sure if a true Englishman would spend the night stark naked in someone's kitchen garden, but you do sound more than a little English to me. I don't suppose you can remember your name? Don't worry, it really doesn't matter. Remembering names is a frightful bore anyway.'

'I must have a name,' he said.

She caught the hint of fear – even panic – in the blue eyes. 'Of course you must. And you do. It simply seems to have got displaced along with your clothes.' She laughed, too gaily. 'After breakfast we'll make enquiries. Why don't I choose a name for you – just for now?' she added quickly, breaking eggs beside the sizzling bacon in the pan.

He looked down at the old coat. 'Choose your husband's name.'

'Rather biblical, I'm afraid. Samuel. Somehow the males in the family always ended up with something cobbled out of the Old Testament.' Her voice dulled. 'My son got saddled with Daniel. I'm Eleanor, by the way. Last of the Hales. Our bunch, anyhow.'

'Daniel,' he repeated.

Morning sun through the window fell across his head and for the first time she saw the long scars under his close-cropped, very fair hair.

She placed his food in front of him then sat down herself, sipping coffee. The raincoat's wide sleeves had fallen back and she recognized hypodermic-needle marks from the anaesthetic and small wounds from the drip-feeds. Not, she knew, the frantic, brutal self-injection of the drug addict. He might be better off if he were, came the thought.

Momentarily, to right her world a little, she played with the idea that he had escaped from the prison. Dartmoor. Which explained the white, near translucent skin. Prison pallor. The gel which covered his body was for the escape: through air-ducts from the prison hospital where he'd been held. Also against the cold. But Dartmoor was too far away. He could not have walked, in the cold, naked, all those miles across the moor? Walked? *Run.* His feet were evidence of his headlong flight. Not from prison. From *them.* They must be hunting him now. Or soon would be. She had to find out for certain.

He set down his cutlery, knife and fork perfectly together, then looked at her. 'Thank you.'

She took a deep breath and rose. 'I'll get you some clothes. Between Daniel's and my husband's there'll be something which will fit. You're lucky I haven't given everything away by now. Should have done really. Morbid. Lucky for you. Now you won't be found in your birthday suit.'

His eyes were still on her but he had retreated behind them.

'Clothes,' she said firmly. 'You wait here. Finish your coffee. I'll draw a hot bath for you – you need it and you'll feel better. I've some ointment for your feet too.'

He might not have heard a word for he followed her upstairs in silence.

She paused for breath. He's ill, he's lost, he's a child seeking security and you're qualified as a psychiatric nurse so sort yourself out and don't get into a blind funk.

'In here,' she said, opening a door to a small box-room

5

converted into a walk-in wardrobe. From a shelf she tugged a thick knitted sweater and a cotton shirt still in laundry Cellophane, then drew down a pair of corduroy trousers from a rail full of men's clothing.

He stood, quite still, facing a khaki military tunic bearing a major's insignia.

'Daniel's,' she said, quietly. 'His number ones. Beautifully tailored. He looked stunning.' The tears were at her eyes, threatening. She drew herself up, furious. 'You must have been army, too?' she asked.

He took the sleeve between his fingers, touched the crown on an epaulette. 'I knew someone.'

'There, you've remembered something. Well done. Now think. Which regiment?'

He ignored her.

She turned to an ancient tallboy in the corner and took new, still packaged, underwear from a drawer. 'I'd buy sets and keep them here just on the off chance he'd get an unexpected weekend leave. Daniel hated packing. The most he'd carry was that bag.' She pointed a thin hand at a weathered brown-leather grip on top of the tallboy; its heavy brass fittings and locks were bright and untarnished. 'Told him he looked like Dr Jekyll in the cinema.' She chuckled at the memory, forgetting for a moment her uncertainty. 'He said he was more Mr Hyde considering the things he had to do in Northern Ireland.' She reached out and touched the grip. ' "What kills us over there", he used to say, "is becoming too weary or too complacent to look over your shoulder every minute of every day." Daniel was never complacent, it wasn't his nature, so I suppose he was simply worn out by all of it. His vigilance slipped and, of course, they had him.' She shook her head in resignation, forcing a sad smile. 'Life goes on – so they say. Actually, it just continues minus the important things with nothing new added to make up for the loss. What *could*, anyway?'

He reached out and squeezed her narrow shoulder.

'Bath,' she said, briskly. 'Or a shower if you prefer, all mod cons here despite being in the middle of nowhere. Come along.'

She left him in the bathroom, then made her way down

to her drawing-room and telephoned the number of the district police station.

'I'd like some information,' she began, addressing the desk sergeant with whom she'd had dealings before – concerning the itinerants she occasionally fed and watered, as she had it. Gypsies, tramps, and thieves, he'd called them when he'd stopped by, unannounced, one morning in a large, brash, shining white police car with the blue light rotating for no good reason whatsoever. She had not as yet forgiven him his bigotry.

She continued, 'My delivery man tells me that he'd heard a rumour of convicts escaping from Dartmoor prison?' The sigh in the earpiece made her fury rise as it had when he had lectured her on her doorstep as though she were some senile geriatric who should have been in a safe rest-home with wall-to-wall care.

'Now, marm,' he started – like other ranks addressing the Queen incorrectly, she thought irritatedly – 'you don't want to go listening to these rumour-mongers. Nothing better to do, I'll be bound, than to try and frighten helpless old ladies with horror stories so that they'll be invited indoors for a nice cup of tea – probably a sandwich as well in your case!'

She fumed silently. 'So you're saying there's no truth in this matter.'

'Not one iota, ma'am. You can rest easy.'

'What about missing persons? Do you have anyone reported as being missing?'

'Now what kind of person would that be?'

'Someone missing from home? Perhaps a hospital? A young man, for instance?'

'Have you been bothered by these so-called travellers in their broken-down old vehicles, Mrs Hale? There's a few around Devon at the moment. If you'd been inside one of their camps, like I have, you'd soon change your opinions – and your habits. I suppose you'd say they're only young so they've got to be given a free rein. I reckon they'd hang themselves with it.' A deep chuckle came down the line.

He even mixes his metaphors, she thought as his patronizing tones continued. 'Would you like me to send a car up to you? Take no time at all to get out there in the big Rover. I'll tell the lads to turn on the old siren – give you a bit of excitement!'

'No, thank you very much. Good morning, Sergeant, and thank you for your assistance.'

She replaced the telephone and sat down.

He was *theirs*.

A sudden thud from above her head caused her to start. Pushing herself quickly out of the armchair she hurried to the bottom of the staircase. 'What are you doing up there?' she demanded.

He came to the top of the stairs, dressed, the pullover knotted around his shoulders, his feet still bare and raw. In his hands he held the leather grip, his face as rigid as his hold on it.

'What are you doing with that?' she snapped. 'Leave it alone. Put it back!'

'Jummy,' he said.

'What?'

His brow was creased with frustration. '*Jummy*? James?'

'McFee,' she retorted. 'How did you know that name? You've been going through Daniel's things. That's very bad of you.'

'He'll die today. They'll kill him.'

'That's a wicked thing to say. I want you to leave immediately. You can keep those clothes but leave that bag where you found it.'

'Jummy brought the bag here to you. He came to tell you that Daniel was probably dead. Inside was a letter and a tape from Daniel – in case he was killed. Daniel said he was now with his father and they were both watching over you. He said he loved you. He said he was sorry for the pain his death would cause you, but that this was not an end.'

Her hand was pressed to her mouth, the blood draining from her face. 'How did you know that? Who are you?' She started up the stairs, her rage overcoming all fear. 'You've broken into my bedroom and read my letters!'

He stood frozen, stunned by the dreadful vision which filled his mind; clear as reality, yet one he could not understand, even less control. Then, he came down the stairs so fast she feared for her life. He grasped her by her frail shoulders: 'You must do something. *Now!*'

'You're quite mad,' she retorted, struggling.

His face was anguished. '*You're killing him.* Don't you understand – I can *see*. Colonel McFee is going to die. An explosion from the air, very soon. You must do something.'

She shook him off, glared at him, then went to her bureau, checked a telephone number in her address book, then dialled it. She waited, her eyes fixed on him. 'I'll just ask for him, I won't be made to look a fool. And incidentally, Jummy McFee's a major.'

A recorded message came over the line: 'For reasons of security, the number you have dialled is temporarily unavailable. Enquiries should be directed to the Ministry of Defence, telephone . . .'

She scrawled the number and extension on to a pad and redialled immediately, meeting, once again, an official stone wall. Angrily she snatched her small book up and demanded another extension. 'Colonel Southby,' she barked, 'tell him Eleanor Hale, widow of the late Brigadier Samuel Hale, is on the line and I wish to speak to him on a matter of some urgency *now*.'

'My dear Mrs Hale,' said a clipped voice after a moment. 'I understand you have a problem. How can I help?'

'The problem seems to be the army's, Colonel. I've just been trying to get hold of a friend of Daniel's, Major James McFee. Everyone seems to call him Jummy. I understood from his last talk with me – he calls from time to time – that he is still serving in Northern Ireland. Unfortunately the number he gave me seems to be unobtainable – security reasons or some such?'

'Ah! There *is* a problem over there at present. Leave it with me for the moment and I'll make enquiries . . .'

'Colonel, I was army before you received your first pips and I know only too well when bad news is being put on the back-burner to be boiled down into a dry, official statement which tells us non-combatants nothing at all. Now *what* is going on?'

'Very well. You of all people deserve the truth. Happened

9

minutes ago. Mortar attack – what they're pleased to call mortars anyway. Vicious weapon. The base HQ caught a direct hit – two, if the reports are accurate. No survivors – that's confirmed. McFee was inside. Killed instantly. Wouldn't have known a thing. Best way if there's no choice. Incidentally, he'd recently received his colonelcy. Well deserved. This is absolutely tragic. If only we were allowed to take the kid gloves off over there . . .'

'Goodbye, Colonel,' she said, quietly. 'And thank you for your frankness.' She put down the receiver. 'Jummy's dead. You were right. Dear God, we might have been within seconds of warning him.' She lowered herself, heavily, into an armchair. 'How many more have to die over there?'

He sat on the chair opposite her, facing the window, his face as bleak as the landscape beyond.

She watched him but saw her husband, reliving the pain of being helpless to aid a tortured soul. Samuel, have they come this far? she asked of the grave and received the answer which had driven him to it. They believe that nothing is impossible for them, now. They've rejected our beginnings, they're manipulating what we have become and they're forging our future in a furnace straight out of hell. Eleanor, they can do things now with the human mind which would shake even you. The ether holds every sound ever made and they have tapped into that maelstrom – driving minds into insanity and not caring. They're searching for the higher functions of the brain we, *Homo sapiens*, were perhaps never meant to use because I believe, like the universe, there is too much there. If they succeed, and I'm so afraid they will, the first to tread that higher road will be burdened with questions for which there may be no answer and we, crass mortals that we are, will no doubt drive him mad seeking answers to our own petty future. If ever such a one should appear, be sure that they have made him and that their plans for him will be only for themselves and their masters. Such a gift – if that is truly the word for it – must be used for the benefit of mankind or . . .

'It's a gift,' she said, firmly, to her young visitor. 'One you must use to save lives. Think of the help you can give to those poor boys in Northern Ireland. You can warn them in advance of bombs, ambushes, snipers. The army would give – '

'*No*,' he started, then clutched his skull.

She reached over. 'I want to help you – for my own reasons. You won't understand this, now, but you're one of those reasons. Perhaps there'll come a time when you will understand. You, or the concept of someone like you, filled part of my life. The worst part. I thought it was over. I believed it was. I should have known better. Listen to me. They've given you an extraordinary power. Something like this was bound to happen sooner or later. Samuel warned of that. They wouldn't listen. They welcomed the possibility of change, even sought it. Now it's come they'll want to use it themselves. That must not happen. I'll do all I can to stop it. All I can to help you. Money, contacts, anything. But you have to get away from them. Away from here. Out there is where you have to be. Use the power.'

He went to the window. 'You said I wasn't born here – in your garden. But I could have been because that's all I know. Waking under the plants, you finding me – that's all. I don't know what's out there.'

Something about the way he stood, the tilt of his head, something, sent a chill through her. No, she protested, don't let it be. Leave me some hope. She wanted desperately to hold him, to search for more – but dared not, afraid of what she would find and, in finding life, confirm death. She wanted her options to be open – at least for a while longer. She needed him to decide. And to do that he needed to know the world.

Her own world was tilting madly and she fought to keep her grip on reality. 'Listen to me. A child knows nothing when it first comes into the world but it learns. Partly by instinct – but mostly by trying. You have to get away. There's no choice – except going back. You have to try. Now not another word till I've finished.'

She sat at her bureau and began writing in a precise, clear hand, first one letter, then another, finally a third – all sealed into envelopes and carefully addressed.

'The police will come here,' she said, finally laying down

11

her pen. 'I telephoned them. I said I didn't need them, but they'll come anyway. It's their way. Can you drive a car? You don't know, do you? But I'm certain that many abilities are dormant in you. If you just do things they'll happen. You've shaved? You found Daniel's razor in his Dr Jekyll bag? Ah! That's why you went to it. There you are: you've shaved and no one showed you how – and you guessed there might be shaving tackle in a travelling bag. Well done. You mustn't be afraid to do things, you have to try. Now listen carefully: I've written down what you must do to get away from here. See if you have any success with the car, otherwise you'll have to walk miles before you get to a major road and even further for a railway station. Also you'll be independent in a car. You can use Daniel's licence, it's still valid. What's the first name that comes into your mind? Quickly!'

'Daniel.'

'Forget Daniel, forget Samuel.'

His pale eyes fought her.

'What?' she demanded.

'Adam.'

'Yes,' she said, with a hopeless smile of confirmation. 'Anything else?'

'I don't understand.'

'Don't try. Just say what you see?'

'Nine.'

'As the number? Nine?'

'Adam Nine.'

Something touched his eyes, then was gone.

'It's all right, you're safe. Please listen: the car is Daniel's. It runs perfectly. I've done all the things he taught me to do when he wasn't here. I turn the engine over, then drive it a few yards, forward and reverse, every day. I don't enjoy that because it's a ferocious beast. There are maps in the car, very good ones knowing Daniel, and it's topped up with everything that needs topping up. I've a checklist he gave me. There's a petrol can and some oil in the boot – and he carried spare water too. Daniel loved that car. He lived in it when he was on leave. Drove it everywhere – always too fast.'

12

She stopped for a moment. 'I want you to leave now. Take these letters, they're all addressed clearly. One is to a former colleague of my husband's. Doctor Erich Hartrampf. He *knows*, do you understand? He's out of it now. All of the originals are dead, like Samuel. Hartrampf's the last. Old, like me. Samuel admired him but feared him also – possibly with good reason, though he always clung to the hope that their shared dream would solve any personal conflict. He never lived to find out and I was never told enough. Hartrampf could still be theirs but there's no one else qualified to help you. You might have to take that chance. The decision will be yours.

The second is to a young lady I've never met but who works in television. She called me a number of times on the telephone after Daniel was taken. She was planning a programme. Soldiers, hostages, their families. How we stood the strain. Whether we experienced any premonition of their death. That type of thing. It all sounded very serious and scientific, not in the least bit sensationalist and she came across as being very warm. Caring. She said she would contact me again. Speak to her, make her aware of the power you have. Others might not believe you – bound to think you're a crank – but I've a feeling she will. At least she'll listen.

'The third letter is to my bankers in London. You'll need that kind of help too. In a way the money is yours. You're the price we paid for earning it.'

Part of the price, she thought, seeing the shattered head; the face she had loved, unrecognizable. Destroyed. As had been her life. Thank God there had been Daniel to live for.

She stood. 'Try the car. In the garage. Keys are in the ignition, the starter is a button on the dash. Start it up, see how you do. I'll sort out more clothes for you. You're slimmer than Daniel by the fit of those trousers. I'll find a belt or braces. Shoes? A pair of Samuel's brogues would probably fit – with thick socks.'

She urged him out into the garden then left him. He entered the cold gloom of the brick garage, edging his way around a long low shape under a dust cover, found a light switch then pulled the cover off revealing a gun-metal grey

13

Jaguar E-type sports coupé. He grinned, then smiled widely, the thrill that coursed through him new and entirely fresh, yet distantly familiar, a brushstroke of memory from some childhood he must have had. A real memory, however vague or fleeting, and his first experience of happiness. For the briefest of moments his fears, his insecurities, receded as he marvelled at the wonder and utter joy a child must feel with each fresh pleasurable experience; for that was how he felt now. The entire world beyond the closed garage doors was uncertain, possibly hostile – but new.

I'm old. I'm a child. I'm growing. Even as I stand here thinking about it, growing fast through my second chance at childhood. Too fast. I'd like to stay here, right here, where I was born today. Or born again? Warm and safe in this house, with its garden to cage me because I am made secure by its boundaries. Yet, out there, somewhere, I am. My life before today exists even though I am standing outside it. I was taken from it to – where? Then brought from that place, naked – like an infant – to here. Or had I run from it? From something that left my mind an empty black hole in my head. What could possibly be that terrible?

Get in the car. Act, don't think. There is insufficient form in your mind for clear thought. If you think too long or too hard, you'll drop through the black hole and maybe never get back out again. Get in the car.

He twisted the ignition key savagely, then jammed his thumb on to the dashboard starter button, allowing the awakening bass growl of the engine to blanket his terrors, and the exhaust boom as he pushed the revs up to blow them away.

Daylight swept in over the long louvred bonnet as Eleanor Hale unlocked the garage doors from the outside. His feet and hands found their own way and the Jaguar rumbled forward.

'There you are,' she called, over the throb of the engine. 'Very good. I've packed a suitcase for you. Clothes, underwear, basics.'

He took the case and hefted it through the hatchback of the coupé with an effort.

She gave him a large leather wallet. 'Money, Daniel's

licence, the car insurance. You've got the letters. Don't come back here, don't telephone. They'll know.'

She faced the rutted track to the house. 'There's only one road to follow for quite a few miles – then you'll start to find yourself on the edges of civilization. That's what they call it anyway. After that you'll have major roads and dreadful traffic to contend with but you'll manage. It's all inside you. Let things happen naturally. Oh! I almost forgot.' She fumbled in her dress and found a watch on a worn leather strap. 'Daniel's. From his school days. A gift from his father. Wear it.' She searched his eyes for a moment, then looked away, quickly.

He held her and for a while she thought he would not go. Part of her said stay. Still, she pushed him down into the car. He took her hand once more, then released it and let the Jaguar's power take him.

She watched the car accelerating away for as long as it remained in sight. When at last she turned away, it might all have been a dream were it not for the open doors of the garage and the emptiness inside.

She closed her mind tight. Not wanting to think, not wanting to remember. And fearing *they* had moved so far forward that even her thoughts were open to them.

It's out of control, she had told Samuel. The very antithesis of everything you profess to believe in; studied, qualified, swore an oath for. It's become no better than what they were doing originally. Worse. You're taking their obscene dream – nightmare – and making it reality. Stop. Give up. Run if you must. I'll be with you.

Except she had not been. Samuel had chosen to run alone. Escape: down the double barrels of his shotgun. A clear message for them: I've left you nothing you can use.

She returned inside, one final task to complete, planned for years.

Upstairs she opened the small safe ensconced under forgotten hats in the bottom of her wardrobe. From this she took a yellowed envelope tied in black mourning ribbon, its wax seal unbroken. Face set, she returned downstairs and, ignoring the twisting knife of her arthritis, wrote one

15

more letter. This done, she took it outside to the hidden place she left mail for the postman to collect.

Finished, wearied by her exertions – and other exhausting emotions besides – she sat in her straightest-backed chair and stared out, across the moors, wondering if *they* even cared that she existed, still.

Oh yes. They'd know.

It was a time for memories – and for pain.

When your life's dream turns to nightmares it is time to die.

Samuel, I miss you.

Danny, where is your spirit? Lord, let it rest in peace. Please.

The Range Rover approached the house thumping into pot-holes, bouncing the small man in the rear against the window and dislodging his rimless spectacles. 'Slow down,' he ordered.

'Bloody dirt-track!' cursed the driver.

The heavy man beside him turned to the rear. 'He couldn't have got this far?'

'He could,' said the small man, flatly.

'She's on the doorstep,' said the driver. 'Must have spotted us.'

'He's been here,' stated the small man. 'She's ready for us.' They halted outside the closed garage. He stepped down, producing a leather identity-card holder from his overcoat.

'Closer,' she said, putting on her spectacles. She read aloud: 'Paige – with an "i". Ministry of Defence. Really? Sorry, I've already given this year.'

Paige gave a brittle smile. 'I'm aware of your sad loss, Mrs Hale.'

'You're aware of everything about me. Condolences, is it? You're so certain he's dead? Is that because you know? Body yours, is it? Go to hell! That's where you're from.'

'You know why we're here. He's blond, hair cut very short, almost six feet, lean. Very pale complexion, looks ill: he is, needs our help. Expert help.'

'Of course he does. But isn't it your philosophy we all

16

do? Sorry, haven't seen a soul for a week – which was when my groceries were delivered.'

Paige stepped back and signalled.

'I'll check the back,' called the driver, already out of the Range Rover.

'He'll do no such thing!'

The heavy man came up to the front door. 'Inside,' Paige told him. 'Top to bottom.'

'Done,' he said, brushing her aside effortlessly.

Paige said, 'I don't want unpleasantness, Mrs Hale.'

'You thrive on it.'

A shout came from the rear of the house. Paige took her arm firmly, led her through to the kitchen and unlocked the door.

'He's been here all right,' said the driver. 'Out there. Vegetable plot. She's had a go at smoothing the soil over but there's a couple of footprints she missed. It's flattened under some of the plants. Kipped out there last night by the look of it. Must have frozen his balls off.'

Paige shook his head and gripped her harder. 'He was exhausted, he was naked. You gave him clothes, you fed him. But then? After that, how did you help him?'

'Go to blazes.'

'Did you give him money? How much do you keep in the house? Enough to get him quite a way I expect.' He moved past her. 'Look for a safe or strong-box!' he called.

He turned to the driver. 'Check the garage.'

'Done.'

'No car?'

'I don't own a car,' said Eleanor Hale. 'I'm too old.'

'Don't waste my time. You let him take your son's Jaguar. Obviously he was fit enough to drive – so where is he driving to? Somewhere you suggested? I need answers, Mrs Hale, and I need them fast.'

The heavy man entered. 'Small safe upstairs, in her wardrobe – can't shift it. Combination lock, she'll have to come and open it up.'

'Take her up there,' ordered Paige. 'She's probably given him all the cash she's got in the house. Find out how much.'

'I'll walk at my own pace if you don't mind,' she said, tugging the heavy man's fingers from her arm.

Paige nodded.

In the hallway she chose a walking stick from an oak stand then began the climb up the steep stairs. Reaching the top she stopped, then summoned all her strength and struck downward with the weighty, solid silver knob of the cane.

The heavy man's face spurted blood: he yelled and lunged at her. Again the silver knob cracked down. He fell on to the stairs, grabbing blindly for her ankles.

She crashed backwards, her skull striking the edge of the doorframe to her bedroom.

'Bloody stupid old woman!' the heavy man shouted.

Paige and the driver rushed up the stairs. 'Get yourself cleaned up,' Paige ordered. 'And don't leave bloodstains.' He needed only a quick glance at Eleanor Hale. 'Throw her down the stairs,' he ordered.

'Do what?' the driver objected.

'Just do it.'

Reluctantly, the man came up the last remaining steps, lifted the body by the armpits, keeping the bloodied head away from him, then let it topple, the neck snapping as it crashed to the bottom.

The heavy man emerged from the bathroom, a towel pressed to his wounds. He looked over the banisters, his face grim.

Paige was in the bedroom, examining a bedside diary. Satisfied, he moved to the wardrobe and pushed clothes aside to reveal the solid grey cube of the safe. Deftly he moved the combination dial through a series of digits then tugged the door open.

After a few moments he came back on to the landing. 'No cash,' he said. 'Stuck out here, she'd keep a couple of hundred, perhaps more.'

The heavy man joined him, two thick Band-aids from the bathroom medicine chest sealing the deep cuts to his forehead. 'Why'd she do it? Wouldn't have made any difference. Christ, there's three of us!'

'Anger,' said Paige. 'Years of it.'

18

'You making this official?'

'There's nothing on record to link us with this place. The police can read it as accident or foul play – it won't matter either way. But we need to get that Jaguar traced, fast.'

The driver looked pointedly at Paige's hand resting on the polished wood of the banisters.

'The only data-bank holding our prints is our own – and nobody has access to that,' assured Paige.

'What about his?'

Paige gave his brittle smile.

'What now?' asked the heavy man.

'Find him before he falls into the wrong hands.'

'If he does?'

'We destroy him so completely there'll be nothing left for a post-mortem.'

TWO

'White-out!' The voice yelled in his ear. He tasted rubber and metal and bile and fear. He turned to the others and saw fixed stares and clenched jaws turned blue-white by the instrument lighting, and terror. He knew they were flying blind and that somewhere – anywhere – beyond the white vortex was the sheer, hard rock-face of the mountain.

He prayed but no one heard him.

The hideous heart-stopping clang and the cascade of sparks came simultaneously. Then the insistent howl of the crash warning klaxon. Then nothing. Nothing at all.

'Major Hale?' questioned the doctor.

He focused on the black face before him, holding it until the other world receded completely.

'Major Hale, you are in Blackwater Clinic, near Camberley. You're unhurt so don't be alarmed. You were found asleep in your car last night by a police patrol in a layby on the A30 not half a mile from here. They woke you up and breathalysed you – negative, fortunately – but you were so groggy they brought you here as a precaution. Being private we're strictly appointment only as a rule but under the circumstances we decided to keep you in overnight. Do you understand?'

He nodded and let his gaze drift around the soft pastels and costly furnishings of the room. He wanted to sleep more but dared not.

'If you want to stay longer don't worry about it, we found your medical insurance ID in your wallet – you're more than adequately covered. Incidentally, you had a large sum of cash on you – that's now in our safe, checked by the two police officers who brought you in. Collect it any time you want to leave. Your XKE is just fine, the nurses are lining up to get a ride in it. You ever decide to sell, give me first call.'

'You're an American?'

'Right. Been there?'

'I don't know.'

'Don't worry. Let's talk. Anything you want to tell me?'

'About what?'

'Last night, when you were found – more or less comatose – you were clutching, and I mean clutching, three sealed hand-addressed envelopes. Policemen have a tendency to suspect the worst and a guy out cold in a car stopped in the middle of nowhere holding sealed letters looks bad even to an optimist like me. You showed all the signs of having taken an overdose of something lethal. Pale, clammy, semi-conscious, disorientated when you were conscious – which was for about four minutes maximum. Frankly I didn't want to touch you – we Americans are paranoid about lawsuits – but, well, let's say this is England not the US. Incidentally, you're fine, nothing untoward in the system.' The doctor paused. 'I noticed you've had some fairly recent cranial surgery – do you want to tell me about it? That could well account for your condition last night.'

'I was in an air crash. It was snowing.'

'Well, you survived. Let's take it from the top. I'm Doctor Ray Livesey, late of Washington DC and now of right here because the girl I married, who incidentally is British like you but with a touch more colour than you have right now, runs the family business. To wit: the Blackwater Medical Clinic. Now you are Daniel S. Hale, you're alive, you're an officer in the British Army, a Guards major to be exact, your home address is given as Raethmoor Farm, Devon and you've got enough medical insurance for me to call you sir. You could well be suffering from some kind of post-operative trauma. What do you remember about yourself?'

'I remember a plane crash.'

'So you said. An airliner? Must have been in the news.'

'No, a small aircraft. Seven of us – and two crew.'

'Us?'

'Men. All men. Uniforms, I think.'

21

'Fixed wing?'

'What?'

'Fixed wing or chopper?'

'Helicopter. Yes, helicopter.'

'What's the matter?'

'I don't know.'

'Is it the crash? Did you just remember it? You look sick.'

'I died.'

'You thought you did.'

'I died.'

'Okay, you feel you died and that can be just as real – but you're here so you didn't. I'm no shrink but I think your problem is right there. You still believe, subconsciously, that you died in the crash. Maybe you want to believe that because the people with you didn't survive? Did they?'

'How would I know? The last time I saw them was . . . then.'

'So when was then?'

'I don't know.'

Livesey hesitated. 'Major, the letters you were holding – one of them is addressed to a Doctor Hartrampf. Erich Hartrampf. His address is Kensington, London. I checked him out. Among the best in psychiatric medicine plus a bunch of other qualifications. Retired. You might have been on your way to meet with him when you stopped last night. I thought of contacting him last night but . . . well, I thought it best to get your permission first – not knowing the circumstances.'

'I have to see him. There are other people I have to see. I made a promise. It's important.'

'Relax. Another of the letters was addressed to a Miss Haversham – London again. I took the liberty of calling her last night late. Thought under the circumstances she'd want to know you were OK. She's right outside.'

'She's *here*?'

'Caught the first train down this morning.'

'She knows about me?'

22

'Like I said: I called her. If you didn't want that I'm sorry.'

'I meant: she knows who I am?'

'Long way to come for a stranger.'

'I'd like to see her now.'

Livesey opened the door. 'He's awake.'

Jane Haversham went straight to the bed and kissed him. 'How are you feeling? God! You look even paler than your mother described on the telephone.' The warning in her eyes stopped his questions. She turned away. 'When will Daniel be ready to leave, Doctor?'

Livesey frowned. 'That's his decision, I can't hold him here – but he needs professional help, that's certain.'

'I'll deal with everything.'

'You understand the clinic can't take responsibility . . .'

'Don't worry, Doctor.'

'Frankly I am worried. I'd get him to Doctor Hartrampf for an opinion as soon as you can.' He turned to Adam. 'Better apply for extended leave from army duties.'

'I'll deal with everything,' she repeated, firmly.

Livesey's frown remained. 'I conducted some tests last night. Won't have the results for a day or so . . .'

'Your reception desk has my contact number,' she said. 'I tend to be out a lot – my job – so leave a message. Incidentally I've settled your fees in cash so you need not make further contact with his medical insurance company. Any subsidiary charges I'll deal with also, on his behalf. It might be better for Daniel's army career if this incident does not become a matter of record. The problem is that nowadays even the most harmless information tends to end up in too many databases. We do understand each other, Doctor?'

'Perfectly. However, remember he was found by a police patrol and the chances are they felt they had to do their paperwork because he was actually admitted to the clinic.'

She pushed her long blonde hair back. 'Well, it's done. I'll bring the E-type up to the front door. Don't worry. Daniel, I've called my brokers and had myself covered to drive it. Will you bring him down, Doctor?'

She was waiting in the car, the engine rumbling and the

23

low passenger door wide open as Livesey left the clinic's reception area with his patient, easing him down into the tight leather bucket seat. He said: 'You survived. Just keep telling yourself that. And don't drive the XKE again until you know you can handle it, OK?'

Jane Haversham reached across for Livesey's hand. 'Thank you for your care – and, I trust, your discretion?'

Livesey nodded. 'I'll be in touch.'

She drove in silence, forming her thoughts, until they reached the slip road for the motorway. There, flooring the accelerator, she sliced through the careering traffic streams making straight for the outside lane.

She had to half-shout over the engine and the wind noise. 'She's dead, Eleanor Hale. The police found her in the early hours of this morning. When you didn't arrive I called her back. The police were there. A patrol car from a country sub-station. I said I was a relative so they told me. Her neck was broken and she had head injuries. It was on the morning news, because of her decoration – we pick up on things like that. I mean TV people.' She turned quickly to him then back to the motorway. 'I'm so sorry.'

He stared ahead, not responding.

'She told me everything she knew. How she found you. The extraordinary business about Northern Ireland. What happened. The confirmation from the MOD. All of it. She said you thought your name was Adam? May I call you that?'

He turned to her.

'So hello, Adam. I'm Jane Haversham, I make TV programmes when I can convince backers I have something worthwhile to hang one on. I've been working on an idea for a long time now without seriously looking at it face to face – and suddenly *you're* here.'

He shouted at her: 'I don't know who I am, where I'm from, if you, this car, this road – everything – is just a dream. I think it is quite possible that I am mad and I'm living in my head.'

She reached sideways, her eyes still on the road, and let her hand rest on his. 'Feel that? That's me. Now if I'm real, so are you. There's nothing in this world – if it's

24

tangible and as real as you are – that cannot be explained. You're not David Bowie who dropped out of space and took over the world. You're not fiction, you're not the movies. You're real. A full-grown man: which means you were born, educated, and all the rest of the other banalities. All we have to do is to find someone who recognizes you – and the way to do that is to put you on television. All right?'

'She wanted me to save lives. That's why I'm here.'

'She told me. You realize that you're going to have to prove yourself? Prove this "gift", as she called it? We live in a world where you've got to show something up front. Eleanor Hale may have witnessed your ability but unfortunately she's dead. That's the brutal truth.'

'They killed her.'

She glanced sharply at him, swerving the Jaguar. A juggernaut's air-horns blared.

'Who killed her?'

'Three men. They killed her twice.'

'Twice?'

'She fought one and she fell – she died then. Another threw her down the stairs. The third man wanted her dead that way.'

She glanced at her mirror, deliberately crossed both inner lanes, braked the car up on to the hard shoulder and faced him. The juggernaut thundered past, horns wailing, rocking the car. 'You're telling me you actually saw this?'

'I *know* what happened.' He looked at her. 'She sent me to you to save lives. I made her that promise. I couldn't even save hers.'

She stared out at the speeding traffic, seeing none of it. 'Jesus.' She found first gear with a crunch and gave the E-type too much throttle, sending it into the traffic trailing blue smoke before easing off and settling in the centre lane.

'How long before it happened were you aware?' she demanded. 'Seconds, ten minutes, an hour?'

'I just know.'

'Can you remember any other occasions when this has happened?'

'Don't you understand?' he shouted in frustration. 'I

25

have no other memories. Everything started yesterday for me. Yesterday morning in her garden.'

She drove without speaking for miles then asked: 'Doctor Livesey said something to you – I just caught it as we left. That you survived? Was he talking about last night?'

'I told him I'd been in an air crash. When I awoke it was as if it had just happened. A helicopter crash in a snowstorm. *White-out*. Someone shouted that. Now, it doesn't seem so real. I must have been dreaming. Or maybe all of this is a dream and the crash was real. In which case I'm dead.'

'I promise you you're not.'

'Well, I'm not who Livesey thought I was. Daniel Hale is dead.'

'Dead but never buried. That's what makes all this so eerie. I knew Daniel briefly – his mother didn't know that but it is a fact. I feel guilty about not having told her; I suppose because I was prepared to use her experience of loss for a programme – or because I was ashamed I might be exploiting my time with Daniel. Doesn't matter now. Quite obviously she never really accepted that he was dead. Believe me, if the IRA get hold of a British army officer working undercover they torture him and they kill him. I've worked as a journalist and I know. Anyway, she's kept him alive in her heart and pretty much everywhere else it seems. His private health cover is paid up to date, the insurance on this car is still in his name. God knows what else!'

'She told you to say I was Daniel?'

'You were Adam.' She smiled. 'Adam Nine. I found that hard to take because there used to be a children's TV character called Joe 90 and I'm afraid, for a moment, I took her less than seriously.'

'I saw Adam – then the number nine. I still do. In my mind. I can't explain it.'

'At least you remembered your first name.'

'I remembered a name. It doesn't have to be mine.'

'It should be. Adam was the first man, according to the Bible, that is. Mean anything? Well, he was made from the earth which from Eleanor Hale's account is where she found you. In her garden. Naked? And she took you in! She must have been an extraordinary lady.'

'I didn't know her. Yet it was as if part of me did . . .' He closed his eyes. After a while, she asked: 'Are you awake?'

'I'm trying to remember something – anything – before I woke in that garden.'

'But there's nothing?'

'Nothing you'd understand.'

'Do you understand?'

'I don't know.'

'Could you have been in some kind of coma? I spoke to Doctor Livesey's wife. She's a surgeon. She asked if I knew anything about recent surgery performed on you. She indicated that you might have been on life-support equipment?'

He turned away, ignoring, or avoiding, her question. 'Have you found others like me?'

After a moment she said: 'Only cranks and con artists. One or two borderline cases of premonition which might hold up to scrutiny but hardly enough to base a programme concept on. Mainly we get retrospective claims and how can we prove or disprove those? I haven't found one person who has convinced me.' She turned. 'Until now.'

'I convince you?'

'You terrify me.'

'Who else do I have to convince?'

'The toughest, most cynical people in the world – and arguably some of the most powerful. People who own television networks.'

He fell silent again.

'Adam?'

'I ran away from something. Something terrible. Eleanor Hale was angry when she died – and afraid. I felt that fear. It was a fear of power. Secret power. I feel that in some way I am part of their power – yet I'm afraid too. More than afraid. Somehow I know I'm not supposed to be here: alive, breathing, living. They want to take me back.'

'Back to where? Look, the only way for me to deal with this is with logic. You woke, naked, in a reclusive old lady's garden – which means you came from somewhere.

27

Somewhere within walking distance because you had no transport and she described you as having blistered and bleeding feet. Somewhere pretty remote because a naked man running through suburbia soon gets himself arrested, OK?'

She fumbled in her handbag one-handed for cigarettes and lit one for herself. 'If you don't remember smoking – don't. Right, back to logic. I have a regular team of researchers who'll be set the task of finding out where you might have walked from. It won't be difficult once we get facts. You mentioned power, secret power – well, even if there's some secret government installation in the area we'll find out where and what it is. Television is a very powerful medium and we use that power ruthlessly when we have to. We'll be ready for them. No threat is as terrifying when it has a face. Let's find out who they are, then we can deal with them. Lawyers, investigators, PR machine, you name it we have them or we can get them. The secret face of government is a sure-fire seller. If that's what this is I'll have no trouble getting backing.'

He slept and she drove in silence, her excitement building, tempered only by the chill of his presence beside her. Who was Adam Nine? She had no answer. But she would have.

They arrived at her Chelsea mews cottage just before midday. She urged him inside quickly, pointed at a settee, turned the TV set to Ceefax, then percolated coffee while listening to her telephone messages.

This done, she sat directly before him on a low leather stool. 'Adam. We have to discuss the business side of this. I work independently – do you understand that? It means I employ myself and go out and make deals. I don't have the kind of capital needed. It's important you understand this because I may have to agree to things that you might not be happy with.'

From his jacket he took one of the letters Livesey had returned to him. 'She told me this would ensure I could keep my promise to her. She meant money. She said in a way the money was mine. I was the price they paid for earning it.'

'What did she mean?'

'She wouldn't say.'

'You saw nothing of her meaning? Felt nothing?'

'Grief. But she closed herself to me. And I felt Daniel. Daniel's presence was as strong as my own.'

She touched him. 'That came from her. She kept him alive. She saw something of him in you – she intimated that on the telephone. She also told me about the letters she'd given you. She knew you'd need guidance and begged my help. I think she wanted to believe you were her lost son. I can understand that. That letter is to a private bank in the City of London. Whatever her reasons she was determined you should have money. She told me that. Adam, please don't feel offended. You'll need that money yourself. I'll raise the finance easily with what I have to offer – but I must be able to negotiate without constantly having to refer to you. I'll need rights and permissions before I can go any further. Also, as I told you in the car, this is a tough business – I'll have to agree on your behalf to some kind of proving run. A test. You won't be believed initially, that's certain. How will you react?'

His pale eyes fixed on her. 'Once I have seen an event, it will occur. Nothing will stop it. It is the one thing I am sure of. The one part of my existence I know is real.'

She looked at him, sensing his fear and sharing it. 'Dear God, are you able to see your own future?'

'Not my future, not my past. Even my present is overlaid with images which aren't part of my life.'

'I don't understand.'

'Then we share something.'

She said, fearfully, not sure she wanted to know: 'Mine? Do you see . . . ?'

'Perhaps. If I do it has no meaning – no understanding for me. I'm tired. Do what you have to do.' He closed his eyes.

Through his close-cropped hair she saw his scars, feeling a surge of compassion and of rage. She knew that Eleanor Hale had felt the same and understood why she had done so much to aid him. This was worse that poverty or the environment or any of the other injustices or idiocies of the twentieth century. A man had been *changed*. She was convinced of that.

She lifted the telephone, her outrage tempered by the needs of commerce.

'World Communications Corporation,' replied a crisp voice.

'Rudolf Moravec,' she said. 'Jane Haversham calling.'

'I'll put you through to the chairman's office.'

'The chairman's in a meeting, Miss Haversham,' said a mellow, cultured woman's voice after a moment.

'Will you get this message to him when he has a moment? Please tell him that if he would like to have the possibility of knowing tomorrow's news today, I have the new technology. It's unpatented and I plan to make a programme about it. He has my home number, I'll be in throughout the day.'

'Tomorrow's news . . . today? He's not very good with ambiguities, Miss Haversham.'

'He understands "new technology" very well and "unpatented" even better, Miss Wolseley.'

'I'll pass on the message.'

'To him personally.'

'In his hand, Miss Haversham.'

She replaced the receiver, colouring slightly, shamed by her approach. 'How else can I sell the idea of a man who can see the future?' she demanded but Adam was already asleep. Escape, she thought, and lifted the phone again and dialled. 'Phillida? I need you and the whole team. I've got the biggest story we'll ever work on. I mean it.'

THREE

'Why is it that whenever some old lady falls down stairs and breaks her neck, there's always somebody who believes she was pushed?' asked Detective Superintendent Peter Foley as he replaced the telephone receiver on his desk at Devon police headquarters in Exeter.

In front of him was Nigel Lewin, young enough to be his son and a permanent lodger in his home – a large gloomy old Victorian property formerly owned by Lewin's parents, both killed in a holiday boating tragedy in their native Wales five years previously. Following that accident and his subsequent successful bid for the house, Foley, a confirmed bachelor, had suggested that Nigel stayed until he felt the need to move on rather than uproot himself immediately. The offer was accepted with alacrity – thus creating a domestic arrangement which raised conservative eyebrows in the upper reaches of the Devon and Cornwall Constabulary. No opinion, though, was actually voiced. Foley, they rationalized as time went on, was after all a Londoner. He was also in their firmament, something of a star – with one or two more years still to shine.

Lewin, characteristically, derived perverse pleasure from the undertones inherent in the arrangement. He dropped in on Foley whenever his position as reporter for the regional newspaper brought him near D Division Headquarters in Exeter, usually purchasing a gift of blooms from a nearby flower-stall as fuel for gossip.

Today he had bought chocolates, hideously boxed, which Foley, a trim, though not without effort, greying fifty-five-year-old, would never eat.

'She the Hale woman?' enquired Lewin, picking out the soft centres by pressure from his index finger.

' "She?" "Hale woman?" Where's your respect? War-

31

time heroine. Nurse. Decorated for working under fire. Late husband a brigadier, Royal Army Medical Corps. Tragic family. He shot himself: both barrels, according to the record. One son, Daniel. Come on, use those grey cells. You remember him surely?'

Lewin popped something squashed into his mouth. 'Guards major? Undercover merchant. IRA lifted him from a backstreet Belfast pub where he was playing at being a boyo.'

'Bloody good at it too, apparently,' asserted Foley.

'Not good enough.'

'How long do you see yourself lasting?'

'I'm neither a soldier nor suicidal.'

'Just cynical.'

Lewin smirked. 'Coming from a career CID copper almost ready to ride, siren wailing, into the sunset?'

Foley glared. 'I clear up mess, I don't rake through it for something even nastier.' He leaned over his desk. 'You're dropping chocolate on the carpet.'

'Never found the body, did they?' asked Lewin, examining the floor exaggeratedly. 'Daniel Hale?'

'Didn't need to. You don't think the IRA have POW camps and observe the Geneva Convention? After they sweated him – hard – they'd have topped him. That's their way. Not like the damn Chinese who'd keep you alive just to torment you or because you'd be worth something as a bargaining counter. The Provos wouldn't see that though; they're filled with the Celtic blood-lust.'

Lewin groaned. 'Sodding Chinese again. You should do something about those nightmares. Keeps me awake. You must have a thing about people being blown to pieces.'

'Vaporized.'

'That's Star Wars, not the prehistoric Korean one you were in.'

'This wasn't TV. *Gone* One minute there's men in the next dugout, whistling, shaving, urinating, whatever – next, a high-explosive shell travelling at supersonic speed comes out of nowhere and they don't exist any more. Nothing. No bits – bones, flesh, tissue – nothing. Vaporized. Atoms. Shakes you up. Eerie. You never believe it, even when you

32

go and stand in the hot shell-crater. We humans need to see a body – even bits of it – to make death real.'

'Strawberry goo?' Lewin queried, holding a mess between finger and thumb.

'You should have lived through one war. Would have opened your eyes a bit. Done all of your generation some good.'

'Falklands? Wasn't that war?'

'The pros fought that for you. Regulars. I mean conscription. National service. Off your soft backsides and out of your hot hatchbacks into grim reality.'

'The new reality is that war is too expensive. It's also unfashionable. Gorby's come down from the mountain with new stone tablets and everyone's scrambling to melt down the Golden Missile before he gets mad. Who was that leaning on you about the old lady?'

'Not your business.'

'Not for publication. Swear to God.'

'Better not be. A Colonel Southby. Something at the Ministry of Defence. Eleanor Hale telephoned him a couple of hours before the accident occurred. He said she sounded spooked. His description.'

'Why did she call?'

'Wanted a Colonel James McFee. Serving in Belfast. Apparently she called his command seconds after it got hit in a mortar attack. You must have seen it on the news. She got a put-off recorded message, knew the form and called Southby at MOD. He had the impression she knew about the attack before he admitted it had occurred. Said it was as if she wanted confirmation. Wasn't her only odd call either. There's a report from the local station desk sergeant – they discovered the body – saying she'd called him the morning of the incident enquiring about unnamed missing persons. According to him, she tended to feed tramps and the like. Sounded peculiar, says he: disturbed.'

'Foul play?' Lewin asked, eagerly. 'Murder on the moors?'

'Don't start that! She's an old person who got careless – and you know that can be lethal. She heard from Colonel Southby about this officer being blown up in Belfast, good

33

friend of her son's apparently, became distressed, went upstairs for a lie-down, woke up groggy, a bit weepy, misses her footing on the stairs and she's another statistic for you media people to ignore or sensationalize depending on what else you've got going on that day.'

'And the call to her local nick? Just chatting up the desk sergeant?'

'She was lonely. Desolate country out there. Don't you go writing anything that'll give us more work. Hear me?'

'As long as I get sight of any new evidence you turn up when you take the house apart later today.'

'Why should I do that? She lived alone, she fell down the stairs, there's no sign of forced entry, nothing apparently disturbed or missing as far as we can tell.'

Lewin nodded at the telephone. 'MOD colonels call chief constables before they call detective supers. I'll bet you a large Scotch any time now your phone will ring and you'll be guaranteeing to run your own personal magnifying glass over the place.' He swallowed the last soft centre noisily and deposited the lurid chocolate box on the desk. 'Maybe I'll get to write it up after all? "Foley's Final Case." I've left you the hard ones. See you later, dearie.'

Foley reached out to launch the box at the closing door but the buzz from his internal phone stopped him.

The mobile phone in Lewin's GTi was trilling as he opened the door. He snatched at it. 'Lewin.'

'Nigel?'

'Who's that?'

'Phillida. Melman.'

'What's happening, Phil? Last time I saw you – '

'Shut up. This is work. Interested?'

'If it's anything like the last lot, no. Definitely, no.'

'Same producer, different story. There's been a death up on some remote farm on Dartmoor. Raethmoor Farm. The owner, a Mrs Eleanor Hale – '

'Fell downstairs and broke her neck. Local news. You don't have a Colonel Southby on your board of directors by any chance?'

'What?'

'Nothing. Go on.'

'You remember Jane Haversham?'

'Oh sure, she sends me down a Cornish tin mine due to be topped up with government nuclear waste, almost gets me buried in it, then collects an award for breaking the story that Joe Public wasn't informed. What's her interest in the old woman? I thought she only took on *meaningful* issues.'

'This is big. We need someone down there we can rely on.'

'But I don't need to know all of it. As usual. What's new?'

'Do you want the assignment?'

'You mean do I need the money? Sure.'

'Right. Hire a helicopter, they can call me for the credit number. And you'll probably need an off-road vehicle – '

'Hang on! I thought we were talking about investigating an old widow-woman who fell down stairs, not going on a sodding expedition?'

The line became muffled briefly then Phillida Melman said: 'Only what you need to know, Nigel, OK? Eleanor Hale found someone in her garden and helped him, on the day of her death. Jane Haversham is doing something on that someone. This person walked there. Walked or ran, hard, from somewhere, let's say, *unusual*. The point is he doesn't remember where or what this place might be. He doesn't even remember crossing the moors. We want you to overfly the area – to find this place, or at least narrow the possibilities.'

'Phil, you're out having lunch, pissed, and making this up as you go along for that idiot, overpaid group of Hoorays you hang out with, right?'

'I'm with Jane Haversham, at her house in Chelsea, and I'm stone-cold sober. We need more information before we go any further. Are you prepared to get it?'

'Do you know where I am?'

'In your car, of course.'

'Outside D Division Police HQ, Exeter. Remember Peter Foley? Detective Superintendent Foley? I live in his house. You got pissed and climbed into his bed instead of mine when you were down here.'

'Dreadful man. Chucked me out, physically.'

35

'He'd chuck me out if he knew about this conversation.'

'Why?'

'Because he doesn't like coincidences – and neither do I. Suddenly a whole bunch of people seem interested in an old lady who lived alone in the middle of nowhere, who made strange telephone calls before she fell down stairs, dead; who according to you had a mysterious visitor who walked to her house from somewhere "unusual" – like maybe a nut-house – and probably killed her though you say he wouldn't remember! That's why.'

'I think you'd better speak directly to Jane.'

'Tell her to speak to Foley, it's his case.'

'I'm putting her on. Don't hang up.'

Lewin lit a cigarette.

'Nigel? Jane Haversham. We've never met but we spoke on the telephone a couple of times during the Cornish nuclear waste site investigation. That was a rough experience you had. You've recovered?'

Lewin grunted. preferring to forget. 'I saw you pick up the award on the box. Is all that blonde hair for real?'

'Absolutely.'

'Ever read Rapunzel?'

'Fairy-tale. What I've got is real life.'

But I don't get to climb up your hair? he thought. 'I'm listening.'

'I don't want to say too much on the telephone but obviously you need to know something of what's going on because of your . . . circumstances.'

'I want to know all of it or none of it – and I don't guarantee to keep confidential any information which the police should have.'

'The problem may be that the police down there might be involved in what could turn out to be some form of conspiracy.'

'In my book conspiracy means secret plotting towards an unlawful end. Serious accusation to be making about anyone, especially the police.'

'This is going to mean wasted time but I want you in on this. Can you drive up to London right away?'

'Quicker for you to fly down to Exeter.'

'No. There's someone I can't leave.'

'The someone from the old woman's house?'

'He's not an escaped convict if that's what you've sur-mised.'

'I'd be following the hunt, avoiding the dog-shit right now if he was – escapes from Dartmoor are national news. And for what it's worth, no one's bolted from any of the area police cells either, I'd have heard. So?'

She fell silent.

Lewin sighed and threw his cigarette out of the window. 'I've got it. The story's so hot you have to keep it cool in case some other network gets a sniff?'

'This story might be hot enough to burn this government out of power,' she snapped down the line.

Lewin paused, suddenly cautious. 'I bet they've never forgiven you for the tin mines?'

'They've given up tapping my phone, if that's what you mean. High Court ruling. That doesn't mean I'm on the Downing Street guest list. However, I'd prefer if we spoke without the aid of electronics. Are you in or not?'

'I'll leave after six tonight.'

'Leave now. Call in and say you're sick. Make up some-thing. You'll be well compensated – and we're perfectly capable of twisting an arm or two on your paper's board if there's a problem.'

'You're really serious.'

'Life is serious. And we believe someone is playing games with it. You've got my address. Get here.'

Lewin put down the dead phone and grimaced into the driving mirror. 'What the hell does that mean?' He started the engine.

Peter Foley pulled his door open. 'Not so fast.'

Lewin stalled the car and swore.

'You'll never make a getaway driver, son.'

'Do you have to creep up on people as if they're crim-inals? And I'm not your son.'

'There's a bit of guilt in everyone: that's what gives us coppers the edge.'

'I'm in a hurry.'

'Just wanted to let you know I'll be in my wellies for the rest of the day – on the moor.'

'Eleanor Hale?'

Foley nodded. 'I could be tied up late. You go ahead and eat whenever you want, I'll use the canteen.'

Lewin hesitated. 'I could be away overnight.'

'Where you off to?'

' "Bright Lights, Big City," ' he sang tunelessly, an imaginary guitar in his arms.

Foley frowned. 'It's your job – the trouble is it can affect mine.'

'Deny all knowledge. Best policy.'

'It's the truth: you won't tell me what you're up to unless I drag it out of you.'

Lewin restarted the engine. He hesitated, then said quickly, 'Look, call this intuition, call it what you like – when you're out there at the old girl's place, check for traces of someone else having been there.'

'What the hell have you heard?'

'See you when I get back.'

Lewin dropped the clutch and accelerated hard out of the car park, hearing Foley's angered exclamation. He swore. That's what comes of trying to be loyal: limit your information and you end up limiting your loyalty. He shrugged the incident off. It wasn't the first time he'd fallen out with Foley and it certainly wouldn't be the last. He'd sort it out on his return.

Peter Foley was angry. Detective Superintendent Foley was suspicious. He strode to his car, removed his hand-tailored jacket to avoid creasing it on the journey and settled himself at the wheel.

He was proud of his BMW cabriolet and drove, as always, with precision. Aware of his position and responsibility, he was a careful guardian of both.

Some of his colleagues on the force damned him as conceited and certainly he had many of the petty vanities confirmed bachelors cultivate, but his opinion of himself was neither overblown nor egotistical; if anything it was his lack of self-confidence which made him appear to strut a little too proudly through life.

He had a horror of ageing and, worse still, dying alone. To counter this, his retirement plans were thoroughly prepared: he would summer in Devon which he had grown to love and winter aboard selected cruise ships, nothing fancy but no tramps either; plenty of people around. That would suit him very well indeed. Money was not a problem: his police pension was generous and most of his investments successful.

Professionally he was acknowledged as a tenacious, often brilliantly analytical detective, past whom nothing slipped. Once, he had based an entire prosecution for murder on minute physical exhibits given in evidence, evidence detected at the scene of the crime by himself and missed by Metropolitan Police forensic experts, winning him a conviction.

If one question mark hung over Peter Foley it was because of his apparently sudden decision made years before, to quit his high-flying career at New Scotland Yard for the quieter – the cruel ones said, softer – option of the Devon and Cornwall Constabulary. No one knew why. Not his then superior in London who had reluctantly agreed to the extraordinary, unexplained transfer request, nor Nigel Lewin, who shared the same living space, usually harmoniously, and who was, despite the age difference between them, his only non-professional friend.

Today, as Foley drove his solitary way across the bleak moorland with only the occasional group of shaggy Dartmoor ponies to add life to the landscape, he went back over his reasoning at the time.

As with many apparently hasty decisions, the motivating factor lay in the past: or the past becoming, unexpectedly – and uncomfortably, part of the present. In Foley's case, the year in question was 1953 when his North Korean captors, under their Chinese allies and masters, sought in the dying months of the war to break him and his fellow prisoners.

Amidst the brutality of the POW camp he had found strength and genuine friendship, sharing the daily struggle

39

with a fellow national serviceman, also a Londoner. Both young men barely survived the ordeal, returning to Britain only to lose touch with each other. Foley's sense of loss hung heavily on him.

Years later, in the sixties, with his police career promising much, Foley embarked, against all good judgement, on an affair with a married woman. What initially appeared to be coincidence concerning her married name became unpleasant fact when, with jealousy controlling his actions, he followed her unseen into the grounds of a mansion in Surrey. From his hiding-place he watched her husband step from his Rolls-Royce and enter the house. Despite the years and the legacy of good living, the lean, bone-hard face Foley remembered from their rat-hole of a cell was still recognizable; the eyes which had displayed ruthless determination for survival still showed that same flinty singleness of purpose.

Foley's immediate reaction was to end the affair but despite his efforts it dragged on and, as his lover spilled dangerous pillow secrets, he learned that the man who had been more than friend, who had renewed his courage and will to survive in extremis, was now deeply involved in less honourable activities.

With his strong sense of duty driving him on, Foley soon had enough evidence to strip away the façade of the successful businessman and lay bare the reality of the cold crime-lord. His dilemma then was how to disclose this without compromising his own career. Worse still, how to avoid placing his informant – and lover – in deadly peril. With prosecution, the truth and ramifications of their relationship must be revealed. He knew, even with her husband behind prison bars, her safety could never be assured.

With the emptiness of the moors surrounding him, he remembered with unwelcome clarity the two barren days he had spent working out what he should do: finally facing the fact that there would be no dramatic intervention by fate to save him from his own reluctance to act positively. Inevitably, worn down and drained, he simply abdicated his position and – as he remembered it – ran for the hills.

Or rather the moors, he thought now: where all things are reduced either by perspective or decay.

In the distance, as he turned off the road, he could see the isolated farmhouse. He scanned the horizon all around, slowing as the track deteriorated, seeing no other dwelling. Lonely place to die, Mrs Hale, he thought. Even lonelier for the living. Let's see if we can sort all this out so that you can be left alone to rest in peace. You didn't have much of that alive, did you? A butchered son and a suicide husband. That's the problem with caring for people: they kill you by dying. Or by changing.

For a moment he was the only person left in the world, watched by the spirits which floated mistily in the hollow. He grinned self-consciously, knowing the moors could get you that way.

The first thump from the BMW's suspension jolted him back to reality.

Lewin's words festered in his mind. 'Check for traces of someone else having been there.' What does that little bugger know? he swore. He had spotted Lewin using his telephone as he had approached his car and sensed wariness – or was it guilt? His anger had subsided but his suspicions lingered. As a professional police officer he distrusted the media in general and investigative reporters in particular. Responsibility without accountability was how he termed their less savoury operations: with overblown financial inducements anaesthetizing any sensitive consciences they encountered. He doubted if Lewin's conscience would need much anaesthetic.

Little Welsh bugger, I'll have you when you get back.

He drew to a halt, acknowledging the waiting scene of crime and investigating officers. 'Pressure from the top on this one so nobody misses anything,' he informed them. 'Right, let's get to it.'

'Sir?' offered a young detective constable as they dispersed. 'I've got the insurance inventory from the old woman's brokers.'

'Lady,' Foley said rigidly, thinking: with influential friends and possible enemies.

'Lady, sir. Sorry. There's a vehicle listed. Jaguar E-type

sports coupé. I've got all the details. It's not here. The car.
I've just checked by radio with one of the first officers on
the scene on Tuesday night. They didn't enter the garage
but did shine their torches through a window at the rear.
No vehicle of any kind on or near the premises.'

'An E-type Jag? Not her car, of course?'

'Registered to Daniel S. Hale. Deceased's son. Army
officer.'

Foley nodded. 'Also deceased.'

'The premium has been kept up and it's road taxed to
date. Listed ownership unchanged,' objected the officer.

'Deceased,' Foley repeated. 'Except in her mind. IRA
lifted him. No body. What do you expect? Put the car on
the national computer at Hendon.'

'It's already on,' interrupted a detective inspector from
the front seat of the Rover next to them. He completed his
radio communication rapidly, climbed out, inclined his
head and walked away from the house.

Foley followed. 'So who's the clever boots, Grant?'

'None of ours.'

'Didn't you ask?'

'Didn't have the access code, Super.'

'You were blocked?'

'Door slammed in my face.'

Foley stopped and surveyed the rise at the rear of the
house, turning full circle to take in the bleak position of
the property once more. You'd need a damn good reason
to choose to live out here. He said: 'Someone authorized a
nationwide trace on the Jag and we're not being told who?
Can we guess?'

'Take your choice: MI6, MI5, Special Branch, C11, Military Intelligence? All the secret squirrels.'

'Ministry of Defence?'

'The car's owner was army – but it's his mother who's
been killed.'

'We'll say "died" just for the moment.'

'There's a whiff about this one, Super.'

Foley hesitated then turned back to the house. 'I had
the impression from the original report that it was all cut
and dried. Had a good run and her time was up. In other

42

words, she wasn't pushed, she fell. That seems to have been the consensus. Agreed?'

'Things change. You've pumped it up yourself, being here, calling us out.'

'*I* was pushed.'

Grant frowned. 'That confuses the issue. If there's some kind of official mess here – though I can't imagine what – you'd think we'd be taken aside quietly and told to have the day off. Wouldn't mind actually.'

'Someone from the MOD instigated this. Nothing official. Personal. We're into old boy network country so we tread easy – like in a minefield.'

'Do you want me to have another crack at the national computer? There's a Hendon old boy network too, and we're both part of it.'

'We're police officers, let's forget the politics,' muttered Foley. So you can safely duck any difficult decisions? he asked himself as he entered the main house.

Nigel Lewin turned into Lennox Gardens Mews in the Royal Borough of Kensington and Chelsea a little after four o'clock. He spotted the sixties E-type Jaguar coupé immediately, noting the mud-spattered number plate.

DSH 42.

Daniel something Hale? he mused. Coincidence? Not when it's parked outside Rapunzel's tower it's not. He smelt intrigue, maybe scandal – and definitely money. Lots of it. Whatever she and her people were up to, he wanted in. He wouldn't mind being in with her in entirely another way as well. He fancied his chances. But later. After he had the story. And the money.

He parked his GTi directly behind the E-type and cracked the heavy door-knocker down once, hard, swivelling his head to take in his surroundings, thinking *mucho* expensive. Well, you're paying for the address, aren't you?

'Traffic bad?' enquired Phillida Melman, drawing him inside.

'Hi, Phil. Engine overheated. You look great.' As in size, he thought.

'Shut up, I've put on at least a stone.'

43

Two, he estimated, holding her for kissing, his hands confirming his opinion. 'Suits you.'

'Liar!'

'We'll check it out later.'

'We won't, I'm engaged to Simon.'

The Jewish property-developer your mother chose, he remembered. He cupped his hand between her thighs. 'Congratulations.'

'Don't!' she whispered furiously. 'Rudolf Moravec's in there!'

'*Moravec*? What's going on? What's the story?'

'It's like we've been given the best present in the world but no one wants to unwrap it in case it explodes. It's this chap. He's weird. That's his Jaguar outside. We've been locked in here since yesterday, not allowed out while Jane was setting up a deal. With Moravec in it's going to be worse.'

'Let's cut and run – flog the story to his competition!'

'Don't even joke about it.'

'And besides, you don't know all of it. Not unless Rapunzel has changed?'

'She's not in the mood for your wit – be warned.'

'Aren't you going to take me in?'

'Wait.'

The odour of expensive Cuban tobacco reached Lewin's nostrils as she returned to the room, closing the door behind her. His irritation started to burn but not enough for his curiosity to get the better of prudence. He was waiting at the farthest end of the narrow entrance hall when Phillida beckoned him through.

Jane Haversham was standing to greet him. He stopped, taken aback. She was taller than his five feet six inches.

'Nigel Lewin,' she said, adding nothing to her spare, almost curt introduction.

Thanks. Would you be more effusive if Mister Big wasn't here? he wondered. Taking in the room he decided not: economy seemed to be essential in her life. No clutter, no small ornaments crowding shelves, no grouped prints, no flippancy. A few possessions, all costly.

'You'll be expected to sign this,' growled the dark, jowly,

dangerous-looking man she had not needed to name. 'It's my guarantee that you don't walk out of here into the nearest telephone box – if you can find one working in this filthy city – and deal with my enemies.'

'I've a phone in my car, Mr Moravec,' grinned Lewin. 'Not that anything like that has entered my mind.'

'It enters everybody's mind. You'll be paid enough to stop you being tempted.'

'What's enough? How big is the story? The impression I got from Miss Haversham is that it's big.'

'She told you too much – or agreed to. When she spoke with you I hadn't finalized my involvement. Now I have. She made an arrangement with you which I don't accept – and as I'm paying *I* make the conditions. Sign the document or leave. I'll pay your time and expenses. Make your mind up. Now.'

Lewin glanced across at Jane Haversham. She smoked, coolly, nothing for him in her face. I'd really like to change that, he decided: see it change; make it change. He looked down at the sum of money the media magnate penned, almost abstractedly, into a space on the document.

'I'm in,' he said, and bent over and scrawled his signature.

'Stay that way. Jane, give him background.'

'You'd better sit, this'll take time,' she suggested.

'Don't I get to meet *him*?'

'No,' she stated, flatly.

'Come on, I've signed haven't I? Jesus, I know who he is. Eleanor Hale's son, right? The army officer the IRA lifted? He's been found alive? Probably a nutter after they'd finished with him. He's killed his old mum and you've got him holed up somewhere cosy. How's that fit your script till now?'

'It doesn't. Things might be clearer if it were true.'

Lewin gestured contemptuously. 'I may be from the sticks but I know what turns Joe Public on, OK? Kidnap, torture. Guards undercover hero and matricide? Perfect. Of course you've got him: that's his Jag outside, for chrissake!'

'He's not Daniel Hale.'

'All right, he's Davy Crockett. What's in a name? So

45

what're you after? You want me to hire a chopper, overfly the area around the old girl's farm – which, by the way, is being taken apart right now by the police – and do what? Look for where the IRA were holding him? On Dartmoor? Are you serious? What's going on?'

She turned to Moravec. 'Lewin might see the transmission tonight,' she said, as if he were not there.

'But not his face,' growled her backer. 'He'll be blacked out on screen.'

'For the moment only,' she reminded him firmly. 'That's our deal.'

'We don't kill the goose before we sell the golden eggs. If there's government involvement in this he could be pulled from under our noses and we couldn't do a damn thing. I won't risk that.'

'You're implying he could be recognized?' said Lewin. 'Of course it's not Major Hale. Not much!'

She ignored him, speaking directly to Moravec. 'The point was to have him recognized. He needs to know who he is.'

Moravec glared at her, his thick neck reddening. 'You're getting too involved, losing your commercial sense. You want immediate airtime when you're ready, production facilities right away and no formal budget limit because you've no idea how deep this thing is going to go. The difficulties and costs involved in rescheduling existing programmes and advertising when you're ready will be enormous. I'm committing a great deal of resources and capital and the only collateral I have from you is him. Let's be clear on this, he goes on open view when, and only when, *I* say the time is right and that'll be when the ratings go through the roof. With the follow-up newspaper and magazine exclusives he'll get all the exposure he'll ever need. You've agreed terms – stick to them.'

Should've gone for it on your own, sweetheart, Lewin advised, silently.

She turned to him, her colour high. 'I want you to do the Dartmoor investigation because I know I can count on you if the going gets rough. And it might. I haven't forgotten how far down the line you went for me the last time.'

46

'Down the mine,' Lewin reminded her grimly. 'Those bastards would have left me down there to have radioactive waste dumped on me. And they got away with it. Nobody went to jail that I know of.'

'People involved in government projects – especially secret projects – can get away with murder,' commented Moravec.

'They almost bloody did.'

'The man we have is not Daniel Hale,' she assured the journalist. 'I promise you that. Nor did he kill Eleanor Hale.'

Lewin tapped out a cigarette from a pack on the low table before him. 'So she was killed?'

'I didn't say that.'

Moravec said: 'Give him the rest or his conscience will have him running to his policeman friend.'

'Not my conscience. The thought of doing time might.'

'We don't know who he is,' she admitted. 'Even after twenty-four hours of enquiries we're no closer to the truth. He appeared – and I use that word advisedly – in Eleanor Hale's garden on Tuesday morning and between then and now we've learned nothing more about his identity. He appears never to have existed before Tuesday morning. Officially existed.'

'Doesn't exist right now, either,' rumbled Moravec. 'He's a non-person. Not a scrap of ID on him except Daniel Hale's papers. All files and databases we can get access to have been thoroughly checked. Nothing.'

'He's got to be somebody,' objected Lewin. 'Unless you're saying he's bloody ET!'

'He's human,' confirmed Jane Haversham.

'You mean you've considered the other possibility?'

'Wouldn't you? Faced with a person who could predict future events?'

Lewin grinned. 'What is this?'

Moravec tossed him a copy of a tabloid newspaper, one part of his media empire. 'Second story, front page.'

'The mortar attack in Northern Ireland? Sure, saw it on the box first, Tuesday night.'

'He knew it was going to happen,' said Jane Haversham.

'He warned Eleanor Hale. Wanted her to do something to stop it. This was Tuesday morning, the day she died. She'd taken him in because of his condition – he saw the attack just minutes before it happened.'

"Saw"? As in vision? And she believed him? An incident in bloody Belfast that hadn't happened yet? He conned her: heard it on the radio or the telly.'

'The news wasn't released to the public until the evening. Next of kin had to be informed by the army.'

'She got her times confused. He must have told her that evening.'

'She called me around one o'clock, Tuesday afternoon. By early evening she was dead. Ask your policeman friend for the coroner's estimate of time of death.'

'She told you he'd predicted the mortar attack? Just like that?'

'He named the officer commanding the base that was hit – a friend of Daniel Hale's. He foresaw his death.'

'Bullshit.'

'I'm committing over a hundred thousand pounds to this bullshit,' growled Moravec. 'And I don't commit capital lightly. Did you listen to your car radio on the way here?'

'Never turn it off.'

'News?'

'On the hour.'

'You remember the lead story?' Moravec nodded at Phillida Melman who brought over a large manila envelope. Lewin noted it had been franked with a time and date: that day, Thursday, 10 a.m. Turning it over he saw four signatures written either side of a heavy wax seal, their business stamp below declaring them to be partners in a law firm. The address was prestigious.

'Not in any way connected with me,' said Moravec. 'Chosen at random from among the top five practices in the country. He, our sleeping friend upstairs, wrote two copies – one for me, the other to be locked in the safe of a former High Court judge and opened tonight. Read it aloud, we don't know the contents either.'

Lewin ignored the seal and sliced through the side of the envelope with a sharp clasp knife taken from his pocket.

48

He scanned the typescript before uttering a word, then read cautiously, disbelieving: ' "Nine a.m., today's date. General Roland Westrum-Laing, attached to the Ministry of Defence, will die as a result of injuries sustained in an explosion caused by a bomb attached magnetically to the underside of his Bentley motor car, below the right-hand front seat. The General will not die instantly as the Bentley is a left-hand drive model. The bomb will be placed incorrectly as he will be driving himself. His bodyguard, Sergeant William Flint, sitting in the front right-hand seat will die first. The General will die before an ambulance can get through the London traffic to him.'

'Accurate?' asked Moravec.

Lewin stared.

'With new technology, you have to get in at the ground floor,' said Moravec, glancing at Jane Haversham with what might on a less predatory face have been a smile. 'And we've done just that.'

'He's a human being,' she replied angrily, not enjoying having her telephone ploy to ensnare Moravec thrown back at her.

'A superior one,' said Lewin.

'Even an engineered one,' Moravec said, darkly.

'What's that supposed to mean?'

'Tell him.'

She said: 'It's a theory. He's recently had cranial surgery – that's been confirmed by a private clinic who had no idea who he really was. He's got no memory. None. He describes having a cold black hole in his head. That made me think of – '

'Lobotomy?' Lewin suggested, wincing.

'It is possible.'

'Sure, possible to cut out a lump of grey tissue. But giving someone a whole new *paranormal* ability? Science fiction. Lead story, *Sunday Sport*: "We Find Fortune-telling Frankenstein." You didn't get me up here for that kind of crap.' He turned to Moravec: 'So buy the answers. You can afford the experts.'

'Call in the high-flyers of the medical profession and we've lost him. If he is somebody's experiment, they're out there looking for him – and what profession do you think they practise? And at what level?'

'Experiment? Medical experiments on human beings? That's illegal. The law – the government – doesn't allow it. Does it?'

'The law is a dinosaur when it comes to advanced scientific medicine,' said Jane Haversham. 'It lumbers behind new advances unable to grasp their significance, never mind their ethical standing. You know what was said in 1977 by Senator Edward Kennedy heading the US Senate Health Subcommittee? "From a constitutional point of view, the frontiers of law for the next twenty to twenty-five years will be in these areas of bio-ethics." And governments? There are many pseudo-medical experimental programmes going on that we don't know enough about, if at all. Military and civilian. Physical and psychical. For example, the Soviets and the Americans are deep into the paranormal: ESP, telepathy, psychokinesis. Have been for years.'

Moravec cut in: 'What we've got here may be just the tip of an iceberg. Understand one thing: this man's a walking weapon for any government who controls him. He can predict the future, which means knowing whatever your enemy plans to do. Knowing unfailingly. For all we know he may have been engineered, adapted, created – whichever – for this purpose. That's a realistic consideration we can't ignore.'

Lewin helped himself to another cigarette and lit it, gazing steadily at the tycoon. 'You mean it's dangerous. All right, you're paying me to stick my neck out. So he's escaped from somewhere? That's what we're looking at?'

Moravec nodded. 'He walked to the Hale farm. Naked. So he escaped without preparation. I crossed three Communist borders in little more than my underwear, a stolen coat, and boots. An opportunity came; I took it. I'd say, so did he.'

'He doesn't remember the hike to the house, naked? Jesus, it gets cold on Dartmoor – and I'm speaking from experience. I've been out with the trackers when convicts were crazy enough to break out of Dartmoor prison. There's

50

no shelter and the wind's a straight razor through whatever you're wearing. Naked? He's not normal.'

'We already know that,' growled Moravec.

Phillida Melman sat reading and rereading the prediction, her face shocked. 'Hasn't anyone thought that this might have saved two lives today? The police should have been told!'

Jane Haversham turned to her. 'They were. Adam told me what was going to happen. He made Eleanor Hale a solemn promise that he would use his ability – his gift, as she called it – to save lives. He trusts me implicitly: almost as a child. I could not betray that trust. The authorities had to be warned, and were. I used an MI5 informant who's been on my payroll in the past. A warning was relayed, unattributably. Obviously it made no difference whatsoever. Adam said they would die – and they did.'

'So he has a name,' said Lewin.

'It's one he remembers. It may not be his but we have to call him something. So, yes: Adam. For some reason he insists he sees the numeral nine with it.'

Moravec exploded. 'If that bombing had failed because of your warning his credibility would have been destroyed. Along with your own – and my investment.'

Jane faced him. 'You don't understand, do you? Adam saw them die – and they did. He's seen the future – in the present – and, for him, it becomes past. It has already happened. Nothing I did could have made any difference today.'

'T. S. Eliot,' Lewin smirked at Moravec. ' "Time present and time past are both perhaps present in time future, and time future contained in time past." Now there's a man who knew how to open a can of worms.'

'Dartmoor,' Jane told him. 'The answer must be there. Or at least the beginnings of it.'

Lewin shook his head. 'Not till I know more about Eleanor Hale. You think she was killed or you know she was – it's one or the other. Can't your Adam tell you?' He caught the silent exchange between her and Moravec. His temper flared, the dormant Celt in him coming out. 'Come on, either you trust me or you don't.'

'At this stage you don't tell your policeman friend anything,' warned Moravec.

'I'm not laying myself open to a charge of accessory after the fact.'

'You face that risk by asking for more information. Or is it simply a question of making the risk worthwhile?' Moravec uncapped his gold fountain-pen and changed the figure on the document Lewin had signed.

Lewin angled his head, read, then grinned: 'Plus expenses?'

'Tell him,' Moravec ordered.

Jane said: 'Adam insists she was killed. Says he knows. Two or three men were involved. She fell after a fight with one of the men and may have died then.'

'You mean her death could have been an accident?'

'Possibly. But they were murderous enough to throw her down a flight of stairs afterwards. Even if they wanted to make it look more of an accident than it did, that's a callous, awful act.'

'This sounds stupid – but did he give a description of these men?'

'No. All he said was she was really frightened by them – and she wasn't a woman who could easily be intimidated. Her courage has been proven and recognized. Yet Adam says – felt – she feared their power. Secret power.'

'You're saying government involvement?'

Moravec said: 'If not actual involvement, tacit approval; certainly funding. Experimental medical projects cost a great deal and even if the private sector could raise the money they'd be open to too much scrutiny.'

'"Tacit approval"?' Lewin snorted. 'They're in it or they're not.'

'Power without responsibility, the political ideal,' said Jane Haversham.

'You mean the old do it but don't get caught?'

'Dangerous speculation,' warned Moravec. 'The truth is that funding of secret projects can easily be lost in Whitehall. There is every reason to believe that Downing Street would have no knowledge of this sort of project. I'm not prepared to risk colossal libel damages without absolute proof.'

'And if we do get proof?' questioned Lewin. 'I wouldn't have thought you'd have wanted to embarrass this government. You haven't done too badly out of their policies.'

Moravec stared at him, hard.

'You assured me you were prepared to go all the way on this,' Jane challenged.

Moravec glowered. 'I sell news: this is a fantastic story, in the truest sense. A unique story. If there is government involvement – whoever the government – in illegal, inhumane, or unethical medical experiments on human beings I'll expose that involvement and the full conspiracy with all the power at my disposal.'

'And you'll make even more money doing it,' grinned Lewin, pocketing one of the packs of cigarettes from the table. He stood. 'I reckon I'll discover something which will make you far more than your expectations, Mister Moravec, and if I'm right I'll expect more than just a fee and expenses. There's something none of you seem to have considered. If any of this has any basis in fact then it's not the faceless *them* imprisoning and experimenting on him that'll be the meat of the scandal.'

'Which is what?' demanded Moravec.

'Where did they get him from in the first place? It's like murder – to kill someone you must first have a victim. Where did they find their victim? And is he the only one? That's the meat Joe Public eats. That's what's going to sell your TV programme and your newspapers.'

The media tycoon heaved himself to his feet, towering over Lewin. 'Find out, prove it, and I'll make you a rich man.'

FOUR

Peter Foley parked his car in the garage of the Victorian house which, despite years of his ownership, still retained so much from the Lewin family's tenure. From the name of the Welsh valley on the front gate to the heavy dark furniture in some of the many high-ceilinged rooms, their legacy was everywhere. Even the absence of the red GTi on the forecourt reminded him of their only begotten son Nigel.

Inside, Foley made himself coffee, his mind churning, his mood dark. He slumped into an armchair to watch the evening news on television and found himself tuned to a chat show on the satellite channel Nigel Lewin was addicted to. He moved to change channels then stopped as the studio lights dimmed and the celebrity host moved across to a screened area. He turned up the volume.

'. . . for centuries people have claimed that they could predict the future. From the ancient soothsayers of the Pharaohs to Nostradamus and on to the modern version, the horoscope writers in our daily newspapers. Some of us believe in prophecy, some laugh, others smugly think we're too advanced to take notice of such superstitious rubbish.

'Ah! I hear the believers say, but there have been documented cases of prophecy which have come pretty close to actual events. But predictions, as with most things paranormal, are open to interpretation, favourable or otherwise. Understanding the meaning of a prediction can be a feat in itself – worse than cryptic clues in *The Times* crossword. Try reading the quatrains of Nostradamus, for example.

'Tonight we may surprise the disbelievers! Concealed behind these screens is someone who not only claims to be able to foresee the future but is in fact prepared to prove it on live television. I should be saying that he has proved it already, for . . .'

A drum-roll heralded a heavy safe being wheeled on to the set on a trolley, halting under a single spotlight.

'. . . inside this safe – which, as you can see, has been sealed with wire by officers of Her Majesty's Customs Service – is an envelope containing a prediction for an event that took place some time today and should already have been reported on the news. Easy! I hear you cry, it's a trick safe, there's a secret way in. Not so, the safe comes from the home of a former High Court judge who's kindly consented to come out of retirement and pass one final judgement for us tonight. But first, let's meet our Future Man!'

A second drum-roll brought back-lighting to the screens, projecting a male figure in silhouette.

'I understand your name is Adam?' asked the host. 'Will you confirm that we have never met or spoken before this moment?'

'Yes,' came the muted reply.

'You claim to predict the future accurately?'

'I see the future. To you, the future is what will happen. To me it is happening or, as with the proof you wanted, it already has.'

'So your written prediction, sealed and witnessed by four eminent members of the English Bar, subsequently locked and again sealed in that safe – you declare, in front of this studio audience and all our viewers, to have already occurred? It is now news we will have heard already?'

'I know you have.'

'Adam, I'm now going to ask our distinguished guest to open his safe. I must point out to the viewers and studio audience that he placed the envelope in there personally this morning after witnessing its sealing and only he knows the combination of the lock.'

Foley put his cup down on the table by his side, watching a tall, ageing man cut through the Customs bonding wire with some difficulty before crouching to work the lock mechanism, his free hand concealing the combination from the probing cameras. The door opened, revealing inside a single, heavy manila envelope. He removed it, put on spectacles, checked the wax seal and closely examined the four signatures.

'All in order,' he confirmed.

The host walked over for the envelope, thanked his guest and returned to the screened area. He held the wax seal out for the camera to focus on. 'Unbroken,' he said. 'The four signatures are confirmed as those written on the envelope before it was placed in the safe. I'm about to open it.'

Once again no response came from the still silhouette.

'Here we go, then.' The seal and thick gummed flap proved tougher than expected but finally the contents were extracted. In a steady voice the host recited the details of the explosion and double murder in Savile Row that afternoon.

He allowed the silence to hang undisturbed for a few moments before turning to the silhouette behind him. 'Adam, I remember a man named Uri Geller who was able to perform extraordinary, apparently paranormal feats. If there is no trickery with this – and to be honest I cannot understand how there could be – what you seem able to do surely must surpass any paranormal powers he claims to have.'

'There is no trick.'

'Can you explain your power?'

'I wish I could.'

'Adam, it must now be obvious to everybody why we have not fully identified you and have also taken the precaution of blacking you out. It is clear that, identified, you would be at extreme risk from terrorist organizations such as the IRA whose activities you predicted so accurately. There's just one question everybody must be asking right now which perhaps you will answer: could you have stopped the atrocity which occurred in London today?'

'What I see has already happened. I know that now. I can't change anything,' came the defeated reply.

'Do you see only the final outcome, or could you follow the chain of events leading to an atrocity such as this one today and provide details to the police? Surely then you could alter the end result?'

'Can you alter the past?'

'No, but one can alter the present. I am in control of my present, therefore, given foreknowledge of what is to come, I can make decisions that perhaps I would not otherwise have made. For example, we have a theatre full of people here: now, God forbid it should happen but there is a chance, according to statistics, that one or more might be involved in an accident driving home. If you could see such an event taking place and warned them now, they might take a taxi home or go by train. You would have saved a life.'

Silence.

'Did you understand the question?'

'You want more proof,' came the heavy reply after a pause. 'I'll write down what you want to know. What you choose to do with it is your decision.'

The host wound up quickly, the ominous response throwing him so that he almost forgot to read the autocue prompt for a forthcoming feature programme on Adam, then moved to his marker to introduce his next guest.

Foley switched off. Bloody IRA. He wondered where Lewin was, determining to drag answers from him if necessary. He felt bone-weary and outraged by the events of the long day. You're getting old, he advised himself: too old to kick back when someone rides roughshod over you. Let it be.

He stretched his long legs out on to a footstool and fell into a deep uneasy sleep almost instantly.

Nigel Lewin woke him.

Foley rubbed his arms, feeling cold, his legs numbed by lack of circulation. 'Jesus, what time is it?'

'Just gone ten thirty. You were out cold.'

'Don't disappear, I want to speak to you.'

'I've had a long bloody hard drive and the sodding car overheated so don't get heavy, OK?'

'How did you know?'

'Know what?'

'I'm too tired for your games.'

Lewin shrugged. 'I was just being clever – you know what I'm like.'

'Let's have it straight. This bit of moonlighting in London – same people as before, are they? The TV producer from that bloody tin-mine disaster. Haversham? She called you, right?'

'I'm telling you, it's nothing.'

'Nothing? I put Eleanor Hale's house under a microscope today because of you. Guess what? There had been someone else there. Four someones. One sat at her kitchen table. An odd one because he was covered in some kind of ointment or jelly which we think he showered off afterwards. They tried to wipe off most of it but there were still traces: on the kitchen table, the legs of the chair he sat on, residue on the sides of the bath from his shower. We also found skin tissue and blood traces in and around the bath. And fingerprints. Lots of fingerprints. They didn't wipe these too well if at all, so they're either very stupid or they didn't care.'

'You've identified the prints?' asked Lewin, warily.

'Not on record.'

'Then they didn't care.'

'What kind of criminal doesn't care whether they leave evidence behind?'

'Head-bangers.'

'Motive?'

'She had a bit of bread – maybe a lot – stashed in the house. They raided the place and had a party while they were at it. Happens, doesn't it? You're the copper. Was she raped? Assaulted? They do that to old ladies nowadays. Yuk!'

'Nothing sexual. Neck broken, back of head caved in. She died from the crushed skull – the neck injury was an extra: maybe because she didn't seem dead or just for kicks.'

'First offenders, that's why the prints aren't on record,' said Lewin, firmly.

'Certainly takes me well away from anything more sinister – which should please you.'

'Sorry, lost me.'

'What you suggest makes sense. Fits very well actually. Drugged-up punks go in, one or more smeared in some as yet to be identified goo, terrorize the old lady, have a ball in the bath, cut themselves in the process leaving bits of skin and blood – small but enough for Forensic to play with – then crush her skull and heave her down the stairs. The problem is there are other factors, possibly another motive, which makes all that garbage.'

'What's that?'

'Wait. Let's take your advice this morning, first. What prompted that? Conscience? A little covering of your own back – just in case?'

'I told you already.'

'And I still don't believe you. I'll give you another motive. Your lady in London, by your own admission and on past evidence, makes programmes with more than a hint of political comment – one might even say bias. She really gets behind a cause, doesn't she?'

'What's sodding politics to do with it?' snapped Lewin.

'The old lady never bothered to vote so that takes her out of the frame. Which leaves son Daniel, doesn't it? Daniel who disappeared into the Belfast lions' den never to be seen again. Heard of, yes. The word came down the line from the informers that he'd been topped, then chopped. Dog food now, apparently. Took it like a man, the IRA boyos are supposed to have said: Should have been one of us. Maybe the informers got paid twice this time? By the bloody Provos as well as the Brits?'

'What are you getting at?'

'He *is* one of them. Now. Alive and turned. They do have a cause, you know. Historical. Older than Marxism – and by God, that's had a lot of unlikely converts. Did you know he'd become a Catholic? A Father McDonnell, interviewed by Special Branch after his disappearance, revealed that truth.'

Lewin wanted to laugh. He was a fluent liar and had a story prepared for Foley's inevitable questioning. 'OK, Jane Haversham is planning a programme about Daniel Hale. She saw the news about his mother and wanted someone local to dig a bit. I'm it. Jesus, you're suspicious! If I were you I'd stick with the head-bangers. Eleanor Hale got in their way – end of story.'

Foley said: 'Daniel Hale is alive. He was found by two police officers asleep in his car in a layby on the A30 outside the town of Camberley, Tuesday night. They woke him, breathalysed him without a result, took him to the nearest hospital – a private medical clinic a couple of minutes away – because his condition concerned them and left him there. He was carrying five hundred pounds in cash in a wallet which also contained his driver's licence and insurance and he was holding three sealed letters not addressed to himself. Under the circumstances, they assumed a suicide attempt: pills and alcohol. They returned the following morning to the clinic – yesterday – but he had already left with a young woman who drove his car for him. A grey E-type Jaguar coupé DSH 42 which we know to have been in the garage at Raethmoor Farm until very recently – possibly even on the day of the murder. The woman was Jane Haversham.'

Lewin shrugged, turned and poured himself a drink. 'News to me,' he said easily. 'Want something?'

Foley said: 'When it comes to the IRA any special pleading I might request on your behalf would fall on deaf ears. Special Branch and MI5 tend to be hard-nosed on that subject.'

'My brain's scrambled, can I go to bed now or is it rubber truncheon time?'

'Ladies of Eleanor Hale's age bruise very easily and a tumble down stairs doesn't cause the kind of bruising associated with the grip of a strong hand which she had on her right arm and left ankle. We found traces of blood on the stair carpet, on a walking stick in a stand at the foot of the stairs, and around the base of one of the taps in the bathroom wash handbasin. Same blood group for all. Not her blood group, nor the group of the one who took a shower. The skin tissue we found trapped in the drain-plug is his. Could be from blistering. What causes blisters?'

Hard running, thought Lewin.

'Burns. Remember the gel in the kitchen and bathroom? Burns can be caused by explosives – and we all know who uses explosives. We've had a demonstration today in London, haven't we? Where you've just come back from.'

This is crazy, thought Lewin. 'So why'd the IRA want

to kill that old woman? Danny's their boy, you say – she's his sodding mum!'

'Until now everyone has accepted the fact of Daniel Hale's death. Everyone except his mother. Deep down she never believed it. You should have been at the house today. She's kept him alive up there. Clothes freshly dry-cleaned and laundered; brand new underwear, socks, shirts. More: car registration, insurance, driver's licence, private health scheme, all up to date. She refused to claim on his life policy. She kept him alive when Daniel Hale wanted to be dead. Or accepted as being dead.'

'You're saying he was in on killing her?'

'I found new packaging from men's shirts and underwear – exactly the same brands as in the house. His. In her dustbin. The last garbage collection was on the Monday. The day before she was killed. She'd become an embarrassment. She could even be dangerous. People might take her seriously. He wanted to be dead. While he was dead he was invisible. The Provos would love that. The E-type was the key. We know from the garbage men that it was there on the Monday: they saw it under its cover as usual. DI Grant chased up the registration on the national computer at Hendon and found where it had been on Tuesday night. A call to the clinic and we had your lady producer driving it to London on Wednesday morning with Daniel Hale as passenger. The clinic were reluctant to pass on her address but it's amazing how the suggestion that police officers might turn up to search premises gets co-operation.'

Lewin's glass was empty. He glanced over at the brandy decanter but made no move towards it. 'So why haven't you gone in and nicked him?'

'You saw Haversham today?'

'You're barking up the wrong tree. Jane Haversham wouldn't get involved with the IRA.'

'Maybe she's not. Maybe it's just personal. Maybe she doesn't know what might be going on.'

Lewin felt relief surge through him and made for the decanter.

'I'll take that drink,' said Foley.

'Cheers,' said Lewin, handing him a brandy and soda.

Foley silently raised his glass. 'You're a computer nut. If I wanted to crack an access code on a computer how'd I go about it?'

Lewin set his glass down. 'You mean illegally?'

Foley took a sip of brandy. 'I suppose I do. Yes.'

'Now I've heard everything. Whose?'

'Police national computer at Hendon. For starters.'

'Crazy! Go in the front door. You're legal.'

Foley sat forward in his chair. 'You ever been caged in, Nigel? You know I have. I can't stand the feeling. I was caged in today. Still am. The bars came down all around and I don't know who operated them. There's a lot of muddying waters from the top but what is clear is that something is going on – being covered up maybe – and the murder of an old lady is of little or no importance in comparison.'

Lewin felt the surge of adrenalin boost the high from the amphetamines he had taken on the drive back from London. Power. Secret power, he remembered.

'I've been blocked from talking to Jane Haversham. Her and Hale. I asked the Met to go in and pick them up and got the can't-do-that-talk-to-Special-Branch excuse. Did that and got bitten by VIPER. Heard of it? MI5 codeword: across the board non-interference directive to all national police forces. Signals an ongoing counter-intelligence operation, we're led to believe, but it could be any damn thing, couldn't it? When VIPER bites you're supposed to roll over and play dead. I'd like to know what I'm not allowed to know. I'd like to give an old lady some peace. I'd like to do my job. Can you help?'

I could, Lewin thought. And maybe you'd ruin everything and I'd be stuck as your lodger in what used to be my home instead of swanning it in some hot place where the girls lie half-naked on the beach in slick rows like a finger buffet, tempting and so easy to pick up.

He said: 'There is someone. He won't come cheap but he'll get results. Which he'll sell to me right after. I'm shattered. I'll fix it up in the morning if you still feel the same way. Maybe tomorrow you'll be back to being the safe, conventional copper I'm used to.'

Maybe, Foley thought.

The next morning Foley awoke to silence. He made his way down across the two cold landings of the old house to the echoing, stone-floored kitchen, dragging his dressing gown on as he went.

Silence. No radio blaring from the window shelf, no heavy rock blasting through the speakers of the powerful stereo system installed in almost every room in the house but controlled from the first-floor sanctuary – boy and man – of Nigel Lewin.

The note was propped against a coffee percolator, wilting from the steam. Foley rescued it and poured black coffee, drinking gratefully as he read:

Dear Heart (Supertec):

How does the world look today? Better? Worse? If you have to be Don Quixote may I decline the role of Sancho Panza because I hate to see grown men crying all over their blotter at work as they pack their desk for the last time. I saw my old dad do it once and it was not a pleasant sight. Also, it's expensive. You tend to lose everything: home, car, the lot. How would you feel without the BMW? This house was part of the price paid for an ageing man's foray against some winter of discontent his hormones had created. He never came to terms with the fact that the home he'd paid for in full was once again a mountain to climb – though he did know he was too old ever to reach the top. You knew, supertec that you are, that they didn't fall, they jumped. My parents weren't the brightest in the world but they knew boats like you know detectiving and I know digging for gold in stories others give up on. Being the Good Guy and Old School you never let me know the truth but I'd worked it out anyway. So you did the Right Thing and let me stay on. God bless you for that, guv'nor, you're a gen'leman and a scholar!

You're wondering, right now: Why this heartpour-

63

ing all over the kitchen table? 'Course you are. Answer: I've slept on all of it, too. Like you did. Or rather, I didn't, not very well anyway. The thing is I'm a little windy. Scared, I mean, not the other thing. The Haversham assignment which I told you about last night isn't quite the way I described it. I think – I feel – that it might become more than a little hairy. They killed the old lady, didn't they! And I don't mean the sodding IRA either.

Foley drank more coffee, seeing the break in the writing and the sudden stiffening of the hand. The banter was gone with the slanting letters and a new serious tone showed in the rigid vertical strokes. Foley had seen such abrupt changes before: in handwritten confessions to serious crimes; in suicide notes. He saw a packet of cigarettes by the percolator. He'd given up years before but now he extracted one and lit it with a match from the ancient gas cooker.

He sat down and continued reading:

You've heard of Rudolf Moravec? Who hasn't? Zillionaire. Owns all the newsprint and TV airtime this side of Moscow – which is roughly where he came from in the first place. Rudolf is going to make me a rich man. Seriously rich. All I have to do is bring home the goodies – which is precisely what I plan to do. As you read this I shall be striving to do just that. Don't, *don't*, I mean it, put out an APB on me because I'll be pissed off. But if perchance I turn up like Eleanor Hale I'd expect you to do something to avenge your dear friend and grateful lodger.

I've written down the name and contact number for your hacker. He's eccentric, gay, and pronounces his name RAFE MYBREE – not Ralph Mayberry, remember that or he'll hang up. Confession time: I was going to cheat and buy any info you get off him for myself – because I really do think we're on the same hunt but going down different paths – but I can't hang around while you plod and maybe I can't see you jeopardizing your career anyway. I'll close with love and kisses because if this does turn out to be my last literary hurrah your reputation will be thoroughly shot!

(If it isn't already.)N.

Foley folded the sheet of paper, got up and poured more coffee, looking out into the sprawling, unkempt garden. Bloody jungle, he thought. He made toast, sat and ate it looking at the note; finally, after wiping his buttery fingers, he read it again.

There's a collective madness that drops over us like a weighted net, he decided. Descending at various times in our lives. This is one. Or maybe it's a virus? The question is, does it start with one person and become contagious or are we all struck down at the same time?

Lewin's note – or the tone of it – did not surprise him. He see-sawed wildly in most things, from his girls to his moods on what Foley called his Celtic days, when he made noises about oncoming personal doom. Young men with literary pretensions tended to go down that route, in Foley's judgement. So be it. He could put up with it. It was better than living alone.

Foley put the note in his dressing-gown, scaled the stairs again and made himself ready to face the world, halting only to advise divisional headquarters, vaguely, that certain enquiries on an outstanding case would entail him journeying to London that day. He was known for his wide-ranging contacts from his years in the capital and occasional forays back there to oil the wheels of inter-force co-operation – and, some said, sweeten his personal network of underworld informers – so his intentions and lack of precise detail were treated as routine.

Not an ordinary day, he thought. There was a feel to it. Or perhaps it was him. He found himself looking forward to the drive up to London. If it stayed dry he would put the top down and let the cobwebs which had built up around him the last few years blow away.

The telephone on the dark, heavy-legged hall table stopped him at the front door.

'Willow here, sir, Scene of Crime.'

'If this is to do with the Hale investigation, Willow, it's been taken out of our hands. Heard last night. Mind, you'll have to pass on your results so you haven't wasted your time. Go on, satisfy my curiosity – what have you got?'

'I don't quite know how to put this.'

'Try words, Willow. But not too many, I'm on my way out.'

'Four individuals were on Raethmoor Farm – four that is apart from the deceased, Mrs Hale. You were convinced that one of these was Daniel Hale.'

'I still am. All the evidence supports that.'

'Sir, I checked with the Met Fingerprint Bureau in case Major Hale's prints had been passed on for ID purposes by Army Intelligence. He had disappeared on undercover duty.'

'And Provo soft-nosed rounds don't leave much of a face. Yes, I know. Had they?'

'Yes. They match with older fingermarks found in the house which we lifted for elimination purposes.'

'And the wrappings we found in the bin – from the underwear and shirts? Hale's prints are on those?'

'The old lady's on the Cellophane are the freshest, the rest are smudged – could be anybody's: shop assistants, other people handling the goods, anyone. The polythene is probably the same but I can't deal with that myself. I haven't sent it off for metal deposition testing yet. Expensive. Gold, lasers, vacuum chambers, all that. I didn't know how far you wanted to go on this one?'

'Someone else's decision now. Are you saying four suspects *and* Daniel Hale?'

'Sir, Hale's fingermarks are considerably older than any of the others, including his mother's.'

'You trying to tell me Hale wasn't there? He's really dead, despite the evidence? . . . Willow?'

'Major Hale may or may not be dead – but one of the men whose prints we found in that house is.'

'When? Where was the body found?' Foley waited, hearing Willow's breathing through the silence. 'For Christ's sake!' he snapped.

'He died in nineteen forty-five, sir.'

'Wonderful! Who gave you that gem of information?'

'Special Branch, sir.'

'Then they need to sort themselves out, don't they.'

'They can't understand it either, sir, but the prints match.'

'Willow, there is no way a man who died in nineteen forty-five can leave fresh fingermarks in a house on Dartmoor the day before yesterday. Or are the Branch suggesting the body has been exhumed – what's left of it – and the prints planted? In any case, if he's dead what's he doing still on file?'

'He's not, sir. Not on file, I mean. The Branch have a Black Museum. The prints in question are there, on display.'

'Bloody stupid. There has to be some kind of mix-up.'

'The chap I spoke to said he was looking at them as he spoke to me.'

'Winding you up. I'll call him and give him a rocket for wasting your time.'

'He really seemed certain, sir . . . I don't want to – '

'Name, rank and extension, Willow.'

'John Baker, sir. Detective Sergeant. Extension 511.'

Foley sat for a moment, pondering. Wind-up? Wilful mischief? The first recorded case of duplicated fingerprints and all that that entailed? Whichever – Willow had found someone who was willing to discuss the case. All the cage doors had not been closed. He dialled London immediately and tersely gave the extension number.

Baker answered the call himself, clearly irritated and unimpressed by Foley's rank: 'As I told your man: I am facing the display case with Fascher's prints right now. There's no mistake this end so I'd say someone's playing silly buggers down there – but don't ask me how they've done it. Sir.'

'What's this villain's name again?'

'Not a villain. I mean not a criminal. A spy: Nazi spy to be exact. Cover name William Miller: real name Otto Horst Fascher. Executed May ninth, nineteen forty-five. Hanged – not shot. Last one we topped, I'd say.'

'For the sake of argument let's assume he escaped the noose – he'd be what age now? Sixties?'

'A civilian in his early twenties still in Britain during war-time got himself a lot of attention, none of it good. Shirker or spy, that was the usual jibe. Fascher was forty-seven, a safe age for a spy.'

'Which makes him?'

'Would have made him well the wrong side of ninety, now.'

Foley paused, then summed up: 'So one supposedly dead man is driving around in his Jaguar, alive if not entirely well, while another gets up from his grave and leaves fingermarks all over a house on Dartmoor!'

'The one in the Jag being Hale? Your chap gave me some background.'

'Correct. Baker, no one down here plays silly buggers with me – they know better. So if you are certain there's no mistake your end then there's only one course of action left.'

'Which is?'

'Exhumation,' said Foley, thinking: and don't anyone scream VIPER because there's no way a Nazi spy hanged in forty-five is involved in any ongoing MI5 operation now.

'Ah!' said Baker. 'Now you may have yourself a problem there.'

'I already have one.'

'This one's called the Ministry of Defence.'

'For an exhumation order? You mean the Home Office.'

'I mean the Ministry of Defence. And strictly speaking anything to do with the late Herr Otto Fascher should be referred to them, even your enquiry. Still secret, the execution of spies – even all that time ago. Powers that be can be touchy, still. I've got the case file right here. Beautiful work: copperplate handwriting for all the secret annexes. Love these old cases – like going back in time.'

'Reference number? Anything to save me sitting in MOD corridors all day?'

'Here we go: "All enquiries to Room 713, The War Office. Army (Department of Advanced Medicine)." Well out of date, probably doesn't exist now – I'll try the computer for a referral. Hold the line.'

Foley could hear soft paper noises he assumed to be password lists being consulted then the gentle clicking of a keyboard. He dragged a chair out from under the hall-table causing a screech from the harlequin tiles then sat down, barely controlling his impatience. 'Anything?' he asked.

'Nothing under Otto Fascher or his British cover name. I'm trying 713 . . . nothing there . . .'

'What about that army department reference?'

'Too long in that form. Okay, let's try this . . .'

Foley waited. He could hear Baker's breath held in check. 'Baker?'

'Sir, I think it would be better if you made any enquiries direct to the MOD.'

'What did you just come up with?'

'Nothing.'

'Nothing you can talk to me about, you mean?'

'Nothing I can get into. End of conversation, sorry.'

'What about the prints? Fascher's. You still say they're the ones found in the farmhouse? I'll need that confirmation when I see the MOD.'

'Speak to them, they'll come back to me if they want me to go any further.'

'What the hell did you punch into that keyboard.'

'Goodbye, Superintendent. Sorry.'

Foley sat, holding the purring phone, staring at it but seeing only a man's fingers punching four digits on a keyboard, hearing the clicks in his mind, seeing the letters. Was it what he saw that changed his mind or had he, too, just been bitten by VIPER?

He took Nigel Lewin's letter from his pocket and dialled the number written at the end.

'Well?' snapped a rude voice.

'Ralph Mayberry?' enquired Foley, pronouncing as Lewin had directed. 'I understand you're some kind of genius?'

'It has been said.'

'I need a key to a door which has no lock.'

'Now that sounds interesting. When?'

'Now,' said Foley. 'I'd better tell you I'm a police officer – but this is strictly private enterprise: no comebacks, not to you, not to me.'

'Give me your name and phone number, I'll call you back.'

'Can't you give me an answer now?'

'Sure – but I need a couple of minutes to check you out.'

'Where?'

'Police personnel database, naturally.'

'Jesus,' breathed Foley.

'No, he's the one who walked on water,' said Mayberry and hung up.

FIVE

He stumbled through the blizzard, away from the wreckage of the helicopter, the fierce shock of the cold squeezing his heart and freezing his lungs. He reached back into his childhood both for escape and for the words to describe the hell he found himself in.

God! This is an awful place.

Scott. He died in the Antarctic. A schoolboy's hero. Glory and all that. Why don't the history books record the pain? Dear God, let me die. I should have died in the crash. Why let me live to face this?

He lay down on the glacier. His vision failed as tears froze on his eyes and momentarily his world cracked, splintered and fell away, becoming white again, too white ever for sleep.

Why do they lie and say cold blesses you with sleep? I'll never sleep again, not while the glare defeats my eyelids so mercilessly.

I'm dreaming, he thought. Or realized. I will wake and be in bed and if she is not already beside me, she will be. It will happen. Look down at yourself, wipe the snow from your clothes and say aloud what you see there. Perhaps she will hear and remember because you remember nothing. Try. Try now.

'I am a dead soldier.'

'Adam!' cried Jane Haversham, over the dreadful sound that came from deep in his throat. She gripped his head, shocked by the cold flesh, and shook it violently.

He awoke, the darkness a door that closed out the storm. The warmth of the bed, paradise. Escape, he thought: but from which? The dream or the reality?

'Thank God!' she breathed.

71

'Tell me what I said.'

'No!' she whispered. 'It was a dream. A nightmare.'

'I wanted you to hear – to remember for me.'

'Adam, you know too much. You knew I heard you and would come to you. Even when you were dreaming, you knew. I can't exist under these conditions. I can't escape them either.'

'Will you stay with me?'

'For a while.'

She came to him, giving herself completely so that he might lose his fear, his confusion, in her. In the darkness something, some part of him distantly, achingly familiar, tore at her. A sudden glimpse of a hard-lost love: brief, longing, too much past hurt and more to come certain – if she committed herself to him. Still, she stayed, curled up to him, until he escaped into the peace she had given.

It was three o'clock: when those who slept slept their deepest. They came in two vehicles, one for themselves, one for him.

He awoke instantly. 'They're here,' he said as if she were as aware as he.

His terror spurred her: she went quickly to the window and edged the curtains aside.

The truck cut off the single entrance – and exit – to the mews, seeming to glow in the darkness as steam, or condensation, seeped from its white cylindrical body. Black shadows moved across the vehicle, mingling with others appearing from the right. She knew she must act now or lose him.

'Stay there,' she ordered and moved carefully downstairs in the dark heading directly for the controls of the house security system, then darted to her powerful stereo, pushed in a CD, spun the volume control to full then began flinging her windows wide open before turning on every light she had.

Outside, her mews cottage was stark halogen white from the security lights, the clamour of the alarms fighting unequally with Chris Rea, crystal clear and in full throat at fifty watts per channel. Within seconds the entire mews was awake, lights snapping on everywhere, trapping silent moving figures on the cobblestones before they turned and ran, pursued only by the noise.

Exhilarated by fear and her small victory Jane ran outside after them but all that remained of their presence was exhaust fumes poisoning the dying night. She silenced the stereo and heard the wail of police sirens and the insistent ringing of her doorbell by her neighbours.

By four o'clock the mews was dark and silent once more, her statement taken by police who wrote silently, their flat eyes hiding their opinions on neurotic women while her neighbours cursed her and the work-day ahead as they tried to regain sleep.

She returned to her own bed because she'd given enough of herself that night. Because Adam was too much for her at that moment. Because she needed the security of her own room, her own bed, and her own ignorance of the future.

A heavy thump and flurry from below woke her. Morning. The silence from Adam's room chilled her. Quickly she pulled on her robe and went there. He slept as though life had deserted him: still and white, the covers pushed off him. Her eyes felt scraped and raw. In her bathroom she splashed cold water on her face then went downstairs to find his grainy silhouette on the front pages of two of the many morning newspapers sprawled on the doormat.

Moravec.

She swore. Their agreement was no press coverage until her programme was made and transmitted – then his newspapers could have a field day. That damned, crass TV show. She should never have allowed it. The last thing Adam needed was a circus!

Immediately, she called World Communications, knowing Moravec was habitually at his desk before others ate breakfast, and was put straight through.

'People from that studio audience are dead and he predicted it,' he growled, cutting her short. 'I've got a head start on the competition and I'm not giving that up. Things change. We have to move with events. I understand you went public yourself last night?'

'Are you having me watched?' she demanded.

'No, but perhaps I should be – just to protect my investment. If my people didn't have sources inside the Metropolitan Police they wouldn't be doing their jobs. You're a resourceful woman.'

'You know who they were?'

'An organization it's illegal to prosecute – even when their own activities are illegal.'

'MI5? How are they involved?'

'Daniel Hale. It's a known fact that Five's been haunted for years by the fear that a British officer with undercover experience – which means knowledge of secret procedures – might go over to the Provos: either by their breaking him or through ideological conversion. I had a call in the middle of the night from Nigel Lewin. It appears that his policeman friend is of the opinion that Daniel Hale could be such an officer. He's theorizing that he killed his own mother because she would not accept the fact of his supposed death – which made her a threat to his new role. Foley's made this deduction because of the apparent reappearance of Hale – with you.'

'Five think Adam really is Daniel Hale?'

'They believe Daniel Hale is alive – that's the word. Anything on him is referred to them directly. They think he may have been turned.'

'Daniel could never be a terrorist. I know.'

'Because he was a hero between your legs? Beyond that you have no conception of how his body or mind might react to persuasion or torture – or both.'

'No wonder you're hated.'

'Hate is an extreme form of respect: I encourage it. Accept the limitations of your knowledge of people and remember I've an empire to keep me informed.'

'So why hasn't Adam been arrested? I mean, openly? Not this creeping around in the night.' She remembered her complete fear just hours before and almost laughed aloud at her flippancy.

'Even I can't buy that information. Perhaps we're not

74

talking to the right people? There seem to be conflicting issues involved here. MI5 is most certainly holding the investigation into the murder of Eleanor Hale in check – so our police sources state – but you know Five's world: this entire Daniel Hale business could be a blind alley for us to follow. Which could mean Five are being manipulated or are being instructed by someone else entirely.'

'How high?'

'Who pulls Five's strings?'

'Cabinet Office? That's laying it directly at the door of Ten Downing Street!'

'Ever read Marya Zaturenska? "In each flower a sleeping snake and the arrows pierce the mark." '

'Is that some oblique Eastern European warning?'

'It's a warning of where our own barbs might be aimed when the time comes.'

'We could never prove it.'

'There are two certainties in any political scandal big enough to destroy careers: there is always someone prepared to jump ship early and always someone prepared to survive at whatever cost to others. I'll shake the political tree and see what, or who, falls out.'

'What about Adam? He's not safe here any more. Last night proved that.'

'Last night proved that those who want him are not prepared to break surface and show themselves.'

'So what do we do – get out of the water?' she enquired, acidly.

'Going public now is one way, yes. The other is to dive deep and hope they don't find you again – but I wouldn't count on it.'

'How did they find us this time?'

'Daniel Hale. His mother, his identity, his car, and if one includes you – his woman.'

'I was never that.'

'Perhaps not – but with his security rating you would have been listed as a contact. You were. A weekend stay. A hotel in Cambridge.'

'Haven't those snooping bastards at Five got better things to do?'

'Naïvety, from you? You're radical and you're media – a positive threat to their secret world and their power.'

'I'll call and let you know what I decide to do with Adam.'

'Not on this line. You may not be tapped now because of the High Court ruling you gained but that can be overturned. If we are playing at the top table, expect everything because it will probably happen.'

'I'll be in touch.'

She felt Adam behind her as she replaced the phone, turned with the newspapers: one look at his pale eyes told her he knew already.

'There was nothing more you could do,' she said, beginning now to understand the weight he must carry. 'You were pressured. It was obvious how you felt.' She set the papers down. 'It says the party was warned but they'd hired the coach and come all the way from Bradford. Didn't want to waste the money. They're reported as saying they thought it was all a trick.'

The telephone rang. She snatched at it, glad to escape his eyes.

'Jane Haversham?' enquired a quick voice, naming a tabloid newspaper owned by Moravec's arch-rival. 'Listen, we know you're involved with *him*, OK? Had it from a source in the studios last night so no point in denials. We're willing to offer serious money for an exclusive. Seen the business about the motorway crash? Incredible! How's he do it? Get him to name his price, add what you want for yourself and we'll meet it. Forget Moravec, we'll sort him out. Court costs, the lot. How's that sound? Is he there with you now? What's your relationship with him? Just professional – or personal too?'

'Get lost,' she snapped and smacked the phone down. 'Damn! This place'll be under siege in half an hour. You don't need this. You're not ready. It'll break you. We've got to leave. *Now*.'

Upstairs she threw things in a case, urging him to do the same. They were ready to leave within fifteen minutes. She stepped out of the cottage first, keeping him back from sight. A couple burst from a car parked near the entrance to the mews, a camera already in the man's hands, a cassette recorder in the girl's. The cameraman halted, knelt like a rifleman, and shot film rapidly.

'The E-type. I'll drive,' Jane said.

The girl shrieked.

Jane turned and saw a man strike the back of the cameraman's neck with a short clubbing downward blow before ripping the slung camera off the splayed figure and tearing out the film.

'Get in,' she snapped, throwing her bag into the rear of the old coupé and herself behind the wheel, momentarily forgetting the starter button, then reversed at speed down the cobbled mews, the monocoque bodywork vibrating madly, the pained whine of the gearbox fighting the growl of the engine. She swerved sharply to avoid the girl reporter crouched beside the cameraman, seeing her mouth an obscenity.

The assailant had vanished.

'Moravec's thugs,' she gasped, her heart hammering. 'The man who attacked the cameraman. The others are his opposition. He's "protecting his investment".'

'No,' said Adam.

'Christ! If you know what's going to happen then bloody tell me!'

'I don't.'

'You know, there's only one thing worse than a man who thinks he's always right – and that's a man who knows he is.' She dropped a gear for a tight corner and accelerated out hard, cutting through the back streets. 'Sorry, I'm bad without sleep.' She glanced at him. 'I don't know what to do or where to go for the moment but I will. All right?'

'Hartrampf,' he said. 'I know too much about everything except myself. He knows. She said so.'

She remembered the strangled sounds and the chilling statement he had made in his nightmare, suppressing the shudder that ran through her body at the thought of opening the door on whatever unnamed horror lay within his closed mind.

She turned the E-type towards Belgravia.

77

Erich Hartrampf stood six feet four and three-quarter inches tall in soft leather slippers on a polished parquet floor the colour of his suntanned, deeply wrinkled skin. His shoulders were rounded, from a lifetime stooping to those smaller than he.

His accent was a curious mixture of Boston and Berlin, his voice strong and unwavering despite his seventy-eight years. 'Terrible news,' he said, ushering them into the study of his hard-edged, echoing, high-ceilinged home. 'I saw the news of Eleanor Hale's death. She called me on the telephone the day she died. She explained.' He glanced at Adam. 'A most courageous lady. A humanitarian.'

'How much did she tell you, Doctor?' Jane asked after he had read Eleanor Hale's letter in silence.

Hartrampf folded the letter and put it in the breast pocket of his jacket. 'I understand she wrote to you too? In mine she expressed some medical opinions. She had once been a psychiatric nurse, quite deeply involved during the war with cases of complete mental breakdown. Military personnel. I regret, of these there were many. Sadly it is in the nature of modern warfare that the mind is possibly more vulnerable than the body: not all combatants suffer physical wounds but there are very few who do not suffer stress resulting from fearing every moment for one's life. Adolf Hitler understood this very well, which is why he was so intent on creating an army of near-robotic humans in his experimental laboratories. You must excuse me, I become impassioned by this. I escaped Nazi Germany – if I hadn't I most certainly would have been forced into aiding his experiments or I would have been killed. I like to believe I would have chosen death.'

While talking, Hartrampf had moved Adam to a tall-backed leather armchair and from behind had manoeuvred an angle-poise lamp above his close-cropped head.

'Very skilful. I would say the best work I have ever seen. Indeed, so good that I wonder if some new advanced technique may have been perfected which I have not followed. In the field of lasers perhaps? At my age one loses touch.'

'He doesn't remember a thing,' Jane said. 'The injury to his head, the operations – nothing.'

Hartrampf gave a brief, tight smile. 'Assumptions can be misleading – if not dangerous. Amnesia can result from a head injury but the majority of cases are due to psychological conflict. However, whatever the cause the fact remains: he doesn't remember. But he *knows*. The question is: is he willing to remember? The mind has its own defence mechanisms, responses that enable the organism to avoid, escape, or mitigate the effects of fear-provoking stimuli – and these can be activated in a split second if sanity is threatened. He is not the first to have sat in this room with no recollection of his prior life – up to a particular moment. What we seek is the event before that moment. One brief moment of . . . whatever shut down his mind.' He laid both of his large hands over Adam's head. 'Young man, if you are willing, I would like to try hypnosis.'

'I need to know,' said Adam.

'Of course.' Hartrampf moved around to face him, his back to Jane, obscuring her view. She did not see what he did or hear the soft words he spoke – all she saw was Adam slumped in his chair. Hartrampf turned to her. 'Don't be concerned. I will not push his mind further than it wishes to go.'

'He has terrible dreams,' she said.

He put a brown finger against his lips then lowered his long body into a chair pulled up before Adam. 'What does the name Adam mean to you?' he asked.

'It is in my mind.'

'Only in your mind?'

'Others.'

'Explain, please.'

'Other minds.'

'You've heard the name? Seen it?'

'In my mind.'

'Only in your mind,' Hartrampf repeated.

'There is nothing more.'

'Nothing more than your mind?'

'And the others.'

'The other minds? How many?'

79

'They change.'

'The minds change? How?'

'They change.'

'New minds?'

'Changed minds.'

Hartrampf's penetrating, washed-out blue eyes fixed on the pale face before him. 'Are these other minds with you now?'

Hesitation. 'I don't know.'

'Where are they?'

Silence.

'Do you miss them? Can you reach out for them?'

Adam's body suddenly stiffened, his face contorting.

'Sleep,' said Hartrampf.

'What happened?' Jane whispered.

'He faced the beginning of the truth, perhaps?'

'These other minds – is he suffering from some form of schizophrenia?'

'One might assume something of the sort.'

'But you don't?'

'I listen.'

'Where is he now?'

'Now? Nowhere. Which I think is where he prefers to be, yes?'

'He sleeps a lot. Has these awful dreams. He tries to escape this power he has. Eleanor Hale did explain . . . ?'

'She tried. Wouldn't you, my dear? Try to escape?'

'It would drive me mad.'

'Or into a catatonic state. Stupor. A coma even.'

'Adam described being in a void. He spoke about feeling death. This was when I first met him. God! That was only on Wednesday – it seems like a lifetime.'

Hartrampf smiled vaguely, distracted, his mind elsewhere. 'I think we must take him down another road. I have spoken on the telephone to the young American doctor from the Blackwater Clinic. Livesey? He tells me Adam believes he died in an aeroplane crash. Obviously, he is alive. This is typical of his dreams? Catastrophe? Death?'

'Last night he had a nightmare. He talked in his sleep.

The last thing he said woke him. He said: "I am a dead soldier." He sounded horror-struck.'

'Very well, we will try evoking this subconscious experience.'

'No! He was in a dreadful state.'

'Perhaps because he was close to facing the incident which shut down his mind, Did he describe this dream to you afterwards? In detail?'

'He wouldn't talk about it but from his rambling it sounded like a continuation of the dream he described to me when I picked him up from the clinic: a helicopter crash in a snowstorm. Except this time he seemed to be outside – exposed, in a blizzard. The cold was intense. He wept, he mentioned Scott, the explorer. Antarctic? For a while he talked like a child.'

'Do you think he dreamed he had survived this crash?'

'I went to him because he was calling me. Don't ask me if he was actually calling or if I imagined it because I can't answer that. The point is I did go to him and by then he was talking about being in the open. I seemed to feel he'd walked away from the crash. Perhaps I was remembering the dream he told me about before. The entire experience was eerie. He was in such a bad way I stayed with him for a couple of hours.' She lit a cigarette, her body language defiant.

Hartrampf gave a small nod. 'So he was alive – walking in a snowstorm – yet he said he was a "dead soldier'? Those were his words?'

'I don't understand, either.'

'He discovered he was a dead soldier?'

'He said something like: "She will hear." He meant me, I know. Then he made that statement. He seemed to be trying to find out who or what he was. He wanted help.'

'Then we must help him.'

'Be careful, please.'

Hartrampf turned away. 'Wake up.'

Adam's eyelids fluttered half-open and stayed there.

'You are very cold. There is a snowstorm all around you. A blizzard. The storm is lessening. Where are you?'

'South Georgia,' came the crisp, positive reply in a voice that might not have been his own.

Jane sat up, startled.

Hartrampf stilled her: 'That is Georgia in the United States or the Soviet Union, please?'

Adam laughed. 'South Georgia, Falkland Islands.'

'That's not him!' Jane blurted.

Hartrampf silenced her with a hard, warning glance. 'Why are you there, please?'

Again the laugh: this time harder, conspiratorial, as if others were with him, listening. 'Because the regiment goes in first to make it easier for the rest.'

'Which regiment?'

'*The* regiment. Twenty-Two, SAS.'

'Tell me please. What is your condition?'

'Our state of readiness?'

'Your physical condition.'

'Bloody cold.'

'Who are you?'

Hesitation. Wariness. 'You don't think I'm going to tell you that!'

'Why not?'

'Go to hell.'

'You think I'm an enemy?'

'Everyone's the enemy when you go in first.'

'I wish only to help you.'

'We help ourselves.'

'The regiment? Your comrades in the SAS? How long have you been with the Special Air Service?'

'Go screw yourself.'

'If I told you that you are dreaming and the Falklands War is over and the British have won, what would be your reaction?'

'Rude. It's only just begun.'

'Very well, let us say that you are not dreaming. You are in fact dead. You were killed by the crash of the helicopter in which you were travelling. You died in the snow. In a blizzard.'

From deep in Adam's throat came the strangled sound of terror.

'Stop!' Jane cried.

'Sleep,' Hartrampf ordered. He turned to her. 'You must respect my professional judgement, otherwise you cannot stay in the same room.'

'He made that sound last night. It's horrible. Look at him, he's out of his mind with fear!'

'No. For the moment no fear. Though he is indeed out of his mind – which is where he wishes to be, I would think.'

'How much more?'

'I want to move him away from this concept of his own death. I believe that he was a soldier in the Falklands, a member of the SAS – and that his dreams are in fact reality, his subconscious trying to tell him about himself. I also believe that someone died. Perhaps many? A comrade he was particularly close to, men for whom he was responsible; deaths he blames himself for and now transfers to himself. It is probable that he was severely wounded himself and felt that he too should have died – but was rescued. He bears every indication of coming quite recently from some medical care establishment of a high order. Quite possibly military. In the field of neurosurgery the British military are leaders. The advances they have made over the years towards saving the lives of soldiers shot in the head in Northern Ireland are quite astonishing. We must return him to this facility.'

'Doctor Hartrampf, have you heard of a British military medical facility in the middle of Dartmoor? I haven't – and I keep up to date on new developments by the government that are bound to cost millions, so it's nothing recent. They're closing hospitals, not building new ones, you must know that. Or is that something you've lost touch with? Adam arrived naked in Eleanor Hale's garden. He walked there. Across the moors. His feet are still blistered. I've seen them. How does a naked man simply appear from nowhere? A man with the ability to predict the future? I want the answer – and incidentally so does he.'

Hartrampf stood up. 'I do not dispute that what we have here is something extraordinary. I have as yet no proof of his paranormal power but I accept your word and that of

83

Eleanor Hale. But there must be an explanation: perhaps also extraordinary yet nevertheless rational. In her letter Eleanor states her opinion that his mind has been "interfered with". Not a medical term – but possibly valid. This "interference" she believes to be not simply brain surgery but something more sinister. Possibly even techniques which could be branded unethical under current thinking.'

'Hallelujah,' Jane breathed.

'You too believe this?'

'I, and others interested in discovering what happened to Adam,' she admitted cautiously. 'At this moment I have people working on this concept.'

'May I ask who are these interested people?'

'Backers. A business corporation.'

'No doubt with interests in the media?' Hartrampf frowned. 'We are discussing fellow members of my profession here. I understand from Eleanor Hale's letter you are a broadcaster?'

'I'm an independent producer of television documentary programmes, yes.'

'You accept I must be cautious under these circumstances. What is it you actually suspect? Unauthorized medical experiments on human beings?'

'*Authorized* medical experiments on human beings. Doctor, we're entering the twenty-first century and we're all expecting scientific advances which must rewrite the current rulebook on ethics and morality. Why shouldn't there be those who've jumped the gun? We've been experimenting on monkeys without their agreement for decades: that's only one evolutionary step from experimenting on man!'

He drifted, time and place meaningless, fear and anxiety muffled by the softness which cosseted him, content to stay exactly where he was for ever. He had a vague notion that he had passed from death into some higher state. He felt peaceful, quite happy with this concept, even forgetting the dreadful echoing sounds that had been part of his existence for so long: sounds from his womb of terror. He drifted backwards because forward was either black and empty,

84

like death, or filled with sudden visions which writhed and coiled as though his mind were a snake-pit and his sanity a trapped, frangible thing frozen by fear. Who am I? he thought, then he heard the whipping clatter above the jet-whine and said: Please God, no! But God's voice took him back anyway.

It was wet and bitterly cold. He stood directly under the whirling rotor-blades by the gaping entrance of the Wessex, the steel deck beneath his splayed legs pushing, irresistibly, up at him before falling away to leave him momentarily in negative gravity. He grabbed the side of the Wessex, secure again, though his stomach had been lost in the bowels of the warship.

'Good luck!' shouted the destroyer's commander, swaying with him. 'Last weather report for the area is bloody awful. You're going to need luck.'

'We'll do the job,' he shouted back and allowed himself to be pulled into the chopper's belly by iron-hard hands.

'Come on boss,' yelled one of the anonymous figures crowded around him, bulky in Arctic warfare order. 'Let's get the bloody bone-shaking bit over with.'

He raised a thumb and the Wessex lifted, dipped sickeningly in a sudden down-draught, then clattered up towards the charcoal-grey clouds.

They reached the island with dawn a broken promise, the inland mountain overlooking the small whaling port directly ahead, the scar of the glacier visible at 1,800 ft above sea level.

He climbed up behind the Royal Navy pilots, pushed his parka hood back and put on the spare flight helmet hanging over the left-hand seat. 'On the glacier,' he said.

'You've got winds exceeding ninety knots coming your way – you want to abort?' said the concerned voice in his ears.

'No.'

'It's your play!'

The machine dipped.

I should have listened, he reprimanded himself, drifting again but seeing all now. Fourteen lives in my hands. I had the choice. The winds came and blew us away. Nothing could stand against their relentless ferocity or survive the chill factor for long. Below, the enemy settled down to safe, warm occupation, while we froze and became completely ineffective.

He knew the helicopters would come for them because that was the Royal Navy's way but also because he'd lived through it already. He knew too what would happen when they did. He wanted to escape the knowledge, the actuality of it, but he knew there was no escape: the dream had ended, the reality begun. He wished he could die right then and not have to face what was to come.

They lay huddled together, their frail bivouac tents ripped to shreds, their strength wasting as the heat was sapped from their bodies. The sound of two approaching Royal Navy helicopters was whipped away by the wind so that they were above them before they were aware of their presence – blades slicing the ice-laden air, crews grim-faced, struggling to keep their machines back from the edge of disaster. He drew from his own depleted reserves of strength to get his beaten men off the glacier and into the machines.

At last, he was in himself, sprawled on the ice-cold steel floor, snow blowing around him, exhausted, weak, his face and fingers destroyed by frostbite, and the part of him that had no fight left wanted him to stay there, even slide out through the open door into oblivion as the floor lurched sickeningly.

'Come on, boss!' They pulled him up and sat him, wedged between two of them, shoulder to shoulder. The crew passed down a helmet and mask and someone put it on him because his hands now were beyond use, beyond hope.

'Welcome aboard, Captain,' said the voice in his ears.

He held the mask over his raw mouth. 'God bless the Royal Navy,' he croaked.

'Amen. And all here.'

The helicopter rose nose-up then lurched sideways, tilting, the engine roar growing with the acute angle.

'White-out!' The voice yelled in his ear. He tasted rubber and metal and bile and fear. He turned and saw fixed stares and clenched jaws turned blue-white by the instrument lighting, and terror. He knew they were flying blind, with no horizon, and somewhere – anywhere – beyond the white vortex was the sheer, hard rock-face of the mountain.

He prayed but no one heard him.

The hideous heart-stopping clang and the cascade of sparks came simultaneously. Then the insistent howl of the crash warning klaxon. Then nothing. Nothing at all.

'Would you like some fresh air?' asked Hartrampf, taking his hand and raising him from the chair. 'I have a beautiful garden. Also vines. In a hothouse of course. Last year was particularly good, my gardeners have assured me that I can add a few bottles of my own label to my cellar.'

He felt drained but not unpleasantly so. He felt also the same cold block in his mind despite the new knowledge of himself. If in fact it was knowledge and not fantasy.

'How much did you learn?' he asked as they walked through the house into the sprawling, wild-looking garden, heavy with plants and flowers, each meticulously labelled.

'A new world at its genesis,' explained Hartrampf, seeming not to have heard his question. 'New species created to counter the harsh effects – the poisons, to be brutal – of modern city living.' He looked down at Jane. 'There are no ethics involved in genetic engineering with regard to plant life – simply necessity. How much did I learn? Young man, you carry a burden of guilt which I deduce as being unwarranted. You talked of being responsible whereas, in fact, you seemed to have little choice in your military decision.'

'You know everything, then? I related it to you?'

'Everything? Absolutely not! *You* know everything. Obviously the rescue of yourself and your men met with disaster. That alone – for a survivor, which you are – might have been enough to cause mental trauma. You survived the terrible ordeal on the mountain only to have hope dashed even as you were being taken from your suffering. But this is not what has cost you your memory. You survived the crash – but what occurred after the crash is what we seek.'

Hartrampf stopped and turned to Jane. 'It is essential

he is returned to the medical facility which was carrying out treatment.'

'Doctor Hartrampf, you're not aware of everything that's involved here. Adam escaped from somewhere, I'm convinced of that. So was Eleanor Hale. Wasn't that clear in her letter? They – whoever they are – are trying to get him back. They tried last night and they'll try again. I daren't even keep him at my own home any more!'

'I understand your concern. Let me help with the problem. Leave him here with me, I have more than enough space to accommodate him. And in the event he suffers further trauma, and it is probable he will, I am qualified to deal with it. You have only kindness to offer, which is not enough. I am being harsh perhaps but accurate.'

'No. Thank you. But I don't think so.'

'You don't trust me?'

'It isn't that.'

'It is precisely that. And I understand your suspicions. We medicos are notorious for closing ranks when scandal appears on our horizon. However, let me assure you that in this particular case I would distance myself completely from those who may have worked on Adam. Remember, please, I abandoned my own country so as to avoid being forced into participating in experimentation on humans.'

'You said so.'

'But you wish proof?'

'Eleanor Hale told me on the telephone that you knew something about Adam. Her late husband knew too. She made no real sense. She seemed either wary of speaking about it or else she was confused. She obviously trusted you enough to have Adam come to you but after everything that's happened – her death, last night's incident, the unanswered questions – I'm not prepared to let him out of my sight until I'm certain just who we're dealing with.'

'Perhaps you mean out of your control, my dear?'

She glanced sharply at him. 'I have a commercial interest, yes, I admit that – but I also have a personal commitment and I think I've demonstrated that adequately.'

'I'm not leaving her,' Adam stated.

'Then both of you must stay here.'

'How did you know Eleanor Hale?' she demanded.

'Through her husband. He was the officer I was interviewed by after I'd escaped the Nazis. He saw to it my professional expertise was not wasted – that I did not rot in a displaced persons camp for the duration of the war. So you see, our friendship goes back a long way.'

'Her husband was an army doctor?'

'A brilliant one. Totally dedicated. I tried to persuade him to come to America with me after the war – he would have made his fortune there – but he preferred to stay in the army. They had a London home in those days – the Devon farmhouse came later. I became involved with him again when he took up a senior military medical post in Northern Ireland. I mentioned earlier the amazing work done to save the lives of soldiers over there. I did some consultancy work with his unit. Nothing in comparison to the things they were achieving. Psychiatric. Helping to reform the brains they had saved from destruction. My part was relatively minor. We lost touch after that and I'm afraid I did nothing about it. I heard later he had killed himself. The strain was simply too great. The work too intense. I should have seen what was happening to him – but, sadly, I did not.'

'But I understood from his son Daniel – I met him briefly once – that he had retired to the Devon house. He'd finished with Northern Ireland. The army even.'

Hartrampf turned to the steamy glass of the hothouse, squinting at the twisted vines inside. He seemed uncomfortable. 'The truth is that Samuel had a breakdown and was forced to retire. He parted on bad terms with the army. He objected to some of the work they were doing in rebuilding the minds and bodies of their young men. This, I think, is what Eleanor meant. She was confused by it all. She sincerely felt her husband had been used and discarded most cruelly. Possibly she was right. You see, as you have said yourself, we are moving very fast in modern medicine – perhaps too fast. But I have to say, when a government demands that the lives of its soldiers should be saved whatever the cost, then sometimes a compromise in ethics might be forced upon those involved.'

'Daniel mentioned the suicide – but he seemed to think his father was still involved in medical work up to the time of his death.'

'Samuel perpetuated this story himself. He would disappear for weeks roaming aimlessly, nobody knew where, then reappear at the farm raving about the wrong direction medicine was taking. His mind by then was not rational. Daniel was not in Devon much at that time: university, Sandhurst, the army, all kept him away. He saw very little of the deterioration. I'm sure he remembered only the perhaps over-dedicated, brilliant man his father was.'

SIX

Nigel Lewin had left Exeter at first light on Friday morning, worn out by lack of sleep, his mind dulled by a night of overactivity and, inevitably, in the early hours, anxiety. He wished he had not popped speed to keep himself awake and on a high after his meeting with Jane Haversham and Moravec in London, knowing that now there was only one way to get himself together: more amphetamines. His black mood was soon made worse when five miles out of the city his GTi developed the same overheating fault which had occurred the day before.

'Shit!' he spat, in raw bad-temper. Now he would have to hire a vehicle for his exploration of the moors instead of using his own and claiming the hire charge.

He stopped at a transport café serving early breakfasts, bought coffee and toast while the radiator cooled, swallowed pills and then, fuming and jittery from the comedown, drove back to a car-hire firm in Exeter where a girl he occasionally enjoyed would – with persuasion – give him a discounted deal and a receipt for the full amount. He left with a Daihatsu Fourtrak off-road vehicle and an inflated receipt after a rushed but pleasant experience in the firm's staff room. The pills were starting to work. He felt great.

'There you go!' he shouted as he drove the tall, virtually brand new vehicle hard, pleased to have exorcised most of the dark devils which rode with him on the long comedown from the pills. He remembered his letter to Foley, grinned at his heavy forebodings then shrugged the matter off. It was a new day and he was going to make it a new beginning.

Rudolf Moravec! Incredible.

If he played this right he could say goodbye to the sticks and be up there in London where it all happened. He remembered all the job applications he'd sent off to the national dailies without result. Well, he'd show them what they'd missed. Soon. Any day now. Don't sodding blink.

He had worked the whole creepy thing out in the night while his mind was still flash-fire-fast from the speed – but now, in daylight after two cups of strong coffee, toast and Hire-Car Linda, it didn't seem so bad after all. Somehow his fresh intake of amphetamines did not enter the equation. As far as he was concerned he knew what was going on – all he had to do was prove it. So get on with it! First things first: location?

How far could their Adam have travelled?

He knew that an experienced, well prepared and equipped Dartmoor walker moving quickly and sensibly, in daylight, could cover a good deal of ground over what was essentially the last great wilderness left in England. But Adam had been without clothes or shoes and had travelled in the dark without so much as a compass.

'So maybe he's sodding Action Man and can read the stars or whatever they do?' he muttered trying to remember what the weather had been like on Monday night. It had been a clear night. The weather had been consistently fair for weeks. Greenhouse effect, he thought. We'll have St Tropez weather here in a few years. More girls. Starkers. He patted the steering-wheel in time with music from the radio. All right!

'Maybe he's JC come down to sort us out?' he asked, peering up at the sky, expectantly.

A low, blood-red Ferrari Testarossa flashed past him airhorns blaring. He lowered the window and yelled: 'Jesus is back and boy is he mad at flash bastards like you!' He left the window down and laughed, banging the wheel enthusiastically.

All right, enough of that, he told himself. Come down. Where're you heading? Think. Even if he was bloody Action Man he couldn't have moved very far in the dark – not across the southern moors where the Hale farmhouse is located – without ending in peat bog up to his chin. OK, so we're looking at somewhere south of Princetown where the nick is because the northern moors are really too far away for him to have reached the farm. Unless he really is Jesus Christ!

He got on to the B3212, driving through villages and hamlets, stopping to apply Lewin's First Rule of Extracting Information: get into the local pub and buy a round but don't be flash with it.

He reached Princetown, knowing from experience he must put more food into his stomach even though the pills, as usual, had killed his appetite. He passed shops selling souvenirs of Dartmoor Prison and pulled to a halt outside a pub, went inside and ordered a pint of local brew. The lounge bar was quiet, the landlord and two customers drinking and conversing quietly together.

'Nice-looking vehicle,' commented the landlord, serving him. 'Japanese?'

'Have one yourself. Has to be, doesn't it? Hired it today. Should've heard what they were asking for a Range Rover. Still, good enough for traipsing around the moors.'

'Tourist?'

'Working. In TV. Looking for locations for a new thriller serial.'

'What's that called then?' asked the drinker on the next stool, a stocky man with a solid jaw ducked into his pewter tankard.

'Title comes later. Something sexy,' replied Lewin glibly, spotting the shirt, trousers, and footwear of a prison guard under the non-uniform sweater and anorak.

'Got a nice friendly pub on your list?' enquired the landlord, laughing but serious.

'Could be,' said Lewin with a wink. 'Tell you what. If you can do decent grub I could fix it to have the crew and cast fed here. Make a welcome change from the catering truck. They drink like fish which'll be good for you.'

'Not if they shut the locals out it won't be,' growled a third man from further away at the end of the bar: much older, a hostile glint in his eye.

'Well, I'm sure it could be arranged properly?' Lewin prompted, glancing hopefully at the landlord, keeping the flow moving.

'Certainly. Sort all that out. Locals come first here. We get many tourists as well of course.'

'Same again,' offered Lewin. 'Another for yourself and perhaps these gentlemen . . . ? You're welcome. Cheers!'

'You from Wales?' asked the prison warder.

'Spotted the leek? Shows, does it?' grinned Lewin.

'Now and then. Got some of your lot inside.'

'Which side of the bars?'

'Both.'

'Well then! Fair, I'd say.'

'Take in the prison, does it? This serial of yours? Better check it out with the powers that be before you start snooping around. Tend to be a suspicious lot out here.'

'We won't be shooting the prison itself. Just the surroundings. Moor, rocks – tors you call them, right? – bogs, the old mines, some of the buildings: getting the atmosphere really. A bit of local life as well.'

'Not a lot round here,' growled the old man. 'Not real locals.'

'Take no notice,' said the landlord, not lowering his voice. 'Hates tourists.'

Lewin grinned and pressed on: 'Actually what we really need to find – like yesterday, because they want to build scenery based on it for interiors – is a building or maybe a group of buildings in the middle of nowhere. Somewhere really remote.'

'Farmhouse and outbuildings sort of thing?' offered the landlord.

'Could be. Depends on location.'

'Better watch yourself creeping around on the moors,' warned the old man. 'There's army firing ranges up around Okehampton and Willsworthy.'

'Saw that in the local paper – but thanks for the reminder.'

'Be reminded right enough with shrapnel up your arse!' the man chuckled, humourlessly.

'There's that survival course place the army runs,' suggested the landlord. 'Hardly old by Dartmoor standards. Not what you'd need, I shouldn't think. Even if they'd rent it out.'

'Can't see your TV stars wanting to rough it around there,' the warder put in. 'Poofs aren't they, most of 'em?'

Lewin stuck a hand on hip and hammed: 'But what *muscles*.'

Everyone laughed, except the old man.

Lewin swallowed lager, his mouth dried by the pills. 'Survival course? You mean shacks? Tents? That sort of thing?'

'Your modern army?' growled the old man. 'No fear. Proper buildings they've got. Central heating, television, the lot. Seen the aerials.'

The landlord shook his head. 'Don't let him mislead you. The original building is Dartmoor granite and dates back to the eighteen hundreds but they've added on accommodation blocks. I've an idea they've expanded a bit recently. Been in existence since the end of the war. Last one. In the early days most people thought it was something to do with spying. Rumours, you know. Cold War was on then and you got some funny government places out in the wilds. Training place, they thought. More above board nowadays. Had some of them visiting here on occasion — not spies, army people — for the beer and the prison. Everyone's fascinated by that.'

'Army? Not one of those civvy outfits? You know: let'spretend time? Yuppies playing at soldiers? Paint-guns, all that?'

'Real thing,' put in the warder. 'They say the SAS use the place when they get bored with the Brecon Beacons.'

'All barbed wire and sentries then?' Lewin enquired, innocently.

'They don't like trespassers,' said the landlord. 'Their prerogative of course. Their land. Government's really. Well, ours at the end of the day. Citizens. Ha!'

'Got to keep a bit of discipline,' said the warder, 'otherwise they couldn't get on with their business, could they?'

'They've got underground tunnels,' grumbled the old man. 'You know where to listen and you'll hear noises from them. Humming. Deep down. Been going on for years. Some fools think it's ghosts or the devil. Latest thing is

95

flying saucers – 'course that suits them fine up there, doesn't it.'

'Don't listen to him,' said the landlord, wiping the bar. 'There's more stories of weird sounds and happenings up here on Dartmoor than anywhere else in the world. Good for tourists, mind you. Fancy trying some of our food – to get an idea for when your crew arrives? On the house?'

The old man had not finished. He put his drink down, hard, spilling some. 'You know what I reckon that place really is?'

'He's off,' groaned the warder. 'Go home, George.'

'Let him have his say,' said Lewin, playing the reasonable newcomer.

'Thank you. They've got a real survival course there and I don't mean bloody army darting about the moor either though they do that as well for our benefit. I mean *survival*. For when it all goes up. Government: MPs, top civil servants, scientists. Not the likes of us.'

The landlord moved to the spilled ale. 'George reckons we're all living on borrowed time.'

Lewin ducked his head into his beer. 'He could be right.'

The old man glared. 'Got themselves a real nice bolt-hole there. Insurance. No nuclear bomb, no chemicals for *them*, that's for sure!'

'Doesn't sound much like one of my locations anyway,' smiled Lewin. 'I'll have a try of your steak and kidney. Another, gentlemen?'

Lewin drove away from the pub, stopped and parked so that it remained in sight. He did not have long to wait. The old man exited on his own and began walking, a little unsteadily, in the opposite direction. Lewin started the Fourtrak and followed.

'Lift?' he offered, drawing alongside.

'What're you after?'

'Just thought we might have a chat.' Lewin leaned over and pushed the passenger door open. 'I pay for information – if it saves me time.'

The old man heaved himself up into the Fourtrak, a sly grin on his ruddy face. 'Thriller serial!' he snorted. 'After the dirt on that army place, aren't you? Caught your look when I said my piece. You from *Panorama* or one of those?'

'One of those,' agreed Lewin. 'OK, we had a tip-off there were strange goings-on up there at . . . what's it called?'

'Don't have a name, far as I know. Not one we know, that is. Strange goings-on? What've you heard?'

Lewin produced a crisp, new twenty-pound note and laid it on the fascia, ignoring the question. 'What about the tunnels?'

The rheumy eyes strayed to the money then lifted to the road ahead. 'Lay another one of those and a tenner there and I'll take you back home and show you something which'd make those buggers back there sit up and think again. You too.'

'What've you got?'

'Like I said, another twenty and a tenner and it's yours. But now, before you see or get told anything.'

Lewin grinned and added more money.

'Drive straight on,' ordered the old man. 'I'll show you where.'

They stopped outside a weary-looking cottage. Lewin followed the old man inside.

'Live on your own, do you, George?'

'Not your problem.'

Lewin shrugged and sat down, without invitation, on a worn chair. 'So earn your money, George.'

The old man went to a tall sideboard, reached up for a small key inside a china cup, unlocked one drawer, removed it and brought it over to sit facing Lewin. 'Took these over the years,' he explained, grasping plain buff envelopes bound together by thick rubber bands. 'Started when I came back after the war. Served my King and Country and got a boot up the backside when it was over.' He jabbed a finger at Lewin. 'I'll tell you, son, we really thought when we voted Clem Attlee into Ten Downing Street that that was it: at last Britain was into the twentieth century, head out of the ground, a bit of realization that it was the working man who created the wealth. Not a bit of it! Privilege ruled then, and it rules now. All right, now there's a different class at the top of the pile – your aristos abdicated and left the country to the robber barons – but it still leaves the working man with nothing when the chips go down.'

'How d'you mean?' pressed Lewin, impatient, sensing gold in the old man but knowing there was no straight shaft down to it. He could barely keep his eyes off the buff envelopes: the prospect of what might be in them was killing him.

'You heard what I said in the pub. That place is a bolt-hole for when the rockets start flying – and there's those who've already booked their rooms. Here, I'll show you some of the buggers.'

The gnarled fingers struggled with the thick rubber bands and Lewin had to fight his urge to rip the envelopes away from him.

Easy, he told himself.

'Started building in 'forty-eight, they did. Here's them working on the original building. Used to be a small explosives factory. Black powder. Had a few of them on Dartmoor back in the eighteen hundreds. See? No roof. Blown off when some poor sod got careless. Killed more'n a few workers you can be certain. Here's one with the new roof on. Place was completed in no time. Best materials. I know, I nicked some.'

Lewin felt disappointment set in. 'You've been watching the place since the end of the forties? Nicking stuff? Can't be exactly very secret if they let you get away with it, can it, George?'

The old face broke into a foxy grin. 'Know what I was in the war? Sniper. Means sitting all bloody day – maybe more – in some bloody uncomfortable hide, not even being able to piss. Lovely stuff, peat, you can cut yourself a hide quick and easy, stick a lump of granite on top for cover and you're made up.'

'So they never saw you.'

'Not when I didn't want them to. Otherwise I made sure they did. Out in the open, walking the dog – dead now – got used to me they did, thought I was a half-witted moorsman. People who get used to you don't see you after a while – ever noticed? 'Course not, you're too young. Everybody

98

takes notice of young people these days. Can't wait for us old sods to die off. Embarrassing, we are. Dinosaurs who can't even make your modern telephones work, never mind understand your computers, eh?'

'OK, so they rebuilt the old building then they added on some concrete boxes – '

'Prefabs first. See here. Nissen huts. Solid stuff came in the late fifties.'

'Where's the meat, George? What you're giving me is a building report I can probably get from the Ministry of Works – and it won't cost me fifty quid!'

The old man pushed himself up, left the room and came back with a white, moulded polystyrene foam package. He split the two halves to reveal the protected contents. 'Ever seen one of those, son? Got it through a gun magazine I get delivered. NVD. Night-Vision Device. Like binoculars 'cept it picks up any available moon- or starlight and concentrates it. Bloody marvellous. You can see in pitch darkness – bit greenish but you soon get used to that.'

'I'm impressed. So you went out there at night and you saw something – what?'

The grin returned, this time self-satisfied. 'This.'

Lewin looked at the photographs as they were fanned out like playing cards on the battered table between them.

'Shot through the NVD,' explained the old man. 'Made up a threaded connector easy as you like.'

'Clever sod, aren't you,' murmured Lewin. 'Hey! That's – '

'Isn't it though.'

Lewin controlled his excitement. 'Well, the place is government-funded, isn't it? You're bound to get them visiting.'

The grin remained fixed. 'Which place? The one everyone sees upstairs or the one underground?'

'There's no proof here of anything underground.'

'Don't rush me. Here's the sequence the photographs were taken in. You can take my word for it or you can check the negs which are automatically numbered and dated.'

'Well sorted out, aren't you?' Lewin observed. 'Camera

99

must have cost a bit?' He looked, pointedly, around the dilapidated room.

'My business what I do with my money. Here we go: party enters the main building after arriving by chopper. Time, just after one in the morning. Normal sort of hour for visiting if everything's kosher? Stays inside for a good hour and a half. I almost fell asleep waiting. Didn't take any more shots in between because I was low on film and low on the means to buy more too.'

'In between what?'

'Going in and coming out, son. Checking everything's five star. See that shot? Entrance to one of the outer buildings. It's blurred because I had to shift fast to get it. Party goes in one building, comes out another. Means they're connected in anybody's language.'

'So a tunnel links the buildings? Could be for convenience in bad weather. Maybe part of the survival course.'

'Tunnel? What they've got under there is big enough to take a full-size truck – and that's just for starters.'

Lewin grinned. 'Come on, George.'

'What d'you call that, then?'

'Some kind of tanker?'

'Refrigeration truck.' A gnarled finger stabbed at the print. 'There's the generator.'

'What's it carrying?'

'Special kind of fuel? Maybe just food? Who knows. But that truck comes regular. Not every week, sometimes you don't see it for a month or so. Then there it is again coming out of the night, white as a ghost.'

Lewin felt a tingle race through his body. 'Go on.'

'Look here. Truck goes into this outbuilding. Garage? Sure. They've got vehicles: couple of Land-Rovers, one Range Rover, so they need somewhere out of the moors weather. Look. Bleeding magic?'

'You photographed this in sequence? Proof positive?'

'All on the negs. Truck goes in, doesn't come out, somehow there's still the same space left for the other vehicles. They've solved the world's parking problem, haven't they.'

'Hydraulic ramp?'

'Electronic lift, more likely. Dead quiet. If that place is

government-funded they'll have the Rolls-Royce of lifts in there, won't they? I tell you, I'd like to see inside some of those underground rooms. Luxury, I'll bet. A few shots of those with the facts to the right papers and you can say goodbye and good riddance to this government.'

'You're dreaming. You've said yourself, that place – whatever it is – was started up in 1948. There's been one or two Labour governments as well since then.'

'Could have been kept from old Clem Attlee – even Wilson, definitely Callaghan. *They* rule this country, who- ever gets voted in. Parliament's a sham just to keep us lot happy – the real government is *privilege*. Power where it counts: behind the scenes. Centuries of it. Generation to generation, cradle to grave. We don't stand a chance.'

'Whitehall? There's a few comrades there, George.'

'Not where it matters, son. Not where it matters.'

'So how much for the photographs?'

'You mean to take away?'

'Of course.'

'It's not just money I want.'

'What then? A medal from Moscow?'

'I want it exposed for what it is: a safe haven for the privileged to deny the working man the equal right of survival.'

Jesus, Lewin thought. Dinosaur is right. Where've you been the last few years? Nobody talks like that any more. Not even the Kremlin. Especially not the Kremlin. He said: 'Sure, George. It'll be exposed – guaranteed. Not sure if the photographs and your word are going to be enough though. There's some big guns involved in this and we'll need heavy ammunition to shake them.'

The old eyes gleamed. 'There's only one way, son. Get in there. Had forty years to work out how. Too old now, of course.'

Lewin's forebodings returned. 'Great.'

'Windy, son?'

'*No.*'

'We hang on here till dark then,' said the old man.

'I've got to call London. I see any phone here?'

'You don't call anyone. Not till this is done.'

101

'Don't you trust me, George? I thought we were in this together? Partners?'

'For different reasons, son.'

'I have to call my boss.'

'Afterwards.'

'Sod off, George. I'll be back in a little while.' Lewin made for the door, heard a smooth, oiled snick and turned to face a Wehrmacht officer's issue Luger automatic pistol with ivory grips.

'Shot the owner of this, oh, Christmas forty-four, driving himself in a Mercedes – the one with exhaust pipes out of the bonnet? Lovely job, top down despite the cold. Celebrating. Or forgetting. On his ownsome. Pissed. One hit, bit too low, caught him here – ' Howard touched his throat – 'but it did for him anyway. Only time I've left my hide to take a look but I'd spotted the bottles of brandy on the back seat through the 'scope. Most got smashed in the crash but I salvaged a couple. And this. Lovely workmanship – a special, not your usual mass-produced job. Engraved, see?'

'Put it down, George.'

'You make us a nice cup of tea, son. Pass the time nicely, that will.'

Rafe Mybree? Sounds like he should wear a tasselled fez, a green velvet smoking jacket, and listen to recordings of the Temperance Seven, decided Peter Foley, locking his BMW securely, aware that anyone with a Stanley knife could cut through the mohair hood in seconds. It was the risk you took if you owned a convertible. He shrugged. Just because society was sick didn't mean his pleasures should go into quarantine.

Mayberry lived, trendily, in a converted warehouse in what had once been Jack the Ripper territory – any closer to the River Thames and it would have needed a hull.

Foley raised the heavy iron knocker on the ancient, solid oak arched door, expecting the crack of a hammer and getting the dull thud of a boxer's gloved fist into the heavy bag.

'Got you,' said Mayberry from somewhere and the door hissed open. 'Stairs in front of you.'

Foley turned back to examine the door.

'Tells me everything about you,' said Mayberry's voice. 'Basically the same as the security arch you'd walk through at an airport which really cared about your life – with a few extra, expensive tricks for the unsuspecting. Also holds back everything except a determined assault by a super-power. Do come up, Detective Superintendent.'

Foley took the stairs, noting the rubberized pads on the wooden treads. 'Why the pressure pads if the door's so secure?' he asked.

'Double indemnity. Technology doesn't march these days – it zooms. Who knows what some clever little bastard with a desk-top PC could design overnight? They also drain you of any static you've built up – which believe me can be a real pain in the ass in my business.'

Foley opened a door at the top of the stairs and entered a vast raftered room.

Jim Reeves welcomed Foley to Mayberry's world from about twenty big matt-black hi-fi speakers aimed menacingly from the beams – then stopped.

'Gimmicky but fun,' said Mayberry, swinging away from viewing the Thames through the vast plate-glass windows. 'Country music's my passion – western-swing preferably.'

'I heard computers were?' said Foley, thinking: so much for the Temperance Seven.

'Computers are my challenge. Drink?'

'What's in the jug? Iced water?'

'Only the best dry martini in the world.'

'Couldn't drive on it. Any alcohol-free beer?'

'Always keep a bottle or two for visiting policemen.'

'Get those, do you?'

Mayberry had set off down the length of the place to a cordoned-off section which might have been for cooking or launching missiles. He called out: 'Around Budget time – or any other tricky manoeuvre the government is planning.'

'I don't want to know,' Foley shouted back.

Mayberry returned and handed him a bottle, a glass

upturned over the opened top. 'Wise man. Stick to the job in hand. What *is* the job in hand?'

Foley took out a pad, wrote two words in block capitals and held it out.

Mayberry gave an insulted snort. 'I sweep the place daily. Just for the exercise.' He pointed at the huge expanse of glass. 'You can't hear it but that, right now, is vibrating with the most extraordinary sonic pulses – anyone aiming a microphone at that for our speech-vibrations is having problems.'

'Nevertheless.'

'Indeed. Well, all right, let's play codenames. The first we all know don't we – naturally excluding all the poor taxpayers out there who pay for our *wunnerful* security service. Nasty things snakes, bite you in the most dreadful places. Where'd this one get you?'

'Probably only in my pride – but at my age that can be painful.'

'But not fatal. Don't be so hard on yourself. By the way, are you gay or is your domestic arrangement with the brash Nigel made for some other, less contentious, reason? If the latter, I'd find some way to let your people know positively because going by your confidential "P" file they really are confused – if not a little disturbed.'

'None of your business.'

'Oh, but it is. There may come a time – please God not – when our transaction today might come out. In which case some of your less sensitive colleagues will certainly insinuate there was something between us – just to add pressure. Now if I know you're definitely not it will make life so much easier when the heavy threats start. I am, you see. Gay, that is.'

'I'm not.'

'Ah well! Life's like that.'

'What about the second name?'

'Genesis. Lovely feller until horrid Eve stirred him up. Women do. Otherwise, it don't mean a thing, Chief Super. What's the background?'

'You forget all of this, hear me?'

'Memory gets wiped when we're through: electronic and biological, OK?'

Foley nodded, though the warning remained in his eyes. 'I have a suspect for the crime of murder. His prints have been found at the scene. Special Branch inform me that those prints belong to a Nazi executed in England during the war for espionage.'

'Straight mistake being out of the question? You wouldn't be here otherwise.'

'No mistake. I was at Special Branch Headquarters here in London before coming to see you. I compared the spy Otto Fascher's prints which are on display in their Black Museum with those taken at the scene of crime. Identical.'

'So the German is alive?'

'Not according to the records.'

'Records are written up by people. People can be got at. I prove that every day.'

'If he were alive today he'd be in his nineties, according to his file. Not realistic.'

'His age could have been faked.'

'I'm satisfied it's genuine. A younger man at that time would have been in uniform. I've seen his photograph. Late forties.'

'So exhume the body. Who cares now?'

'That's the point: somebody does. I wanted sight of the body and was told I had problems. Normally an exhumation order goes through the Home Office but in Fascher's case there's a referral to the Ministry of Defence. More than a referral, an instruction: all enquiries to the MOD – or else.'

'Defence shouldn't be involved. Someone's blundered or was over-zealous. If the Home Office has something they want to keep under wraps they could perfectly well duck behind the One Hundred Year Rule. Section Five (1) of the Public Record Act. A World War Two spy case listed as an ongoing file? Still running? Nonsense. You've hit some old war-time War Office minute that someone's forgotten to cancel.'

Foley glanced out of the window as the decapitated superstructure of a vessel drifted across the glass, absurdly close: he could see rivets and rust-runs on the metal. A seaman waved.

'He can't see us,' said Mayberry. 'The glass is reflective from the outside. Be like an oven in here on a hot day if it wasn't.'

Foley drank beer and grimaced. 'My contact tried the Branch's own computer records with what little information he had: Room 713. The War Office. Army (Department of Advanced Medicine).'

Mayberry grinned. 'That's where you got the name from. Did you get your contact to try it?'

'I suggested he try the army reference so he keyed in something which could have been the acronym then got cold feet – or a heavy command to stop – because he cut me dead.'

'You saw him key it in?'

'No, I heard the keystrokes. It was a telephone conversation. I was still in Exeter at the time.'

'So you're guessing. Who are these people?'

'The department doesn't exist. Never existed, so I'm told.'

A look of glee lit Mayberry's eyes. 'Except you know it did 'cause the Special Branch officer told you so. You didn't actually see it though? Now they're saying: sorry, bit of a balls-up, brought you all this way for nothing, there's no written instruction to go straight to MOD and have your toe-nails pulled out for being nosey, but no, you can't dig up old Otto anyway! Close?'

'Very.'

Mayberry sighed. 'Why are government department coverups so inept? Is it the people, or the system? You didn't push it?'

'One deliberate lie is always a prelude to others. Besides I'd have been muddying waters I wanted to swim through with you.'

'Absolutely right. Well, now I'll ask the questions – and the answers I get won't be lies. That's the great thing with databases – the information has to be factual, otherwise what's the point?'

'You're assuming the MOD instruction was something

which should have been lifted? The Special Branch chap said on the telephone he thought the Thirty Year Rule might apply, in which case restrictions should have been lifted in nineteen seventy-five.'

'To the basement,' said Mayberry, rising. 'There are thousands of outdated minutes, instructions – whatever – on paper files which only come to light when someone pulls them: the result of slack admin and of course the sudden switch to chip technology. Nothing sinister in that – except I believe I'm hearing the classic slow grind of bureaucratic wheels moving as one department drops a clanger and the reverberation echoes through the corridors of power. Sound a bit portentous? Whitehall has that effect on me.'

They entered a cool, white, air-conditioned room. Foley was expecting a mass of computer hardware but surprisingly there was very little. Or it was well concealed.

'What do we do?' Foley enquired, as Mayberry sat down and swivelled a monitor screen towards himself.

'We? You sit there on that chair, no objections, no comments. I ask questions: sometimes you answer them, sometimes . . .' Mayberry splayed long hands '. . . answers arrive. Oh, and you make coffee from that machine on the wall between times.'

'Whatever you say.'

'Aren't our policemen wunnerful.'

'How do you get away with it?'

'Because the law hasn't kept pace with technology. One day it will change – but by then I'll be living on a small Caribbean island without even a telephone.'

'You couldn't exist without all this.'

'You wanna bet? Question: did you say your Special Branch chap accessed the MOD computer or their own? There is a crossover limited-information link between the two.'

'The referral to the MOD was on paper. He actually had the original case file – commented on the penmanship.'

'I thought war-time counter-espionage was handled by MI5, not Special Branch?'

'It was. He may have drawn the old file from Curzon

Street or they let the Yard have it years ago because of the unusual nature of Fascher's prints – he didn't say.'

'Unusual, how?'

'Don't conform to any normal pattern. Known as accidentals. Very, very rare.'

'So he saw the referral, and —?'

'Tried the Branch computer records with Fascher's real and cover names, got nowhere, so I suggested the army reference. Then he clammed up.'

'We'll go the same route.' Mayberry drew a modem towards him then did things with his equipment, tapping sudden bursts into his keyboard, occasionally consulting something inside a drawer down to his right. 'Anchors aweigh! Have to go around the world a bit so they don't know where we're coming from. All part of the game. Silence please.' Foley looked down at the floor, feeling distinctly uncomfortable. The air-conditioning whispered in the background, like his conscience. 'We're in,' Mayberry stated, finally. 'No! Stay where you are. Good. The German's full name, please?'

'Fascher, Otto Horst.'

'Negative. Cover name?'

'Miller. William Arthur.'

'Negative.'

'Try the War Office room number. Seven-one-three. He did that next.'

'Negative.'

'Then he said: "OK, let's try this," worked the keyboard – end of conversation.'

'Four keystrokes?'

'Four – then the command.'

'Army (Department of Advanced Medicine). Right? ADAM.' Mayberry stopped. Peered, then stabbed the keyboard, fast.

'What the hell was that?' Foley demanded, rising.

'Sit down. Something that might give the average Special Branch officer a minor coronary if he came up against it unexpectedly. Sort of thing I get used to – but I can imagine the effect on mere mortals.'

'Are you going to tell me what?'

'Big Brother is watching you and just who do you think you are, little man, messing in something that's strictly for the grown-ups who run the country and probably some of the world too.'

'You mean that's it? You're not prepared to go any further?'

'Not down that route. Don't know who'll come knocking if we do.'

'They can trace us?'

'If I'd stayed in long enough – which I didn't.'

'What now?'

'VIPER. Let's see what the connection is between your murder case in Devon and an ongoing MI5 operation.'

'I can tell you that. Daniel Hale. British Army major working undercover in Northern Ireland, lifted by the IRA and reportedly butchered by them – literally. The murder victim was his mother. She'd more or less kept him alive – on paper – which proved embarrassing and dangerous because I think he's alive and working for the Provos.'

'You think the IRA killed her?'

'I think her son may have killed her. Maybe to prove his commitment to them. That's a common tactic of terrorist groups – which is why undercover penetration of them is so hazardous.'

'If that is the situation, why are you so put out that it's been taken away from you? You know the form with anything political – and Irish political is worse.'

'Change of life.'

'You're supposed to be worrying about your virility and your index-linked pension – not playing fast draw computer games with the powers that be.'

'I'm a policeman. A very good one. Part of being a policeman is making things add up. At this moment very little does. Look at it my way. I have a murder, suspects, possible motive, and evidence, including fingerprints. My enquiries tell me that two of the men involved in the crime are supposedly dead yet my evidence shows them to be up and walking. Next, MI5 put a block on enquiries into my chief suspect – Daniel Hale – then some heavy government warning comes down on number two – Fascher – whose prints are all over the scene of crime!'

'Coffee,' interrupted Mayberry. 'Black and bitter.'

Foley went to the machine on the wall and worked it.

Mayberry said: 'ADAM is another ball-game entirely. I think there's no connection at all between it and VIPER – or indeed your murder case.'

'But it turns you on,' observed Foley, shrewdly.

'Oh, that it does, officer. Gets the adrenalin going like mad.'

'You want to get in there.'

'Indeed I do.'

'How?'

'We have the Official Secrets Act, the Americans have the Freedom of Information Act. Between the two is something we're pleased to call the Special Relationship – though I have a suspicion we're being cuckolded by the Krauts these days. You wouldn't believe some of the traffic between the State Department and Bonn. Changing times, dearie. However, when we have a secret we usually share it with our American cousins, who promptly share it with whoever knows where to find it.'

'And you do?'

'That's my world.'

Foley sipped his surprisingly good coffee, looking at Mayberry over the rim of his cup. 'Actually there is a connection between ADAM and VIPER. It may be just coincidence but I always view coincidence with suspicion.'

''Course you do. What is it?'

'Dead men who won't stay dead.'

Mayberry nodded then stood up. 'This is a not a lewd proposition – but how do you feel about staying here overnight?'

'Why?'

'International time zones. Also there are certain relatively safe periods which I prefer to use. I want to penetrate the GDN – Government Data Network – which will give me access to every government ministry including unnamed departments, i.e. the security service, MI5. I'd really rather

110

go in over the weekend but you're a man in a hurry – and you're paying.'

Foley considered for a moment, Nigel Lewin's note that morning preying on his mind. He should do something. But what? Put out a search party? Ridiculous. 'I can't tell anyone I'm here though, right?'

'You smooth criminal. See how easy it is to fall into bad ways?'

Wunnerful, thought Foley, grimly.

SEVEN

Immediately after Jane Haversham's angry telephone call from Lennox Gardens Mews early on Friday morning, Rudolf Moravec had arranged a luncheon meeting with Lord Brennay, Euro MP and board member of several Moravec companies, and urged him to bring with him his closest friend, Richard Wardlove, Minister for the Armed Forces at the Ministry of Defence.

They met at the New European, Moravec's newly opened club, its membership list filled with rising stars of the coming era of European power. Some said, cruelly, that the real reason for the club's existence was that Moravec, a Russian, a Jew, and a peasant by birth, had been black-balled by every establishment club in town. They were, in part, correct. Moravec craved acceptance by the British establishment – there were those who said that he would give half his empire and both his daughters' hands in marriage for a knighthood – nevertheless, he did not invest great sums of money simply out of pique and, as he had predicted, the New European had almost immediately become the temple for high priests and acolytes of the New Order, all seeking influence and power in the days to come.

If ever a man thought himself destined for power, you are he, thought Moravec over lunch, studying the film-star looks of Wardlove and hearing the smooth, confident voice which had just enough of Eton and Oxford professionally roughed out to avoid putting off the street-smart young go-getters while retaining a reserve to flatter the hopeless social ambitions of the constituency flowery-dress and hat brigade whose influence he knew should never be underestimated.

'Wouldn't mind a soft spot on your satellite TV station if we lose the next election,' laughed Wardlove, loudly enough to mean it.

Brennay glanced up, shocked, from his lobster bisque. 'Surely you don't think . . . ?'

'Not a hope!'

Moravec's index finger lifted a millimetre off costly white Irish linen and more vintage Krug appeared.

'Excellent!' said Wardlove.

'There are no "soft" spots on my networks but there's a place for you any time if you want it, Mr Wardlove.'

'Jesting. Not my style actually.'

Moravec waived tasting the Krug. 'Just pour,' he ordered, dismissing the waiter. 'Politics is a most precarious profession, don't you think? Of course if you have private means, as you do, there is at least a buffer against losing your parlimentary seat, career, and ambitions.'

Wardlove grimaced. 'Don't even talk about it. Anyhow, I'm not as well off as the press make out, your papers included. Took one hell of a financial beating when the marekts crashed. Wife almost walked. Shopping trips curtailed and all that. Well, less comfortable than before, I should say. Don't want to plead too much poverty; voters don't like it. Lose confidence.'

'Quite right,' agreed Brennay, accepting his sole eagerly.

'You've put on pounds since I last saw you,' warned Wardlove.

'Haven't I!' Brennay patted his ample stomach. He looked across at Moravec. 'Earned a good few too.'

'I don't have your directorships, Bertie.'

Moravec raised his glass. 'To the government, long may its rule continue.'

Wardlove hesitated, sipped then studied his host 'Why do I get the feeling you know something I don't?'

'Perhaps because I do?'

'Oh.'

'Got that sudden sinking feeling, Minister? Remember the Profumo affair? The number of Tory MPs who've told me the first they heard of that scandal was over a meal – lost their appetite immediately of course.'

Wardlove glanced sharply at Brennay who ducked his head to his fish, eyes fixed firmly on his plate. 'This is a set-up, Bertie?'

'Brennay is merely the go-between here, don't vent your anger on him. Besides, you may have reason to be grateful to your old school friend at some date not too far distant.'

Wardlove leaned back in his chair, sensing opportunity in whatever issue was about to be raised.

Brennay stood up. 'I've, er, a call or two to make, back soon, carry on without me for the moment.'

Moravec shifted his bulk, took a mouthful of filet *bleu*, and drained his glass. 'Make nothing on our steaks. Absolutely the best in the world.' He touched his large ears. 'Profits come from using these, in this place.'

'I'm not for sale,' warned Wardlove. 'In case you've been given the wrong impression?'

'I'm not buying. I'm offering you an unconditional gift which you may exploit if you wish. Or, of course, you may reject it.'

'You don't offer free gifts, Moravec – even in your rags. There's always a price to pay. Seems even this lunch isn't free after all.'

'I'll forget your momentary lapse because I'm certain you'll apologize in a few moments.'

'I doubt it.'

'I could have gone to the opposition but I think you can do more with my free gift when the time comes – as I believe it most surely will. Here's my advice: when you return to your desk this afternoon, personally instigate an enquiry into the medical treatment of servicemen. Specifically, you wish all information on organ transplant operations within the armed services. Also, you require accurate details of records held on organ donors and recipients – if by any small chance such operations have indeed taken place.'

Wardlove stared at the magnate, in silence. 'What are you telling me, Moravec?'

'Only you can discover that. I can tell you what I think. After that it's up to you to decide what you want to do. What, indeed, you want to do with the rest of your life. Very few men are given the opportunity to face a once-in-a-lifetime decision which could give them everything they dream of. In your case, Minister: power. And I mean real power. Top table.'

'Tell me.'

Moravec did.

'You're mad!' exclaimed Wardlove. 'They wouldn't dare!'

'Wouldn't they? Given the freedom to experiment, the funding, and – shall we say "human resources", they might not care.'

'This would crush any government if it's true.'

'And make the man who uncovered it.'

Wardlove raised his glass. 'I apoplogize for my crass-ness.'

Moravec dipped his large head. 'You understand the risks of course? The problem with any conspiracy is that one never quite knows how far the tentacles reach.'

'Are you suggesting Downing Street?' Wardlove mur-mured, alarmed yet excited.

'Your position is better than mine to answer that, Minis-ter,' said Moravec.

'Good lunch, sir?' enquired Wardlove's private secretary on his return.

Wardlove grunted.

'I'd heard the food at the New European is the best in London?'

'A good lunch in our world, Tillis, rarely has much to do with culinary standards.'

'Company below par?'

'Lord Brennay ducked out after the main course.'

'Sounds as if it wasn't à deux?'

'Le patron himself made the third.'

'Moravec? You realize that will make the gossip columns, especially since it wasn't that long ago you condemned his investigative reportage of brutality in the army.'

'Do you think I don't know that? I wasn't told he'd be there. Lord Brennay is not flavour-of-the-month with me at this moment. Anyway, it's done. What's on this after-noon? I was hoping for an early start to the weekend.'

'Nothing to hold you here. Nothing that the under-secretary can't handle, that is. I'll arrange your car now if you like?'

'Bloody marvellous. Tell you what, Tillis: best decision I ever made asking for you instead of some weepy female who couldn't handle my off days – or her own for that matter. Last private secretary I had was guaranteed to turn sour once a month and make me feel guilty if I dared to even hint at anything resembling leisure.'

'The business of government is not conducted entirely from Westminster – or indeed from the ministries, sir.'

'Indeed not.' Wardlove grinned. 'I think I'll take you with me to Downing Street when the day comes.'

Tillis let his eyes rest momentarily on his master. 'It is within your capabilities, sir, if I may say so. I'll have the car brought around.'

'Tillis, there's something you can do for me this afternoon. Well, you can instigate it at least. Might take a few days to put the whole thing together. Here, I've made some notes of what I'm after. Read through them and set the wheels in motion. Make sure my name is on the enquiry, understand?'

'Certainly, Minister.'

After Wardlove had departed, Roger Tillis read and reread the notes he had been given, trying to work out the reasoning and motive behind Wardlove's unexpected enquiry. His thoughts flew. Written in the car on the way back from lunch? Obvious, from the worse than usual scrawl. Raised over lunch at the New European? By Rudolf Moravec himself? Not Brennay, that fat fool only went to luncheon for one purpose: eating. Moravec had set it up.

Why? What was behind it?

Tillis was bewildered. His master was treading on dangerous ground, involving himself with a man who had many enemies both at Defence and in Westminster. If Wardlove was prepared to risk his reputation – perhaps even his career – it meant the stakes were very high. Or he was being used. Tillis knew what he had to do: obey his master, then betray him.

By nine o'clock that evening he was sitting in a Hampstead pub, drinking steadily from a pint glass of lager

116

with a double tot of Scotch on the side for bite. The place was crammed with young revellers who made too much money and seemed intent on letting that fact be known as loudly and as drunkenly as possible.

'Seen her on the tee-vee!' one brayed as a plump woman pushed through their ranks. 'Sort of Leftish Miss Piggy. Hey, that your toy-boy?'

'Ignore the bastards,' she said, plumping down opposite Tillis.

He leaned over and pecked her cheek. 'We can't discuss this in here!' he protested in a harsh whisper.

Someone wolf-whistled.

She beamed as he sat back. 'Perfect place, we're friends and those morons will soon find someone else to pick on just as loudly. Which suits us fine. Listen to them! They think the world is an extension of their bloody public schools.'

'It is,' said Tillis, with controlled anger.

'Easy, Roger. Well, what is it?'

'He had lunch with Moravec – '

'What!'

'That idiot Brennay set it up without letting on – which means Moravec planned it. Anyway he came back and did the "Oh lord, it was a drag" number, but it soon came out who was there because he knew I'd see it in Nigel Dempster.' Tillis gulped the Scotch and lifted the lager. 'Cheers.'

'Cheers.'

'I could tell something was up but couldn't nail it, then he made his usual "I'm going home" noises and put in his instruction for the enquiry as if it were an afterthought, which is always a dead giveaway with him. Absolutely nothing to do with lunch or Moravec. Not half!'

'What enquiry?'

'Wants to know the state of health of the bloody army.'

'What?'

'That's the general thing. What he's really asking is, have there been any transplant ops done? Who got done and where the bits came from. Names, addresses, the lot.'

'Are you thinking what I'm thinking?'

'I've certainly been thinking. How dirty is your mind?'

'Not half as dirty as theirs, apparently.'

'The organ-donor sales racket they made such a fuss about?'

'Precisely. Roger, *if* – let's just dream for a moment and pretend we've won the pools and the next fifty bloody general elections – *if* Moravec's got a sniff of a bit of free market enterprise in the beastly British army with a few godforsaken squaddies selling their bits, or – oh, heaven shine down on me – actually not knowing they've sold them, we are going to take this bloody government to the bloody cleaners! Christ, Roger.'

'You have got a dirty mind.'

'I know, isn't it *lovely*.'

Mary McCarthy squeezed herself into her rusting Austin Mini, the worn engine grinding into life as she started her journey to the opposite side of London. One of her head-lights was out, causing constant flashing from oncoming drivers. She ignored them as she did most things she considered trivial.

She had left before Tillis, after congratulating him and inciting him to further effort. She was glad to get away, not only because she was bursting to pass on his infor-mation but also because she found him vain and pumped up with self-importance, and his reaction to her flattery confirmed it. She saw people as birds or animals, and Tillis, undoubtedly, was a peacock.

Well, he can flare his feathers all he likes as long as he delivers the goods, she thought, blinking at another head-light flash.

She smiled. The position she was in at that moment – being able to decide who would receive her knowledge – was one she had occasionally dreamed of. She toyed a little with her decision, knowing all the while that it was not the leader of her party who would be the recipient but instead the man who, like herself, stood squarely on the political left and made no bones of the fact.

Yes, she decided, a good attacking performance from him in the House when the time came to blitz the govern-ment with the full dreadful story, and his place as rightful head of the party would be assured. As, in turn, would her own lesser position.

'Bugger off!' she bawled at a flashing driver, put her sole headlamp on main beam and left it there for the rest of her journey.

She parked behind Westminster Hospital and walked, always conscious that she was of ongoing interest to both the security service and Special Branch because of her known affiliations with certain Irish radical political figures and suspected links with others who favoured more direct revolutionary action.

She backtracked, entered the hospital through the front entrance, took herself up a couple of floors then exited via a staff entrance after a moment with an Irish nurse who was both her occasional lover and courier for The Cause.

Her direction was towards the Houses of Parliament, her destination a first-floor apartment close enough to Big Ben to hear the harmonics.

'Mary,' she announced breathlessly into the door entry-phone.

'You should have called.'

'This is vital.'

The door buzzed and opened. She climbed heavily up the curving stairway, her fat arm pulling at the mahogany rail.

He was waiting, his door open. 'You should lose weight.'

'Tell me something I don't know,' she gasped.

He glanced at his watch as they moved inside. 'I'm speaking at a crisis meeting arranged by the Health Service workers' committee, Shepherd's Bush Green. We have to stop the privatization bill going through whatever the means.'

'I know. I've something which might help.'

'Sit down. Drink?'

'Bless you.'

'Irish as usual?'

She accepted the generous measure and drank deeply. 'Well?'

She began.

The Member of Parliament listened in silence, standing

119

by his Adam fireplace, occasionally adjusting the position of silver-framed photographs fulsomely inscribed by various radical political rulers of the third world, some, surprisingly, still alive and in power.

Finished, she awaited judgement.

He took her tumbler and poured, less generously. 'You are driving, I take it?'

She nodded.

He said: 'Wardlove has two choices. He could admit to having instigated an enquiry into military medical records and be prepared to go all the way with it: name names, embarrass the government, put his own position in jeopardy – and, perhaps, come out of it smelling like a potential future party leader.'

'Which he sees himself as already.'

'Or he could duck it, run to Downing Street screaming blue murder . . . or red, rather, being as he'll blame us for suborning a member of his staff. Your own source does realize his name will undoubtedly be published, when things heat up?'

'No.'

'Ah! Well, these things happen, don't they.'

'We all pay a price.'

'A destroyed career is quite a price to pay. He won't duck out, will he?'

She opened her scuffed, patchwork vinyl bag and removed a small, surprisingly pristine cassette recorder.

'You taped all of it?'

'Every beautiful word – including his phone call to get me to the Hampstead pub.'

'I'm glad you're on our side.'

'Yours,' she corrected, firmly. 'The rest have sold out. They're so hungry for power they've bankrupted their ideals.'

'Yes,' he agreed, his eyes, quite suddenly, alight. 'And they'll come crawling when there's food to eat.'

'At your table.'

The politician gave a thin smile. 'Where there'll be a place set for you, my dear. You'll come to the rally, I hope?'

Mary McCarthy smiled at herself in the battered Mini's cracked driving mirror, angled as ever nowhere near the rear window. Not bad, she decided. A good night's work. After the workers' rally she would drive to Notting Hill where she knew a café with hungry girls. She grinned. She'd give one something to eat. That was if she failed to pick up a nice juicy nurse in the crush on the green. God, she felt randy. She squirmed in her squashed seat, her fat thighs spread, the rim of the steering wheel pressed into the tight ridge between her bulging breasts and stomach. She shifted position, the smile still on her chubby, florid face.

The Jamaican mini-cab driver coming fast the opposite way, his radio control urging him to beat the gathering crowds at Shepherd's Bush, saw a single headlight on full beam blazing at him, too close to the central white line. He spun the window down fast, the night air like a cold punch as he stuck his head into the slipstream to yell his usual obscenity at crazy motorcyclists. For a split second before the impact his brain registered the tilted shape of the rusted Mini and the blind eye of its offside headlight. He never saw the heavy, clothed projectile burst through the Mini's disintegrating windscreen, jammed solid as the car spun wildly, ending up on its side narrowly missed by traffic in the opposite lane.

Police presence was heavy in the area because of the rally and an officer on foot was at the scene within moments, with two mobile units wailing to a halt behind the gathering crowd.

'What's your game?' the breathless constable demanded of the man going through Mary McCarthy's handbag.

A second man, leaning over into the upturned car, held out an opened leather ID case without withdrawing his head.

'Oh,' said the officer.

'Dead, the other driver too,' said the man with the handbag, pocketing letters and a diary. He handed a small cassette recorder to his colleague who slipped headphones on and listened, eyes blank.

'Got crafty in her old age,' said the handbag man, grimacing as he ripped at the filthy lining. 'Technical! Who'd have believed it?'

'You were following her then?' asked the young constable, hovering, letting his colleagues hold back the crowd and do the reporting. This was his first encounter with the shadow world of MI5.

'Him,' said the man, almost to himself. 'Fat Mary just picked a bad day to do business. We couldn't resist it. Been tomorrow we wouldn't have had enough people to cover.' He looked up at the young officer and smiled. 'Government cuts,' he said as chants of protest floated towards them from the green. 'Same all over, isn't it?'

Feedback from the tannoy and wild cheers heralded the introduction of the rally's celebrated speaker.

'Hartramp?' barked Rudolf Moravec into one of the array of telephones on his massive desk at the World Communications Corporation. 'The doctor the Hale woman wrote to? Psychiatrist? Are you out of your mind? Get him away from there.'

'He's used hypnosis – ' Jane Haversham attempted to explain.

'I said: get him away from Hartrampf.'

'No. It was Adam's decision and it's the right one – he's learning about himself. Hartrampf knows what he's doing.'

'Does he? If he digs too deep he may wipe out Adam's paranormal ability. Which leaves him normal – and us nowhere.'

'That risk exists – but for Adam's sake his past must be uncovered.'

'Not until we've capitalized on his power. What's the matter with you? You're risking a once-in-a-lifetime opportunity. You can't know how far his abilities might develop, or how fragile they are.'

'Please listen to me. Adam is going through hell every moment he exists in this state. With Hartrampf's professional help some of the pressure can be taken off him. We don't as yet know his true identity – but we're getting there. Through hypnosis we've discovered he's an SAS officer, or was. He was left to die on a glacier in South

Georgia at the start of the Falklands War. A helicopter crash. He was the sole survivor.'

'Now you listen. I instigated enquiries at the highest possible level today. If I'm correct, there's going to be a political crisis very soon. A government which prides itself on its human rights record might have to defend itself against charges which would make the Kremlin's forced psychiatric treatment of political prisoners seem positively humane. Use your brains instead of your emotions: members of the medical profession must be involved, there is no other conclusion to be drawn, and until we know who they are we keep Adam away from all doctors other than those I have in my pocket.'

'Hartrampf's achieved a breakthrough. Adam wants to carry on with the hypnosis therapy. If I don't go along we could lose him altogether. The only hold we have on him is me. You know our legal position: no contract signed by him – in his present mental condition – would hold up in court. I'll keep you aware of progress. I'm sorry, but this is the way it has to be.' She rang off.

Moravec lifted one of his private lines, punched in a number then said: 'Chapman? Absolute priority, get your best people on to this: in-depth background on one Doctor Erich Hartrampf, now retired. Address, Eaton Square, London. He had a connection with an Eleanor Hale, died a few days ago in an apparent accident at her Dartmoor home, Raethmoor Farm. Reported nationally. War-time heroine. We did something ourselves. I want the connection. Cost is immaterial. Get back to me.'

'A Doctor Raymond Liversey on two,' said his secretary's voice through his intercom. 'From the Blackwater Clinic, Camberley. He insists Miss Haversham gave him your number.'

'Put him through.'

The American's voice sounded worn. 'Mr Rudolf Moravec? I'm sorry about this, sir. I know you're a busy man so I'll be brief. I've been trying to get hold of Jane Haversham regarding a friend of hers all morning. The matter is urgent. She left a contact number on her answerphone – yours, apparently.'

'Don't apologize, doctor. Would the friend be Daniel Hale, by any chance?'

'You know him?'

'Jane's producing a programme on him for my satellite television company.'

'Is there anywhere I can get in touch with Daniel or Miss Haversham?'

'Doctor Livesey, I have exclusive exploitation rights on Daniel Hale – obviously his health and well-being are of great interest and, of course, concern to me.'

'Of course,' Livesey said, flatly. 'I guess you've had a medical team working flat out on him. I had the results of my own tests this morning and I've worked non-stop since then.'

Moravec remained silent.

'I understand your caution, sir. A vaccine synthesized from Daniel's blood cells would be worth a fortune – but then I'm talking to the man who'll soon be arranging the deal with the drug conglomerates. That's typical of my life. I make the hit but someone else gets the run.'

Moravec twisted right around in his chair, so that he had a towering view across the Thames and London. 'I'm not a completely greedy man, no matter what my enemies may say. Perhaps some of the details of your tests differ from the work I've had done. We could work out a financial arrangement, fee or percentage, if this was the case.'

Livesey brightened. 'Sure. You can have sight of my work any time – but I doubt if I've done anything your people haven't. I'd like to have seen their faces when they discovered the difference in Daniel's blood cell structure – and the potential!'

'I wasn't there, I'm afraid.'

'You should have been, sir. The very real possibility of defeating a killer virus like AIDS doesn't stare you in the face every day.'

Moravec stood and looked down to the grey river thirty-nine storeys below. 'Doctor, never decry your own efforts. Come up to London with your results. I promise you it won't be a wasted journey. Let me make a suggestion: I'd already arranged a meeting with our own medical consultant for tomorrow morning. Top man in the field. Doctor James Shirer?'

'Oh yes, sir. I've seen his TV specials. The one on AIDS – *The Wrath of God* – was important. Excellent production.'

'Yes. If you can attend the meeting I'll get my secretary to call you with the details and arrange a car to pick you up.'

'I'll be there. I look forward to meeting with you.'

'It will be my pleasure, Doctor Livesey.' Moravec replaced the receiver and called his confidential secretary: 'Blackwater Clinic, Camberley. We already have background information on the place. Get me the current financial state of the business and of one of the partners, Doctor Raymond Livesey. At the Regent's Park penthouse, eight o'clock tonight.'

He turned back to the sweeping view.

So they've found a way to defeat the "wrath of God"? And that, too, they kept secret. What else? Well, grace may be given of God – but knowledge is bought in the marketplace. He smiled: power is a wondrous thing, the years fall away when you grasp it and you are young again. He stared out through the plate glass, beyond the river. All the world was out there. The old world. It was finished. Something new had been born – or created, or engineered – and nothing would or could ever be the same again. Yet a spectre hovered in his mind, from childhood: an image, not from real life but from a wall poster. He could see that image now. Cropped, very blond hair on a noble head with pale eyes penetrating a distant future with a purpose that would not be denied. He saw himself, too. An urchin in rags, he stared up at the face, his own hopelessness made complete by it. It humbled him more even than the war which raged around him, engulfing his country, destroying his family and, with time, much of his race.

He had seen that face – or its real-life counterpart – again. Yesterday. A face that saw the future. Read it. And possibly could even make it.

He turned back to his massive desk. Forget the past. Profit from the future. And if the past has already formed the future? Then make damn sure you're the man in the poster and not the wretched urchin in the rubble with air in your belly and nothing in your eyes.

Better still: be the man with the power to put the face on the poster and the poster on the wall.

He touched his intercom. 'Get me Doctor Shirer.'

'He's using the Marbella villa at the moment, sir. Left Heathrow yesterday.' The mellow, modulated voice paused. 'His mistress joined him this morning.'

'Fly him back immediately, alone. Unscheduled flight. Charter something – with no trace back to the corporation.'

'I understand.'

'Have him taken immediately to the Regent's Park penthouse. I want him there tonight.'

'He'll be there, sir.'

Moravec sat very still, his mind working. AIDS. Genetic engineering? Have they discovered a cure or have they put right their own mistake? Accident? Or intention? The face on the poster came back. Echoes. Targeting a particular social group viewed as 'undesirable' in some quarters? Selective destruction by 'natural' means? What they could do to one group they could do to others. Where would it end?

He made another call, to an agency whose headquarters were in Victoria, London, but whose services and expertise were spread across the world wherever terror or conspiracy were a threat. His confidence in the organization was complete. He trusted them with his life; they supplied the team of bodyguards who secured his safety around the clock. He knew they were more than capable of safeguarding his most recent investment.

Adam sipped cautiously at the single glass of burgundy Hartrampf had permitted him, the taste detonating a sudden explosion of memories, so many, so fleeting, they died like sparks in the chill pit of his empty mind.

'Adam, are you all right?' asked Jane, watching him closely.

'Perhaps the wine is too heavy?' said Hartrampf, pouring a small measure from a bottle of hock on his massive oval dining table. 'Try this instead.'

126

'We'll have your real name soon,' said Jane, smiling.

Hartrampf smiled, too.

Adam tasted the hock and his world shifted. He saw strangers before him, yet the wine, the heavy furniture, were – if not familiar – then *comfortable* within his mind. He drank again, this time draining the glass, then held it out confidently. '*Bitte?*'

Jane stared at him.

Hartrampf poured, appearing not to notice the use of his native tongue.

He was on a train, the smell of steam and cinders strong. And he could smell the sea. The engine pulled forward with a jerk as the wheels spun, then bit. He worried about his suitcase on the rack above. The case was heavy. If it fell it would hurt somebody. It would also kill him, though not by its weight. By its contents. The transmitter would hang him for sure. They were moving now and the country-side was quite beautiful: sunshine, summer smells pouring through the partially opened window carrying a hint of smoke which made him a student again, travelling hard, third class but not minding it, to his university at Heidelberg. A uniformed man entered the carriage and his heart contracted but he only wanted his ticket, not his freedom, not his life.

'Adam?' questioned Jane, concerned. 'Are you sure you're all right?'

'Yes,' he said, though he knew that the train was taking him to his death and there was no way he could get off it.

'He needs rest,' stated Hartrampf. 'He should sleep now.'

'We'll sleep together,' said Jane, going to Adam. 'I'll be there, don't worry.'

Here, he said in his mind. Not there.

Doctor James Shirer arrived, disgruntled and frustrated, at the duplex penthouse apartment overlooking Regent's Park, the World Communications Corporation's official London guest-house, his mood made worse by Moravec's absence.

'You're in the blue suite, Doctor,' announced the male housekeeper, in his black and stripes looking every inch the top hotel executive which was precisely what he had been before he had sold his services, his discretion – and sometimes, he thought, his soul too – to Rudolf Moravec.

'I'm in the ruddy dog-house, chum,' snapped Shirer, a pugnacious-looking Scot whose sandy-red hair was the beacon for the notorious temper beneath. 'Where's he keep his cigars and his bloody brandy?'

'There's a meal prepared, Doctor.'

'What's that got to do with anything?'

Moravec entered without apology, made a dismissive motion with one large hand and took Shirer's arm with the other, propelling him out on to a long glass-enclosed balcony, lush with plants, overlooking the park.

'This had better be good,' complained the Scot.

Moravec pointed at one of a row of wicker chairs. 'Sit down and listen. Take your mind off your woman until I've finished and you just might find yourself with enough money to stop her screwing around behind your back – and maybe afford a divorce settlement on your wife too.'

'I need a drink. Flying does it every time.'

'I need your brain. No alcohol until we've finished – which could be the whole weekend. I'll arrange a girl to lower your libido.'

'No thanks, too dangerous these days.'

'Yes,' agreed Moravec with a tight smile. 'Which is precisely why you've been brought here. How much would you give for a sample of blood which purports to contain antibodies which could defeat the AIDS virus?'

Shirer snorted. 'My right arm. Bugger my right arm – all of me from the neck down! With the obvious exclusion of my reproductive organs so that I can test the synthesized product personally. What's all this bullshit?'

'Tomorrow morning you're going to sit down with a young black American doctor who just might have paved the way for you to enter your dubious paradise.'

'You're being conned.'

'If I am – and I've every reason to believe I'm not – then you're the authority who'll prove it.'

'Just like that? Here? Great laboratory!'

'I'm not looking for a prolonged testing programme. That can come later. Any equipment you need will be supplied. What I need is the answer to a simple question: is the sample of blood you will examine different from normal human blood?'

'What's that mean? Undiseased blood? Common blood type? What's normal?'

'I'm looking for a difference. A subtle difference or even a starting difference. I didn't study medicine.'

'Different meaning abnormal?'

'Possibly, yes.'

'Mutated?'

'Again, a possibility.'

'We are definitely talking human here? Not something derived from animal experiments? Genetic experiments? A biological chimera?'

'Meaning precisely?'

'An organism made up of two genetically distinct tissues.'

'I'm looking more towards advanced human.'

Shirer sat forward, his quick brown eyes fixed on the media tycoon. 'You've found some bugger who's been out there playing games he shouldn't be – right? Genetic games which could make our worst nightmares step right out of the bloody shadows and send the human race screaming back into the primaeval swamp in one generation.'

'Surely that's an exaggeration?'

'Oh, is it? Just how long has it taken for the AIDS virus to take hold? How far has it spread in that time? Exaggeration? Don't hold your breath? So who's the arsehole? This black American wonder? Or is he just the delivery boy?'

'I don't know.'

'Then you'd better find out. For all our sakes. Genetic engineering behind closed doors with the gloves off is *dangerous*.'

'What does the name Hartrampf mean to you?'

'Erich Hartrampf? In relation to this? Involved in early genetic research: the dark age when we saw everything and understood nothing. Well, not much. A little further on

129

from Mendel and his peas maybe. Early fifties, before Watson and Crick went into the model-making business and gave us a shape to work on. Gave it all up – Hartrampf – decided there was more money in psychiatry, which there is, and flew off to the Promised Land. America, not Israel.'

'Seems a drastic change?'

'Perhaps it was then. Not now. The *raison d'être* of genetic engineering as some view it is to create something as near damn perfect as one can. Which includes behavioural aspects. Perhaps even especially behavioural aspects. For example, genetic engineering on a grand scale for social purposes – not that I agree with it – could ensure that our prisons were populated only with a decreasing number of old lags in a couple of generations. Mind you, we'd probably end up with a world full of bloody boring people. Anyhow, Hartrampf made his pile over the water and got himself in with some high-powered people. The Pentagon crowd. I heard a rumour that he was involved with some sensitive government project. Mega-bucks budget. Telekinesis, that kind of thing. Yanks and the Russians spend more on research of the paranormal – parapsychology – than we do running our wretched hospitals over here. They reckon the next generation of weapons will be controlled by human thought impulses linked to computers. They're serious – and they're probably right. Spend enough money and you can make anything work.'

Moravec stood up. 'You can have that drink.'

'What did I say?'

'One word.'

'Which word?'

'Nothing you'd understand at this point. I needed a link. You just gave it to me. "Paranormal." Even if this AIDS business amounts to nothing you've earned your retainer this year.'

'Don't know what you're on about – but I'll take the drink. a large brandy.'

'You'll know soon enough.'

Shirer studied the tycoon as he poured cognac from a crystal decanter at the bar at the furthest end of the lush balcony.

'You know who's experimenting illegally, don't you, Moravec?'

Moravec returned, handed Shirer his cognac and savoured his own, staring across at the darkened park and the rearing shapes of the zoo enclosures. He thought he heard some caged animal shriek in pain but knew the sound could never penetrate the sound-proofed glass of the penthouse balcony. 'Not yet,' he said.

EIGHT

'Time to go, lad,' said George Howard.

'Don't you ever sleep?' Lewin muttered, dragging himself out of the battered armchair in Howard's cold Princetown cottage. He swallowed more amphetamines, dry.

'Been watching you taking them pills. Need them, do you? Keep you awake? Gave us those during the war. Me, I'm an old hand at staying up and bright. Chucked mine. I can catnap for a couple of minutes and you wouldn't know it. Good as a couple of hours' sleep if you do it right.'

'You're marvellous, George. Must have been told that all your life – mostly by yourself.'

Howard chuckled. 'Good to hear you've got a bit of spunk left in you. You're going to need it.'

Lewin glanced at his watch.

'One a.m. on the button,' said Howard. 'Be two thirty by the time we get there. They're going to be a bit slack around about then – every bugger is. Should be able to drive quite close in that fancy motor you've got. Not *too* close, mind. I reckon they've got equipment to pick up the sound of approaching vehicles: they always seem to know when something's on the way.'

'You mean we have to walk.'

'That we do, son. Do a lot of that round these parts. Famous for it really.'

'Just don't get us lost and stuck in a bog.'

'Pigs might fly.'

'They sink, just like us.'

Howard chuckled. 'Cuppa tea, a bit of toast, and we're off, OK by you?'

'Who's going to be mum?'

'I've got the gun, lad.'

'You don't need that now, do you?'

'I'll decide that.'

They were on the road within fifteen minutes, Howard's directions precise, heading them south across the moors.

Lewin's mouth was as dry as dust, the effects of the amphetamines cutting off his saliva. He ached for a pint of beer but knew his stomach would reject it after the pills.

He wondered where Peter Foley was and if he was awake also, and decided probably not. Past it. Poor old sod. Not me, I'm going to keep going till I fall over, even if it's in the gutter when I've just reached thirty. No bloody geriatric ward for me.

'Hard-top finishes in a while,' advised Howard. 'No matter, plenty of good tracks for a way yet.'

'Terrific.'

'Ever used one of these, son?' He indicated the Luger.

'I'm a reporter, not Billy the bloody Kid.'

'Thought not. I toyed with the idea of letting you have it when you go in there but you'd be more of a danger to yourself than anyone else, I reckon.'

Lewin glanced sideways, sharply. 'You think I'll need it? We're only doing a bit of trespassing.'

'You are, son. I'm sitting waiting for you to come out.'

'That's not an answer, George.'

Howard shrugged. 'All depends what they're hiding down there, doesn't it?'

'Something that brings cabinet ministers out in the middle of the night according to your photos.'

'You know what I think.'

'A bolt-hole for the privileged? Don't see it, George. Never get down it in time, would they? Need a fair bit of warning to get here from London, even by chopper. Four minutes isn't long enough and that's all the time there's supposed to be if it's a surprise attack.'

'Wars don't start that way, lad. There's a build-up. You've seen it on the telly. Loads of tension, diplomatic notes going back and forth – then your actual ultimatum. If they bother with one of those. The bastards who've got themselves booked in that place won't be sitting around for no four-minute warning. That's for poor chumps like you and me. You'll see, when it really comes down to it, there'll be plenty of squaring off before anyone throws a punch. That's nature, son, us and the animals – not too much difference between us when you get down to the bone.'

The Fourtrak thumped, hard, into a pothole, lurching wildly. 'Shit!' Lewin cursed.

'Be like this from now on,' Howard chuckled.

'I bloody hope you've got the safety catch on that old relic.'

'Never, be like having a woman with a rubber on, that would.'

'Everyone does it like that nowadays, George, haven't you heard of AIDS out here in the wilderness?' Lewin snapped, nervously.

'Self-inflicted. That's my view. Don't worry, I know fire-arms like you know how to eat them pills.'

'Piss off.'

'Cut the engine and roll her to a stop,' ordered Howard.

'What?'

'You heard. Do it. *Now*. And kill the lights.'

Lewin complied. 'What's up?'

'Nothing, I hope. I was gassing away to you and not watching where we were.'

'Are we there?'

'Couple of miles away.'

'A couple of miles. Christ, it's pitch black out there. We couldn't see a step in front of us.'

Howard unzipped the canvas bag he had at his feet. 'We'll see.'

'Torches? They'll be seen for miles.'

'Not underground they won't be. I told you I'd found a way in.' Howard pointed into the blackness. 'Over there. Disused tin mine. I rigged a sling and pulley system – oh, months ago – down the main shaft. Underground, there's a whole series of workings which connect up making a regular network of tunnels. They thought they'd be clever, see: reckoned no one would be fool enough to go down there so they use some of the tunnels as airways for their filtration systems – which is how you get in, son. I am bloody marvellous, aren't I.'

Lewin sat still and silent, facing Howard in the darkness. 'You said nothing about going down a tin mine.'

'Didn't ask, did you, son. Claustrophobic are you?'

'The last time I went down a tin mine I almost didn't get out.'

'Well you've got me to hold your hand this time, haven't you.'

'Fuck you, George.'

'Not the way to speak to someone who's going to make you famous.'

Lewin caught the silver glint of the Luger, then felt it press, coldly, against his face.

'We've come this far, son, might as well go all the way. Leave the keys in the ignition.'

Lewin stepped down from the Fourtrak into the blackness, stumbling beside Howard, gripped by the old man's surprising strength. He could just make out the ruin against the stars, the old granite engine-house and chimney like a fist with one accusing finger raised to God in admonition for the destruction of an entire industry and the lives of its workers. Now he could see the silhouetted tors, the moor rock formations, black as night and shaped as if to strike terror. A landscape as pagan as its origins, with the land rolling away like deep swells on a black sea. He felt cut off, abandoned, surrounded by emptiness with God only knew what beneath him.

Write it up, he told himself, write it in your mind and keep your terrors behind that dam. Milton did it for you, centuries ago; you're stumbling in his footsteps. This same entire bloody experience. 'Of dire chimeras and enchanted isles, and rifted rocks whose entrance leads to Hell.' There, in front of me.

'Once we get inside I'll turn on the torches,' said Howard. 'You want to stop those pills, son, your nerves are shot.'

Lewin felt the grip on his arm tighten as he was drawn inside the ruined structure, as if the old man sensed he was about to bolt.

'The sling is up ahead. Safe as anything, used it many times.'

'I thought you said you hadn't been in there,' snapped Lewin, hearing the quaver in his voice and knowing he could not control it.

'Not in *there*, son. Been down the mine many times.'

'What was all that bullshit about your hidey-hole and being able to hear the humming of the machinery?'

'No bullshit, son, I have my hole for taking the shots and like I said in the pub, if you know where to listen you hear things. Down there is where.'

'How far down?' asked Lewin, querulously.

'Shaft goes down, oh, fourteen, fifteen hundred feet.'

'Fifteen hundred feet in a home-made sling at the end of a rope that you leave here in all weathers – and only a couple of torches for light. You're a raving lunatic.'

'Calm down. The shaft goes that deep but there's tunnels off it at different heights all the way down. We get off maybe a third of the way down. Safe as houses.'

'Whose? You place is so derelict I could kick the bugger over.'

'Still got your sense of humour then?'

'You hear me laughing?'

'Listen, the sling is a professional job: mountain-rescue equipment, nicked it from the mountain-rescue post up by Princetown. They got another soon enough. Rope's from the same source. Best stuff, guaranteed for years.'

'You should be in the Dartmoor nick.'

Howard gave a hard laugh. 'They think I'm an old bugger who lost a few marbles along the way. Same as the bunch down there think. I can get away with murder on these moors, son.'

'Yeah. Mine for starters.'

'You'll be OK. I'll look out for you.'

'Makes me feel really good.'

'You go first, son.'

'Fuck you!'

'Sorry, but that's the way it has to be. Do as I tell you and you'll be right as rain.' Howard switched on his torch. 'There's the sling on the wall. Stop right there and don't look down.'

'Oh *shit*.'

'Like I said: don't look down.'

Lewin knew he would never take another step in his life. He was rooted to that spot and would stay that way until his legs gave out and he'd topple into the shaft and that would be that.

'Feels like it's sucking you in, doesn't it lad. Think of it being six feet deep, the old mind likes having something it can handle.'

Lewin croaked: 'They dig graves six feet deep.'

Howard's shoulders heaved. 'So they do. Here you go. Knapsack first, over your chest. Good, now slip this over you. Easy now.'

'I'm not going down there!'

''Course you are, that's why you're here.'

'You do it, I'll pay whatever you ask. Please.'

'Too big, son. Need to be your size to get through their ducting system. Too old as well, I'd stiffen up in there and be stuck for the duration.'

'Duration? The bloody war's over, you old fool.'

'See you're feeling better already. Hold still now. Right.'

Lewin shrieked as he swung into space, the gaping black pit looming beneath his jerking legs.

Howard took an end of rope and struck at him, hard. '*Quiet!* Sound carries miles out here. Be still or you'll lose the sling, then you've had it.'

Lewin hung stiffly, slowly rotating, certain he was about to die. The harness bit into his body but he was sure he could feel himself slipping out of it.

He dropped, screaming.

Howard calculated depth by the knots he had placed in the rope; after some moments he stopped Lewin's descent and secured the rope to a stanchion. He lay flat, his head over the edge of the pit.

'Can you hear me?'

From below in the blackness came a low gurgling sound. Howard hung his arm into the shaft and switched on his torch.

Lewin's face, deathly white and glistening wetly, turned upward to the light.

Howard hissed downward: 'You're all right, son, done

well so far. Now, swing yourself forward a couple of feet and you should be right in line with the second level tunnel.'

The face stared upward, panic building in the eyes like a runaway fire.

'Son! *Do it now or you're a dead man.* Hear me?'

Excruciatingly slowly Lewin's body began to swing, by inches.

'That's it. Good. Keep that up, you've only got to cover a short distance. Stick your legs out in case you're not in line with the tunnel. Don't want you crashing into the rock, do we?'

'Fuck you, George,' Lewin's voice wailed upward.

'That's more like it. OK, I can see we've got it right. There's a safety grip on the left – take hold of that and pull yourself into the tunnel. Good. *Good.* Now rest, take a few deep breaths – but take off the sling first.'

Howard pulled the rope upward the instant it became slack until the sling was in his hands, then leaned over the edge.

'Can you hear me?'

'I'd hear you better if you'd get your arse down here.'

'I'm not coming down, son.'

'What!'

'I've had a think about it and I reckon you'd be better off if I was on the surface.'

'*I'd* be better off? Stop pissing around, George.'

'In the knapsack there's the camera, all the directions you need, flask of water, gum, biscuits, smokes – '

'I'm not on a fucking hiking holiday!'

'Just listen. If I'm down there with you there's nothing we can do if they find this place and toss the rope down the shaft, right?'

'George, you bastard, you're telling me that if they catch me you're not about to be trapped as well – right?'

'You see it your way, son.'

'Get down here.'

'No.'

'*George.*'

'You're on your own. Better make the best of it.'

'Chuck that harness down!'

'Not until you've got the photos.'

'Please, George.'

'Won't do you any good, son. Best get on with it, that's my view.'

'From up there. Great!'

'You've got no choice. Do as I say and we'll get what we want.'

'I'm not going anywhere.'

'That's right, son. You're not going anywhere without this sling and it's not coming down until you've done the job.'

'You bastard. I'll wring your neck when I get up there.'

'You do that, son – but you'll need the sling.'

Lewin drew back into the tunnel and out of the beam of Howard's torch.

Howard waited, rolling a cigarette then pulling hard on it.

'All right, George, I'll do it.'

Howard waited, rolling a cigarette then pulling hard on it.

'All right, George, I'll do it.'

Howard smiled, letting the smoke drift from his nostrils. 'Do what, son? Go down the tunnel, have a kip for a bit then come back and tell me you couldn't get in?'

'I'll get in.'

'How do I know?'

'I've got the camera, haven't I?'

'You bring something out of there.'

'What?'

'How do I know? Anything. Something from one of the rooms.'

'Then you'll bring me out.'

'Of course. And don't fall and break the camera – those tunnels are full of junk.'

'You're all heart, George.'

'I'll be up here waiting.'

'You'd better be.'

Lewin ducked back into the tunnel, surprised that his anger had reduced his terror. He still felt jittery but knew that most of that was due to the pills. He examined the

139

contents of the knapsack, studying the hand-drawn diagram of the workings Howard had included with his directions. His mouth felt as if he had eaten ashes. He unwrapped a stick of gum and chewed steadily, relishing the sharp taste of spearmint.

He had a long walk in front of him and his panic flared again at the thought of his torch breaking or the batteries running out, then he found a smaller back-up torch in a side-pocket. He rested against the rock-wall, feeling the sweat on his forehead turning icy. For the first time he became aware of cold and shivered despite his padded anorak. He wished he had worn gloves and thicker socks.

'I'm off now, George,' he called. 'Don't bloody be asleep when I get back.'

The familiar chuckle drifted down to him with the acrid smell of the hard hand-rolling tobacco the old man preferred.

Right, *move*.

He started forward, forcing back the memory of his nightmare experience in the Cornish tin mine the year before, not grateful for the knowledge, the preparation it had given him. He could write a treatise on the nature of his surroundings, imprinted in stark terror and bound in blind panic. A long tunnel hewn through solid granite, its ceiling well clear of his five feet six inches, under his cautious feet, rotting sleepers and rusted lines for carts which had long since given up hauling mined rock. And water. Pools, red from the granite. Streams down the walls. Air made humid by it. The constant, maddening drip of it. Everywhere.

He remembered the water most of all. They had hoped he would drown in it – though they later denied knowledge of his presence. Naturally. Don't think about it, you silly sod. Like that old bastard George said: don't look over the edge. Rapunzel owes me for that and I know how I want to be paid. Her. All of her. On all fours so that I can grab that blonde mane like reins and give her a hard time. A real hard time.

The tunnel split. He shone the torch on to Howard's hand-drawn diagram, the constant drip of water now so loud he feared a wall of it was bearing down on him. Only

140

in your mind, he advised himself. He took the left hand fork, edging past a fallen cart with rust crusted like blood all over it.

He was coming down from the pills and mentally counted the number he had left. 'You want to stop taking those pills, son, your nerves are shot.' George, if I stop now I'll just squat here in the puddles, going nowhere. So screw your advice.

He swallowed two, drinking deeply from the water flask because the dry catch at his throat warned him of dehydration. Ten minutes, he thought, and I'll be *up*. In the meantime just keep moving. He checked his watch. How long had he been walking? Five minutes? For ever? Should have checked when you started but your mind was full of other things then: like screaming panic and thoughts of murder. Keep moving. 'Listen for the noise of their machines,' George had written in block capitals as if it were his commandment. 'When you hear it, look for the filters and you're in.' In where, George? The kingdom of heaven? Or hell?

Adam, he thought. Is this where you came from? The wet bloody bowels of the earth? No Eden, is it? No wonder you did a runner. He laughed and the sound shattered on the granite in a rock-fall of echoes.

Then he heard the hum. Expensive, he thought. Deep and rich with heavy undertones, a creamy bass of the kind you get only from the very best speakers. Heavy investment in plant. Good way to judge the size and importance of any project.

The beam of his torch caught the dull gleam of stainless steel and his heart thumped. So, in or out? The entire sodding media world for the asking, enough bread from Moravec to tell them to go screw themselves and buy a bright, leggy lovely for compensation – or? Or, nothing. The same nowhere job, the same nowhere prospects, old Foley's face over breakfast for the next thousand years, the same thick, unimaginative, petty little birds with as much class as a docker's armpit. No contest.

He set down the knapsack, found the tools Howard had included and began working.

'California, here I come,' he breathed tunelessly to the basso profondo accompaniment of the machinery buried somewhere beneath the bleak surface of Dartmoor.

Peter Foley sat, relaxed, gazing at the Thames, a Drambuie in his hand and a cigarette in his mouth. Bugger it, he thought: I've got a couple of years to go in the job, not a lot of ambition left to burn up the calories, a fat pension and no dependants to drain my enjoyment of it, so what the hell? I might die a couple of years early but I stay thin. Vanity at your age, Foley? Why not? If you don't take a good look at yourself who else will? He lit the cigarette.

'A rupee for your ruminations, your honour?' asked Mayberry in passable Peter Sellers Bombay English.

'Vanity.'

'Ah! "That reverend vice, that grey iniquity, that father ruffian, that vanity in years." It's creeping rot, not vanity. Only youth suffers real vanity in believing it's immortal.'

'Shakespeare had the advantage of observing our weaknesses; besides, he was a genius so not subject to them.'

'Anyone who locks himself away for years believing others are going to take notice of his outpourings has got a fair old slice of human weakness. You call it genius, some might call it conceit.'

'But not you?'

'I, in my own way, am blessed with genius.' Mayberry lifted his chin haughtily.

'And not a little conceit.'

'Touché. Not your average sort of bobby, are you, Chief Super?'

'I hope not.' Foley sipped his liqueur and watched a dredger working under floodlights on the far bank of the river. 'I wonder what they find?'

'Mud. Centuries old, with the stink of history.'

'I meant abandoned things – perhaps even concealed things. Forgotten murder weapons from forgotten cases. Chucked back. A life discarded, retribution denied.'

'Is that alcohol talking or a copper who feels guilty about all the cases he'll leave unsolved?'

Foley sighed. 'Bit of both. Trouble is, the public sees our

job in black and white. Crime equals conviction equals punishment. Nowadays it's getting to be crime equals compromise equals negotiated conviction equals reduced punishment.'

'It's a complicated world. I bet you long for the fifties: Johnny Ray, Frankie Laine, and the death penalty.'

'The fifties? That's the best part of a lifetime ago. Jesus!'

'Unless you're young, like Nigel Lewin, in which case it's someone else's lifetime – like Alfred the Great.'

Foley turned away from the river. 'I'd like to show you something. In my jacket beside you, inside pocket, a letter. Read it.'

'From Nigel?'

'Himself. Almost hysterical in parts.'

Mayberry reached for the jacket and read the rambling note Lewin had left Foley that morning. After a moment he glanced up, cautious. 'I assume you know?'

'Know what?'

'Ah! Well, best leave it alone.'

'You want a busted arm? Out with it.'

'Under protest, your honour. Young Nigel's a pill-popper. Speed and sleepers: uppers for acceleration, downers for brakes. Surprised you of all people haven't spotted it. Mind you, he's no junkie . . .'

'They all think that,' snapped Foley, shocked by the depth of his anger. He felt betrayed. 'How'd I miss it?'

''Cause you weren't looking. When was the last time you looked – really looked – at Nigel?'

'I'm a copper, I should have spotted it.'

'He only did them when he wanted the lift.'

'You mean when he was under pressure.'

Mayberry shrugged. 'I take it from what he's written in this doomy missive – despite the fact he says you're "going down different paths" – that the hunt he's on has the same prey at the end as your own?'

Foley reached for the Drambuie bottle. 'Bloody good question. Trouble is I don't know what I'm hunting, do I? Got all the choices though! Sublime to ridiculous. An army officer who's defected to the IRA and murdered his old mum? A conspiracy by MI5 to pervert the course of justice?

143

The ghost of some old Nazi dropped over here in the last war and topped by us?'

'You're thinking like a copper. Too small.'

'That's what I am,' growled Foley.

Mayberry quoted from Lewin's letter: ' "Peter, if this is what I think it is and it's exposed, let's say it's big enough for the history books." Now if that doesn't hint with lead boots of *heavy* political conspiracy I don't know what does! This Haversham assignment he mentions? Jane Haversham? He's worked for her before. She eats political intrigue; probably sleeps with it as well if it means getting hard information.'

Foley sipped the liqueur and lit another cigarette. 'You know about the last time Nigel got tied up with her?'

'I know he went through something *dreadful*. He wouldn't discuss it. Unusual for the little braggart.'

'Got himself trapped down a disused Cornish tin mine. Supposedly he had inside information that the place was being set up as a dump for nuclear waste.'

'It was. I saw the programme – it won an award.'

'A tin mine is normally constructed with one shaft sunk deep and tunnels carved out from it at various levels. Nigel, stupid bugger, decided he'd bribe one of the waste handlers to get him down there then found the character had set him up. That's Nigel's story anyway. He was down on one of the mid-levels, protective suit on, oxygen pack, the lot – really thought he'd fixed himself up well – then he heard running water. They were flooding the place with him in it. He'd have been up to his ears in water – possibly contaminated – in no time. He scrambled out. Just. He should have been in hotter water legally but no charges were preferred. Could have had him sewn up if they'd wanted to. Trespassing on government property for starters – and he broke locks at various points, so breaking and entering as well. I thought he'd go down for a couple of years. And I had Special Branch knocking down my door! Lucky little bugger.'

'Lucky he had Jane Haversham behind him. Never underestimate the power of the media, especially television.

That wretched box is the eye *they* want you to see through – "they" being whoever you choose to be influenced by.'

'Not Special Branch's favourite lady. He wouldn't have been down there if he hadn't been mixed up with her.'

'Nigel's headstrong – and easily influenced by women, more's the pity.'

'You seem to know him well.' Foley hesitated. 'He's not . . .'

'One of the silent but deadly bisexuals who're currently spoiling it for all you heteros by passing AIDS on to all those bosomy blondes you drool over? Definitely not. Not AC-DC as the really naff comedians say. Nigel is dedicated to laying any woman who doesn't fall over with her legs open the second she's clapped eyes on him. Reassured?'

'Only about his sexual habits.'

'Well, if you're truly worried about him, do what he says not to: put out an APB or whatever it's called this side of Hollywood.'

'And spoil his scoop? I'd never hear the end of it.'

Again Mayberry scanned the letter. 'I'd think about doing *something*. If this is some sensitive government project like the Cornish nuclear-waste dump Haversham exposed . . . well, you'd be surprised how prone to accidents secret installations are. I've hacked into so-called safety reports for interested parties and I've seen how easy it is to lose a statistic or two.'

Foley reached for Lewin's letter. 'I wouldn't know where to start. I don't even know where he is.'

'Haversham must know.' Mayberry pointed at the note. 'And Rudolf Moravec. He's the one who seems to have promised to make Nigel a rich man if he brings home the goodies. The question is, what are the goodies? And where?'

'It's Saturday tomorrow.'

'You stop investigations because people aren't at their place of work?'

'This is not an investigation.'

'Make it one. Nigel's record proves he's liable to get himself mixed up in assignments which have dubious legality and that letter suggests he's currently involved in something which could interest the forces of law and order. Improvise.'

'You mean lie.'

'Whitely. While you're doing that, I'll ask your other questions, electronically. As Nigel suggests, we might well be hunting the same prey.'

Foley crushed out his cigarette. His mouth tasted foul and he regretted starting again. 'Let's hope it doesn't bite back.'

'Call Moravec now. Arrange a meeting for tomorrow.'

'Number? He's hardly likely to be in the directory.'

'You've come to the right place, sweetheart,' said Mayberry, in appalling Bogart. 'Wait right there.' He got as far as the entrance to the long room, disappeared then stuck his head around the door-frame, neck extended. 'ET phone home,' he droned nasally. 'You never know, Nigel might be tucked up in bed with some brainless beauty he's picked up on the way.'

'Worth a try.' Foley stretched for the telephone. What's a nice copper like you doing in a joint like this? he asked himself. Busting the law and associating with criminals with deviant sexual habits. So changes the world.

His Exeter number trilled in his ear then stopped and Nigel Lewin said: 'This is the Lewin residence. Himself speaking. Sorry, not here, leave a number and I'll get back to you. Oh! If you want Peter Foley, he's not in either. Try calling . . .' Foley waited for the message signal. 'Nigel, I'm here at Mayberry's – call me immediately you get in. *Immediately*. Understand?'

'Still gallivanting?' enquired Mayberry, returning.

'Usual cheeky message on the answerphone. Changes it every time I record one. Little Welsh – '

'Moravec,' Mayberry reminded him. 'London office, London apartment block, Bucks mansion, or Scottish estate with huntin', shootin', and fishin' built in? That's just British real estate. You want Switzerland, West Indies, et al?'

'I'll try Haversham first, the number's on Nigel's note.'

'Moravec scare you? Imagine him in his underwear.'

'I'd rather it were her, thank you.'

'You're so *straight*!'

Foley dialled, listened for a moment, said: 'Please repeat,' then made notes in a black flip-top pad.

'Anything you say will be taken down and may be used in evidence,' intoned Mayberry gravely.

'Answering service. She left two alternatives: World Communications London Office –'

'Moravec.'

'And a Doctor Hartrampf.'

'Never heard of him. Try Moravec's London apartment.'

'Where did you get these numbers?'

'Silly question.'

'You're a ruddy electronic peeping Tom.'

'I rather like that! May I use it?'

'Number?'

Mayberry gave it. He moved closer, enjoying himself. Foley waited, the receiver pressed to his ear. He cleared his throat. 'Mister Rudolf Moravec, please. Detective Superintendent Foley of the Devon and Cornwall Constabulary here.'

'That'll shake him,' mouthed Mayberry.

'Shut up,' Foley snapped. 'Yes, sorry, I'll hang on.' He reached forward for another drink, changed his mind and sat back, his face determined but apprehensive.

'Moravec,' stated a deep, rude voice.

'Ah, sir! I'm terribly sorry to be calling at this late hour –'

'Don't apologize, Detective Superintendent, I imagine you're calling regarding Nigel Lewin.'

'I am, sir. How did you know that?'

'Lewin is doing some research work for one of my companies. Research that I have a personal interest in. We have it on record that he lives in your home. Exeter? I'm cursed with a memory that never forgets detail. Is there some problem?'

Foley hesitated. 'I'd like to speak plainly, sir, if I may.'

'I'm listening.'

'You're a powerful man, with powerful means at your disposal.'

'I try to temper that power with humanity.'

'Sir, I have no idea what young Nigel is investigating on

147

your behalf but the fact is he left me a disturbing letter in which he hints at there being some risk to himself. Considerable risk. I must confess, his state of mind, as it comes over in the letter, doesn't sound encouraging. You wouldn't care to comment?'

'On his state of mind? I'm not qualified, Superintendent.'

'On the cause, sir. Would you mind informing me of the subject of this research?'

'You have to understand, in my business the essence of success is to be ahead of one's competitors. We have an investigation going on of some importance to the public. Naturally, through our various media outlets we have many investigations running and this is only one of them. I'd like to help but I really don't see how your knowing the subject of our research will ease your concern regarding Lewin. I have to say he seemed perfectly balanced to me at our meeting on Thursday. Do I take it this interest of yours is personal and not professional?' Moravec's voice hardened. 'If not . . .'

'Personal – and confidential,' Foley confirmed, quickly. 'You have my word on it.'

'Very well, I'll make a point of contacting the relevant people to ensure any news of Lewin comes to me immediately. Let me have your number.'

Foley covered the receiver. 'He wants this number?'

Mayberry considered, then shrugged.

Foley read off the number then added: 'I'll be here – most of the day tomorrow?' Mayberry nodded confirmation. 'Goodbye, sir, and thank you for your time.'

Mayberry refilled Foley's glass. 'That was a bit of a cop-out – no pun intended. Threatened you with his legal heavy artillery, did he?'

'Unspoken ultimatum. If my business was professional and in the rough direction of whatever Nigel is up to: war.'

'On your feet, may as well bring your drink too.'

'Where are we going?'

Mayberry pointed downward. 'Medicine seems to be a common factor in all this and it may have slipped your notice but you've just been given the name of a doctor.'

'Haversham's answering service? Hart- something.'

'Hartrampf. Interesting name. While we're digging you can tell me *everything*.'

'I can't do that! This is part of an official police investigation.'

Mayberry halted and turned. 'Don't be bloody silly. They took it away from you, remember? Why? Because you're not one of the élite who are in the know. You're not trusted. You're PC Plod who stuck his size fourteen boots where they shouldn't have been and I'll bet you your virginity that if they knew about the games you're playing here with me, they'd cut you off at the knees. Maybe even at the neck.'

Foley reddened. 'So who're *they*?'

'Who they always are – and always have been. The people who really run the country, not the jokers who get voted in or out every time the plebs decide they'd like a change. Whitehall, Peter Foley. Whitehall and its tentacles, which cover the length and breadth of this sceptred isle.'

'Interesting,' murmured Mayberry, studying the VDU screen.

Foley sipped his third coffee. Seems like only yesterday I could sit on stake-out from midnight through till six without drooping an eyelid. What happened? 'What's interesting?' he asked, wearily.

'Hartrampf was a German national. Got himself a Brit passport just a few months after he came over here – that wasn't easy in those days.'

'Which days?'

'Immediately after the war. Your average Kraut was laying traps for rats in the ruins of the Third Reich then.'

'He was a doctor. We needed those badly so the rules got bent? If he was offered rationing in England against rat-meat at home there was no contest. Where're you getting all this or aren't I supposed to ask?'

'You've told me all you know so I'll return the confidence. Just don't use it against me when you go back to being a law-abiding, boring old copper again.'

'Less of the old.'

149

'Hartrampf's obviously listed with his professional body. I'm just peeking into their data-bank.'

'Easy as that?'

'Wars are going to be fought this way, you know, in the future.'

'Everyone attacking each other's computers?'

'Put simply, yes.'

'Better than killing each other, I suppose.'

'Oh, we'll get around to that – always do.' Mayberry paused, stuck his hand under his chin and made a face at the screen. 'Curiouser and curiouser.'

'Hartrampf?'

'You did say this murder victim's name was Hale?'

'Eleanor May. Son Daniel. Abducted and believed murdered by the IRA.'

'I've just found daddy.'

'Where?'

'Side by side with old Erich Hartrampf – well, young Erich in those days. Mid-twenties and something of a boy genius. Erich I mean, not Hale senior. One of the future men of the time: great theorists, brave new world, all that. Apparently at the age of twenty he wrote a thesis – this is well before Crick and Watson – on the possible existence of so-called regulator genes which give instructions to ordinary genes. Genes with very ancient roots conserved from the time when there was a common ancestor to man, insects, and mammals. A kind of genetic hierarchy. The ruling class get in everywhere.'

Mayberry frowned, his face lit by the glow from the screen. 'He wasn't a Jew. He seems to have been apolitical – *slightly* difficult in Nazi Germany, I'd say. Did nothing violent in the war. Well, who did? Spent all of it in Germany, apparently. Awesome talent in medical science. Altogether a jolly good case for British citizenship, I'd say. Bonaparte was wrong – we're a nation of pragmatists, not shopkeepers.'

'Brigadier Hale?' Foley insisted.

'Erich's mentor – and seemingly Erich's boss for many years.'

'That would follow, he was also a doctor – military kind.'

'Oh, *quite.*'

'What's that supposed to convey?'

'Well, I figured I'd get bored with the Brit end of the medical profession so I'd already popped into our Atlantic cousins' basket of goodies, keeping it handy just in case – and how right I was, as ever. Here we go! Wait, let it all roll. OK, we're closing in: Hartrampf and Hale were both involved in the medical monitoring of troops and observers during the period of extensive nuclear testing in the nineteen fifties. Not straight doctoring, you understand, Peter Foley. Research. Ask me where they conducted this research. And it wasn't on Bikini Atoll or any of the other blighted islands either.'

'America?'

'No, sir! Their results went to America, which is confirmed here most succinctly, but that is not where they put their heads – and whatever else – together and no doubt came up with a whole bunch of nasties which the great unwashed, once again, was never informed of. Think of somewhere out of the way, somewhere forbidding to keep out prying eyes. Somewhere the government – via the army – owns whole tracts of?'

Foley put down his cup. 'Dartmoor.'

'Wunnerful.'

'What's that prove?'

'You're the detective?'

'Pretend you are.'

'It proves nothing but it does provide a link which might help you in your search for young Nigel.'

'You're saying that this place on Dartmoor – assuming it still exists – is what this is all about? Some sort of secret testing place? Treating victims of unreported, unpublicized nuclear accidents? That kind of thing?'

'The concept would be somewhere in Jane Haversham's ball-park, wouldn't it? On the basis of her past record? A classic cover-up. An entire organization to keep the public from hearing the bad news and leave safety records squeaky clean!'

'*Army* Department of Advanced Medicine. Why Army?'

'They started it. Nuclear weapon tests came under military jurisdiction. They've kept control, or it's convenient the way it is because of the security aspect. Who knows?'

'You said Hartrampf was into genetics? Where's the connection with radiation victims?'

Mayberry sighed. 'What effect does radiation have on genes?'

'Fries them?'

'And mutates them.'

'That's Hartrampf's interest? Frankenstein monsters? If he wasn't a German – and from that period in their history – would you come to the same conclusion?'

'Mutations aren't necessarily monsters. Species develop through gradual mutation. Even ours.'

'But you suspect that there are those who are not waiting generations for something to develop?'

'Perhaps.'

'And perhaps Eleanor Hale wasn't murdered by her son – or the IRA.'

'It was your theory.'

'It fitted the circumstances.'

'You made it fit the circumstances.'

'Go on then. Who killed Eleanor Hale? An escaped mutant?'

'You did say there were some bizarre aspects to the crime. The gel smeared around the place, for example.'

'Some skin treatment. Maybe for burns.'

'Radiation burns?'

'Now who's making things fit? Listen, mutants don't steal cars – they probably can't even drive.'

'All I've said is there was – could still be – some type of secret government medical facility on Dartmoor involving radiation victims and research. Dartmoor is where Eleanor Hale lived and where she died in suspicious circumstances. Daniel Hale, who must have lived there at some time, has been seen with Jane Haversham who would bend over backwards – possibly even forwards – for any story involving a government cover-up. She employs Nigel who happens to live close to the area and knows it well. Seems to me there's more than a wild chance that the place you'll find Nigel is on Dartmoor!'

'The car. The E-type Jag,' Foley insisted, stubbornly. 'Whoever nicked the car killed Eleanor Hale. Whoever nicked the car is in some way connected to MI5 – or is of interest to them. All right, secret medical research. That brings Five in. So I'm back where I was when I arrived here yesterday. MI5 are in charge, I'm temporarily redundant – and if any of this comes out, permanently redundant!'

'You arrived here determined to fight MI5. VIPER, remember? And what about Nigel?'

'All right! So go ahead! Get into Five's operational files! You want to risk fifteen to thirty years inside, I'll go along.'

'Just as long as we don't have to share a cell,' Mayberry grimaced. 'You're way too prickly.'

'Give me something to do to keep me awake.'

'Can you handle a keyboard?'

'We don't ring bells on our cars these days, you know.'

'Use that station there. Swear on your pension you didn't see me do this.'

'Do what?'

'Put you into New Scotland Yard's up-to-the-minute incident report.'

'Christ!'

'Look at the alert status! Terrorist attack in London? It says an armed incident.'

Foley's eyes were fixed to the rapid flow of words on the screen. 'That's the car! The Jag. See? E-type Jaguar, gunmetal grey, DSH 42. That's bloody Daniel Hale's car.'

'Bloody might be right. Look at the number of casualties.'

'Fatalities,' corrected Foley.

Mayberry moved rapidly to where he'd left his notes. 'That's Hartrampf's current address,' he said.

'What?' Foley asked still reading.

'In front of you on the screen. Where the incident took place. That's Hartrampf's London address.'

'Are you certain?'

'I've written it down from his Medical Association listing. I'm certain. Looks like your murderer just went serial.'

The information stopped: a reference came on screen, diverting enquiries to a numbered section.

'The Met just got bitten,' Foley said, unsurprised, satisfaction on his face. 'VIPER.'

NINE

He sat, completely alone, in the cell. Knowing, with dreadful finality, that when he walked from it he would never return. Unless whatever there was on the other side, if anything, gave him a nostalgic tour for the hell of it.

Hell? Nice thought right now! He smiled but felt only a hard grimace break his face. You're scared shitless so you make jokes. Come on, you bastards, get on with it!

Not even the Führer can help you now, Otto, he told himself. He knew his own name and strangely that gave him comfort. Momentarily he thought he was dreaming. Relief flooded through him, freezing the instant he heard the double crash of the horror at the end of the corridor outside his cell.

The stench from the mess in his lavatory bowl sickened him as it would those who came for him. It was an indictment of his fear; it revealed, too well, his inner turmoil, giving the lie to his outward calm, his show of courage for an audience of three. Three, until they entered the chamber itself when, dear God, they would become four and he would become nothing.

Nothing.

They send a priest to tend my soul in its hour of extremity yet my body they have threatened to feed to pigs.

You'll aid our war effort, one had sneered. Adolf won't like that, will he?

Adolf won't know. Adolf is as cut off from the real world as I soon will be. Permanently.

The sound of the heavy iron cell door opening was his signal to stand upright: rigid, prepared, ready for the worst. But his legs, like the stench from the putrid bowl, betrayed him and he stumbled forward, his knuckles barking on the cold, gritty stone floor.

155

'On your feet, Otto. No good begging for mercy now,' the cruel one jibed.

'Shut up,' snapped the other, who, he had learned over the weeks, had compassion in his soul despite the bombs that rained down every night, some of which he, Otto Horst Fascher, failed spy of the glorious Third Reich, had personally directed on to their targets.

He heard the priest mumbling.

Is that what you do, Father, when the work you must carry out in God's holy name leaves you barren, with nothing left but words to read, like an automaton, from a book given to you by Him for guidance? Thou shalt not kill. Say the commandment as you stand by me, Father – but not too close – on the trap-door to oblivion.

Is there nothing better you can offer me than a place in heaven? How about a seat outside on the pavement at that café I remember in Heidelberg? Sunshine? Girls? Just one girl to sit beside me? A few hours? Make it mid-morning, so that I'd have the afternoon with the girl, somewhere soft, somewhere cool, the shutters open and damn the prying world. But make it before the war. Say, when I was thirty? Young enough still to learn and old enough to know better. Hear me, Father? Price too high? The devil would buy my soul for that much without even a flick of his tail. Your God wants it all, of course. So did mine. That's why they're killing me today.

'Time,' said the one with compassion.

Has run out, he thought and walked through the doorway.

The brick walls of the corridor were gloss-painted, dark green and creamy yellow. He saw high, lush Austrian meadows and thick mountain milk. Everything his eyes locked on to evoked a memory and he wanted to roar with the pain of it but was so stunned he half-believed they had hit him.

This can't be happening.

He heard the crash of the final test at the end of the corridor.

It is.

He had planned, even rehearsed, his refusal of the hood

156

but now with only a door between him and the horror beyond, he longed for its gift of blindness.

The door opened, hushed, as if well oiled to silence any sound that might recall that other door set in the floor.

He closed his eyes and they led him forward like a blind man; his shoes, stripped of laces, loose and cumbersome on his feet. He wondered if they would fall off when he reached the end of the rope. He knew they would. They would be free of him. Free of the stench of his fear. Everything now seemed to have life – or at least the prospect of being among the living. Except himself. I'd trade places with you if I could, shoes. Better down at the bottom of the pit than hanging, crookedly, broken-necked above it.

The hood slipped over his head. Silken, almost chilled. He had expected coarseness and stifling heat. It feels that way because your blood burns in final protest. An ache coursed through him, so overwhelming he thought he must die from it: desire for all that was going; regret for all that had never been. He felt he was no longer there although the droning of the priest confirmed that he was.

'. . . in the sure and certain knowledge of everlasting life.'

Now, he thought. They'll do it now.

He felt the broad straps bind him, arms tight to his sides, legs hard together. He could smell the leather and other men's sweat. Also their fear. The hood was nothing now. I am one great sensing being, he thought: every atom of me radiates with life at the moment of my death.

The sting in his arm was exquisite pain and he sent blessings to the one with compassion for sparing him the final horror. He drifted away. Too quickly. He wanted life a moment longer.

He awoke in darkness. Alone. The bed was firm and so large he had to stretch to find its perimeters. He got up, naked, his body drenched in sweat and moved to the glow beyond the curtains.

The street lamp was almost level with the window. He stared at it, then down at the rows of cars parked along the sides of the square. He saw the dull gun-metal of the Jaguar directly below.

He almost screamed out loud. Dear God. Who am I?

He saw clearly, the tanker drive on to the square, felt the cold from it chill him, freeze him to the spot. It was not there. But it would be. He knew.

He dressed urgently, fear driving him. He knew her room was across the corridor. Stealth seemed a natural part of him and he moved with it in the dark, finding her door, slipping inside, sensing her on the bed just hearing her breath. He stopped it, one hand over her mouth.

'Adam,' he rasped. 'Not a sound. Dress. They're coming for me. *Now*.'

She prised his fingers off her face, rolled away, threw on clothes, her breathing short and fast from fear. The worst kind. Of the unknown: the unseen.

She moved to her case but he pulled her back.

'Just my bag,' she hissed. 'The car keys.'

'*Quickly*. Carry your shoes.'

They moved as swiftly as they dared, their bare feet noiseless on the polished wooden floors. Nothing hindered their passage. They stepped out into the square, the street-light holding them momentarily in its pool, then they raced for the Jaguar, the keys already in her hand. He heard her gasp a shocking profanity as the lock resisted before turning. Then they were inside, the engine growling low as she pressed the throttle as if it were soft and alive, the car rumbling threateningly, easing its way around the square, then out and away.

He reached over, under the steering wheel.

'Christ! What's that?'

'Heckler and Koch, nine millimetre automatic pistol.'

She turned, hearing, sensing, now seeing, a change in him. Harder. Confident. 'Daniel's,' she said, resignedly. 'No point in asking how you knew it was there. What happened back there?'

'The dream has gone. The crash on the mountain. Now there's another dream.'

'It wasn't a dream. It happened – and you survived.'

'I didn't survive the new dream. If it was a dream.'

'Tell me.'

'They executed me. Hanged me. Here, in London. I was

158

a spy. A German. My name was Otto. Not Adam. Otto Horst Fascher. The war was close to an end, I felt that. They still hanged me.'

She turned briefly, feeling drained. 'This time it is fantasy, Adam. Even if you were only eighteen at the end of the war you'd be in your sixties now. Take a look at yourself.' She pulled the Jaguar to a halt. 'Will you please tell me why we had to leave Doctor Hartrampf's?'

'I did.'

'They were coming for us?'

'For me. You don't matter.'

'Why bother to wake me then?' she snapped.

'They'd have killed you. I meant you don't matter to them because they don't need to keep you alive.'

'But they need to keep *you* alive? Suddenly you seem to know a lot more about them and their intentions than before.'

'Hartrampf called them.'

She looked out through the windscreen. She could see Buckingham Palace in the distance, realized they were on the Mall and couldn't remember driving there. 'Hartrampf called them,' she repeated dully. 'Called who? You overheard this? Was there a name? An English name this time which we could work on?'

His voice had ice in it. 'I don't need to hear.'

'I'm sorry.' She dropped her head to the wheel, aching for sleep.

He hauled himself out and came around to her side. 'I'll drive.'

'Drive where? Let's go back to my place. They won't come back.'

He pulled her out. 'They haven't left.'

She dropped into the passenger bucket-seat, stretched her long legs as far as they would go in the footwell and let her head loll against the window. 'Adam, you'd better find us somewhere safe to sleep or I'll be out of this noisy, cramped car and up the road banging on her majesty's door begging a bed for the night. All right?'

'I think it's better if I leave you now.'

'Try it.'

'Where is Wandsworth?'

'Here in London. What's in Wandsworth?'

'The prison. Perhaps the grave?'

She shook her head wearily, eyes closed. 'The spy's grave? Wasting your time. I don't think spies rate tombstones.'

'Nothing. No marker?'

She pushed herself up. 'Adam, listen to me: forget the dream. You are an officer in the Special Air Service who's suffered injury and a horrifying, traumatic experience. Perhaps the only safe place for you is with them. The SAS. Amongst those who know you. Jesus, you couldn't be much safer!'

'You don't understand.'

'You expect me to? Come on. Nothing like this has happened to me since – oh, forget it! See it my way – there's no way I'll see it yours!'

He sat silently, his face set, eyes blue-ice in the dashboard glow. 'I have to go back,' he said finally.

'Back where.'

'*There.*'

'No. You don't have to go anywhere. We know who you are. That's enough. Now we concentrate on the gift you've been given. We use it, we give you back your past and slowly you'll accept it. With your powers the whole world is yours – you don't need to go in search of anything. Christ! I thought we were running away from these people?'

'We know who I am? Do we? What if we only know part of who I am? What if, inside me, in some way we can't begin to understand – but they can – there are others?'

'Don't!'

'Otto did not die by the rope – he died by a needle. An injection. Here. I felt it. In my arm. Or perhaps Otto never died. Perhaps they killed his body but saved his soul. Can they do that now?'

'I don't want to hear this.'

'Can they take souls and keep them inside a live body, like insects in a bottle? Can they do that now? *Tell me!*'

She screamed at him: '*No!* No, they bloody can't! I don't

know, for chrissake, what anyone can or can't do any more. You're the fucking future, you tell me.'

'I think they can do something terrible. I think I *am* something terrible. That's why they want me back so badly. That's why they killed Eleanor Hale and they're prepared to kill you.'

She felt the cold rise through her and tears spill and wanted desperately to be alone, away from him, all knowledge of him forgotten – her life back to where it was just days before.

He put his hand on hers and she moved away, afraid as much of him now as of the unknown figures who hunted him. Within and without. She wanted to leap from the car and run. But knew it was too late. It had been too late right from the beginning. She heard herself gasp in realization of the truth of his words: the unexplainable, unimaginable truth. There, right next to her. Not in flesh, but there, still. No SAS officer, no German spy, yet both of these. But also, she felt, she almost heard in the voice, could almost see behind the eyes – as surely as Eleanor Hale had done – the presence of Daniel Hale.

'Jane?'

'I'll be all right. Just don't touch me.'

She sensed his withdrawal but could do nothing to stop it. Daniel, she thought, remembering the biting humour, the boyish charm, the hint of wildness beneath, and above all, the aura of danger which came off him, like static, even when they had made love. Especially when they had made love.

Eleanor Hale had known. Which was why she had sent Adam to her. She had known where he had come from and possibly how he came to be what he was. The words of her letter, which had appeared in part to be the ramblings of a mildly eccentric old lady, began now to have real meaning: 'The price we pay for our children's future may be their lives. Daniel is dead. I accept that now. They have killed him. Yet, even in death there is life.'

They?

Not the IRA.

161

'The price we pay for our children's future may be their lives.'

Jane felt the tingle run through her; adrenalin banishing fear, forcing the unknown into the light. The letter! Eleanor Hale's letter to Hartrampf was the key. If Hartrampf had betrayed them, as Adam insisted, then he was involved in the conspiracy. Possibly from the start.

A flash of memory came to her: Daniel Hale beside her, naked on the hotel bed, she exploring the wound scars on his hard body. His words: 'If my father's theories had come to anything the next generation of bloody squaddies would have had self-healing wounds and he'd have put himself out of business.'

Hartrampf had come out of Nazi Germany and Daniel's surgeon father had ensured he continued practising medicine.

When had Hartrampf come out of Nazi Germany? Before their nightmare world of medical experiments began, as he had suggested? Or after time had run out for Hitler and his hellish works? Had Hartrampf done what so many other Nazis had done: offered their conquerors something they could not refuse, in exchange for freedom? Or perhaps, in Hartrampf's case, freedom and facilities to carry on his work?

She lit a cigarette and drew deeply. 'Eleanor's letter to Hartrampf,' she said, after a moment. 'The answers we need are in there. Some of them. The rest are out there on the moors.'

'And in me,' said Adam.

'Yes.'

'I'm different, aren't I?' he said.

She laughed sharply. 'That's what we term understatement.'

'I mean completely different. From you. From all of you.'

Yes, she thought, and God help you because we human beings have a shocking record when it comes to *that*.

She pushed the thought aside. 'We have to get hold of that letter.' She pictured Hartrampf's darkened house with its tall rooms and oversized furniture, remembering her little-girl feelings as she sat watching him read the letter,

162

probably planning, even then what he would do. She shuddered.

'We must go back,' she said.

'They may be there.'

'Good!' she snapped. 'This time the police will have to believe me. Did you see when they'd arrive? Back there in the house?'

'I saw the truck in the square. Night time. I was barely awake. Fear drove me.'

'I don't see we have any choice – not if we want the truth and an end to this blind running. How long do you think we can keep this up?'

Adam started the engine.

Neither noticed the innocuous-looking saloon pass the opposite way after their U-turn on the Mall or saw it repeat their action with a surprisingly deep exhaust growl and little suspension roll.

In the car, one of its two occupants spoke into a short-wave radio. 'Looks like they've changed their minds.'

'We have a situation here,' came the reply. 'Two vehicles. One refrigeration truck, one Range Rover. Halted at Hartrampf's house. We count nine white males. Victoria says hold, observe – and follow if necessary. Our charges are your responsibility. Immobilize if necessary and hold.'

'Understood. We have Jaguar heading back your direction. Repeat. Your direction.'

'Hear you. We now have Hartrampf speaking with one white male, five feet four or five, spectacles, dark to balding. From activity, they know our charges have gone. Hartrampf is entering Range Rover. Driving off now with truck. We'll maintain surveillance distance.'

'Understood. Good luck. Out. Victoria, do you copy? Our charges our heading back to Eaton Square.'

'Maintain surveillance, unit one.'

'Affirmative. Out.'

'What the fuck's going on?' demanded the driver.

'Doesn't matter, does it? We just stick with them.'

'What's the score, then? Refrigeration truck?'

'The old boy's a quack, isn't he? Maybe they're body-snatchers. Your modern Burke and Hare?'

'Berk and who?'

'Bloody ex-paras, all the same, brain-damaged from oxygen starvation.'

'There's a car following us,' said Adam.

Jane shifted to look through the mirror on her side. 'Do you want to try and lose them?'

'We're almost at Hartrampf's – there's the square.'

'That's *them!*'

The front of the approaching Range Rover seemed to explode as its battery of auxiliary lighting was switched on. Close behind it, the white truck swung out blocking the road, figures in protective clothing emerging from it.

'Reverse!' Jane yelled as Adam sat still and rigid. 'Adam!'

When the bastards come for you it'll be to kill you – whether then or later, said a voice in Adam's mind, the Belfast accent harsh. My advice is take a few with you, Danny boy.

He got out of the car, the Heckler nine millimetre in both hands, blasting rapid fire into the advancing figures then shifting instantly to the blinding lights.

When they've got a vehicle, forget the driver, he's got his hands full and his mind's on the driving. Knock out the one beside him first because he's already got you lined up for the kill.

The Heckler flared again. The Range Rover's windscreen crazed and a heavy, bloodied figure rebounded from the front passenger seat through the shattered glass on to the bonnet, blood from the hole in his forehead soaking the surgical dressing covering stitches over his left eye which had been opened to the bone by the solid silver knob of an ancient walking-stick only days before.

There may be more boyos in the back but they've got to shoot around their comrades and through an opaque windscreen so you can bet the bloody Pope's riches against the pockets of a Belfast wino that the one nearest you will open his door and start blasting from behind it because a car door is full of all sorts of lovely things like glass and padding and mechanisms which deflect rounds, so go for the head-shot to be sure. Speed is important, Danny boy, because you want to keep them in disarray but remember: be deliberate, because nothing scares the boyos more than a man who knows what he's doing, especially when what he's doing is killing. They're good but they're not as good as us. No one is.

Adam began to move forward.

For a brief moment, an unnatural silence hung over the scene. Even the deep throb of the truck's engine and the hiss of steam from the Range Rover's punctured radiator seemed muted. From nearby houses came shouts and a long scream which might have been that of a child. Lights came on nervously then were extinguished. One of the men in protective clothing crawled aside from the approaching figure, coughed and died.

If ever they get you alive, Danny boy, say goodbye to all you love because they're animals when it comes down to it. Get my meaning, laddie? Don't give them the pleasure of your pain and humiliation. Deny them, son. Deny them, and you've won. Even dead, you've beaten the scum.

A small man opened the rear door of the Range Rover, his spectacles caught by the street-lighting, his face white and beaded with sweat, but determined. 'We're taking you back,' he said.

Adam heard: Throw her down the stairs.

Daniel, came the cry; anguished, lonelier than death.

I'm coming, mother. Home. Through the night, through the cold. I'm lost, I'm blind. I'm no one. Help me.

Adam shot Paige in the face, twice.

Hartrampf scrambled across the rear seat but Adam reached out and held him, the burning-hot barrel of the Heckler pressed against his temple, singeing the blood-spattered grey hair.

'Don't,' Hartrampf pleaded.

'Who am I?'

'I'm out of it now. I swear to God. Please *don't*.'

'My mother's letter?'

'Oh dear God! *I didn't know*. It's their choice who they use.' Hartrampf fumbled at his jacket. 'Here, read it. She wanted me to help you.'

'You were taking me back.'

'You don't understand.'

'Who am I?'

'It's not that easy.'

'What am I?'

Through his terror, pride filled Hartrampf's eyes. 'You're the future.'

Adam shook his head. 'I'm the end.'

Hartrampf's brain exploded over the rear window.

Adam walked back to the E-type, the sound of police sirens strident in the night. People in night clothes stood cowering in their porches not daring to approach closer.

Jane was gone.

He kept walking.

The insistent bleating of his bedside telephone dragged Rudolf Moravec from a troubled sleep plagued by images from his horrific childhood.

'Moravec,' he grunted, trying to clear his mind.

'Serious problem,' said the chief executive of the security agency Moravec employed.

'Yes?'

'Not on the phone. Two of my people are on their way to you now – should be there in minutes.'

'My investment is secure?'

'Alive. Wait for my people. I suspect your editors will be trying to get through to you so I'll get off the line.'

A discreet knock came from the door.

'I think your people are here,' said Moravec. 'We had better meet.'

'Afterwards.' The line went dead.

Moravec called: 'I'll be out in a moment, have them wait in the study.' Hastily, he slipped a silk dressing gown over his pyjamas, washed sleep and bad dreams away in icy water – and went immediately to the penthouse study.

Jane Haversham sat ashen-faced on a deep-green chesterfield. The two men from the security agency, looking shaken, stood heads together speaking quietly but heatedly.

'Wake Doctor Shirer,' Moravec snapped at the hovering housekeeper.

'Already done, sir. He's dressing.'

'Get him, now.'

'Of course, sir.'

'I want all of it,' growled Moravec. 'Nothing left out, understood?'

Jane looked at him, her eyes red from weeping. 'Don't blame them, they weren't involved.'

'They're paid to be involved.'

'We were just surveillance, sir.'

'From the beginning,' snapped Moravec, impatiently.

One of the row of phones on his massive mahogany desk trilled. He snatched it up.

'We've got a "funny",' said the editor of Moravec's highly profitable tabloid newspaper. 'Major shooting incident. Here in London. Bodies everywhere. Eye-witness reports of victims wearing protective clothing – no accurate description of type or purpose. Police arrived, armed, because of the gunfire reports, took over the scene, cleared it, gave no explanation and left.'

Moravec cast a heavy glance at his visitors. 'D-notice received?'

'I'm expecting the call.'

'Keep me informed.'

Moravec put down the receiver. 'Where's Adam?' he demanded. 'He had better not be one of the bodies I've just been told about.'

'He's the one who did for them,' said one of the men.

'Who're you?'

'Peters, sir. This is Shaw.'

Shaw said: 'We were operating under your instructions. Us and another mobile unit were based on Eaton Square and controlled from Victoria – two units in case our charges were split or the target left to make a late-night contact. The lady here left the Eaton Square house at one fifty-three: we logged the time. The man was with her. We weren't given their names – only the doctor's.'

Jane interrupted. 'Adam *saw* the truck entering the square. *Their* truck. Do you understand?'

Moravec nodded.

'He woke me and we left immediately. We got as far as

the Mall. I don't remember how I drove there. I was still groggy from being woken in the middle of the night. The second night in succession. I'm shattered.' She stopped, tears spilling from her eyes. She brushed them angrily away. 'Damn it! I've never seen people shot to death just yards from me. He killed them all, every one. Some of them weren't armed.'

'Shot all nine, sir. Our other unit confirms,' offered Shaw.

'Ten with the doctor,' corrected Peters.

Moravec stared at him.

'Hartrampf,' said Jane. 'Adam shot him.'

'Shot dead, sir. Last one to go. Spent a minute talking to him first. The old boy gave him something from his jacket. Could have been papers? Documents?'

'Eleanor Hale's letter,' said Jane. 'That's why Adam and I went back to Hartrampf's. God, how I wish we'd kept on going. I made him go back.'

'What's the importance of the letter?' questioned Moravec.

'It's crucial. I'm certain the truth is in there.'

James Shirer entered. 'What the hell's going on?'

Moravec said: 'You know Jane Haversham. She's just had a severe shock. Take her into one of the guest rooms and look her over.'

'I'm fine,' she protested.

'I'll decide that,' said Shirer, drawing her away.

'We should have been warned he was armed,' Shaw protested.

'There'll be a bonus,' said Moravec. 'I didn't know he had a weapon. He might have got it from Hartrampf's house.'

'We're material witnesses to murder.'

'Everything will be dealt with. I assume your other unit is holding him?'

'The only thing they're holding is their sphincter muscles. Don't worry, they're with him, close, but not too close – on foot, like he is. They've both got portable telephones so communication's no problem. Victoria will know their location – I'll call them.'

Shirer returned with Jane. 'Nothing a good night's sleep won't cure,' he said.

'He's going to Wandsworth,' said Jane, glancing pointedly at Shaw and Peters.

Moravec pressed a button on his desk summoning the housekeeper. 'See these men get something to drink,' he ordered. To Shaw he said: 'Tell Victoria I want to be kept informed of every movement he makes. Tell them also I can't have him running free as he is, there are other interested parties and now the police as well. Find a means to pull him in without more people getting killed.'

'Risky.'

'Your company exists on risks.'

'Calculated risks, sir,' corrected Shaw.

'Wandsworth?' questioned Moravec as the two men left.

'You'll find this hard to believe,' warned Jane, dropping on to the Chesterfield.

'I sell newspapers. Nothing is too hard to believe.'

'Do you want me in on this?' asked Shirer.

'I think we need a medical mind to make sense of it,' advised Jane.

Moravec nodded and lowered his big body into the executive chair behind his desk as she told her story.

'Schizophrenia?' she questioned Shirer. 'Purely mental? I mean, imaginary – not a physical state?'

Shirer inclined his red head. 'More or less. Although in extreme cases a schizophrenic will dress the part of the new personality even to the extent of a change of physical appearance: wigs, clothes, make-up, that type of thing.'

'I mean physical, doctor. Actually being.'

'I'm not with you?'

'Adam is more than one person.'

'Believes he is.'

'*Is*.'

'Ridiculous.'

'What is memory?'

'It's too late – or too early – for a debate on metapsychology.'

'Answer her,' growled Moravec.

'In everyday terms? We all know what memory is – we've all got it, though sometimes we wish we hadn't.'

'Very well,' said Jane. 'Where is memory?'

'Where it's always been – in your overworked brain. Electronic impulses flashing away, reminding you of the worst bits of your past.'

'Only electronic impulses? Nothing – sorry to labour this point – physical? Cells? Molecules? Tissue?'

'Sure, there's cells and tissue, we're all made of the stuff.'

'Could you isolate memory – the cells in that part of the brain which stores memories . . . if that's how it works?'

'You've been looking at those studies done in Michigan, right? Flat-worms, rats: scotophobin?'

'No. But if it's relevant I want to hear it.'

'Psychologist in the States came up with the theory that memory molecules float around all over the body's nervous system but you can't get a response from them until they end up in the brain. Experiments were conducted on flat-worms, the simplest creature considered to have a brain. Very mild electronic impulses were passed through a bath of water containing the worms which, as any of us would, reacted to the shock. The next stage was to turn a light on the bath two seconds before the shock was due. Quite soon the worms reacted, in classic Pavlovian fashion, to the light as if it were the shock itself.

'The interesting, if bizarre, part of all this was that the worms were then cut in two – flat-worms grow a new head or tail if this is done – and the newly generated tail-based worms remembered the light before the shock sequence. So it seems, in flat-worms anyway, that memories are not stored solely in the brain. Further, flat-worms being some-what cannibalistic, it was decided to chop up the conditioned worms and feed them to hungry new worms. Bingo! When the light went on in the bath the new worms reacted exactly as if they had been conditioned.

'The same transferability of memory experiments were tried on rats, mice, hamsters, chicks – even goldfish – with positive results from a number of the laboratories involved. Inevitably an experiment was conducted to cross the spec-ies barrier: the brains of rats or mice trained to shun dark-

170

ness – which they normally prefer – were made into a mush and injected into hamsters. The injected hamsters soon began shunning darkness. One neurochemist has reported that with coded molecules he has isolated the specific substance that caused a conditioned rat to shun darkness. The material turned out to be a peptide with a complex amino-acid sequence – peptides being molecules formed by two or more amino-acids. It has since been synthesized although efforts to replicate the synthesis have been inconclusive.'

Moravec lit a cigar. 'Are you saying that memory can be synthesized and transferred from one being to another? Human beings as well?'

'Possibly. Given time and pots of money. Conditioned thought is what you're really asking about. Something most aspiring dictators would give their jackboots for, eh?'

Moravec glared hard at Shirer through a cloud of blue smoke.

'What did I say?'

'Doctor,' said Jane. 'The question I need answered is: could it be possible for the memories of one man – his essential identity, his feelings, his skills – to be transferred into another human being, another brain in another body?'

Shirer grinned, 'You're not pinning me down on this one. I'll tell you one thing: some of the things the medical profession considered pure science fiction a decade ago are now everyday practice. Earlier this evening I told Moravec that given enough financial backing the impossible can become probable.'

Jane turned to look at Moravec. 'Adam is a so far unidentified captain of the Special Air Services Regiment; he is a Nazi spy hanged in Wandsworth prison at the end of the last war; he is also, and I know because I've seen it, felt it, heard it, and almost smelt it on him, Daniel Hale – whose mother sent him to me in the first place because she sensed the presence of her son just as I subsequently did and who, unless I've lost my nose for intrigue, was somehow involved in all of this some time in her past. That wasn't Adam who mercilessly killed those men tonight: it was Daniel Hale. I remember Daniel describing to me how he had been trained to deal quickly and ruthlessly with a vehicle-mounted ambush for his undercover duties in Northern Ireland.'

Shirer turned to Moravec and smirked. 'This something you've cooked up for one of your rags?'

Moravec's expression was menacing. 'How many deutsch-marks, how many lives did the Nazis invest in medical experimentation on human beings? An unlimited number, is the answer. How much would medical science give for the results of those experiments?'

Shirer thrust out his chin. 'You know damn well no one touched the stuff – it was out of bounds, completely unethical. Besides, the argument is academic: the records were destroyed.'

'If the records were not destroyed? If ethics didn't exist?'

'They bloody do!'

'If an environment, a place, an establishment, utterly secret, was created where they did not?'

'Couldn't happen.'

'*If?*' Moravec demanded, his fist a hammer on his desk.

'If such a place existed, I'd expect to see Lucifer rising from it because it would be the nearest this sick bloody world will ever get to building hell.'

Moravec growled: 'Expect it.' He turned to Jane. 'Use our facilities. I want the name of this SAS captain and of the Nazi. I want to know if they're alive, dead – or missing and if they're officially recorded as being dead I want to know where their remains are to be found.'

'The German's name is Fascher . . . Otto Horst Fascher. Adam felt he was him in the moments before his execution at Wandsworth. Trying to get hold of the identity of a living – even missing – officer in the SAS is impossible. I know, I tried doing that for a programme on Northern Ireland.'

Moravec scowled. 'Hartrampf was definitely involved in this?'

She nodded. 'Adam was certain of it. That's why we ran.'

'So Hartrampf's assertion of Adam's identity as an SAS captain could be a fabrication for some purpose of his own?'

172

'No. I was there when he took Adam through the entire incident.'

'Suggestion? You admit Hartrampf had him under hypnosis.'

'Not unless he has perfected a telepathic link. I witnessed every word, every gesture.'

'Would you discount the possibility of a telepathic link – knowing Adam's abilities?'

Her face showed her tiredness and strain. 'I can't discount that.'

Shirer cut in. 'One moment. If you are accepting all this as having credibility then you have to consider the fact that the identity Hartrampf brought out under hypnosis need not be this man's true identity at all. He could be any of the three people you've mentioned – or none of them. Correct?'

Jane shook her head. 'I knew Daniel Hale. Adam is not him. Not physically.'

'The Nazi would be too old,' added Moravec, impatiently. 'If he isn't the SAS captain we're no further forward. He could be anyone.'

'Or no one,' said Shirer, half to himself.

'Explain that,' Moravec demanded.

Shirer's eyes shifted between them. 'Assume I believe all of this. If the mysterious "they" have managed to do the things you are suggesting, it is more than possible that they have taken their playing God to the ultimate conclusion. Test-tube babies are an accepted thing these days. A planned – I mean genetically planned – human being created from human sperm and ovum in an artificial womb is perfectly possible. In fact they're virtually doing that already in the States: selective breeding, a choice of sperm donors to achieve the desired result. Private medicine of course, very expensive. That's more genetic manipulation than engineering.'

'So what's to stop the process going one stage further?' questioned Moravec.

'Because genetic engineering, as I've already said, is bloody dangerous. One slip and you could let loose something that could cause the beginning of the end for human life as we know it. Ever wondered why there are so many viruses around today with the ability to change – to protect themselves? Why bacteria we thought we had under control are suddenly causing hysteria in the world food markets? Look a few years back when a few misguided – and I'm being kind – scientists were working blind in the genetic field and you might find your answer.'

Jane stared at Shirer. 'Are you implying that Adam might be a . . . *creation*?'

'Wasn't the original? Although admittedly divine if one is a believer.'

'Why then give him memories from others?'

'That's part of what you have to find out, isn't it?'

'Guess,' she said.

'I never guess.'

'Reason, then.'

'Reason only works when you know all the facts. All we have here is near-fantasy.'

'Then fantasize. If you had created – engineered – a human being, why would you give it memories from other humans?'

Shirer breathed out. 'In the world of fantasy I'd say you have a couple of possibilities. One: your Adam is part of an experimental programme, an advanced laboratory rat. Perhaps a failure in their programme who managed to escape? Or, and way out in left field even for fantasy: they were attempting memory-cell transference for the purposes of utilizing skills that would otherwise be lost on the death of the "donor" mind? Or rescuing secrets from a brain in coma? God knows. I don't even want to fantasize about it – it's Frankensteinish enough to be both horrific and plausible and I want to sleep at night.'

Jane persisted: 'Why a nineteen forties German spy? Any skills, any secrets he had would be redundant now, surely. And why two young army officers? They can't be that difficult to train, even accepting they were both specialists in their field.'

'Because they were available?' offered Shirer. 'The Nazi due to be executed so who'd miss him? Two army officers conveniently "missing in action" so no explanations as to cause of death necessary!' He smiled wryly. 'Even in the world of fantasy one must have available bodies for experimentation.'

'The disappearance of which should not prompt awkward questions,' interrupted Moravec. 'That's what young Lewin had in his ambitious mind.'

'Who's Lewin?'

Jane answered: 'A young field-researcher I use on occasion. Very determined. Liable to take risks sometimes but good. He's on Dartmoor now – where Adam first appeared.'

Shirer walked over to a drinks table and poured himself a healthy measure of Scotch. 'If these people – this establishment – do exist, your young man would be advised not to take risks in their vicinity. History has proved there are few more ruthless professions than medicine – or certain members of it – when it comes to advancement of its techniques or theories. Don't forget, not all that long ago in historical terms grave robbing was an accepted method of gaining bodies for hands-on anatomical experience. Times may have changed, advanced if you like, but remember this: Burke and Hare gave up grave robbing because it was more cost efficient to murder.' Shirer gave his wry grin once more. 'That could be termed business expansion in our free-market economy.'

'That's not funny,' glared Jane.

'It was not meant to be, Miss Haversham. It was a comment, laced with suitable irony I thought, on the values of our times. You and Moravec are out to make money from this story, hence you've sent – and I quote you – a determined young field-researcher liable to take risks out to where you think the sharp end of this business might be. I'm here because I too want to add to my already excellent life-style and Moravec here has proven time and time again that he can do that for me. There's one thing that worries me though. You see, not everyone in this world is out for big bucks. They may be a forgotten breed but they still exist out there. Idealists – to whom money means less than nothing: the ideal is all. The twenties and thirties saw the rise of modern idealism, the sixties saw its peak and subsequent decline. Since then we've all been busily making lots of lovely money and to hell with anything else.

'Meanwhile, if Moravec is right, a ruthless group of idealists have our long-term future – as they perceive it, naturally – all planned out on the drawing board. Or more correctly, the genetic map. And we either won't have any choice in the matter because when they implement their genetic changes we won't know they're occurring, or, we'll gladly aid and abet their scheme of things because every mother wishes for a whole, normal child, born without mental or physical defects. Given the choice between this and abnormality, however slight, there's no contest.

'Perfection is a human ideal, all of us when it comes to our children desire it. Well, we've almost reached the stage where we can demand it: order it ready packaged. The question is, who does the packaging? Medical experts of course. Trained for the job. Would a prospective mother ask the man or woman who could produce for her a physically and mentally perfect child what that person's views were on the future direction of humanity? I doubt if such a question would even enter her mind. She would think only of her child. An idealist in a position of such awesome responsibility might, however, think of the creation of a new generation. "New" being the optimum and contentious word. I may be an old sinner but even I would hate to see the time come when God's – or if you prefer, Nature's – hand was taken from the conception of our children to be replaced by man's, misguided by worldly forces.'

'That's what we're trying to stop, Doctor Shirer,' Jane said coldly. She glanced at Moravec. 'At least I am. I'm not in this for financial reward.'

'Lewin is,' Moravec growled. 'He's driven by the promise of it – I deal with men like him every day.'

'You buy and sell us,' Shirer smiled, grimly.

TEN

The deep bass hum was a live thing, the air-duct a steel tentacle of the main body, vibrating at a constant pitch, jangling Nigel Lewin's already taut nerves.

'Come on, let's be having you then,' he growled in heavy mock Devon to release some of his tension.

He tried to calculate the extent of his uncomfortable, crouched progress but gave up.

Too bloody far. Screw you, George.

The beam of his torch was kept lowered and smothered by a handkerchief so all he saw was the ducting at his feet, feeling, as he progressed, the slight tug on his clothes as air was sucked into whatever lay ahead. For a moment he imagined a great razor-bladed fan waiting to slice into him but he knew that image came from the pills and fear so forced it down.

The grid of light in the blackness beyond the beam of his torch halted him. He crawled forward cautiously, looked down through the inspection panel and saw the machinery which created the hum. Computerized, state-of-the-art. And bloody expensive, he confirmed, recalling his earlier appraisal of the sound. God bless the taxpayer. He examined the grille. The release mechanism inside the duct was uncovered so exiting the shaft would be easy, but the thought of exposing his presence did not appeal. Retribution for his penetration of what might be an ultra-secret government project could be swift and painful or very long term.

Sweat trickled from his scalp, stinging his eyes.

Do something.

What?

Stay in the shaft, relatively safe, and see where it leads? Maybe find another grille to peer through? Or get

177

out and be the bloody hero everyone and his dog wants you to be?

Suddenly his bright fantasy of well-filled pockets and limitless topless beauties on white sands dulled.

Sod Moravec, sod George. I'm ducking out, going back to old Peter Foley, public sentinel and general good egg. Life in the fast lane is too bloody hairy.

But Moravec's promise of riches lingered.

Sod it. Go for it. Rapunzel will cheer and let you climb up her hair – all the way.

He took the tools from the rucksack and worked on the hatch cover, his fingers gripping the inlets to stop it falling away, praying the chamber really was empty. He squeezed his slim body through the aperture, hanging momentarily, then dropped, his trainers absorbing the impact. He turned around, fast, like a startled rabbit, his heartbeat frantic.

Easy. Come down.

The area seemed deserted. He glanced around searching for a central control point, found it, saw from the technology that human beings were superfluous to the operation and headed for the stairs leading to the sole exit.

He stopped dead.

Life. Shit. Now what?

Go for it.

He stabbed the control and waited, his eyes searching for closed-circuit TV cameras.

Idiot. Security will be at the top. Only lunatics like George who creep around derelict tin mines would know about getting into this place through its arsehole. Which puts you right in it, doesn't it? If I get out of here, George, I'm going to stick your head up your own arse, I swear to God.

The door slid open.

He stepped inside, turned and saw the legend above the numbered floor-level touch-controls:

'ADAM.'

His heart thumped.

Say it again, Rapunzel?

'It's a name he remembers. For some reason he sees the number nine with it.'

Lewin reached out and touched the digit. The floor pushed at his feet and an electronic, synthesized voice warned: 'Level Nine. Biological hazard. Protective clothing must be worn at all times.'

He threw himself at the emergency stop but the doors were already opening.

Two figures stood waiting, hooded, trunked and hunchbacked, their silver skin hanging in folds.

'Exit and don protective clothing,' ordered the flat nasal voice.

'Bollocks,' he retorted and stabbed the control to go back down. The lift doors remained open, the machinery silent.

The voice repeated its message.

'Go fuck yourself,' Lewin hissed, backed against the lift wall, terrified.

'Level Nine is a biological hazard area, all authorized personnel must wear protective clothing. Release controls for elevator held on Level Nine may be activated only by security personnel. Report nature of difficulty or incident immediately.'

Lewin stared out at the suspended suits. 'You've got no choice, son,' George's voice told him.

He moved quickly, tearing off the knapsack, straight for the suits. He saw that they were designed to be stepped into on their stands, did this fast, pulled up the long front zip, stepped off the stand and felt the weight of the backpack, his nostrils catching the rubbery smell of compressed air being fed automatically into the visored hood.

One giant step for mankind, he mimicked, his nerve going fast. Don't get straight back into the lift, maybe it's on a time sequence.

He turned ponderously, taking in his surroundings. A control room: two swivel chairs before electronic consoles; a large rectangle of glass, darkness beyond. He shuffled towards the glass and pressed his visor to it.

He stepped back.

What the hell?

The white shapes in the gloom were tantalizing.

Camera. Take some bloody shots. You're here, you've come this far, taken the risks – so do the job.

Then he saw the airlock.

'You're mad, Lewin,' he said aloud. 'Fucking crazy!'

He fumbled through the knapsack cursing the integral gloved fingers of the suit, saw with relief that George had made the film in the camera ready and shuffled to the airlock, cold fingers of sweat clawing all over his body.

Lord, let me do this one thing and get out safely and you can name your price.

Frantically he searched the consoles for something – anything – which might be the opening control for the stainless steel door with its spyhole.

Come on.

There.

DECONTAMINATION LOCK.

He touched the control and the curved door slid silently away. He stepped inside.

The synthesized voice said: 'Entry and exit procedure will not be authorized until decontamination cycle has been completed.'

'I'm with you, baby,' he murmured and activated the controls.

The outer door closed and the lock filled with a fine mist. He closed his eyes. After a moment the inner door slid aside and he stepped into cold, silent darkness, broken only by the blue-white glow of ultra-violet light from some concealed source and chirruping electronic sounds. The chill seeped through his protective suit and lay on his skin like frost.

'Jesus, it gets cold on Dartmoor, Mister Moravec . . . There's no shelter and the wind's a straight razor right through whatever you're wearing. Naked? He's not normal.'

If this was home, no wonder.

He shuffled forward, his breathing shallow but a gale in the hood, approaching one of two rows of long white containers set amid twinkling pin-lights and snaking cables.

He pushed up the heavy cover on one.

The blackened figure inside lay suspended in glutinous liquid: fingers, toes and penis charred to stumps; the face featureless, as if melted.

180

Lewin backed away.

Oh Christ.

The cover stayed open on thick gas-filled struts.

No one lives through burns like that.

The charred chest swelled then deflated, the breathing motion so slow it seemed the next expansion would never come.

Die. I wouldn't want to live like that. Die.

Lewin stared in horror at the destroyed face and the screwed-on transparent cap over the scalp which protected terminals, wires, and tubes containing liquid, both red and colourless, exiting the skull. Involuntarily his eyes followed their path to a smaller container beside him. The heading on the card affixed to it read: 'PILOT'. The large container had an identical card, heavily detailed with medical notes and patterns which to Lewin resembled supermarket bar codes; the heading was 'PILOT 1982 (FALKLAND ISLANDS)'.

They wouldn't dare.

They bloody have, haven't they?

Lewin's fury burned, he heaved up the cover on the smaller container and recoiled from the sight of a human brain imbedded with tubes and wires. He slammed back against the larger container, turned to steady himself and saw one milky white, blinded eye staring up at him.

He gagged and stumbled backward.

Bastards. Sick bastards.

His fury now was uncontrollable. He wanted to destroy everything around him, certain that unimaginable horrors lay in the other containers, other hideously deformed and wounded men who had not been allowed to die.

Bastards.

He fumbled with the camera, all thought of riches and fame gone, his sole purpose now to expose what surrounded him. He took two shots of the mute, staring, blackened figure, his own face contorted in horror and pity, then turned and moved to the containers on the opposite side, pushing up the cover on the first.

He froze.

He man inside was naked, lean and hard, his pale body unblemished, his hair shaved to his scalp which bore the

181

only scars on his body: fine precise lines, perfectly healed and barely visible. Needles were imbedded in his arms, the tubes from them taped to his white near-translucent flesh. His entire frame was enmeshed in wires leading from the electrodes continually stimulating his musculature to a pulsing bank of computer-controlled electronics. To Lewin, the perfection of his physique in the presence of the pitiful charred form opposite was obscene. He fought the over-powering urge to rip out feed-tubes and wires, raised the camera and flashed off two more shots.

The man's body stirred, disturbing the sluggish suspension he lay in. His eyes opened. Lewin, half in panic, fired off another shot. The man blinked and began to rise. From somewhere came a shrill sound. Lewin retreated into the open air-lock, the blue eyes in the raised, shaven head fixed on him, cold and empty. He jabbed the control and stood, rigid, as the chemical spray enveloped him.

This is what he ran from. He awoke, naked, like the others in the tanks, somehow got out and ran headlong across the moors into the night, out of his mind with terror – just like I am. I'm in hell. I've died and I don't know it. Help me, Jesus. Ask anything, Lord – you've got it, I swear.

The inner door slid open.

They were waiting for him, dressed exactly as he yet still their aspect was terrifying. Two pinioned him whilst a third moved behind him and did something to his air-supply pack. His visor seemed to mist over, he felt huge yet tiny at the same time. Kill me, he raged in silence. Don't use me. The threatening black wave engulfed him.

George Howard sat against the hard rock, knees pulled up to his chin, arms hugging them against the seeping cold, the unbroken darkness around him solid, like black marble.

'Come on, you little bugger,' he murmured, forcing down his growing apprehension. 'Get out of there!'

He had the Luger beside him, the toggle-action forced against his buttock so that he knew exactly where the weapon lay. His eyes ached as though the black cold was exerting pressure against them. He longed to switch on his torch but his old sniper's instincts warned: Never expose your position.

He sat close to the deep shaft, dangerously close in the darkness, but he needed to be on the lip to see the approaching glow of Lewin's torch as he made his way back down the tunnel.

The sound froze him rigid: a strange rustling, like crisp leaves brushing against each other: not from below, but from the direction of the engine-house at the entrance to the mine, getting closer, the distance shortening between it and the yawning pit beside him. He wanted to edge away but knew he must stay rock still. His fingers found the icy nickel of the Luger, one curling through the trigger-guard, taking up the pressure ready. You have the advantage, his never forgotten training told him: you know the enemy is coming; they're only guessing you're here.

Light flared, brighter than day, and behind the wide beams, caught in their halo, he saw the enemy formed in white and silver, skin loose and crinkled, black cyclops eyes glinting above trunks curling from grotesque heads. He clawed himself upward, heart banging, the Luger coming up, his finger already jerking on the trigger in spasms of terror, the explosions ear-shattering in the enclosed space.

One figure fell and his fear lifted as he knew he could hurt them, then orange and yellow flared in the blinding white glare and a searing stab pierced him, dropping him, jarringly, to his knees then over on to his side where the cold hard rock became a black grave a thousand feet deep.

A metallic voice blurted in agony from the figure on the ground, bloody beneath his right collar bone. 'Where'd he get a fucking gun?'

Another of the figures stooped for the fallen Luger and examined it. 'War souvenir,' he said, then walked to the edge of the shaft and directed a powerful beam downwards. Stepping back he touched the communication panel on his left arm. 'He'll never be found. Contamination?' he enquired of the one unarmed member of the group.

The big, visored hood shook negatively. 'Their vehicle will have to be dealt with,' the man reminded him.

'Bog,' ordered the leader. 'Now.' He tossed the silver Luger into the shaft. 'Old fool!'

They left the ruined minehead like alien beings, the material of their protective suits rustling in the still, cold night.

Daniel Hale sat alone on the Underground platform bench, examined his watch, perplexed. He hadn't seen this old thing in years – had chucked it away in a drawer when he'd been given his stainless steel Rolex. Christ, that was before his cadet days at Sandhurst! Have to get another strap, he decided; just about had it, this one.

He was utterly bewildered. What was he doing on the platform of a London Underground station? Or more precisely, what was the station doing in Belfast?

I'm dreaming, he thought and smiled broadly, relief rushing through him. Had me going for a bit there. Thought the old mind had finally cracked with the strain. Well, I'll just sit back and enjoy it. Maybe there'll be something juicy in it – though God alone knows where you'd do it in this windy, filthy hole. Dreaming about the bloody Tube? I *hate* the bloody Tube!

He had bought a ticket from a machine, he knew that. He also knew that he was going to Wandsworth – but not why.

Wandsworth? All he knew about Wandsworth was that they had a prison there mainly filled with East End thugs.

He was going there for a friend.

Which friend? Dream friend or real friend?

German friend.

Sorry, wrong dream, don't know any Krauts in London. Or Britain for that matter. Last lot I had anything to do with was at some stinks and bangs course run by the Huns for their GSG9 counter-terror squad. If I was in charge of this dream I'd be in the mess, first floor, Duke of York's Barracks, sinking a few before chasing a dolly or two down the King's Road.

Duke of York's? Hell's bells, I'm a Guardsman, not SAS. How'd that notion get in here?

He turned to a commotion at the furthest end of the

platform and saw a pack of young blacks ruthlessly knocking people aside, ripping possessions from them as they moved closer to him.

Nothing really hurts in a dream. They're not having the old watch. Sentimental value and all that. They'll have to bleed an awful lot before they get it off me.

He stood up, preparing himself, and felt the pressure of the automatic against his middle back. The gun felt too light and that concerned him.

Never, even when you're dreaming, son, step out in hostile territory without a filled magazine in place and one round in the chamber.

Thank you, Sar'n't Barrett, you advice is always heeded but I'm not in charge of this dream and for the life of me I can't tell you why the Heckler is light. Too light. Maybe even empty?

The group of youths had surrounded a middle-aged couple who meekly, almost eagerly, began handing over their possessions. The woman struggled vainly with a glistening ring on her wedding finger. One of the youths swore at her, withdrew a machete from inside his short overcoat, slammed her hand against the postered wall, sliced through the splayed fingers, bent for the rings in the dirt, pocketed them and kicked the severed digits on to the track. The woman's shrieks echoing down the tunnel mated with her husband's outraged wail. The youths felled them both and moved on.

It's a dream, Daniel Hale reminded himself.

He heard movement behind him and saw two hard-looking men further down the platform, one white, one black, dressed casually but soberly.

Now where did you two charmers come from? Never spotted you – not that I was looking. Still, a bit sloppy. Going to give it to me from both ends are you, my dears? Time to wake up, Danny boy.

'Hey, skinhead! You're next,' one of the blacks shouted as the pack came at him.

Skinhead? He touched his scalp; felt the stubble. It's a dream, remember.

185

The pack came at him and he wanted desperately to go for the Heckler but his instructor's voice warned:

Never pull a gun unless you're certain it's loaded. If it isn't they're likely to kill you instead of just beating you because as far as they're concerned you meant to kill them. Remember there's always a useful deadly weapon on or near you even when you're unarmed. I could make you a candidate for a white stick with a bunch of keys. In between the fingers, son. Doesn't take a moment but your assailant will spend the rest of his life in darkness wishing he could turn back the clock.

Training works even in the subconscious, thought Daniel, dropping into a crouch and snatching a cluster of discarded ice-lolly sticks from beneath the bench. He came up fast, the sticks like daggers in his tight fists, striking instantly at the face of the first to reach him. The young man squealed and doubled over, fingers clawing at the jagged wood splinters piercing his ripped flesh. Daniel kicked the bowed head back up, hearing the vertebrae crack and not caring, jabbed his elbow deep into the gut of another who had leapt on him, feeling the weight leave him, butted a third who came at him head-on, felling him – then saw the flash of knives and the raised machete as the remainder backed off preparing to close in for the kill.

It's only a dream, Danny boy.

He barely stopped himself from maiming the man who came up behind him, seeing, just in time, the snob-nosed revolver and the ID card in his hands.

'You're all nicked!' the man bawled, causing the pack to break and run, leaving their injured and dead on the platform.

A train thundered out of the tunnel.

The man's grip on Daniel's arm was ferocious, his head jerked towards a tunnel marked 'NO EXIT'. 'It's OK!' he yelled over the noise.

The train squealed to a tortured halt, hissed, and the doors rumbled open. The woman with the bloodied hand was down on her knees while her husband dementedly banged on a carriage with his fists. The guard shouted. Someone bawled an obscenity.

'Now,' snapped the man. 'We go now or you've had it and you're not taking us with you – got it?'

'His weapon?' queried his black partner.

'No way! That's *well* dirty.'

'Watch him then.'

'Count on it.'

Daniel grinned. 'It's only a dream.'

'Some fuckin' dream,' said the black. 'Move.'

They pulled him into the tunnel and he let them, wearying now of the fantasy, trying to force his awakening.

They left the station for the Edgware Road and made straight for the car they had abandoned outside.

The black took the wheel, pulling away immediately they were in.

'Nice and easy, Joseph,' said the other.

'Sure, nice and easy. Get on the fuckin' phone and tell Victoria we're not takin' him far – just to the nearest nick.'

'You know we can't do that.'

'I don't know anything right now, OK? The guy's a crazy.' The black hand shifted the driving mirror to view the rear. 'You're crazy. How come you're worth so much?'

Daniel smiled and saw reflected a blond, cropped stranger grinning back at him. His skin went cold, his brain numbed and an animal-like sound started to rise from deep within him. He struck out wildly.

'Shit! Hit the bastard!' the driver shouted, swerving the car violently as he ducked the blows. 'For fuck's sake do something!'

The man in the rear locked both arms around the madly writhing figure, pinioning him, then jerked forward with a head-butt.

The hood slipped over his head. Silken, almost chilled. He had expected coarseness and stifling heat. It feels that way because your blood burns in final protest, he decided. An ache coursed through him, so overwhelming he thought he must die from it: desire for all that was going; regret for all that had never been. He felt he was no longer there although the droning of the priest confirmed that he was.

'. . . in the sure and certain knowledge of everlasting life.'

Now. They'll do it now.

He felt the broad straps bind him, arms tight to his sides, legs hard together. He could smell the leather and other men's sweat. Also their fear. The hood was nothing now. I am one great sensing being, he thought: every atom of me radiates with life at the moment of my death.

The sting in his arm was exquisite pain and he sent blessings to the guard with compassion for sparing him the final horror. He drifted away. Too quickly. He wanted life a moment longer.

I'm not dead, decided Otto Fascher's mind. No elation, no joy. Only puzzlement and the will to survive. And instincts which screamed: *hostile territory*.

'How's he doing?' questioned the driver.

Fascher felt fingers on his wrist. 'He'll live.'

Which means you die, thought Fascher. He opened his eyes a fraction, saw the driver reach between the seats, punch buttons then lift something to his ear.

'Victoria, we have our charge. Please advise our next action.'

Car radio? thought Fascher. Advanced type. Didn't matter if it was a crystal set, the fact they had it in the car made them police or MI5. He took stock of his situation, his quick mind unusually sluggish but getting swifter by the second. Fascher was proud of his intellect – and of his natural cunning. Wait, he urged himself, listen, watch, assess – then strike.

His head rested against the window, the darkened streets a blur to his fractionally opened eyes. He was impressed and puzzled by the car: so silent, so well sprung? Yet it was no limousine, no Rolls or Hispano and certainly no *grosse* Mercedes Benz: the driver's seat was pressed against his legs so it was quite small. He let his head loll so that he could peer downward at the door locks. No handles? Something recessed into the door? Ah! Safety devices to stop prisoners fleeing from the car. Clever. In Germany the Gestapo simply removed the handles from the rear. The British were always so inventive. He admired that trait in them. As, he knew, did the Führer.

The Führer.

Was he still alive? Was the war still going on? Surely not. Germany was spitting its last drops of blood on its own streets when the British police had arrested him on suspicion of espionage. Suspicion? How quaint the British could be with their strict adherence to the niceties of the law. Turn the tables: make this the Reich and the Gestapo would have dragged him screaming by the hair into the torture chamber where they'd fry his balls first then tell him why he'd been pulled in.

But the British had won the war – with American help of course: which meant the Jews had done it again. Auf wiedersehen, Adolf: you tried, you failed, and probably took poor Germany with you. And all our superior technology? Have the Allies got that now? The great rockets? The bomb you hinted could destroy entire cities? All our great advances passed to the Jews and their vassals? It could so easily have been different. If only the British had seen the light, perceived that the future truly belongs to those who grasp it with both hands and drag themselves forward to it. But the pack can always destroy even the strongest lone wolf when they mass and turn on him. Farewell then, my Führer, I know you wouldn't have let them take you alive.

'His condition is good,' replied the driver to a question. 'There's been another incident. Possible fatality. Details later. We're keeping off main roads to be safe.'

Had hostilities not ceased? wondered Fascher. He peered out again at the dark streets rushing by. Blackout still? Perhaps pockets of Luftwaffe still operated?

You're fooling yourself.

Think back.

Needle.

Pain from a hypodermic.

How long have they kept you unconscious?

Why did they save you?

Who saved you?

British Fascists? They might have kept the armed struggle going, our ideals alive? What did the driver report in his radio? Another incident – possible fatality? If I could escape and link up with such an organization I would truly have served the Fatherland well.

The car lurched. Fascher took the opportunity to let his head left. He could see the back of the driver's head now.

A negro?

He would never have believed it of the British. A negro in their counter-intelligence service? Even in war-time that seemed outrageous. He had never even seen a black British policeman in the two years he had been active in Britain. In the colonies perhaps. But in Britain?

What year was it? He had to know.

He gathered himself for action, feeling extraordinarily young and supple. How old had he been when they finally cornered him? Forty-seven on his forged William Miller documents to guarantee he was safe from conscription but in actuality he was forty-four. And you felt every year of Miller's supposed age, didn't you, Otto? Now, for reasons he could not understand, he felt young and fit. The drug they had used on him perhaps? Some euphoric side-effect?

His right hand hurt, sharp pain as if he had cut it very recently. He thought he could feel the sticky dampness of blood. His? Theirs? And how his head *throbbed*. They had sandbagged him, that was certain. Snatched him back from his rescuers. Well, for sure, he was not making a second trip to the scaffold. This time they would have to shoot him – and not by firing squad either.

The car-phone buzzed. The black snatched at it. 'Right,' he said after a moment and replaced the phone. 'The Regent's Park address,' he said to his colleague. 'Report to the man himself?'

Regent's Park? thought Fascher. His last interrogation had taken place inside the school they had commandeered opposite Wandsworth Prison. He had seen the name as they had driven him in: the Royal Victoria Patriotic School. Regent's Park meant big guns. 'The man himself?' Undoubtedly, from the respectful tone of voice, someone most senior in the British counter-espionage hierarchy. More interrogation? They already knew everything about him, which meant they were after information on his rescuers. The problem was he had nothing to give them, so he'd suffer a lot of useless pain because they would never accept his explanation of being drugged and remembering nothing of his escape. Even he found that hard to believe.

How long had he to act? Where were they now? Come on, *schwartzer*, get off these gloomy backstreets and show me a landmark I know.

'He's still got the automatic,' said the black. 'Take it off him while he's out.'

'Told you on the station, I'm not handling a murder weapon, Joe. You want it, you stop the car and get it.'

'The guy's a nutter. You've seen what can happen when guns and nutters mix. Just get it off him, Harry. Here, use this.'

Fascher had difficulty staying slumped, his body rigid: he had a weapon on him and they had not disarmed him. The rest of their conversation meant nothing. Murder weapon? Nutter? He heard only the fact he was armed.

Where was the weapon? Jacket? Trousers? In his belt? There was pressure against his lower spine but he dared not move from his slumped position. He tried to remember handling the gun but nothing came, except a brief, absurd flash of being cold in a very noisy aircraft, checking a heavy, unfamiliar automatic pistol, a hallucination he put down to the drug.

He sensed the figure next to him tense, then felt hands searching quickly and expertly. A yellow cloth appeared under his barely open eyes as the man checked under his armpits and his breast pockets. The yellow vanished, then the man said: 'Here you go: small of back. Told you he was a pro.'

'Flipped. Hope we never get that way.'

Fascher reacted faster then he believed possible: turned, locked one hand over the man's wrist and drove the heel of the other up, under and through the cartilage of his nose, sending bone-splinters into his brain. Ignoring the spurting blood and body in spasm he retrieved the gun from the seat and jammed it against the driver's neck.

'Stop the car, *schwartzer*,' he ordered.

The driver cursed under his breath and pulled the car into a space. He swivelled his eyes to the sprawled form on the rear seat. 'If he's dead there's about fifty blokes who'll never give up till they hang you up by your balls.'

The stench of voided bowels filled the car.

'He's dead.'

'Then so are you, you fucker.'

Fascher drove the gun viciously into the tight black curls. 'People of your race don't speak to their superiors in that manner.'

'What century are you living in, man?'

'I need answers.'

'Then you don't need me – I'm hired help.'

'What happened to the people who helped me escape? You arrested them? Where did you take them? Wandsworth Prison also?'

The curly head shook slowly from side to side. 'You're talking a language I don't understand, man. You're sick.'

'My English is perfect. I spent my childhood here. I'm not ill – I've been drugged.'

'Jesus,' murmured the driver.

'Which are you: police or MI5?'

'You think the ID we flashed was real? A con, to get you out before they chopped you up for good. We should have let 'em do it. Right now I'd help. Harry was my mate.'

Again the gun dug in. 'Police or MI5?'

'We're private. Watchers mostly though sometimes we're doers if the going gets rough – or personal.' A pink and black thumb jerked towards the back seat.

Fascher shifted, agitated now. 'You're lying to save your life. Give me real answers. What is the state of the war?'

'Which war?'

'*The* war, idiot. The war against Germany.'

'Oh! That war? You should've said so. Tell you what: you tell me what state you'd like it to be in and I'll give you the latest news, OK?'

'Answer me! Have we lost?'

'We won. Make you feel better?'

'The Allies won?'

'Allies? Sure.'

Fascher nodded. 'Inevitable. This underground movement – British Fascists? How powerful are they?'

The driver sighed. 'Look, give me the gun and I'll take you somewhere where you can be treated.'

'Answer me! The force which engineered my escape – how established are they?'

'I don't know what you're talking about, mister. OK? All I know is two teams were put on to this job; round-the-clock, expense no object, and we had to make sure you weren't snatched by persons unknown. Brief was we could use force if necessary. That's a laugh! You went and did the job for us, didn't you?'

Fascher felt the sweat start to fall from him: his mind seemed inhabited by insects with razored pincers. He felt that he was existing in a familiar, yet strangely alien, world peopled by beings whom he could neither communicate with nor understand – despite his speaking their language fluently.

Worse, he had the dreadful feeling that it was he who was an alien. A despairing wave of loneliness swept over him; he felt he was the last human left alive, surrounded by spirits who shifted away each time he reached out for them. Could he be dead? Had the execution taken place after all? Impossible! He bled, didn't he! His painful hand was proof. And he had just killed a man: which made him tangible – not a spirit. Could it be that death was not how men conceived it at all? Perhaps it was a transference of the soul on an earthly plain, laterally, to another human, rather than ascension – or descent – to wherever. If he was to retain his sanity he must know whether he, Otto Fascher, still existed. The horror of his predicament chilled him; yet, whatever the risk to himself, he had to know. Or go mad.

'You have a radio in this car?' he demanded.

'Radio and telephone. You want to call someone?'

'I want you to ask those in authority to confirm or deny the death by execution in Wandsworth Prison, London, on May the seventh, nineteen forty-five, of a German national named Otto Horst Fascher. His cover name was William Arthur Miller, his crime espionage.'

Something in Fascher's voice made the driver ignore the

gun at his head and turn towards him. 'You look terrible, man. Let me get you to a hospital.'

'Just ask the question.'

'Ask who?'

'Your people. The police, MI5. The authorities.'

'I'll ask Victoria to advise, okay? That's my HQ. Understand?'

'Don't advise them where we are or I'll kill you.'

'I believe it,' commented the negro, bleakly.

Moravec lifted the ringing telephone. 'Who wants him? Very well, this is he. Wait.' He clicked fingers at Jane Haversham who was on another line, making notes on a pad. 'They have him.'

Jane said into her telephone: 'I know it's difficult but call me immediately if you get anything,' and put down the receiver.

The driver's voice came metallically through a speaker on Moravec's desk.

'Sir, I'm to ask you some questions – just a minute.' A rustling came through the speaker and the driver's faded voice asked: 'What was that name again?'

A sharp curse came down the line. A voice with the merest hint of an accent said: 'Otto Horst Fascher. Officer in the Abwehr. Executed May nineteen forty-five, Wandsworth Prison, London. Crime espionage. Confirm this. No lies or your man here dies.'

'Adam?' Jane blurted, involuntarily.

'That isn't Adam,' growled Moravec.

'It is. He changes, I heard it happen at Hartrampf's. Adam! This is Jane. Tell us where you are, we'll come for you. You'll be perfectly safe.'

The voice said: 'Did you hear my question?'

'*Adam!*'

Moravec made a cutting signal. 'We have the information you require,' he said smoothly, but glaring at her. 'Give us a moment please.'

She wrote fast: 'YOU CAN'T TELL HIM HE'S DEAD!', tore the sheet and thrust it at Moravec.

He ignored the message holding his hand out for her notes.

She shook her head.

He stood towering over her and pulled the pad from her grip. 'You heard Shirer,' she pleaded. 'Those could be Fascher's memory cells in Adam's brain – which makes the problem physical, not psychological. Gods knows what damage might occur!'

'Answer!' demanded Fascher.

Jane said: 'You can't take the risk.'

'I'll kill your man *now* if you don't answer,' Fascher warned.

'He means it,' confirmed the black's voice through the speaker. 'He's already killed my mate.'

Jane turned away.

Moravec read aloud from her notes: 'Otto Horst Fascher, executed by hanging for the crime of espionage, eight fifteen a.m. on May the seventh, nineteen hundred and forty-five. Wandsworth Prison, London.'

The gasp through the speaker was plainly audible. After a moment a shocked voice asked: 'Place of burial, please?'

'We don't have that information.'

'You're lying. The execution is a lie!'

'We'll try to find that information for you. They probably buried the body in the prison.'

'Find out.'

'It isn't that easy in the middle of the night. We may need to contact the Home Office and that's impossible at present.'

'Who informed you of the execution?'

'We have specialists who record such information.'

'I must have the place of burial. Do you understand? Your man's life depends on your getting it.'

Jane rapidly punched numbers into another phone. 'Come on, wake up,' she breathed.

'We need time,' Moravec stalled.

'I'm waiting. Your man too.'

'Don't take too long,' warned the tight voice of the driver as he gave the car-phone number.

Jane spoke with relief into the telephone. 'Roy Parker?

Jane Haversham. I'm really sorry to wake you again . . . I didn't? You took so long to answer.' She looked up at Moravec, lines of strain showing around her bruised eyes. 'Yes, it is a fascinating case, I agree. Mister Parker, sorry to interrupt but we need urgently – I mean right away – the place of burial of this spy Fascher. You do? *What!*' She listened, eyes blank, not noticing Shirer reappear with Shaw and Peters. She insisted: 'You're certain? Of course, yes. That's right. Well, you are the expert on the subject. Thanks again, goodbye.'

'You have it?' demanded Moravec.

'More,' she answered, her tiredness gone. 'Fascher was supposed to be buried in the grounds of Wandsworth Prison. A Home Office directive arrived the morning of the scheduled execution ordering the body to be handed over to an army medical section for, and I quote the directive, 'scientific purposes'. The body was released without objection – one assumes no one much cared what happened to the body of a Nazi spy – and was driven by army vehicle to an unspecified destination in Devon. My contact, Parker, the acknowledged expert on the subject of German espionage operations in both world wars, interviewed various retired prison guards with regard to the Fascher case during his research. One of them told him that the soldier driving the truck made a comment about "going from one nick to another'. Questioned, the soldier admitted they were heading for Dartmoor to take delivery of another corpse but warned the guard not to repeat that because their final destination was also in that area and was, quote, "hush-hush".'

Shirer had listened intently to every ward. 'The Home Office directive presumably must have been countersigned by an officer from this army medical section? If you had a name you could break this wide open.'

'I have a name,' Jane said quietly. 'An army medical officer was present at the execution – it was he who delivered the directive. His name was Samuel Hale. Daniel's father. He was accompanied by an army nurse named Eleanor Pagett-Lisle. I'd stake my career that later she became Eleanor Hale.'

'Just one moment,' said Shirer. 'Nurse? Why? Nursing care is for live patients, not corpses.'

'Exactly, Doctor.'

Moravec broke in: 'You telling me this German is still alive?'

Jane shook her head. 'I very much doubt it – he'd be an advanced geriatric – '

'And a vegetable if they'd been lopping off parts of his brain over the years,' Shirer interrupted.

Moravec asked: 'They'd have to keep him alive if they wanted to use parts of his brain, surely?'

Shirer corrected him. 'You can keep cells alive virtually indefinitely under the correct conditions.'

'What's going on?' asked Shaw, the taller of the two security-agency men, both of whom were bemused by the exchange.

'Your man's got a problem,' explained Moravec.

'Which man?'

'Gave his name as Nelson.'

'What's his problem?'

'Listen.' Moravec reached for a telephone.

'Wait! What are you going to tell Adam?' Jane demanded.

'He's not Adam. Perhaps he never will be again.'

'Daniel Hale was temporary, Fascher followed. Neither one is the real Adam. Physically. He – whoever he is – is still there. I can talk him back, I know it.'

'Shirer?' Moravec questioned.

'Come on, you don't expect an opinion? We're talking revolutionary neurosurgery here – and God knows what else. Advanced medicine. Experimental. Futuristic. A surgical quantum leap! I'm positively medieval compared to it.'

'That was the medical section named on the Home Office directive,' Jane cut in, pointing at her pad.

Moravec scanned the lines of pencilled notes. 'Where did you say the name Adam came from?'

'It was the only name he recalled according to Eleanor Hale. He told me himself he saw the name, with the number nine.'

Moravec slashed underlining on her notes and tossed the pad back over his great leather-topped desk.

'What is it?' Shirer asked, seeing the expression on her face.

Moravec explained: 'Army. Department of Advanced Medicine.'

'ADAM,' she said, quietly.

'Nine?' queried Moravec.

'Number of an experiment?' offered Shirer.

'That's inhuman,' Jane exclaimed.

'Where's humanity come into this?' said Shirer. 'Fanatics – and it seems that's what we're dealing with – don't have the word in their vocabulary. Your Adam isn't anything more than a number to them. Yes, an experiment. One of many. And one that bloody failed, by the mayhem he's caused. These people aren't after improving medicine, they're after improving – *perfecting* – us poor defective human beings. They're delving into the unknown; messing around with things they don't know enough about is another description for it. The scientific term is eugenics. The Nazis had an entire programme for it, as Moravec here so rightly pointed out. Their holy grail if you like: the development of their "master race" by selective breeding and, probably, knowing how advanced they were in other fields of science, genetic engineering as well – in some crude form.' He paused, reflective. 'Or perhaps not so crude. Perhaps they were further advanced than we've been led to believe – and that knowledge has been the basis for continuing secret research and experimentation. I hope not. The most profound and terrifying observation I've ever heard on the subject is: "Lurking behind every genetic dream come true is a brave new world nightmare."'

Shaw's frustration boiled over. 'What's Joe Nelson's problem?'

Moravec answered: 'Nelson is all right – for the moment. I'm afraid the man with him is dead.'

'Mitchell! How?'

'I don't know the circumstances.'

'Your bloke did it?'

Moravec nodded.

Peters mouthed a crude obscenity. 'We should have been warned. So where's he now?'

'Holding Nelson.'

'What's he after then?'

'The answer to a question. If he's given it – it might kill him,' explained Jane.

'Tough.'

'He might kill your man first.'

'Nelson can handle himself.'

'With a bullet in his brain?' asked Moravec and lifted the telephone again.

Otto Fascher grabbed the car-phone at its first tone.

'We have the information,' Moravec's deep voice rumbled.

'Tell me.'

'Otto Fascher was not executed on the day in question. To our knowledge he was never executed.'

'Explain.'

'We have documented evidence that he was taken from Wandsworth Prison that morning, possibly unconscious because a nurse and doctor were present.'

'Taken where?'

'Dartmoor, in Devon.'

Fascher felt part of his world slip, his consciousness threatening to go with it. Cold fingers seemed to press on his brain, numbing parts of it and areas of his body. His vision fragmented.

Hold on. Even if this is death, hold on. Nothing is as bad as the void that is waiting.

He was terrified by the thought – the voice? – that was not his, yet was clear in his mind. He knew it, yet did not. He also knew, yet did not, the meaning of the warning. Like a man near fainting with fear on a narrow high ledge knowing unconsciousness meant death, he dragged his consciousness back fraction by fraction from the void.

Then he saw, perfectly, a soft face with concerned eyes, neither beautiful nor plain but to him infinitely lovely. He felt her hand on his brow, the coolness of something pass over his face, the rasp of stubble as it brushed his jawline.

Her voice said: 'Must the driver crash us about so?' and through his floating he too felt the jarring thump of the vehicle's suspension being tortured.

'Slow down!' he shouted, wishing only to please his vision.

'Do what?' queried Nelson. 'We're stationary, mate.'

'What's the matter?' Moravec's voice asked.

'Drive to Dartmoor,' Fascher ordered.

'You mean Broadmoor,' Nelson muttered under his breath. 'Look, Dartmoor's a bloody big area – and this isn't the vehicle for the job. I'm not the man for it either. Tell you what, I'll just get out and leave you the keys, OK? I'll even give you a few quid for petrol.'

'Drive,' Fascher yelled and ripped out the car-phone.

'He's crazy,' said Shaw, as the speaker on the desk cut out.

Shirer said: 'Moravec, I think it's time the police were informed.'

'Call the police, and that place and what they're doing in it will never be exposed. It'll be shut up tight and its existence denied. I've a duty to inform the public.'

'You've a duty to your shareholders first.'

Moravec turned to Jane. 'What's he going to do? Guess.'

'He's going home.'

'Home being this Army Department of Advanced Medicine? We have no idea where it is.'

'Home. Daniel's home. Raethmoor Farm. Couldn't you hear it in his voice? The Fascher part of him is barely holding on. He'll go back to being either Daniel or Adam – whichever one it is, he'll go back to the farm. Adam ran there from that place – it's really all he knows of the outside world. I know he'll go back.'

Shirer said: 'Adam may have done the running but the part that is Daniel Hale obviously guided him. Drove him.'

'What drove him, Doctor, was fear. The fear of being neither dead nor alive. He described it as a void: a knowledge of existing while dead. His description was horrific.'

Shaw snapped: 'We've got to do something. *Now*.'

'Take me to Raethmoor Farm,' said Jane, firmly. 'It's the only choice we've got.'

'You mean, Joe Nelson's got,' reminded Peters.

Moravec was already on the telephone. 'Well, find him and get him there now!' he growled, thumping the receiver down. 'Our helicopter will get you there faster. The pad is on the roof of the Worldcom building. Shirer, you stay, there's work for you to do here.'

ELEVEN

Richard Wardlove woke his wife and made love to her with an intensity which had been lacking in the past year of their five-year marriage. Half asleep but awake enough to enjoy the event, she wondered briefly – and with momentary panic – if he was having an affair and this sudden, heavy desire was the physical manifestation of his guilt. She dismissed the thought. Harriet Wardlove knew her husband had been having an affair for most of his life with something which precluded other women including herself: power. His middle-of-the-night urge was his insecurity showing, the backwash from some new power game he had entered. Something never seen by his peers.

Wardlove rolled on to his back, conceding defeat in the one battle he could never win: satisfying his wife's own desires once they were aroused.

The bedside telephone, like all the others in Wardlove's various homes, rang very loudly.

'No!' Harriet Wardlove exploded.

He snatched the receiver, recognized the voice in his ear and pushed his wife off him.

'Oh God,' she moaned.

Wardlove took a quick sip of mineral water, his expression fixed in shock.

'What's wrong?' Harriet hissed.

He shook his head, angrily. 'Prime Minister, I have absolutely no idea where he might have got that information from. Yes, I agree, it must have been leaked from within my department – yes, someone close to me, to have got out so quickly.'

'What in heaven's name were you trying to prove?' shrilled a hard voice, quite clear, from the earpiece.

Wardlove's eyes darted to his wife's. 'I was given information. I felt it necessary to check on its authenticity. To follow upon it at least.'

Harriet Wardlove pressed her ear to the receiver.

'You had no business authorizing an investigation on an issue as sensitive as this without consulting me first. It really is the height of irresponsibility.'

Wardlove's eyes hardened. 'Are you implying, Prime Minister, that this story is authentic and you are fully aware of the facts?'

'The accusation is of course patently absurd. No government – no British government – would approve of the sale of bodily organs from unwilling, or indeed willing, donors whether they be in the armed services or not. However – '

'Excuse me for interrupting, Prime Minister, but is that the content of this accusation? The illicit sale of transplant organs?'

'Of course, haven't I made that clear?'

'No, I'm afraid you haven't,' Wardlove retorted, choosing his words carefully. 'Until now you've only intimated that an accusation has been made publicly, by a member of the Opposition, concerning an investigation I'd set in motion within my department. As the accusation has been made without the protection of parliamentary privilege I shall naturally be taking legal advice on the matter. The leak is unfortunate and I'll see that whoever is responsible is disciplined – but you know full well, Prime Minister, that leaks cannot be stopped; they're part of politics.'

The Prime Minister's voice turned to steel. 'Very soon there'll be a knock on your door. You will greet this person who will appraise you of a particular, highly sensitive, matter. You will give him your fullest attention. When he is done you will sign the document he will present confirming that you have been fully informed of a top-secret project concerning both the military and medicine – but not this ridiculous tabloid-fodder story of the illicit butchery of British soldiers for the sake of profit. How could you possibly treat such a fabrication with anything more than the contempt it deserves? I have to tell you I'm most disappointed, indeed dismayed by your lack of good judgement. I shall of course expect to be informed of your source: tomorrow at Downing Street, ten o'clock sharp. I wouldn't go back to sleep if I were you: people from the security service tend to drive very quickly.'

Wardlove stared at the purring receiver.

'What's going on? Richard?'

'Wait.' He leapt out of bed, darted naked from the room, returned with a small notebook and dialled a number. A voice answered surprisingly quickly, given the hour.

'Yes?'

'Moravec? Richard Wardlove. I won't apologize for waking you . . . You were? Then you've heard the news?'

'No. You tell me.'

'The government's been accused of running a programme involving the sale of transplant organs extracted illicitly from members of the armed forces.' Wardlove named the radical left-wing MP who had made the accusation. 'He must have heard of the investigation I put in motion on your behalf.'

'I made a suggestion which might further your long-term political prospects – no more.'

'Ye gods, you did a lot more than that! You virtually accused the government of being involved in some kind of Orwellian experimental-medicine programme using fatally injured servicemen as guinea-pigs.'

'I'm sorry, this is a terrible line.'

'You heard all right. Listen, you bastard, the opposition have got the wrong end of the stick but instead of laughing it off, the headmistress is taking – no, ordering – me into her confidence. What I want off you is very simple and if I don't get it I'll pull every string I have to make your people's rotten dirty jobs more difficult than they already are.'

'Go on.'

'I need to know who gave you the information regarding the programme in the first place. I have to give the Prime Minister my source and if I admit it's you my career is over. I want your source, Moravec. I need it now.'

'I'll give you an acronym. ADAM. You've just used part of it. You've a fine brain: work it out. Think it through and I'm certain you'll have the answer very quickly.'

'The answer is your source?'

'Find out what lies behind that acronym and you may have the answer to all your problems – it might even be your door into Ten Downing Street.'

'I've been summoned to bloody Downing Street first thing. I need a *name* – now.'

Moravec considered: 'Very well. Hartrampf. Doctor Erich Hartrampf.'

'Don't know him.'

'And you never will. He died tonight. Killed by persons unknown – or that's what the official verdict will eventually be. Listen to the morning news.'

'If he's dead what good is it me naming him as a source? He can't confirm it.'

'He can't deny it either! Good night, Wardlove, I expect we'll be in touch in the future. Incidentally, when you've finally solved the acronym be very careful indeed as to who you repeat it to.'

'Are you threatening me, Moravec?'

'On the contrary. I'm warning you.'

'Fat bloody Jew,' Wardlove swore and slammed down the receiver.

'*Moravec?*' Harriet gasped. 'You've involved with Moravec? Are you insane? The party will crucify you if this comes out! Are you going to tell me what's going on?'

He reached for a message pad, wrote boldly: 'ADAM.' 'Here, you're bloody good at *The Times* crossword. Solve this.'

'What does it mean?'

'Don't be completely thick! That's what you're supposed to find out.'

'Is this important?'

'Vital.'

'What are you doing?'

'Getting dressed. We have a visitor. Soon, according to Mount Olympus.'

'I'll need a clue. I've not enough information.'

'Something I said is part of it. Right at the end of the conversation? The M must be Medicine.'

'You said "experimental medicine". That doesn't fit.'

205

'I said "Orwellian experimental medicine" if you need the bloody transcript verbatim!'

'That's right, you did. O is no good.'

Wardlove knotted his tie quickly. 'Hurry up.'

'All I've got to go on is M. I need more. A-D-A? You must know more and not realize it.'

'ADA? Somebody's aunt? Anno Domini? Christ, I don't know. A could be Army or Armed – this does involve the armed forces.'

'All right, Army. So: Army something something Medicine. What are you doing getting mixed up with Moravec? Thank goodness we're not short of money.'

'I'll come through this – as I've always done.'

'From the look of you this isn't your normal wrist-slapping offence.'

'Shut up, D. Defence!'

'All right, say it is? Doesn't really make sense, even allowing for the missing A. Army Defence something Medicine?'

'Doesn't need to – it's just a convenient name for another bloody secret government department.'

'Department! Army Department of Medicine. What medicine? Experimental but starts with A? Orwellian? What was Orwell?'

'Bloody Red.'

'Ahead of his time, you idiot. Advanced. Army is a prefix, don't you see? Army – Department of Advanced Medicine! ADAM. Does it mean anything?'

Wardlove stopped brushing his hair, a wolfish grin on his handsome face in the mirror. 'Yes. Could be. Started with the army but it spread? Grew with extra funding? One of those outrageously expensive, unexplained defence projects which nobody but the top Whitehall mandarins seem to know about?'

'Who fob you off with silly answers when you make enquiries?'

'Oh, never silly. Convoluted, even plausible. That's if you get an answer at all. Usually you're asked why you're interested in the first place. Then you're read the bloody Official Secrets Act.'

'But you're the minister. One of them, anyway.'

Wardlove laughed. 'Ministers are temporary – like governments. Sure, we're given the helm every so often, we might even get to navigate – but they provide the charts and run the engines. Christ, if the truth were known, it's their bloody ship!'

'Richard! You sound like a Socialist.'

'I sound like a realist who knows precisely what he's talking about.'

A chime came from low down in the rambling country house.

'Who the hell is that at three in the morning?'

'Whitehall come calling,' said Wardlove. 'You stay out of this. This is men's business – and it's also top secret.'

'And more bloody lies?'

'Sanders,' said the moustached man on the doorstep. 'You'd have been called, I imagine. Sorry about the knock-up in the early hours, not out usual style. Fought the last war to stop all that, didn't we?'

'Who're they?' enquired Wardlove, spotting the second car parked on the gravel sweep.

'Just in case.'

'In case of what?'

'You needed to be shown the facility. May I come in?'

'Shown? At this time? Where's the facility?'

'Army land. Dartmoor.'

'Dartmoor? I'm supposed to be at Downing Street by ten!'

'As I said: just in case. I'll brief you and then we'll decide, shall we? May I come in?'

Wardlove stood aside, finally, unsettled by the hard-faced men slumped in the second car.

'Beautiful home,' said Sanders as they walked into a sprawling low-beamed room dominated by a vast granite fireplace. 'Tudor of course.'

'I'll take the briefing before the compliments if you don't mind.'

Sanders nodded and sat without being asked. 'Why don't you make yourself comfortable.'

'You can send the heavies away. I've no intention of driving to bloody Dartmoor – or anywhere else for that matter. Not tonight, Josephine.'

Sanders gave a mean smile and stayed in his chair.

'Do you want me to tell them?'

'They stay.'

Wardlove felt his blood rise, controlled himself and sat.

'What prompted this enquiry of yours?' asked Sanders, taking out a silver cigarette case and removing a cigarette. 'Do you mind if I smoke?'

'My wife hates it.'

Sanders considered, tapped the cigarette on his case then replaced it inside with a small sigh.

'I was given information alluding to the mistreatment of servicemen under medical care.'

'Really? This is treatment within the medical branches of the services or are we talking civilian here?'

'Within the service structure.'

'Name?'

'What?'

'Name? Name of your informant.'

'I don't have to tell you that.'

'You do. And you will.'

'I've agreed to inform the Prime Minister. You're exceeding your authority and you're also bloody rude.'

'In the matter of the defence of the realm there are no limits to my authority, Mister Wardlove. You should know that.'

'We're talking about army medicine here, not bloody enemy action.'

'There we are! You see how poorly you've been informed. Misinformed, actually. I believe we can sort this out very quickly. Let me say this – warning you first that everything you hear in this room is subject to the Official Secrets Act and the terms and penalties therein contained.'

'Christ, first day of term,' Wardlove muttered, arose and poured himself a stiff whisky and soda.

'Not for me,' said Sanders.

Didn't offer, thought Wardlove, still disturbed by the men in the second car. He hoped Harriet didn't start prowling around the house half-naked as she was prone to do when she hadn't had enough. They'd do a job on her, for sure. Bloody East End thugs hammered into shape with hard discipline and training, then ordered to do practically the same things they'd undoubtedly have gone to jail for if they hadn't signed up with Her Majesty's guardians of freedom. And she'd enjoy it.

Sanders was talking.

'Say again?'

'I asked: how well have you been briefed on our biological warfare capabilities?'

'Not much. Who is, for Christ's sake? We don't even have a cohesive policy, do we?'

'Nevertheless the other side have the weapons so we must too.'

'Fine by me. What's this to do with squaddies in wretched army hospitals?'

'Some of those squaddies in those "wretched" army hospitals have been put there by biological weapons.'

'Enemy usage?'

'Our usage. We have to test these weapons – no matter how dangerous – because, very simply, our men have to be protected. We must gain knowledge of how best to protect them.'

'You're telling me we're testing biological weapons on our own men?'

'Of course not. Not in the sense you mean. To test new protective clothing, new vehicles, sealed enclosures, to develop counter measures we must use human subjects. Obviously the strictest safety regulations apply whenever these exercises are carried out . . .'

'But sometimes they fail?'

'Sometimes an unforeseen accident occurs. A suit is punctured, a seal may be broken – that kind of thing.'

'And a poor bloody squaddie ends up spewing his lungs out in hospital.'

'Crudely put, yes.'

'Is there another way of putting it?'

'The public could be badly affected by such emotive terminology. If the media got hold of this, that is precisely the language they would use. Certain areas of the media, that is.'

'Probably,' said Wardlove, carefully.

'You had no ideas in that direction, did you, sir?'

Wardlove glanced up from his tumbler. 'Absolutely none.'

'I'm relieved to hear that. So you wouldn't mind telling me your source?'

Wardlove locked eyes with Sanders. 'First, you answer a question.'

'Fire away.'

'The name ADAM – or rather the acronym. Mean anything to you? Codename for this operation, perhaps? The name of the organization which looks after these accident cases. I worked it out as being Army Department of Advanced Medicine,'

'Where did you get the name from?' Sanders queried.

Wardlove watched him take out his silver cigarette case, extract a cigarette and put it between his lips, lighter poised.

'Didn't you hear the question?'

Wardlove's throat had dried out. He tried to swallow a mouthful of Scotch. 'Hartrampf. Doctor Erich Hartrampf.'

Sanders lit his cigarette and walked to the window overlooking the gravel sweep. 'Doctor Hartrampf died tonight. Violently. He was part of a highly sensitive long-term project – retired because of his age but his expertise was still called on regularly. Because of the extreme sensitivity of this project, Hartrampf was under constant observation – audio and visual – as were all members of the team, past and present, operative and retired. You never spoke to Doctor Hartrampf, you never communicated with him in any way. You didn't know Doctor Hartrampf. You didn't even know of his existence.'

'Look here – '

'She's in the bedroom,' announced one of the hard-faced men from the door.

'What's he mean? Damn it, if they've touched my wife – '

'Take him upstairs,' ordered Sanders.

Stark fear gripped Wardlove. He lurched for the crystal

210

whisky decanter and hurled it at the door, immediately going for another containing cognac – missing with both. The two men crossed the room fast, pounced and had him armlocked in seconds.

'Upstairs,' Sanders repeated. 'In the bedroom – with her. Make it look good. Tie him up with one of his Eton ties, that'll add a touch of radicalism to it. I think you'll have to rape her to make it convincing. Just the two of you. The others can sort out down here.'

'Who are you people?' Wardlove screamed, eyes bulging in sheer terror.

'We're the future, Mister Wardlove. A pure British future. How would you describe what's out there now – in the present? Muddle? Chaos? It's worse: it's nothing. The end of a race. The end of a line of pure breeding that conquered the world. This small island once ruled much of the globe – not because of the quality of our weapons or their mass, but because of the quality of our people. That quality hasn't all gone, yet – but it's being diluted with every passing year. A few more generations with things going on the way they are now and you'd be lucky to find a pure-blooded Anglo-Saxon in the British Isles. We're making certain that never happens.'

'Listen, for Christ's sake, I share some of your ideals.'

'Some? Mister Wardlove, that's not enough.'

'All of them!'

'Take him away.'

'Moravec! Rudolf Moravec. He knows. He told me about ADAM. He was my source. If you harm me he'll know. He warned me. He'll print the truth!'

'He doesn't know the truth. Like this Prime Minister and all the prime ministers since the end of the last war – none has ever known the truth. They believe what they're told. Politicians all want to stay in office so when you tell them that something dreadful is going on – unavoidably, naturally – they move heaven and earth to help suppress the spread of that knowledge. Which is how the project has survived, and been so well funded, in secret for so long. Nobody really knew the truth. Even if they did, would they dare to be the one to blow the whistle? To admit they didn't know? Would the voters believe them? Too many imponderables for a politician, I think. Especially one who wishes to stay in power – and I don't think any other kind exists. Do you? Goodbye.'

Sanders walked out on to the gravel, his heavy brogues crunching with each step. A sharp scream reached his ears followed by a longer one, then a series of yelps. He heard a man roar. Then silence. Then, a double blast from a shotgun, explosions so close together he could imagine the gun shifting in expert hands from head to head, side by side, very close.

Sanders nodded. Another unsolved murder for the people to leer over in their morning newspapers and on their TV screens. Motives: envy, lust, blind violence. The Roman games played out again – or elements of them – for the degenerate masses. While the media emperors played the tune?

Rudolf Moravec, he reminded himself.

Yes.

Difficult.

Also, the Haversham woman.

Matters to be decided at a much higher level. He or others would be given instructions in due course.

He pondered briefly about the left-wing MP whose ill-informed ranting had caused the problem but decided that very few people took him seriously anyway. Best left alone to stew in his own poison. A careful, very discreet watch was always kept on him. And the source of his information? The McCarthy woman was already dead meat: even if she had survived the crash she could have been pulled in on any number of counts from sexually molesting under-age girls to providing aid and sustenance to Her Majesty's enemies. It might have been entertaining to pull her in for a week or two and allow her Irish comrades to start believing she was writing the IRA operational handbook just for us before releasing her. The clown in Wardlove's office? A nothing. Not worth bothering about. He'll be so scared tomorrow morning he'll become the fastest political convert in history. With any luck he'll hang himself. The black American doctor from the Camberley clinic was an added problem: he had undoubtedly carried out a thorough examination of his unexpected patient. His life hung on how thorough he had been. Others would be investigating that at that very moment.

The lights went out in the house.

'Good thing they don't keep servants, sir,' said the waiting driver of the first car.

'Good thing for the servants,' observed Sanders, seeing shadowy figures leave the house, making for their car. He entered his own. 'It's up to the police now,' he smiled.

The big white and orange Rover shrieked to a halt behind the third fire-engine in line. Two policemen jumped out, arms thrown up against the sudden heat and smouldering, whirling ashes.

'That's her,' one pointed, indicating a distressed Asian woman in a nightdress, its hem wet and soiled, a red ambulance blanket over her shoulders.

'Looks bad,' said his colleague. 'Best go easy.'

'Come on.'

A team of firemen ran past with a hose fat from pressure, almost knocking them over. 'Out of the way!' one bawled. A huge crash followed his words and sparks burst in a fire-cloud over the scene.

'Shit!'

'That's it! Roof's down!' one of the firemen called to a poised ambulance stretcher team. 'Sorry, lads.'

The team leant the stretcher against an ambulance. One of them glanced at the sobbing woman, then turned away.

The policeman hovered, awaiting their moment.

A red-headed white girl comforting the Asian woman murmured something, causing her to turn.

'Mrs Livesey?' one officer enquired of the Asian.

'Doctor Livesey,' corrected the red-head, fiercely.

'You and your husband are both doctors?'

The red-head gave a withering look.

The two officers glanced at the inferno that had been the Blackwater Clinic.

'We have to ask a couple of questions. Sorry.'

'Can't it wait?' snapped the red-head.

213

'It's all right, Moira,' said Susheela Livesey. 'What do you need to know?'

'We received a call from your husband, reporting possible intruders?'

She wiped tears away, brusquely. 'He heard – thought he heard – noises from the administrative section.'

'That's where, ma'am?' asked the second officer.

She pointed to the heart of the fire without looking.

'Did he go and check things himself? We always warn callers to use extreme caution under these circumstances.'

'My husband's an American from New York City. He would never consider doing anything that stupid. He knows cornered criminals can resort quickly to violence.' Now she faced the fire and the tears streamed.

'But he er . . . . went in there? Doctor Livesey?'

'He went into the laboratory in the same block. I begged him not to. He wouldn't listen. He was frantic.'

'Why? Why did he go in there? Something special?'

The second policeman shifted uncomfortably. 'Nothing dangerous, was there? Something we should know about?'

Still looking at the fire, she shook her head and smiled. 'Dangerous? Hardly. Life-saving. A miracle. He thought he had won the Nobel for certain. And now this. Why? Senseless. Cruel.' She slumped and the red-head caught her, enveloping the small body again.

'Perhaps you'd better go to hospital, ma'am?'

'This is a hospital, you idiot,' the red-head retorted.

'Moira!'

'It's all right, Doctor, we understand.'

'So your husband went into the lab after the fire started?' the second officer persisted.

'Correct,' the red-head answered. 'We both tried to stop him. He just pushed us off. He was very fit.'

'Do you know what he was after, miss?'

'We took in a patient. You brought him in. Police. Last Wednesday. Early hours. Thought it was an attempted suicide. It was something to do with him.'

'You're who?'

'Moira Wilson. Nurse. Here. Well . . .' She glanced ruefully at the burning ruin.

214

One of the officers murmured an aside. 'Dave Barnes mentioned something about that – him and Thompson together. Got a good rucking a couple of days later for not bringing him straight into the nick.'

'How was it to do with this man, Miss Wilson?' asked his colleague, nodding acknowledgement.

Susheela Livesey lifted her face. 'She doesn't know – nor do I. Not completely. Ray, my husband, wouldn't say anything beyond the fact that he believed he had found the basis of a possible cure for AIDS.'

The policemen glanced at each other.

She bridled. 'You think he'd give his life for nothing? It had to be genuine!'

'Can't you carry on where he left off?' said one, placatingly.

She shrieked wildly, piercing the noise of the fire and the hoses: 'It's *burned* – can't you see!'

Nigel Lewin awoke naked on the floor of the windowless stainless steel cell, his short legs splayed out before him, his mind half-numbed.

Cold. Why was everything so sodding cold?

'Lewin?' a voice from somewhere enquired. 'Identify the amphetamines you are using.'

'Am I nicked? I want a solicitor.'

'You have illegally entered a sensitive military area. Any civil rights you have are suspended. Answer the question: the substance?'

'Speed. Look in the waistband of my tracksuit bottoms – I've a few left.'

Silence.

Lewin scratched at his arm, dislodging a small surgical plaster. He peeled it back, seeing the red needle-prick and blued flesh. He felt hazy yet sharp, nerves taut.

The floor came up and slammed into his testicles. He shrieked, his body arched, shaking wildly.

The power died.

He slumped, trembling, a hammer pounding in his chest. 'You bastards,' he croaked, dragging himself up, his limbs

215

made useless by the electric shock. He fell, raging blindly at his unseen inquisitors.

'Lewin, we know your name from your press card. You share an address with a senior police officer?'

He gasped. 'Lodger. I'm his lodger, OK? He'll be wondering where I am. Let me go. Please?' He found he was dribbling and wiped it away in disgust.

'The old man. Your relationship with him?'

'What old man?'

'In the engine house. We let him go.'

'Let *me* go.'

'We need answers.'

'All right.'

'Your relationship?'

'With bloody George? Money. Fifty quid. I wanted to know a bit about this place. He seemed to have some ideas.'

'Ideas?'

Fear was returning. Darkness, white shapes; *level nine*.

'Where's George?'

'Escorted to his home. His ideas?'

Gave up his Luger just like that, did he?

'Thought this place was a luxury bolt-hole for senior government figures in case of nuclear war. Dartmoor Hilton. Great stuff for the radical comics. Papers, not alternative comedians, OK?'

'And what did you think?'

'I'll listen to anyone. I was trying to sell a story.'

'Not seeking locations for a film company?'

What big ears you've got. 'That's the way we work. Tell people you're press and it costs. Listen, let me go, I haven't harmed anything. Just kick me out on to the moor – I'll make my way back. As far as I'm concerned there's no story here – no nothing. All right?'

'You may have been contaminated.'

'I feel fine. Brilliant.'

The shock threw him across the cell.

'Why'd you do that?' he screamed.

Silence.

He heard a slight hum fade and die.

'Come back!' he shouted.

Nothing.

He slumped to the floor, tears threatening but his fight holding. 'Bastards!'

Sod you.

He scanned the cell carefully. Nice government grant for this little lot. Amnesty International inspected and approved, is it? I'm getting out of here and I'm going to have you. Hear me?

Have who? Ministry of Defence? George's photographs and at least one of the poor sods on level nine said yes. And *he*, whoever *he* is, just admitted military.

But who said: Go ahead, do it and don't worry about public opinion because they won't be told? Minister of Defence? The Cabinet? PM? Some secret bloody Star Chamber that Joe Public doesn't know exists?

Go ahead and do what? What was the point of keeping the pathetic, charred horror on level nine alive? He was beyond any medical breakthrough. Beyond hope. Except a miracle. Were they miracle workers? If they were, Jesus Christ wasn't in it with them: he wouldn't go along with electric shocks to the balls.

He shifted position, uneasily. They're going to come back – and they'll do it to you again. Face it.

A new voice said: 'Who sent you here?'

Lewin scrambled to his feet. 'My paper of course.'

'We checked and were told you'd suddenly taken time off. They weren't pleased.'

'All right, I took a commission, freelance, good bread. It's a free world. At least I bloody thought it was!'

'Commission from whom?'

'TV company. I've worked for the producer before.'

'Jane Haversham?'

Lewin's anger spilled. 'Why ask if you know? What's all this about, then?'

'Rudolf Moravec was at the Chelsea mews cottage meeting on Thursday. Haversham confided in one of our people. We need to know more regarding him.'

'Moravec? Listen, I'm a reporter from the sticks – don't ask me what someone like Rudolf Moravec thinks or does.'

'But you know his intentions regarding our young man?'

217

'Adam?'

'That's what you call him?'

'That's what he calls himself.'

'First impression on his mind. It would follow. This facility of his, his apparent precognition. You witnessed this yourself?'

'I was shown proof. I didn't see him. I asked to, they said no, OK?'

'What are Moravec's intentions?'

'Come on! Mega-bucks – for Moravec.'

'He doesn't understand.'

'*I* don't sodding understand! All Moravec understands is making money, all right?'

'This is beyond money.'

'You're living in the wrong decade, mate.'

The original, harder voice returned: 'Moravec is interested in the origins of our man. That's why you're here.'

Our Man, Lewin repeated, silently. God speaking? Our creation. Real fear hit him, worse even that the shocks. He wanted to curl up on the floor, in the corner, but there was nowhere to hide. Not from what he'd seen on level nine.

'I'm here for the money. Please let me go.'

'Who else knows?'

'Knows about Adam?'

'About us.'

Lewin slumped. 'Look, I keep telling you. I don't know what's going on here. Just don't tell me, OK? I don't want to know. I just want out.'

'The young woman at the meeting. Who was she?'

'Phillida Melman. Just a gofer, like me. A nothing, all right?'

'We need names brought up at the meeting. Anyone involved or to be informed?'

'Eleanor Hale.'

'We know about Eleanor Hale.'

'I don't want to know.'

'Anyone else?'

'Her son, Daniel.'

218

'That was the start of the problem,' said the voice. hard edged with recrimination as if to another.

'Let me go.'

'You entered level nine.'

'I'm all right, I swear.'

'You don't understand.'

'I'll trade information if you let me go.'

The shock lifted him high, pinning his body to the steel wall. He screamed. The power died. He dropped, hard, on to his knees. He smelt singed hair; then vomited.

'Lewin?'

He lifted his face, tears streaming, his voice a series of gasps. 'They had a theory. Someone was performing illegal medical experiments – on people. They wanted me to find out who. They thought it might be sanctioned by government. Adam escaped from wherever these experiments were being done. That's as far as they got. I was to find the place because I know the area. That's everything, I swear it.'

'What did you think of their theory?'

Lewin was racked by a fit of retching. 'Wait! Please don't. No more. I told Moravec what would really sell was finding out where the people used in the experiments came from. I said I could. I'm bloody clever like that!'

'Yes,' said the voice and the hum died.

'Fuck you,' murmured Lewin. He smelt something that was not his singed hair, or his vomit; an odour, faint and tantalizing. And threatening. He tried, desperately, to raise his bowed head but couldn't. The fight drained from him. Amid gathering shadows he wished he had told Peter Foley everything.

Foley telephoned his Exeter home again, taunted once more by Lewin's smiling, recorded voice. He stabbed at the cut-off tab and glared at the purring receiver. 'I have to call a colleague,' he told Mayberry after a moment. 'I can guarantee his discretion.'

'Guarantee all you like but don't give this number and don't tell him where you are and who you're with.'

'You'd better listen in.' Foley dialled Detective Inspector

Grant's Exeter home. A blurred voice answered, struggling to sound sharp.

'Grant? Foley. Wake yourself up.'

'Hang on.'

Foley heard water being gulped.

'God! Throat like a camel's crotch. Super, you're man-of-the-week and no one can find you. Call in, you're wanted.'

'Who by?'

'I noted the names in my book. You'll have to hold again, sorry.'

Foley covered the mouthpiece. 'Something's up. Listen.'

'I'd be surprised if there wasn't,' commented Mayberry, still tapping mysteriously into his keyboard. He lifted the telephone on his work-station.

'Got it. A Colonel Southby. Ministry of Defence. Wants you to call him urgently. He's renewed that message at least three times I know of. Left his home number – because of the weekend. Got a pen?'

Foley wrote in his flip-pad.

'Also some bigwig from Whitehall. Listen, he's been on to the top brass – like I said, you're a wanted man.'

'Never mind about that. Name?'

'It's your pension. Name's Nesbitt: that's double "t". Oh, he's a *Sir* David, though that probably won't bother you either.'

'Which patch of Whitehall is his? One of the funnies, is he?'

'No. Comes under the umbrella of Environment, Department of – so he says. Chairman of some policy study group: Ecology and Human Resources. You're to contact him immediately. Immediately was yesterday, by the way.'

'Grant. The car. Daniel Hale's Jag. It was used in an armed incident in London tonight. A serious armed incident. Not a siege, so it's over now. I want you to request that the vehicle is either turned over to us or that we have access to it. We have priority. The car was taken from the scene of an ongoing murder investigation. Ours. Previous to the Met incident.'

Grant was silent.

'You there?'

'Can't do that, Super. We *had* a murder investigation. They shut it down: remember VIPER? Doesn't belong to us any more. You're not thinking straight. Obviously this shooting is part of MI5's operation. Bloody IRA, I shouldn't wonder. I'm not bucking a hands-off order. Sorry. I've my career to think about. Wife, kids, dog, mortgage.'

Mayberry clicked his fingers then drew one across his throat.

Foley nodded. 'I understand. No problem. Grant, listen, I didn't call you.'

'See you when I see you then. You are OK, Super?'

'Never better.'

'Remember what I said? There's a whiff about this one. Best stay downwind.'

'I hear what you're saying.'

'But you're not listening?'

'Good night, Grant.' Foley put the receiver down. Mayberry matched him then immediately lifted his again, listened for a couple of seconds then put it down.

'Tapped?'

And recorded,' Mayberry confirmed. 'One day the Brits will stop muddling through and update their bugging equipment. Jesus, we invent the best there is.'

'What do you think?'

'Grant tends to be your confidant on cases? That a known thing around the place?'

'It's accepted. We work well together. He's sharper than most.'

'Then he'd be the one, wouldn't he? The one they'd pick on. I'd say they've got a recorder on voice activation, and some poor devil half-asleep or bored out of his mind monitoring.'

'Don't see it. I've given them – whoever – no reason to be concerned. And your electronic peeping you say is secure. And you haven't mentioned me? Correct?'

'I'm not their source, Peter Foley. They've picked up young Nigel, I'd guess. Even if he hasn't involved you directly – told them about his letter to you, that is – they'll have found out he lives with you. That would be enough to cause them to act. Consider their position: they've got the media going for them, hard. Moravec's a pretty big gun in anyone's terms, even if Nigel's his poor bloody infantry. You've got your teeth firmly into a case they want dropped – then you make a sudden trip to London and duck into cover. They have to act to protect themselves. I would. Wouldn't you?'

Foley stood up, agitated, almost too tired to think. 'We don't know who we're dealing with. Who to fight.'

'Southby is the MOD Colonel who called you initially regarding Eleanor Hale?'

'Yes. He was concerned by her telephone call – and the "accident".'

'I'm not the detective here but I'd say that makes him clean. He brought you into all of this.'

'True.'

'Call him.'

'Is it safe?'

Mayberry shrugged. 'God knows. How far do the tentacles spread? If his line is tapped they must have known about his call to you – which involves your Chief Constable, as he was the one who put you and Southby together. Correct?'

'I suppose so. Yes. Correct. *Christ*.'

'I somehow doubt it. The matter could have been shunted into some police siding and lost, couldn't it? It didn't have to come to a star like you.'

'I could have been the siding – in his view.'

'Oh dear, we are low, aren't we? Have another coffee.'

'I'll call Southby now,' Foley said, decisively.

'At this hour of the morning? My word!'

'Bollocks.'

'Two of my favourite things.'

Foley glared, dialling.

A crisp but tense voice came on the line almost immediately. 'Southby here.'

'Colonel, Detective Superintendent Foley. Sorry about –'

'Where are you? London? Your chap said you'd come up. I need to see you – right away.'

'What's the problem?'

222

'Not on the telephone. If you can't get to me I'll get to you.'

'Address?'

'Apartment just down from Hyde Park Corner. Towards Bayswater. Know the area?'

'I'm a Londoner originally.'

'Good man. Take this down.'

Foley wrote.

'Right away then. Where are you?'

'Rather not say.'

'Understood. Don't delay.'

'I'm leaving now. Goodbye.' Foley stood, turned towards Mayberry. 'Will you find out everything you can about this Nesbitt character?'

Mayberry sat, still and serious. 'Knight of the realm, no less! Chairman of a policy study group. What was it, Ecology and Human Resources? That covers an awful lot, doesn't it? The environment we live in and us who live in it. Serious power, and a subtle – quite beautiful actually – cover for wielding it. Power over the land, sea, air – and the people. There's nothing they could not legitimately dip their clever fingers into. Maybe we've finally got a face and name for *them*?'

'Can you hack into Nesbitt's organization?'

'Peter Foley, there are some things one never messes with because one instinctively knows when one is out of one's depth, and I hate water closing over my head.'

'You're saying this is as far as you go?'

'Absolutely.'

'What about Nigel?'

'Nigel – if they have him – will either be released or end up as an accident statistic.'

'Why the sudden change of heart?'

'Because when someone as powerful as a Nesbitt comes out from under the murky Whitehall grey and takes a long hard look at you then you know the time has come to reassess your commitment to toppling windmills. The windmills usually win.'

'Nesbitt called me, not you.'

'Correct. And I don't intend for his interest to expand in my direction.'

'I'm certainly not going to mention your involvement.'

Mayberry smiled. 'The strength of real power lies in the fact that it encompasses almost everything. Nothing, no one is free from scrutiny. Minute scrutiny if need be. That is why and indeed how small groups of powerful men can rule banana republics – or superpowers.'

'Britain is not a totalitarian state.'

'Everywhere is a totalitarian state. It's only a question of the degree – or the subtlety.'

'You're more cynical than Nigel Lewin,' observed Foley settling his jacket over his shoulders. 'But thanks for your help up to now.'

Mayberry ducked his head at a monitor. 'I've more reason to be. Suggestion, Detective Superintendent. Go home. Do your time. Collect the pension. Enjoy life.'

'Forget tilting at windmills?'

'They've always been there, they always will be.'

They had climbed up to Mayberry's amazing front door.

Foley said: 'Don't worry, I'll not say a word of what you've got here.'

Mayberry winked as the door hissed open. 'Come up and see me some time,' he said, in perfect Mae West.

Foley stood outside alone, the scent of the river strong after the sanitized environment of Mayberry's computer room. Something hooted. Ship? Owl? The Ripper's ghost, having a laugh at his perverse compulsion to hunt on, courting his own downfall? The strains of country music drifted down to him: Faron Young's recording of 'It's Four in the Morning'. He looked at his watch. 'Not bloody funny.'

He walked to the BMW, grunted when he saw the convertible's hood was unscathed, checked tyres and lights then got in.

'Let's see what keeps you awake till four in the morning, Colonel,' he muttered, starting the engine.

Southby was a sandy man. Hair, eyebrows, moustache: all of him. And tall, with quick amber eyes which swept over

Foley as if sizing him up for battle. But his own battlefield days were over, the solid hawthorn stick propped against a stiff left leg as evidence.

'Inside,' he urged.

From the hard-edged spartan furnishings of the apartment, Foley knew no woman shared the soldier's life. Tended it, perhaps, temporarily, paid or otherwise; but definitely did not share.

'Sit. Do yourself a drink if you like. I've the usual things, there on the table.'

'I'm all right, thanks.'

'Good for you. Wish I had your resolve. Do me a Scotch, splash of soda – will you? Hate this leg. Bloody crab most of the time.'

'Where'd it happen?'

Southby's lips twisted under his moustache. 'Bloody Ireland. Russians – via the Czechs – handed out some new experimental high-velocity rounds to the Provisionals. Took one in the leg getting out of a vehicle. One entry wound, about fifty exits: wiped out all the important bits. Probably get more response out of one of the new artificial bolt-ons – but hell!'

'I'd feel the same.'

'Good. Thanks. Cheers.'

Foley had given himself a tonic water. He sipped, waiting.

Southby stretched forward, his face a grimace. 'Here. For you. Someone like you, anyway. Policeman. I've opened it as you see – instructions were for me to read it then make contact with the officer in charge of the case. That's you.'

Foley stared blankly at the bulky slit-open yellowed envelope, the thick wax seal intact, dark red and cracking a little from age, the initials SJH intertwined and proud.

'I've put the explanatory note inside,' said Southby. 'Read that first.'

Foley extracted a single sheet of high quality notepaper.

The printed address stated Raethmoor Farm. He looked up. 'Eleanor Hale?'

'Quite.'

'How did you get this, Colonel Southby?'

'Forget the "th". As in sou'west.'

'Your first name's not Rafe by any chance?'

'Charles. Why?'

'Doesn't matter. The letter?'

'Post. First class. Yesterday. Thought it might be a letter bomb at first but I saw the postmark and immediately thought of that bright, bloody marvellous old lady. Read it.'

Foley sat a little further back into the hard, buttoned leather chair. Eleanor Hàle's copperplate hand was exquisite, with only a slight wavering in the strokes to give away her age. He read:

My dear Colonel Southby,

I must put aside pleasantries and get immediately to the heart of the matter. Please find enclosed a last statement written and sealed by my late husband Samuel whom I know you met on various occasions. If my memory serves me well these were usually in action when my husband was visiting trouble-spots which we British are so good at being drawn into. It is for that reason – you only relatively recently being brought into the mainstream of things so to speak – that I pass, and please forgive me for doing so, this responsibility, this dreadful weight, on to you.

When you receive this letter, I suspect that I shall have left my home here on the moors, quite possibly having given a most plausible explanation for my disappearance. Do not believe it.

Equally it is possible I shall have been the victim of an attack by criminals or suffered an accident. Fatally in either instance. Once again I urge you not to take any explanation of my death at face value.

Please do not consider me a deranged old woman until you have read the statement I bequeath to you. You will see that it is sealed and that the seal remains intact. I did not need to read the contents myself as I know – God forgive me – most, if not all, already.

That which I don't know I have no wish to add to my already heavy-burdened conscience.

Treat what you read as fact, Colonel. Do not be tempted to think that such things could not happen – either here in England or for that matter in any civilized country in this racing-headlong-to-destruction world of ours: it has happened before and it is happening now.

I realize that by placing my husband's memoir, his legacy, in your hands I am, wittingly, endangering your own life – therefore may I suggest you make contact with the police officer who may be in charge of any enquiry into my disappearance or death and show him this letter which he may accept as an affidavit of my fears for my life and safety.

When you have read the enclosed you may wonder why I've been left alive for so long after Samuel's suicide. I too have considered this. I think they either thought another unnatural death at Raethmoor might have been suspicious or, more likely, they simply considered an ageing, reclusive woman no threat to them at all. In the latter case, they were right. I was no threat. While I lived. But perhaps in death, with your help, and God's blessing – for it is truly He who has been betrayed – I can bring retribution down on the heads of those who carry out this devil's work.

One final word of warning which again I beg you not to dismiss lightly. These are powerful men: unelected, unaccountable, and unidentified, with powerful forces at their disposal: they believe utterly in the correctness of what they are doing – as once did my husband – and this makes them deadly. Remember your Keats? 'Fanatics have their dream, wherewith they weave a paradise for a sect.' Ruthless fanaticism can only be halted if it is devalued by reason. I tried to be the voice of reason to Samuel but his mind, his sensibilities, his humanity, had all been pushed too near the edge of the precipice. The shotgun was his way of stopping himself falling into the pit. He couldn't save himself but at least he saved his soul. God bless him, and you, and any you choose to recruit in this fight for man's integrity. Forgive me once again for placing this burden upon you.

    In gratitude,

      Eleanor Hale

The wavering hand was fear, not age, thought Foley.

'Don't dismiss her as a churchy old biddy whose marbles have gone,' warned Southby.

'Believe me, I have no intention of doing so.'

Foley took out the remaining contents from the thick yellowed envelope.

'You were army once. I checked. I suggest you give yourself a real drink before you look at that,' advised Southby, utterly serious.

Foley caught something unreadable – but disturbing – in the soldier's eyes. He got up, found cognac and gave himself a little. He began reading, saw the date of the heading and was a child again, sitting on one of the grassy hummocks which buried his school's soon-to-be-obsolete air-raid shelters in unmarked graves, wondering what would replace the sights and sounds of war in the promised peace. But Samuel Hale's world of that time was not one for children. Even in their worst nightmares. Foley walked in a suicide's footsteps, saw through his eyes, lived the torture that had led inexorably, down the years, to the hour of the gun. He read, but he was *there*.

TWELVE

1945

Enemy air-raids were so rare by then they could have held the final meeting in one of Whitehall's surface buildings perfectly safely had it not been for the need for absolute secrecy. As it was they met in the bowels of the underground complex, with pipes, like intestines, gurgling and bubbling, leading to or from no one knew where.

Samuel Hale waited with impatience, resorting to glaring fixedly at the willowy intellectual from some Oxbridge college – brought in, he decided, as a sop to democratic procedure – who droned on for too long with all the weary moral arguments against the mission. Indeed, against the entire concept.

Hale shuffled his notes together like a gambler with cards. In a way, that was what he, and others equally committed, were: gamblers with man's future in the pot, the stakes enormous, the risks higher – but then they were certain there was no other choice.

The decision by the Americans to use the new minimally tested atomic weapon with its deadly side-effects had forced all the players to the table, aware that if they were to win in the long term they must play the most devious hand of all: to steal from the enemy that which would soon brand him inhuman in the eyes of the world.

The protesting don wound up: 'In closing let me say this: if God Almighty returns to this earth in some distant future to seek the descendants of Adam, be certain that if the footprint he finds does not match that of his original creation he need only seek out the heirs of the men in this room tonight to apportion the blame. And most particularly, that man there!'

Samuel Hale smiled bleakly, nodded perfunctorily at his critic and arose.

'Gentlemen: if God Almighty did come down at some future time, he would be entitled to an explanation for any change in the genetic structure of man as he planned and created it, and our heirs would have no difficulty in justifying their deeds. Be certain of this: the use of atomic energy as a weapon – or even as a tool – will cause change in human beings. Radiation triggers gene mutation, we are well aware of that – and potentially damaging sources of radiation are expanding rapidly. The invention of television combined with the techniques of mass production developed during the war could mean that by the end of the century even the humblest homes might possess such a device for entertainment. From these devices flow a small but constant amount of radiation. Also, when our supply of fossil fuels becomes seriously depleted we shall undoubtedly turn to atomic energy to power our cities, our industries. These power stations too will leak small but constant levels of radiation into the atmosphere. There will be other sources as time goes on. Do not doubt this.'

'You're exaggerating, surely,' snapped the don.

'Am I? Does anyone know enough about the atom and its lethal potential at this time to take the risk that I am not?'

'We don't need persuading,' interrupted the chairman of the group. 'Or convincing. We are well aware that the Russians are within striking distance of this Nazi facility and that this operation is necessary to your research.'

'Essential,' corrected Hale.

'Very well – essential. But how do we justify such an operation to a public soon to be appraised of the unspeakable horrors perpetrated by the Hitler regime? If we condemn these acts – as surely we must – we cannot in the same voice say we intend to use the results of experiments made on people taken from these dreadful concentration camps.'

Hale's face displayed his alarm. 'The work done in this particular experimental unit must not be made public! This is not the butchery of sadistic quacks given a free hand in

230

the camps. From the technical information passed on to our intelligence service by the informant inside the establishment we know just how important, how serious this work is. The fact of this facility having been kept utterly secret until the dying moments of the war is evidence of that. It is absolutely vital for us to get those results. If we don't, the Soviets most certainly will – with all that that entails. I say again: the people must not be told. To do so would provoke an outcry which would finish the project and kill all our hopes of making man a stronger animal to face an uncertain, possibly hostile, environment in the future.'

'You realize you're advocating conspiracy on an historic scale?'

'All history is conspiracy. How else do events which forge change materialize?'

'You ask too much,' complained the don, knowing his cause was lost but desperate to leave his mark on the battlefield.

Hale shook his head. 'Our children's children might well say I didn't ask enough. When you are in danger of losing your life in battle you do not reject a weapon dropped by your enemy because it has been used to kill your comrades!'

'That is hardly a fair analogy.'

'Fairness does not enter into the matter. Survival is simply a question of who is the fittest. The best adapted. To be the best adapted is our task.'

'We are agreed,' confirmed their chairman. 'The operation shall be mounted and carried out with all speed. The results of the Nazi experiments shall be taken immediately to the place designated for the purpose of evaluating and furthering the work and shall be funded from the Secret Vote until such time as permission to continue is withdrawn by us or our successors. We understand you have a suggestion to cover the actual purpose of the unit?'

'Department of Advanced Medicine. We could come under the Ministry of Health umbrella.'

'No. You open yourself to too much scrutiny. Health is simply . . . too public. The location for your work is on land owned by the Ministry of War?'

'Dartmoor. The army use a considerable area of the moor for training purposes and also for trials of new types of gas and, I understand, a research and experimental facility for biological weapons.'

'We may be able to inject additional funding if you have some – at least ostensible – army connection. An extra budget to draw from if the need arose. Such a project must entail enrolling the very best minds and they won't come cheaply.'

'The Germans we offer amnesty to will work unpaid,' stated Hale. 'That will be the basis of the deal.'

'For a fixed period. We are not Nazis. We won't sanction slavery. You're presuming you will bring the top people out alive?'

'That is the intention.'

The chairman stood. 'Very well. So, Army Department of Advanced Medicine? Try, somehow, to tie your work in with whoever has control of this germ-weapons facility. That sort of thing tends to keep people from prying. Afraid they might catch something!'

Hale nodded. 'Regarding our need for experimental subjects? We discussed this at an earlier meeting. Prisons? Men due to be executed?'

'We agree to your using the . . . remains . . . of those who are without direct next of kin or who are to be executed for spying. Please remember that any actions you take regarding your work are entirely your responsibility. We will deny any knowledge of your activities. You will exist as part of an army research department with links to their medical corps, which will benefit you materially. No record has been kept of this or any previous meetings. They simply did not take place. The same applies to the German operation.'

'Understood,' said Hale.

'You had better be given an army rank. For the sake of good order.'

They filed out, leaving him to deal with the commando officer who seemed absurdly young to be a silent killer. He thought of them as barons: equally as powerful as those who had forced John to Runnymede and the Magna Charta.

ADAM, Hale mused, afterwards. Apt for the creation of a new man or, more accurately, an adaptation of the old. But he did not feel at all like God. God would not be terrified of being dropped by parachute in the dead of night.

They moved like shadows and killed in silence, the garrotte and blade their chosen weapons, striking in darkness near the heart of the enemy whilst invasion forces launched their attack on his armoured flanks.

'What'll we find when we get in there?' murmured their young commander, his blackened face close to Hale's.

'Horror,' came the taut reply. 'And knowledge. Years of research. They've had the time, the freedom, and the means.'

'So your ends justify their means?'

'I'm not here to judge – just to appropriate.'

'Will it be worth the human cost?'

A black-clad figure emerged from the darkness and slumped before them, rank vomit on his breath and staining his tunic. 'Secured,' he gasped, turned away and retched drily.

Hale started forward. 'You've signed away your right of protest. You, your men, I, were never here. What we take out never existed. Neither history nor the British government will ever record any of it. Forget it all.'

'And what about the future?'

'The future is why we're here,' said Hale and started forward.

They entered hell and it was cold.

The chamber was dully lit, refrigerated, and filled with complex electronic equipment and glowing glass tanks: the victims inside these floated in liquid suspension with rubber tubes exiting body orifices while unknown substances were fed into major veins. Beside these, smaller tanks contained various body organs connected to the still, barely breathing, hairless white forms. Two held human brains, a third, a complete severed head.

Hale caught sight of this and turned away, his rapid breathing visible in the chilled air.

The officer gagged. 'Oh Christ!'

Recovering, he moved hesitantly towards the tank and lowered himself to his haunches, facing the white, shaven-headed, seemingly sexless face.

The eyelids flickered, then opened wide, the eyes a mute scream.

He drew back in horror. 'That's not possible.'

Hale came up beside him. 'They've made it possible. Everything in here is alive although I'm certain that no one here is quite the same as when they arrived.'

'What are we going to do with them?'

Hale laid a hand on his shoulder. 'It's probable they would die the instant we removed them from their conditioned environment. The truth is they died as soon as they arrived here. What you're witnessing is artificial life. In our lifetime we shall see many people kept alive on machines who might otherwise have died.'

'Never. That's something out of Frankenstein.'

'It will happen.'

'What good are these – things – to you? What good can come of this, for God's sake?'

'The records of their time here, the work done on them, are vital to us. Some have been subjected to stresses, forces, environmental conditions, which none of your men – notwithstanding their supreme fitness – could hope to survive. Others have been the subject of experimental organ transplantation – and survived. Think of the lives that will save in the future.'

'It's barbaric.'

'We now consider surgery at its infancy to have been barbaric, yet those crude beginnings have given us the life-saving techniques we have today.'

'That's entirely different.'

'It's not. Certainly what the Nazis have done here is cruel and perhaps crude – but it has been effective. This is a new beginning for man.'

The young officer turned away from the face, his eyes brimming. 'And the end for humanity.'

'One day you'll understand.'

'Nothing will ever make me understand this.'

Hale turned, walking towards a group of shivering prisoners dressed in pyjamas and held in a tight circle by grim-faced commandos. He called out four names.

The men hesitantly identified themselves just before others in the circle gave them away.

'These go back with us,' Hale ordered.

A very tall man shouldered his way through the group, his blue eyes shrewd. 'They might be the top men but I know more about the project than all of them together,' he said in good English.

'You think your evidence in defence will be better regarded than theirs?'

'You're not putting them on trial. You're planning to use their brains, not to punish them.'

Realization touched Hale's eyes. 'You're the one who made contact with our intelligence people. You have plenty of nerve. We thought you were dead for certain, after your information dried up.'

'I stopped because it was the only way to get you to move. To get you over here before it was too late. I'm alive and my mind is as good as my nerve. My name is Erich Hartrampf. I think we share the same dream.'

Hale glanced quickly around the dreadful chamber. 'Perhaps not the same methods in achieving it.'

'When there are no restrictions, excesses are inevitable.'

'I shall remember those words, Eric Hartrampf.'

'Then you will take me back with you?'

Hale nodded.

'What about the rest of these ... people?' the young officer demanded, white with anger and shock.

'What would you do with them, Captain?'

'Shoot the lot! No trial, no jury, no humanity. They don't deserve any.'

'Then do it. Quickly. Afterwards set your explosives to destroy this place completely. I want no recognizable trace of what it was used for when the Russians come smashing through here in a few days' time.'

The officer ducked his head at the glowing glass tanks. 'And them?'

'There's nothing we can do. I'm sorry.'

'They're living dead anyway.'

235

'Then they'll find peace,' said Hale, and meant it.

The destruction had been total. Foley could almost feel the heat and blast of the high explosive as he lived with Hale through those final moments in the heartland of a dying but dangerous enemy.

He took up the second, stapled, group of pages, eager to return to Hale's world, his need for answers urgent.

'To whom it may concern,' the heading proclaimed.

Me, thought Foley. I'm the one sitting in judgement.

Familiar with the outpourings of suicides, he knew what would be on the sheets: an apologia aching with self-blame, self-doubt, hopelessness, and lost will. He wanted no part of it, yet knew he was already too far down the bitter road to turn back.

Southby read his mind – or his expression. 'Expect you've read a lot of those? Suicide notes? This is more than just that. It's an indictment. Of himself and of an ideal he became disenchanted with.'

Foley nodded, sipped his cognac, not tasting it, and read:

Eleanor, my dearest,

This is not for you, for you already know all there is to know. It is, however, for you to pass on when the time is right. You will know when. When you have done so, protect yourself, for they will surely attempt to destroy you. Forgive me. There is no other way. None. Not while retaining what is left of my sanity. My integrity and all those other idealistic things went by the board so very long ago.

So goodbye, my dearest, this is not an end but perhaps a better new beginning than the dream I had.

They? asked Foley of the finger pointing accusingly from the grave. Tell me who *they* are and I'll give her justice.

He read on:

I assume whoever reads this will be someone trusted by my wife; someone she considers strong enough to

236

carry this burden and accept the dangers of being in possession of this knowledge.

You will already have read my account of the meeting of the steering group in 1945 and of the mission they sanctioned. Those events were, in part, the beginning. The dream before the nightmare. Or, the dream which became the nightmare.

A group of us, research scientists in the field of genetics and equally disturbed members of the team involved in the development of atomic weapons, met to bring our concern for the human race into the open. War-time secrecy was killing free debate and the politicians and the generals held the future in their hands: their dangerously misguided, inexpert hands. I became our group's spokesman – their leader, although we rejected that sort of concept as a matter of principle. We decided that going to politicians of whatever persuasion would be a regressive step and we would never put our ideas, our dream, into the hands of generals or entrust it to any military mind. The power it could give either group could be awesome – and lethal. Indeed it may well prove to be so. But not, thank God, in my lifetime.

Therefore we went instead to the oldest power grouping in this great land of ours. Oldest, in the sense of the longest serving, having the greatest history, an imbued sense of tradition and honour and generally being above politics despite the fact they have their own chamber in Parliament.

The 'facts' we placed at their disposal were our detailed and deeply researched view of how the world as we knew it would be changed by the power of the atom, as both weapon and tool. The danger of mutation of the species was our greatest fear and therefore our most strident warning. We knew that mutation would occur. Monsters might be created. However, this was not the worst of it. We were convinced that, genetically, man would be changed. Changes would take place on a massive scale and be made irreversible by propagation. 'Normal' man as we

237

knew him would become a minority within two to three centuries. The mutants, baser versions of *homo sapiens*, would have power by numbers.

The greatest danger in our argument was that Adolf Hitler had, in another direction and with political motivation, put his distorted ideas into practice. His theories could be viewed as not dissimilar to ours. Hitler saw man as being already divided and sub-divided. A present state. We forecast the actuality of this but for a future time. A time would come when the best of what is in us would be removed, wiped out, lost from the blueprint of life we all carry. Our cause, our dream, was to create a strain of man so pure, so strong genetically, that he could withstand anything the future would bring.

Foley looked up at Southby.

'Hardly believable, is it?' said the Colonel.

'They were advocating a master race.'

'Not just advocating. The worst is yet to come.'

Foley read on:

The men we dealt with followed our reasoning but were far from convinced at the outset. It took months before any hard decisions were taken. We needed finance and influence desperately and only they could help us. We lived in fear of the growing Socialist movement in Britain which permeated intellectual levels like a disease. If the Socialists got wind of what we proposed they would hound us to our graves, for our ideas were, to them, heresy: worse, to their rigid, blinkered minds we advocated the heinous philosophy of their deadliest political enemy, the Fascists. For the Socialists, the political war was not yet won: indeed it was only just beginning and we, if they discovered our existence, were the enemy.

Finally, because our backers feared the spread of Socialist doctrine to the masses and, ultimately, its establishment as a political force in Britain, they gave us everything we needed. Including the means to steal from under Hitler's nose the results of ultra-secret work done by the cream of his scientists.

How stupid we are to believe that a nation which at that time was more advanced than the rest of the world in every scientific field would have only quacks and charlatans conducting sadistic, pseudo-medical experiments with pointless results! That happened certainly, but it was no more than the excesses of degenerates. The *real* minds were hard at work researching the secret of life; rebuilding man to as near perfection as was possible.

We all became willing victims of our post-war propaganda. After all, who wants to think of himself as less than perfect if he functions normally already?

The concept of the blond blue-eyed powerful Aryan may be a myth from early history revived to satisfy a madman's racial fantasies but the blueprint for the genetic engineering of such a man or woman is no myth: it is reality. Colouring is merely a matter of choice and perfect physique may be sculptured in the womb – or in truth, before the womb, even before conception. We found the first of the future men in secret bunkers deep in a German forest and we destroyed him. Then we stole the blueprints to start again in England.

That is when the nightmare first lifted the edge of the dream and crept into our secret beds.

I suppose, in retrospect, I should have known that the direction we were taking was so close to Hitler's perverted visions that unless a firm hand was kept on the tiller we could soon stray on to dangerous rocks. The problem was we were all young men, idealists, who were simply too weak against the forces which were ultimately to control us. We had no strong leader, no one who could stand up against either the will of the Germans we had brought back or their depth of knowledge. They were years ahead of us. Decades. We were children, they the teachers. Worse, a kindergarten class within the walls of their university.

They soon convinced us, somehow, that their route

was the best one to follow – despite our moral objections. In very little time afterwards they had the men of power and influence eating out of their hands. Nothing was too much to give. Not if they could deliver the dream.

The problem was: whose dream was it now? And what *was* the dream? Certainly not one of saving man from himself any more. With each passing year it became more a matter of creating a model who would fit, without demur, into a society in which he made no decisions. In fact the very foundations of his being would be decided by others. Before birth.

No longer was it future man we were planning but pliable man, programmed man, his genes engineered for the role he would play out in life. Illness abolished; health written in. We started to believe that this was how God should have planned it. Except God has an infinite number of combinations which He rarely, if ever, repeats in human beings, and we poor humans with our limited intelligence and vision can only produce mass mediocrity – like cars on a production line, colours and options varying but to what degree?

The Germans won the war. Our war, if not the world war – although sometimes I wondered if they had not won that too.

Inevitably Erich Hartrampf gained overall power and used it ruthlessly. The men who backed us – new members entering the conspiracy all the time – saw him as genius personified. The answers to all their prayers. His promises were the promises they might have asked for themselves. He fed them the bread they ate, the drink which quenched their thirst. All without exception wishing for – planning for – an ordered world. A uniform world from which the degenerates, the protestors, the under-achievers, the non-contributors would be eliminated. Not by force, which could provoke violence and civil strife, but gently, silently, secretly before the first heartbeat of life.

But Hartrampf needed more bricks to build their world and told them so. Subjects for experimentation.

Britain had no concentration camps, no ready supply of live human guinea-pigs. The prisons occasionally could be persuaded to give up their hanged dead but Hartrampf – and yes, all of us – needed life to improve life. So we became worse than murderers. We stole God's promise of Peace at the Last and kept life going so that we could perpetrate whatever atrocity – for that is how I came to see our experiments – we decided upon.

As part, however spuriously, of the armed forces we could not have been better placed. There was no better source for young men with no regularised home life, no families, no questioning next of kin: young men who join the forces to become part of a ready-made family and sign away their right to life for Queen and Country.

We began with victims of accidents who fitted the criteria; then, as Britain's minor wars came and went, our supply grew. Our installation bored deeper into the earth, seemingly heading further and further towards hell whose role it seemed to have taken over. Except hell burnt red and we existed in a white world as chilled as a corpse.

This is the truth. Perhaps not all of it because towards the end they more or less locked me out of the important policy meetings and experiments. But enough is here for someone to read and believe – and be outraged by. Who knows how far they've gone since? I shan't because I'll be dead. Their greatest fear is that one of their new strains might manage to escape and propagate. This would be like setting a match to a world dried by drought. Inside every eugenicist's dream is a nightmare waiting to get out. Be certain of one thing. The conspiracy is no longer limited to Britain. Hartrampf spent many years in America, ostensibly practising psychiatry but in reality involved in secret government projects researching the possibility of developing psychic and paranormal abilities in selected human beings. He became for a while engrossed in the concept of 'mixing minds', interconnecting brains at higher-function levels, patching one

241

or more into the receiving brain. He even authorized transplant surgery between subjects with this end in view. His theories, his studies, his results, were considered very seriously indeed at the highest level. Taken to the ultimate, we could be looking, biologically, at something not too dissimilar to a master computer and its terminals. The question is, whose mind shall be master and whose the terminals.

I leave you with a warning. I no longer know who the people are behind what we used to call the ADAM Project but know this: you'll find them amongst the most powerful. By the dawning of the twenty-first century this evil work will be under way in Britain, in America, in Europe, West and East – because frontiers mean nothing to those who control the real power in our world. In time the conflict between differing political ideologies will cease to have meaning, and the barriers will fall because the pursuit of power will no longer be a question of force or coercion but of planning in the womb. East or West, their ultimate goal is total control of the masses by the most cost effective – and certain – means and the ADAM Project is forging the first links of the chains to shackle weaker man to whatever limited future may be allowed him. Therefore, whatever action you might decide to take, take with extreme care. Your life to them is worth only the use your mind and your living body can be put to. Which is why I have made certain that nothing is left of my own brain. I do not wish to enter the world of the tanks where the only reality is the cold and, as I've always believed since the time in Germany when I witnessed with Captain Heatheridge the severed head's eyes open, an awareness of horror at the edge of death-denied.

Perhaps it is all too late. The price we have paid for our children's future may be their lives. When your life's dreams turn to nightmares it is time to die. Goodbye and may God aid you. I cannot believe He could forgive me but, very soon, I shall know.

Samuel Hale

Foley put down the document, absolutely silent.

'Do you believe it?' asked Southby.

'Beyond any doubt.'

'What do you plan to do about it?'

'Tread very carefully.'

'I'm willing to help. The thought of using soldiers . . .' Southby trailed off, his disgust and barely controlled fury halting him.

Foley pulled his shoulders back, his neck aching, more weary than he had been in years, his own outrage tempered by his realization of the probable depth and scale of the conspiracy before him. How far have they come since 1945? What new horrors exist in their secret places? How many secret places? How many indoctrinated 'future men' are ranged against us ordinary, thick human beings? He shook his head, not in defeat but in awe.

'Colonel. This is too big. Too big for just you and me. They killed an old woman. Brutally. That's my direct involvement. My case. They took that away from me. Easily. And who the hell are *they*? These people?' Foley's finger stabbed at Samuel Hale's denouncement. 'I understood I was halted by Five, our own security service. If that's not true, then who the hell else can get away with using Five's powers, Five's channels with impunity? If it is MI5, that's even worse! What do we have here? A secret state within the state? Conspiracy on a scale that doesn't bear thinking about. Whom do we trust? Somehow I've got to break this down into terms I can handle. Like dealing with Freemasons on the force: you don't know if some action you take affects one of them – which means all of them – until quite suddenly you've proved Newton's Third Law and the frailty of your own long-term career planning. I'm trying to get this into manageable proportions for a half-way bright, nearing retirement copper who enjoys an ordered, reasonably quiet life with the option to live what remains of it without threat of sudden termination. I'm saying we'd have to be damn sure about anyone else we showed the Hale document to. Damn sure of anyone we even breathed of its existence to.

'I want to break these people, sure I do. So do you. Show me how! I feel exactly as you do about their using wounded servicemen, Colonel. It's too close to a recurring nightmare I suffer from: Korea, nineteen fifties, I'm in a trench, I hear a shell coming in fast, very close. Too close. It hits. Explodes. I scramble over to the crater. Where there were men, there's nothing. Vaporized. *Nothing*. I stand there and I realize that I was one of the men and I'm stranded until I can find my body. It's a sensation I could live without. Short of actually dying I can't imagine feeling more alone than at that moment. I can understand what Samuel Hale is – was – talking about.' He stopped, drained his glass and put it down, too carefully, on the table. 'Also, I think they might have a friend of mine. Nigel Lewin, a newspaper reporter. I think he knows more about all this than we did until we read that document.' Foley reached into his jacket and found Lewin's note. 'Look at this.'

Southby read in silence. Finally raising thick sandy eyebrows, he handed the note back. Pain made him shift his position; he winced, facing Foley. 'These are people with power and obvious influence. We're agreed on that. Their shadow world has survived, expanded even, over a very long period. They're clever, ruthless, and certainly not stupid. Eleanor Hale was an old woman who knew too much, perhaps was getting troublesome and could, just conceivably, have fallen downstairs and killed herself, so perhaps her murder was a calculated risk on their part? But I really can't see them getting involved in the murder of a newspaper reporter. That's ham-fisted and they're not that, are they?'

'Another calculated risk? People can vanish very easily in a wilderness like Dartmoor. They'd be aware of that. I've also learned that Lewin has a drug problem. Nothing heavy – but you mention drug abuse to an overworked coroner and he's likely to bring that stamp down on a death certificate before your objection's even formed. I'm a fool, I should have spotted he was on something long ago and I should have gone after him myself, this morning. Yesterday morning. Christ!' Foley shook his head, wearily.

'It was bloody obvious he was intending to march straight into real trouble – he's near perfect at doing that.'

Southby finished his own drink and levered himself up. 'You look dead beat if you don't mind me saying so. I suggest you lay yourself out on that settee for a few hours before you even consider any action. You're no use to your friend at the point of exhaustion.'

Foley agreed, gratefully. 'I wouldn't send men on to the moors in the middle of the night. Frankly, I doubt if I could convince my superiors that Lewin is into anything other than self-imposed isolation because he's found a hot story. He's done that before, I'm afraid, and policemen of any rank don't easily forgive, and never forget, time-wasters. To get a full-scale search going I'd need to produce a witness to his being last seen in a disturbed state on or heading for Dartmoor – or if I'm suggesting foul play, provide due cause for suspicion. I don't have either. The last statement of a suicide isn't proof – it might even prejudice any hope of an early search or official enquiry. Young Nigel would have to be out of touch for a lot longer than he has been before the police or rescue services get called out. I'm afraid whatever needs doing I'll have to do myself. Solo.' He glanced at Southby's rigid leg. 'I can't see you trudging around Dartmoor.'

'Doesn't mean I'm helpless though,' Southby countered, then paused, thoughtful. 'That commando officer who led the raid into Germany with Hale?'

'Heatheridge. Captain. No first name given.'

'I could use ministry records to track him down. There weren't that many commando officers. Hale described Heatheridge as young. In war-time a captain could be in his early twenties easily. Be in his late sixties now but he'd still be listed, alive or dead. Get him to talk, even off the record, and it gives you a start – and credibility. If he confirmed Samuel Hale's written statement, I'm damn certain I could convince the right people, safe people . . .'

'If he's alive would he be prepared to tell his story?'

'He was the beginning. If he knew the end as we do, I'd say yes. For God's sake, he was a soldier too!'

'We haven't reached the end. I wouldn't want to guess at what they've got hidden away from the rest of us mere mortals.'

'All we can do is attempt to convince people of the truth.'

'Truth and reality are concepts people shy away from when they are unpleasant, Colonel; thirty years as a police officer have taught me that. Can you get at your records before Monday?'

'Forgot about that. Impossible on weekends – unless you're Downing Street.'

Foley remembered Mayberry, gave an ironic smile but said nothing. 'How secure is your telephone?' he asked.

'Ordinary line. I don't talk ministry business on it. I've a protected device for emergencies. In the main, illegals – they're the spies we don't know about – and terrorists don't go in for phone taps: difficult to access the system and harder to place if you do get in, no matter what the movies pretend. If they want to listen, they use directional microphones or fake a break-in and plant bugs. Don't fret, this place is swept regularly – including the lift and the corridors outside. I'm on the Northern Ireland desk so I do get priority. Neighbours get vetted too. Don't know it of course. What're you up to?'

'Best you don't know.'

Southby nodded. 'Get myself ready for bed, then.'

Foley lifted the receiver and dialled.

' "It had to be you," ' crooned a good, light tenor. 'Hello, Superintendent,' said Mayberry's wide-awake voice.

'You're too clever for your own good. What are you doing still up?'

'Waiting for your call, sweetheart,' Mayberry's Bogart rumbled. 'What have you got?'

'Thought you wanted out?'

Mayberry sighed. 'I do.'

'But you can't sleep.'

'Curse of high intelligence, dear boy.'

'Use it then. Commando officer. Name of Heatheridge. Could be alive, could be dead. Last record I have of him is somewhere in Germany, 1945. Secret mission.'

"Course it was,' Mayberry said, archly. 'That's all you've got? No given names?'

'Nothing.'

Foley could hear Mayberry's fingers pecking at his keyboards.

'What are you into? Can you say?'

'Only mildly illegal: my mode of entry, not the contents. Post-war army lists, openly published; my way saves you time. Good thing the name's out of the ordinary. I've only a handful here for the period. Where the blazes have I heard that name recently?'

'Means nothing to me,'

'Tee-vee. Sure of it.'

'Search me.'

'My lucky day.'

'Sod off.'

'Of course!'

'What?'

'Don't you watch our elected rulers on the box? No, our policemen are supposed to be above politics, aren't they? There's a Heatheridge in the House. Old-style Tory. Backbencher. Long-term rebel. Never made the front of the class – and won't now.'

'Age?'

'Ancient. Well, older than you. But fit. Seen him in action. Tough as teak. I can get chapter and verse on him if you want.'

'Can't be that easy.'

'Are you doubting my genius?'

'No. I mean he – Captain Heatheridge – is more likely to be a recluse living in the middle of nowhere after what he'd seen. Not serving as an MP.'

'Why? Because that's how Eleanor Hale lived – and died?'

'Because if I'd seen what Captain Heatheridge saw I'd want to get away from my fellow man pretty damn quick – and for a long time.' Foley could hear rapid clicking as he spoke. 'Are you listening?'

'To every sparkling word. Fact is, some run away from horror, others run directly at it. Same reaction, different

247

direction. Look at the two of us. I'm all for getting out of this and you're breaking your neck getting in deeper! What's the difference between a hero and a coward? One's got no sense of direction. Guess which?'

'What are you doing? Checking the others?'

'Playing the hero,' Mayberry reacted, sharply. 'I could do without the interrogation on an open line. Forget the others: they don't fit or they're dead. Dicky was a Hussar. *Delicious* uniform. He also had no sense of direction: won himself a DSO.'

'Awarded when?'

'1945. Just made it, didn't he?'

Foley fell silent.

'Bells ringing, Superintendent?'

'Any information as to what the action was? Or where?'

'Something valorous and important to the Allied invasion behind enemy lines. Which could have made him – '

'A commando,' growled Foley.

'So be happy. You've got a result.'

'I wanted a man – maybe a broken man – who would spill everything he knew once confronted with the truth. And I've got most of the truth. In writing, right here in front of me. And it's so bloody terrifying that faced with it even your wit would dry up. No, the last person I need is an MP who won't say anything in case it screws up his career.'

Mayberry discarded his bantering tone. 'Going by his parliamentary record, Heatheridge isn't the kind of man who values personal political advancement too highly. Loves a cause. Sticks his neck out. He's well known for defying his party whip, yet he's survived – which makes him special. A word of advice, Superintendent, from my overworked paranoia department: if you're going to approach him, do it well away from the Palace of Westminster. That place is the ultimate establishment club and the establishment, like the human body, has defence mechanisms to protect it when threatened.'

'I'm one of those mechanisms.'

'You're not. You're a police officer. You protect "decent" people from villains. That's your brief, that's your world, and it has nothing whatsoever to do with the world I'm talking about. You talk of the "funnies" and the "secret squirrels" and make them sound tame, even cute. They're neither. They are protectors. And they're killers if they're ordered to be. I'm the fly on the wall, Foley – trust me.'

'I hear you.'

'What about Southby?'

'He's read everything I have. Read it first.'

'And he's in?'

'Yes.'

Mayberry hesitated. 'You know the whole truth?'

'As it was in the beginning.'

'Is now and ever shall be, world without end, amen?'

'I hope not,' retorted Foley, with feeling.

'Worse than we thought?'

'Worse than we could dream.'

The clicking of the computer keyboard stopped.

'What've you got, Mayberry?'

'Insatiable curiosity, dear boy – fighting my natural cowardice.'

'Which is winning?'

Foley heard the swish of a laser printer. Mayberry asked: 'Heard of a club called Willie's?'

'You being funny?'

'Willie as in Nelson, country singer. Named after him. They do an afternoon session on a Saturday – that's today, dear boy. I'll be there from mid-day till four thirty.'

'Address?'

Mayberry gave it.

'I'll be there,' Foley promised.

'I'll be waiting. Oh, Superintendent – come as you are, high-heeled boots and rhinestones are definitely *out*.' The line clicked dead.

'Development?' enquired Southby from the door, wearing a dressing gown, a pillow and rug tucked under his free arm.

Foley put down the telephone. 'A Richard Heatheridge. Right sort of age group, won the DSO in 'forty-five for some behind-the-lines mission, now a Member of Parliament – Tory of course. Somehow not what I expected.'

'Saves you a great deal of footwork if he's Hale's captain which sounds more than probable. Can't say I've come across him before but frankly I avoid MPs like the plague. Our own ministers at Defence are all I need, thank you.' Southby frowned. 'One thing: if he's in that sort of position, with that sort of knowledge – ' his stick came up, directed at Hale's legacy ' – quite likely he's been bought or silenced with the Act. Or both.'

'That has occurred to me.'

'And we still face him with it?'

'Is there a choice?'

Southby smiled. 'Run away from it? Leave it to history to take care of? While we still can?'

Foley accepted the rug and pillow. 'Will you, Colonel?'

'My running days are over, I'm afraid. Sorry I can't do you a bed.'

'Right now I'd take the floor if that's all there was.'

The brass clock chimed. Foley glanced at it, cursed and removed his jacket, hanging it carefully over the back of a chair before stretching out on the settee. 'Tell me, Colonel, you move in those circles: where do you find an MP on a Saturday?'

'Not in the Palace of Westminster. He'll have some sort of London place – they usually do – or he's left for the weekend. Leave Heatheridge to me, I'll run him down. Don't worry, I'll tread carefully too. Get some sleep or you'll be no use to anyone.' Southby turned off the light and morning edged the heavy green velvet of the curtains in cold grey.

Foley closed his eyes, oblivious to birds singing, his mind filled with an obscene horror: a severed human head, eyes opened in a silent scream. *They've made it possible*, he heard Samuel Hale say and knew he would never dream his nightmare of the trenches ever again.

THIRTEEN

Jane Haversham ran back to the lights of the helicopter, head down, her long blonde hair made a maelstrom by the down-draught from the rotors.

Shaw helped her back inside then shut the door, diminishing the engine noise. 'Deserted. Doors locked. No lights, no car. We're here before them.'

'If they're coming at all,' snapped Peters, his partner.

Jane turned to the pilot. 'Dawn's coming up, I want you to do a sweep of the area.'

'What sort of radius?'

'How far can an SAS officer travel on foot in one night?'

The pilot grinned. 'This trivia time?'

'I'm deadly serious.'

Shaw said: 'Minimum distance for selection purposes is forty miles in twenty hours over mountain terrain. That's carrying a back-pack specified weight fifty-five pounds.'

'That sounds like expert knowledge?' she questioned.

'Fact,' said Shaw. 'He's with the regiment, isn't he?'

She nodded, looking away from his accusing eyes. 'Was. He barely survived after being dropped on to South Georgia at the start of the Falklands War. His group got trapped by a blizzard in the mountains and a rescue attempt by helicopter ended in a disastrous crash. All we know is that he survived somehow and was brought back to somewhere around here. Some experimental medical facility, we think.'

'We should have been told who we were dealing with.'

'I agree. But I wasn't told that you people had been called in – and Moravec didn't know of Adam's SAS connection at that time.'

Peters snapped: 'We're here to get a job done – getting Joe Nelson back in one piece – so let's get on with it.'

'We'll stay here, miss,' said Shaw, firmly.

'No, absolutely not.'

'We're staying,' agreed Peters.

Shaw looked directly at her. 'We're not going to tackle him. If you think you can talk him round that's good news for Nelson. Good news for us too if he's SAS. We'll wait under cover. All right?'

'You're not giving me any choice.'

'As much as Joe Nelson had, miss.'

They left the Bell and blended into the gloom.

The pilot turned enquiringly.

'He wasn't in good shape,' she said. But he had the strength of terror to push him on, she reminded herself. 'Use the farm as a start point and I'll tell you when to stop.'

The pilot smiled.

'I don't know how far he ran!' she flared.

'OK, but I'll have to watch the fuel.'

The Jetranger lifted.

Spotlights blazed, blinding white. The pilot threw an arm up to his eyes, the helicopter yawing wildly, rotor-blades slicing dangerously close to the ground, churning up a dust-storm.

'I have to put her down!' he yelled, killing power, the machine hitting the ground hard, the spin of the rotors dying with the jet-whine.

Bulky figures in combat fatigues emerged from the gloom into the lights closing around the aircraft, automatic weapons at the ready, faces smeared with camouflage paint.

A very senior uniformed police officer stood with an overcoated civilian beyond the encircling soldiers, his face turned away from the swirling dust.

A voice blared from a loud-hailer: 'Leave the aircraft singly and lie face down on the ground. Do it now.'

Jane could see the roughly handled figures of Peters and Shaw being forced into the halo of light. Peters' face was a mask of blood, his nose misshapen, his eyes angry. Shaw appeared to shrug his shoulders in resignation.

'Out,' ordered the pilot, removing his head-set and seat-belts with deliberate movements. 'No argument. Do exactly what they say. They're serious.'

Jane stepped out first.

'Get down!' the loud-hailer roared. 'Now!'

She knelt slowly on the soft soil.

'Forget your clothes,' snapped the pilot, pushing her down hard.

The soldiers shifted menacingly.

'It's all right!' the pilot shouted.

Four soldiers rushed forward dragging them further apart. Jane gasped as her legs were kicked open and hard hands moved between her spread thighs then, expertly, over the rest of her body.

'Clean!' one of the soldiers barked.

'This one too!' yelled another.

'On your feet!' the loud-hailer blared. 'Now!'

Jane pushed herself up, angry and humiliated, her colour high in the lights. 'I'm an accredited journalist – ' she shouted, then gasped, winded by a punch in the back.

'No talking,' growled the soldier.

'You creep!' she snapped.

He grinned.

'Shut up,' advised the pilot.

The senior police officer approached, the overcoated civilian staying back behind the lights. He read aloud from a typed sheet: 'You are charged with contravening the conditions of the Official Secrets Act – '

'I demand access to a solicitor immediately.'

'Your civil rights are temporarily suspended under the emergency powers of the Prevention of Terrorism Act.'

'You're mad! None of us are terrorists. I tried to tell you I'm an accredited journalist and television producer. I have every right to investigate any – '

'You are further charged with aiding a known member of an illegal terrorist organization – namely, the Provisional Wing of the Irish Republican Army – by supplying confidential information regarding a secret Ministry of Defence facility, while knowing this information was to be used for the purpose of illegal penetration of the said facility and of the removal therefrom of certain experimental substances with the intention of endangering human life. You will be

253

held in custody without access to a solicitor until further enquiries have been completed.'

'Get that chopper away from here quickly!' came a barked order from the direction of the civilian.

'I don't believe this,' said Jane, and suffered another thump between her shoulder-blades.

'Clear the area!' came another order.

As she was led away, the civilian approached. 'He's not with you? Where is he?'

'Who? I want to know who you're talking about. Who is *he*?'

'Don't be stupid. Daniel Hale, of course. We've known for months he'd gone over to the IRA. Had to be just a matter of time before they thought of using him to penetrate the biological weapon centre we have here. Too bloody obvious. His father was in charge of it for years! Typical IRA, think everyone's as thick as they are.'

She halted, ignoring the push at her back. 'Cover-up! Beautiful, glorious, *foul* cover-up! You can't hide the truth for ever.'

He moved closer, his eyes hard, confident, even smiling. 'The facts are the truth. What facts do you have? Something lurid for the tabloids? Forget it all, you'll find life easier that way.'

She glared at him. He walked on.

She stood still, Adam's words clear: 'Eleanor Hale was angry when she died – and afraid. I felt that fear. It was a fear of power. Secret power.'

Now, she understood. Understood their indifference to her threats. Understood the fact of that power but not the how or even the why of it. She was desperate for that knowledge.

'Wait! I knew Daniel. You must know that. You know every other damn thing. So who is he?'

He shrugged. 'Very well. Someone we saved.'

'And kept.'

'In real terms he was already dead.'

'His gift? Seeing the future? *Your* work?'

'The capacity for precognition exists in all of us – our lost primaeval sixth sense if you like. In some subjects it

254

has not been entirely suppressed despite centuries of genetic change and development: hence you get the occasional genuine precog – very rarely, admittedly – amongst all the charlatans and frauds. Isolate the carrier genes and it becomes possible in theory to engineer anything from a full-blown human oracle to teams of precogs acting as a human early-warning system against missile attack down to the lowly foot-soldier able to detect an ambush around the next bend. Our work continues.'

'He's just an experiment to you.'

'He's far more than simply that.'

'How did you know we were coming here?' she demanded.

'It was inevitable. He'd come back, we knew that. It was simply a question of when. And of course how much damage was done while he was out. We've had Raethmoor Farm under surveillance since the unfortunate business with Mrs Hale.'

'Damage? To whom? Him?'

He paused. 'Stay there,' he ordered the soldiers and led her aside. 'To the future. Not that I'd expect you to understand that.'

'That utterly bewildered being is what you see for the future? He's your model for the new man?'

'He's part of it. A relatively small but important part. Some day you – the world – will be grateful for the work we have dedicated our lives to: the advances we have achieved and will still achieve.' He threw an arm out, almost in anger. 'That's a sick world out there. Humanity under mortal threat from virtually everything we do or produce. From the deadly filth of pollution, from our own self-indulgences, from epidemics we encourage because our morality is in the gutter with the rest of the filth. Becasue no one seems to have the will to cry – enough!'

'Except you? Whoever you people are?'

'Except us.'

'Who gives you that right?'

He smiled, sadly. 'You really don't understand, do you? We all have that right. No, the responsibility. The blueprint of life is in all of us and it is our duty to save it from

255

extinction. Or possibly worse: deterioration. The human gene pool, which is what determines our genetic quality, is already deteriorating. We're heading slowly but surely into a genetic twilight. It's probable, continuing as we are, that in each future century the number of genetically defective people dependent on medical technology to survive will increase by eight per cent. In six hundred years – a drop in the ocean of man's development – the majority of the world's population will become seriously defective, genetically. We are devaluing man with our own actions. Destroying ourselves. To counteract this we must make changes. Genetic changes. Re-establish the order. Strengthen the strain.'

She looked up at the faltering night. 'In other words, play God.'

'God isn't above – he's ahead. If God exists, we exist as His creation: therefore the abilities He endowed us with should have no frontiers beyond our human physical and mental limitations. And those can be adapted, expanded. This can be done: it has been done. Why were we given free will if it is wrong to reason? To choose? If your ship is sinking do you drown simply because water is a hostile environment and the act of swimming must be learned and is therefore unnatural – therefore wrong? The will to survive is indestructible. We're ensuring man's survival. Nature is looking after itself, haven't you witnessed that? Changing. Adapting. Protecting itself against our excesses.'

'But we want the choice! We *all* need to choose what changes are to be made to us, to our children and theirs. Not just some select group of élitists.'

'A consensus? A referendum? Democratic debate? We'll still be here on doomsday, discussing it.'

'So you plan on making the choice for us?'

'It's already been made.' He signalled the soldiers. 'Take her away.'

'Wait, damn you! You're advocating the creation of a superior race, a master race. How are you going to sort us out? Mass screening at birth? Terminate genetically defective babies? How will you deal with us, the transitory ones, the ones you didn't engineer – the lower orders?'

'We – our heirs – won't need to. The best adapted will survive, the rest will perish. Natural selection. Evolution.'

'But it's not natural, don't you see? You're engineering the changes.' She screamed at him in frustration, in outrage: 'You don't have the right to change life!'

But he had turned and walked away. Indifferent.

Joseph Nelson knew his life teetered on the same edge as his captor's sanity. He drove cautiously, as though he had a live grenade with the ring-pin half pulled balanced on the car's dashboard, his window down against the lingering stench from Mitchell's voided bowels, despite the body having been dumped at the first opportunity by his crazed captor.

Otto Fascher barely hung on to reality. The car kept dissolving, replaced by an aircraft of a design he had never encountered. He was in the aircraft. Could see out from it. It had no wings. The noise crucified his mind. He wanted to cry out for help. To anyone. God. His dead mother. Even the *schwartzer*. But the negro was not in the strange aircraft. Men in bulky combat uniforms inhabited it; soldiers, armed with automatic weapons quite new to him, men who smiled grimly at him with respect, with camaraderie. But he knew none of them.

He screamed.

'Take it easy,' said Nelson. 'Sun'll be up soon and we're already on Dartmoor. You sure you know where you want to go?'

'Home,' said another, deeper voice from the rear.

Nelson's blood ran cold.

'It's not far now. You part of the team that got me out of the station?'

Nelson stared ahead at the road, not daring to look around.

'Come on?'

Now, thought Nelson, if you're going to survive, do something *now*, because he's *gone*.

He saw the figure lean over on to the front passenger seat, the arms folding around the seat-back, the hands

257

clasped together, the chin resting almost contentedly on the head-rest.

Why's he dumped the fucking gun? Because that's not *him*. That's someone else. He's a raving schizo. Move now. Now or never.

Casually, he pressed his seat-belt release. 'Not me. Those were other guys,' he answered, arms braced on the wheel, then hit the brakes hard, twisting fast, his fist connecting with a double-knuckle punch to the waiting temple.

Nelson's anger exploded: he grabbed the stunned form and head-butted him, following up with two short, cruel blows to the face with his fist for good measure. He jumped out and heaved the now unconscious figure on to the deserted road, dragging him along the metalled surface, swearing and kicking, until he reached the scrub some yards further back.

'That's you on Dartmoor – bastard!' Nelson swore and lashed out a final kick. Back at the car he found the automatic on the back seat, lifted it with a ball-point through the trigger guard, returned to the unconscious figure and dropped it beside him.

He drove off, the sun a sliver of gold on the horizon. He had mentally noted the last telephone box they had passed and headed for it. There were two calls he had to make: one to Victoria to report in, the other, anonymously, to the local police. He hated the thought of the long drive back to London and would have given anything to be able to stop off somewhere and sleep – but Mitchell had a wife who had to be told. The thought of that was crushing. He should have killed the crazy, murderous bastard. He heard again that chilling change of voice and the word 'home'. He shuddered, his eyes fixed on the road ahead and firmly off the bleak moors shrouded in grey morning mist. He needed buildings around him and the smell of the city to get his head right again. This place was only good for crazies. And it reminded him too much of his Jamaican mother's childhood horror stories of walking dead. He pressed down firmly on the accelerator.

'Come on, Danny boy,' one of them sneered, putting the

boot in for what might have been the first or the thousandth time: he could not tell the difference any more, his body numb, the nerves switched off by his brain. Survival, he reasoned. The body is protecting itself; shutting down to preserve sanity. He felt euphoric, he rather thought he actually smiled.

'Funny is it then, you Brit bastard?' Again the boot went in.

'That's enough,' said the bearded one. 'Leave something for the executioner.'

That's it then. The deed was finally upon him. Well, he'd had time to prepare himself, that was one saving grace.

Grace? Had he acquitted himself well enough to achieve it? Was his the right cause in the eyes of God? Yes. They had no interest in God despite their hypocritical genuflecting towards Rome. He was more Catholic than they, despite being a convert. He was nearer to God than they in every sense. God was just another instrument they used to promote terror. They were butchers, hacking at the living carcass of their own land, selling its future to whoever provided the hatchets. God damn every one of them.

'Sing us a good old rebel song then?' said the sadist, pulling him off the stone floor and back on to the solid torture chair. 'Hear you're good at that.'

'You'll not get a word out of him – he's a plucky devil,' said a third, much older man. 'You've near-killed him already and not a word passed his lips.'

There was a woman in the room. He had seen her between bouts of unconsciousness. She was attractive but unkempt. And bright. He'd spotted that in her eyes. He had the feeling that it was she who had seen through his cover and had him snatched. His weak spot: women. He'd been told that – warned – so many times.

They think of their women as we think of our men: hard-nosed squaddies who do the rotten, dirty, most dangerous jobs because that's their place in the pecking order.

Actually, not so, sir, he'd begged to disagree. Officers do rotten, dirty, dangerous jobs as well. Us, sir. And their women – the most effective of them anyway – are usually

259

highly political and therefore more motivated than your run-of-the-mill Provo with a stripped-down Kalashnikov stuffed down his trousers. Generally they're intellectuals who swapped the Bible for *Das Kapital* at university and the guilt of the confessional for the release of pure violence.

Pure violence, Major? He remembered the arch query.

Certainly, sir. Violence, if you are totally committed to it, has no side, no comeback, morally. It's an act, a deed one commits and walks away from, cleansed. You've purged yourself of the urge, your victim has received the most you can give – other than your love. Sir.

Been reading too much psychology, Major, that's my view.

Yes, sir.

'This is useless,' observed the woman. 'It's also dangerous. We've kept him in one place too long.'

'They've no way of knowing where he is,' sneered the sadist.

'They've every way of knowing. They've got tracking equipment now that would give you nightmares – if you had enough brains to dream, that is.'

'You Belfast cow!'

'What do you think they have in their helicopters? TV sets for football? They can pick out a group of people in a house which they know normally has only a couple of occupants even though no one steps outside the door. Thermal imaging. And that's just one of their techniques.'

'Expensive toys. One AK-47 and a good finger on the trigger will bring them down to ground level with a nice bang.'

She shook her head with frustration. 'The only thing you'll get at ground level is the SAS creeping up on you on their bellies – and you won't hear their "nice bang". I think we ought to move. Straight away.'

'The executioner is on his way here. We stay,' affirmed the bearded terrorist.

'One of you do it,' she said.

'No. They're breaking in a new lad. You know the test. There'd be bad feeling.'

She shrugged and left the room.

The sadidst amused himself for a while with the portable generator and the crocodile clips but gave up.

'Maybe we should do it,' he said, worried now. 'He's half-dead already – aren't you, Danny boy? Maybe she's right. We ought to move along.'

'It's the test,' said the old man. 'They don't like it when they lose an opportunity.'

'Be here any time now,' said the bearded one. 'Take it easy.'

The door opened and the farmer put his head around it. 'Van coming.'

That'll be them, then. Get him outside, be easier for the cleaning up.'

I'll go fighting, he promised himself. Not a lamb to the slaughter. A soldier. A man, at least. He wished he wasn't naked. He reached pathetically with swollen, broken fingers for his clothes.

The cruel one brought his revolver down on his hand. He fell. 'Modest, are we, Danny boy? Jesus was naked when they crucified him, did you know that? The loin-cloth was made up by the Pope.'

The old man pushed his trousers across the flagged stone floor with a foot. 'Give him a bit of dignity, he's earned it.'

'I'll give him dignity – with my boot!'

A searing white flash froze the room. He reacted faster than any of them despite his injuries. He knew. His head was tucked down, hands jammed over his ears before the thunderous explosion. He stayed down, flat as he could, as rapid, deadly accurate, short bursts of automatic fire ripped his captors apart.

He felt a sharp, quite dreadful, pain in his head and a strange taste in his mouth. Ricochet, his dying mind said. Of all the bloody luck!

Take me home, boys. Don't leave me here in this abattoir of a country.

He regained consciousness face down in rough scrub. Turning carefully on to his side, he tested his body. The hard metal of the automatic dug into his bruised ribs. He winced, pulled it free and sat up slowly.

261

His hand went instinctively to his head.

Shaved?

Well, it had been.

Grown a bit since then.

When?

God knows.

How the bloody hell did I get here?

Sort yourself out, Hale!

He knew his purpose was to go home. Back to Raeth-moor. Back to Mother. Fine. But that didn't answer any of the questions attacking his mind.

There was one universal answer and he shrank from it – but it had to be faced. Amnesia. He fingered the long scar on his scalp exploratively. Somehow the bloody marvellous army surgeons had saved his life, got him away from wretched Northern Ireland, back to England, cracked the old head open, found the offending round from the ricochet, sewn him up or whatever they did to skulls, then promptly lost him. Or rather he'd lost them because to tell the truth, he didn't feel completely on top of the world.

Well, you did get a severe kicking!

How long ago though?

Enough time for the op and a bit of a lounge around.

Weeks? Months? Feels more like a couple of minutes!

The gun? The Heckler? It was his emergency stash in the old E-type. What the hell? Oh bugger it. On your feet. March. Danny boy's coming home, Mother. Put on the old bacon and eggs – with all the extras, as Pop used to say.

He looked down at his clothes as he marched, his soldier's mind in top gear, heading true as a die in the right direction. My cords, shirt, sweater. Pop's jacket? Pop's Lobb brogues? I can't get into those, can I? Never thought I could anyway. There's racks of them up in the loft. Worth a mint these days. Try the lot on when I get home. After breakfast and a good jaw with Mother, naturally. Wish I didn't feel so bloody lousy.

He heard the whipping sound of rotors and dropped to the ground, not knowing why. Choppers were friends, weren't they? But some part of him felt threatened. He flattened himself against the moss, the peaty smell of it strong in his nostrils, grateful for his father's tweed jacket which in his view, for the moor, was better in colour than any army camouflage rig.

The helicopter flew directly overhead, heading north. For a split second he saw himself inside, in Arctic order, armed to the teeth with hard but friendly faces around him, fear and exhilaration in his belly – which meant imminent action. He smiled at himself: just like a bloody schoolboy! You're in the army, you don't have to daydream about it any more.

He pushed himself up, wincing, then moved on.

Soon be home.

March.

He crested the rise and saw Raethmoor, feeling oddly as if he were seeing it for the first time, and yet as if returning. But returning a stranger.

Bloody prodigal returns, he chuckled, inside. She'll kill me for not writing. Sorry, Ma, been busy dying a little. Where were you? Didn't they tell you? Could have done with that small, firm grip to help me keep a grasp on the old reality.

But something told him he *had* seen her. Recently. Days only.

You're dreaming, Danny boy. Or the bloody moors are getting to you as they do to the superstitious and the feeble-minded. Maybe after taking a full metal jacket nine mill in the brainbox, feeble-minded is what you've become? Rather have bought it than that, given the option. Which you weren't.

God, he was cold. His fingers felt numb with it. Dead, almost. He jammed his hands under his armpits, the brush of rough tweed on his fingers making him wince. Soon warm up in front of the old Aga, hands around a bloody great mug of tea. Nothing like it.

The light was improving and the lines of the rambling property were becoming clear. Mist hung, as it always did at dawn, over the low-roofed outbuildings where, once, he had laid some ravishing beauty in a pile of rank straw he had thought was fresh. She didn't mind at the time though, did she, Danny boy? Only afterwards when she had to

263

come into the house with the back of her dress giving the game away. Not that Ma had minded, really. Understood male needs. Female too. Dad, of course, wasn't there. Not that far away but still, not there. Actually he wasn't there when he *was* there. Miles away. Some intellectual nirvana. For ever the future man: searching, delving, once even caught him praying for the salvation of the human race. Not religion, mind you. That was never Pop's hang-up. Worse really, he wanted to know the secret of life so that he could spill the beans and make everyone's lot that much better.

Me, I think the human race are a bunch of animals who woke up one morning to find their tails had gone and they had a tongue instead. As the majority speak through their arseholes anyway it seems a shame the tails had to go – natural gag if you see what I mean?

'Who the bloody hell are you talking to?' he demanded, aloud, moving faster down from the ridge now. Definitely going round the twist. Feels like I'm sharing my thinking space. G'arn, get out of there, give me a bit of peace.

Daniel?

'Yes?'

She's dead, Daniel, I'm sorry. I saw it happen. We saw it happen.

He stopped and dropped to his haunches, both hands crushed to his head. 'Don't!' he bellowed.

It's true. You know it's true. Inside.

We were here?

We ran here. From there.

Oh God, no!

Daniel, we can't go back. You know that, don't you?

He looked up, seeing Raethmoor almost entirely clear now, his soldier's eyes probing the dark spaces and the cover. 'We can't go forward. They're here.'

I know.

There were other voices. Many. Where are they? Is there only you now?

I feel another but he is dying, Daniel. He doesn't understand as we do. They gave us his hands, ours – mine – were finished.

Which one were you?

264

I was Timothy.

Tim, I remember. You always made me feel cold when you reached me. I'm cold now.

So am I, Daniel. I never want to be cold again. Do you understand me?

Yes.

Go down to the house.

They'll take us back.

I can see, Daniel. I know the way forward. You can trust me.

Do you know what . . . comes after?

Yes, Daniel.

Tell me.

You can't tell it. You only know.

He looked across, past the house at the clearing moors, the rock tors breaking through the mist like soldiers through battlefield smoke.

Will I miss this very much?

It will always be with you, but in perspective, a part of something greater, yet still valued. There'll be no regret. I know.

Tim?

Yes?

Shall we walk down now?

Yes, Daniel.

Will I know what to do?

I'll know. Just enjoy the morning.

I shall.

Take the gun from your belt and put it inside your breast pocket with the letter you'll find there.

Should I read the letter?

It isn't for you, Daniel. It's for Jane.

I remember Jane. Beautiful. Sunny. Brighter than me in all departments.

She is beautiful. She's here, Daniel.

Good. Right then. We'll go down together.

He came down at the rear of the house, smiling as he saw the rear garden gate he had long before christened Hobo Heaven after his mother's unfailing charity to life's failures who passed this way.

Two figures in camouflage rig appeared from behind masonry.

The gun, Daniel, the Heckler. Quickly. But don't fire!

His hand flew under his jacket.

'*Stop!*' The order was barked but too late: one soldier fired, two rounds, placed to kill.

He lay on his back. There was no pain.

Tim? You there? You know this is not enough.

Don't worry.

'He's going,' a voice said close by, tight with anger. 'Get that fool out of my sight.'

'He went for his gun, sir!'

'You should have let him shoot you, you idiot. Come on, we have to move fast!'

Don't worry, Daniel.

She's here, I can feel it.

Yes.

'Let me go to him,' Jane pleaded, her face silver with tears.

'For God's sake! Very well. You've a minute, till that chopper gets here, that's all.'

She knelt over him. 'Adam?'

She doesn't know our names?

She knows what she has to do.

Are you certain?

As certain as death.

And peace.

Yes, and peace.

She put her hand over his heart, ignoring the blood, gasping at the erratic, fading beat, feeling with the back of her hand the weight of the gun in his breast pocket and the sharp edge of an envelope.

She took the envelope, opened and read the letter. Then deliberately lowered herself over him, feeling the wet warmth seeping through her clothes, and extracted the gun.

'Miss?' said one of the soldiers, standing back, understanding grief – and death by the gun. 'They'll be here to take him in a minute.'

She shook her head, her back to them, kneeling up, the gun pressed hard to the centre of his forehead.

'*Miss!*'

She pulled the trigger and kept on pulling long after the magazine was empty and his brains were no more.

The letter, caught by a quick morning breeze, skittered on to the moors.

Raethmoor Farm
Dartmoor

Erich,

Despite all that has happened: Samuel's death; the hell you built together; your interference with the best of God's creations – the human mind and body; the legacy of horror you left to be perpetuated by men perhaps even more misguided than yourself; still, I offer you my forgiveness: perhaps my last act if your successors have their way. On one condition. As you read this you will have before you one of your children. If my mother's instincts are correct, and they always have been, they have taken what remained of my son and robbed him of the Eternal Peace which God promises us all. Release him, Erich, I beg you. But spare him more pain when you do it for he has suffered enough.

Daniel's soul is in your hands. Let it fly free.

Eleanor Hale

FOURTEEN

An unscheduled meeting of ministers was convened in the cabinet room at Ten Downing Street for eleven o'clock that Saturday morning, the subsequent briefing giving the explanation: matters involving security in Northern Ireland – which was a standard catch-all, halting penetrating questions by even the most hard-nosed political hacks.

'First of all,' said the Prime Minister, 'I feel a moment's silence is in order in view of the appalling, quite barbarous, murders of Richard Wardlove and his wife Harriet at their Hertfordshire home last night. I understand the police are doing the best they can but, in private, admit to being less than confident of apprehending the perpetrators. Genetic fingerprinting is a possibility – Harriet Wardlove was brutally raped so evidence of that nature is available – but of course this technique is confirmatory and there seem to be few if any clues to the identity of these monsters. Perhaps this might be an opportune time to show ourselves utterly committed to a policy of very harsh sentencing for capital crimes such as these.'

Murmurs of approval echoed around the long coffin-shaped cabinet table then died as a formal silence was observed.

The Prime Minister broke it: 'I've called you here because there is sure to be press speculation regarding the armed incident during the early hours of this morning, here in central London. A vague account has already been given on radio and television.' She nodded to the cabinet secretary who stood and went to the double doors, allowing entry to a straight-backed man in civilian clothes who was not offered a chair.

'Colonel Masterson of the security service will brief you

on the facts,' explained the Prime Minister. 'They are subject to the Official Secrets Act.'

Masterson gave a curt nod. 'An officer of the Coldstream Guards, Major Daniel Hale, was kidnapped by the IRA some months ago while working undercover in Northern Ireland. You will probably recall his name from media reports when it occurred. He was tortured by the Provisionals but also, according to reliable informants, was subjected to prolonged brainwashing techniques, aimed at turning his allegiances around so that he might be used against us. Possibly this was instigated or aided by the fact that shortly before his kidnapping Major Hale had become a convert to Roman Catholicism.'

One of the seated ministers objected: 'If the fact of this religious conversion was known then why on earth was this officer allowed to carry out an undercover role where his loyalties would by the very nature of his work become – to say the least – blurred? One does not become a Roman Catholic overnight, the process of instruction is lengthy. The intelligence people must have had more than enough time to analyse the situation?'

'There are many Catholic officers and men serving in Northern Ireland without suffering spiritual or ideological conflict,' said Masterson.

The Prime Minister interrupted. 'We're not here to conduct an enquiry, only to be appraised of the facts. Continue, please, Colonel.'

'The army has, as you know, a great deal of land in the Dartmoor area. One section is occupied by a top-secret research unit working on a programme for the development of certain experimental biological weapons. Actually, the synthesizing of certain strains of germs which, after genetic engineering, would in their new form have a controlled period of effectiveness. The idea obviously being that, once this period was over, our own men could walk perfectly safely into what was previously a lethal environment. These experiments have been quite successful. Progress is satisfactory, according to latest reports.'

'How wide is the circle of knowledge on this?' someone enquired, quietly.

'Extremely limited,' answered the Prime Minister, her tone an unmistakable warning.

'How did Major Hale get to know about this?' enquired the Home Secretary. 'That is what you're leading to, isn't it?'

'Precisely. Hale gave information to the IRA that this facility existed. He knew about the facility and the work carried out there because his late father, Brigadier Samuel Hale, was for some years in charge of the project.'

An uncomfortable shifting of bodies occurred around the table as realization of a looming major security scandal sunk home.

'Bad choice,' someone muttered.

'In retrospect, yes,' agreed the Prime Minister. 'However, Major Hale was an exemplary officer in all respects and his father's role in this Dartmoor project was of course secret. Brigadier Hale was generally known to be a senior officer of the Royal Army Medical Corps, nothing more. Colonel?'

'Thank you, Prime Minister. Once the IRA had this information from Major Hale, as we know from our own informants they did, their plan was to achieve a propaganda coup by penetrating the facility and then releasing information – disinformation, I should say – that we were intending to use these weapons in certain areas of Northern Ireland.'

'Sounds more like old-style KGB thinking,' put in the Home Secretary. 'IRA's style would be to try and steal the stuff. Or just blow it up.'

'It does have that stamp,' agreed Masterson. 'Plotting was ingenious. They sucked in members of the media very cleverly indeed. Whether they actually targeted Rudolf Moravec's empire we'll never know but they almost succeeded in making it their disinformation platform.'

'Sounds completely bloody Irish to me,' muttered the Defence Secretary.

The Prime Minister said: 'Moravec himself being taken in surprises me greatly.'

'Had to be big money involved,' someone offered.

'That was the bait,' agreed Masterson. 'Moravec was

270

persuaded by a young woman named Jane Haversham, a freelance television producer he uses often and known to us as something of a radical, that a man she had once had a short-lived affair with had, quite suddenly, lost his memory and in its place developed the gift of precognition. Probably realizing that even Moravec's worst rag would have a hard time selling such a story convincingly, she offered proof of her former lover's ability: advance warning – prophecy, if you prefer – of a bomb attack on a senior British Army officer in London. Name, date, time, place. All spot-on.'

'General Westrum-Laing?' asked the Home Secretary.

Masterson nodded. 'This so-called prophecy was announced in a theatrical manner on television. A sensationalist stunt, typical of Moravec's approach. The prediction was of course accurate. It's not at all difficult to predict the future if you've already planned it in advance – which of course was what the IRA had done.'

'This woman Haversham,' enquired the Energy Secretary. 'She's the one who contrived to get someone inside the disused Cornish tin-mine site we were investigating as a possible nuclear waste dump, right? I have to say this: I had sight of her file and there was nothing which even hinted at IRA sympathies. She's not even actively left-wing. Green certainly, over-zealous perhaps – but not a terrorist fellow-traveller. Not from the information I saw, I must say!'

Masterson sighed. 'A security file only tells what we know and that's probably only what they want us to know. However, I'll agree in this case you're probably right. She thought she had a marvellous story and this clouded her judgement. The man she had the affair with was Major Daniel Hale. He was the IRA's stalking-horse. She was entrapped by a call from a private medical clinic near Camberley where Daniel Hale had been placed overnight after being found in an apparent near-coma by a police patrol. The clinic was the nearest hospital and Hale's condition seemed serious, possibly critical. We believe that this was achieved by drugs. There is a theory that the doctor in charge of the clinic, an American named Livesey – some-

271

thing of a revolutionary himself during the sixties – might have administered these drugs himself prior to planting Hale near to the clinic, ripe for a passing police patrol. There may be some truth in this as Livesey was killed last night when the clinic was fire-bombed. It's entirely possible that he was silenced by the IRA. Anti-terrorist squad officers are sifting discreetly through the ruins of the building at this moment to see if anything remains of the device used. The press will not be informed of a possible terrorist link.

'However, to go back to the woman Haversham: Livesey found – conveniently – a letter addressed to her on Major Hale. He called her on the telephone in the middle of the night and she agreed to aid her former lover. She travelled down the next morning by train and drove Hale back to her Chelsea home using his car. She kept him there while she made financial arrangements for his story with Moravec. Moravec was completely duped into believing he had a modern Nostradamus on his hands. It was precisely the type of story his tabloid editors would eat up. I can imagine he was already counting the millions he would earn. We know he'd planned coverage on his satellite TV network along with press and magazine features.'

'The man's a fool,' muttered the Defence Secretary.

'But his media empire could still have done irreparable damage to our world image if they carried such a story as the IRA intended,' stated the Prime Minister.

'All lies.'

'But with enough truth to make the lie credible. The work being done at the experimental facility is a fact – how we intended to use their products could easily be open to erroneous but believable interpretation.'

'Accepted,' grunted the Defence Secretary. 'But what was Major Hale supposed to do? Forecast some catastrophe at the base which the IRA would make fact? As with the killing of General Westrum-Laing?'

'All he needed to do was say it existed. That he'd seen it. A "vision" or however you describe that sort of nonsense. The point was to have him believed.'

'Have the IRA penetrated the facility, Colonel?' enquired the Energy Secretary, firmly.

'No, sir. However, the site is now compromised.' Masterson turned. 'Your decision regarding this must be made without delay, Prime Minister.'

'We'll make our collective decision without haste,' her deputy interrupted, breaking the thoughtful silence he had maintained throughout. Heads around the table angled towards him.

'Could we get back to the fire-fight on the streets of London?' asked the Home Secretary.

Masterson nodded. 'Nine of the dead were members of the security service attempting to apprehend Daniel Hale. The tenth was a psychiatrist brought along by us because we had firm information that brainwashing had been used on Hale and specialized professional help would be needed very quickly. The psychiatrist in question has long been used by us. Hale's mind had obviously been pushed to its limits because he simply went berserk, killing everyone. Haversham, according to eye-witnesses, was driven away by two unidentified men, thought at the time to be IRA but we have since learned they were members of a private security company employed by Moravec to watch over Hale. We know the company well and expect their full co-operation in tidying this up.'

'Why private security?' asked the Home Secretary.

'Moravec afraid his competitors would brandish a fatter cheque to his golden goose?' suggested the Energy Secretary.

'Probably,' said Masterson. 'Or perhaps he thought the IRA would try and get Hale back. He believed Hale had escaped, of course.'

The Deputy Prime Minister enquired, almost apologetically: 'The protective suits? The white truck? They were mentioned in the first radio report soon after the incident happened. This was in the early hours – I couldn't sleep and spent a while reading with the radio on. Heard those details then, but there was nothing about them later.'

'D-notices were issued,' said the Prime Minister, patiently. 'That was raised earlier.'

'Was it? I understood that the D-notice we discussed involved Rudolf Moravec's organization. I don't recall mention of the BBC being subject to one? Obviously you had a very early start to your day, Prime Minister. You too, Colonel Masterson. Sending out D-notices to catch the morning news broadcasts.'

'The matter was treated with the utmost urgency,' she stated.

Masterson explained: 'You have to understand that we are dealing with unknown factors with these new synthesized germ strains. They are still very much experimental. We are certain that neither Haversham nor Daniel Hale got anywhere near the Dartmoor facility but no chances were being taken. The protective clothing and the special sealed and refrigerated truck were precautionary measures. The D-notices were applied immediately to avoid any question of public concern. Panic, even.'

'And is there reason for public concern? For panic?'

'Absolutely not, sir. Neither Major Hale nor Jane Haversham were in any way contaminated. As I said, the special equipment was brought in purely as a precaution.'

'So where are they now? Hale and Haversham?' asked the Home Secretary.

'Hale is dead. Haversham killed him. Shot him with his own gun. Emptied what was left in the magazine into his head. Undoubtedly realized she'd been duped and perhaps discovered that Hale had killed his own mother whom we believe suspected a change in her son. The brainwashing would do that and a mother would spot a behavioural difference. We know Mrs Hale communicated this disquiet to Haversham. The police haven't proven he did kill his mother but on available evidence it seems likely. Hale was definitely seen driving his car – a distinctive, old, Jaguar sports model – away from the house on the day Mrs Hale apparently fell down stairs sustaining a broken neck. However, she died from a fractured skull before the fall. Forensic evidence confirms this.'

'Has Haversham said Major Hale admitted to this murder?'

'She's severely shocked at present so interrogation is not advisable, according to medical opinion.'

'Whose medical opinion might that be, Colonel?' enquired the Deputy Prime Minister. 'The police surgeon?'

'Actually an army doctor. The scene of the shooting was relatively close to the experimental facility.'

'Is Haversham to be charged with Major Hale's murder?'

The Prime Minister answered: 'Under the circumstances, it might be better if no official charges are brought. If we charge her with Hale's killing we must justify those charges. We will have to admit to certain things, or worse, as far as the reaction of the media will be concerned, refuse to comment. To do anything further on this matter will simply achieve what the IRA intended all along: the public revelation of this top-secret facility. There is also a wider issue involved here. I've been advised this morning – ' she looked directly at her deputy ' – by an extremely accurate and reliable intelligence source we share with the Americans, that the Russians have no fewer than eight secret biological weapons research sites . . . Colonel?'

'Zagorsk to the north of Moscow, Pokrov east; Omutninsk, Penza, Sverdlovsk, Kurgan, Aksu and Berdsk spread eastwards, Prime Minister.'

'Thank you. And they continue experimentation in this field despite their president's much-acclaimed stand against chemical weapons – a fact which I know the Americans were about to exploit in the propaganda war. Obviously the public revelation of our secret facility will torpedo that propaganda initiative for Washington, apart from causing us to appear out of step with the changing times once again. Bearing all this in mind, I plan – and I need the cabinet's support – to bury the entire business. For ever.'

She waited.

'You've silenced Moravec with a D-notice for the moment, Prime Minister, but how can you guarantee the silence of Haversham if she's as radical as is suggested?' questioned the Defence Secretary.

Masterson answered: 'Apparently Haversham had developed some extraordinary idea that Major Hale was not Major Hale.' He suppressed a smile. 'Not entirely, that is. She believes, quite sincerely, that he was in fact three or more other individuals in the same body. Or was it mind? I didn't quite grasp her explanation. However, she insists his condition was not one of schizophrenia. She appears confused and seems oblivious to the whole issue of the biological weapons facility. Insists there's some Nazi-style racial conspiracy going on.' He smiled drily. 'I don't see her being taken too seriously.'

'Now *that* sounds like the kind of story Moravec would spend money on. Where'd she get this idea? Don't tell me – the bloody IRA?'

'These trendy TV types see fascist conspiracies every-where,' offered someone.

'Moravec's a Jew,' reminded the Home Secretary. 'Believes he's unloved if not actually persecuted. This is sore ground for him. If he's not effectively muzzled he'll have his teeth into that angle, fast.'

'We're on top of the Moravec situation,' stated Masterson.

'Can we get away with a cover-up?' demanded the Defence Secretary. 'The last thing we need at the moment is another scandal concerning the armed forces after this business of Wardlove and his insane transplant enquiry. Obviously our hearts go out to the family but, hell's teeth, what was he thinking about?'

'Someone must have given him information to prompt him into such an action,' said the Deputy Prime Minister, glancing up from his notepad.

'Well of course there's a leak in my house!' snapped the Defence Minister, viciously. 'My problem – and I'll deal with it.'

'We must decide,' said the Prime Minister.

'I'm not certain we've had all the facts,' her deputy protested, gently.

'There are no more facts, sir,' said Masterson. 'Unless you wish to be appraised of the technical side of this experi-mental work.' He glanced at the Prime Minister. 'The security aspect . . . ?'

'Need to know,' she stated. 'And none of us have that need – nor any real understanding of this type of work, I'm sure,' she added, raising a few smiles. 'Gentlemen?' She received their affirmations with a satisfied nod. 'Bury it,' she ordered.

Masterson's eyes smiled as he gave a slight deferential bow to his masters, closed the doors to the cabinet room and merged once more with the shadows.

The Deputy Prime Minister arose, eager to be away after allowing the tide to sweep over him as usual, wondering if he should have fought harder this time. Something was wrong. He detested cabinets where decisions seemed to have been made beforehand; where the feeling that the touch of some unseen hand had directed events lingered long after business was done. Issues concerning the Americans generally prompted that feeling but he was not at all sure that in this case it was the hand of Washington at work. Above all, what he truly disliked was that it all seemed too pat. Masterson's explanation had tripped out so easily. Where were the loose ends? Real life had loose ends. Where were they? And there was the business of the intelligence information from that 'extremely accurate and reliable intelligence source we share with the Americans'. Well, they'd involved themselves pretty damn fast! Those meetings were always held at Chequers and he was certain the Prime Minister had not left Downing Street after the Commons concluded business on Friday afternoon. So who brought the information? Who read her mind, understood her dilemma, gave her precisely the information exposing Soviet hypocrisy she needed as her shovel to bury the entire business? Who broke established – agreed, with the Americans – procedure? Talking of procedure, why had he not been invited? His presence at a personal briefing immediately following delivery of the latest information and forecasts was also established. No word had come from Downing Street. Only the dawn summons which had dragged him from sleep he had dropped into barely two hours before. He felt the chill, aged fingers of the House of Lords reaching for him – and the not-so-gentle push in the back towards them.

You have to fight, he heard his wife say, as she always did.

Fight what, my dear? he enquired silently as he made his way out to his car, choosing not to linger. Another battle lost. Never fought, he corrected himself.

'What was the meeting about, sir?' shouted a familiar voice from the usual Downing Street hunting pack of reporters.

He smiled, blinked at the camera-flashes as he always did. 'I'm sure you'll be told,' he called, ducking into the car. 'Home, Robert.'

'Town or country, sir?' the chauffeur enquired.

'Definitely country.' There, you've made a real decision. Now go back to sleep.

Southby, still in his dressing gown, stood over Foley, shaking him awake, telephone in hand. 'One of your people. Grant? In a public call-box.'

'What time is it?' croaked Foley, his head banging.

'After ten.'

Foley fumbled with the receiver, propping himself up against the arm of the settee, silently cursing tobacco and alcohol. 'Grant? How'd you find me?'

'I gave you Colonel Southby's number, remember?'

'Right. Not awake yet.'

'Got a cold?'

'Bloody cigarettes.'

'You gave up.'

'And I will again. Today. Believe me.'

'Super, you've got to get back here. I don't know what you've been up to but they're screaming for you – softly, which makes it worse. Got the heavy hand on the shoulder: Chief Constable wants you. Did the questioning himself: "Where's the Superintendent? London? London where? Contact number? Surely you have a telephone number, Inspector? Have a think about it. He must have mentioned something. Some old case needed warming over, that his story? It's the one I had anyway. Checking his famous snouts, perhaps? So why call Special Branch? Sit a while in the outer office, put your feet up, have a cup of real coffee – nothing from a machine up here. Pretty young thing to make it too. You could get used to it, I'm sure." Thought for a moment he'd really taken to me – maybe even believed me – then I looked at his eyes.'

'I'm sorry.'

'Wouldn't have minded an upward shove, actually.'

'Just a question of how long you'd stay there.'

'That's a lot you just said.'

'I'm probably wrong. He's being leaned on, I'm sure. Heavily. He's human – all he wants is a quiet life and he's got a rogue officer threatening his peace and order. Just hope that's what it is because the alternative . . . forget it. Grant, you watched his eyes – they're not his questions, are they? So where are they coming from? Really coming from?'

'You tell me.'

'Nesbitt? Sir David Nesbitt? That name come up at all? He was the one after me yesterday, right?'

'Everyone was after you yesterday. Still are. No, Nesbitt wasn't mentioned. Have you called him?'

'And risk having to admit I'm continuing an investigation I've been ordered to drop?'

'How's he involved?'

'Don't know exactly – but in a big way.'

'Listen, whatever you're on to can't be so big you'd risk your pension for it?'

Foley remained silent.

'All right, say it is that big. What can you do about it? Peter Foley, London drop-out, currently a Devonshire copper ready for pasture.'

'Thanks.'

'It's true. This thing's got "political" stamped all over it. You're out of your league. Jump ship. Come home and mow the lawn. Take that cruise you're always on about.'

'I've the rest of my life for all that. Grant? Listen to me. You're best off out of this, hear me?'

'I hear you. I'll decide when I have to throw you to the lions.'

'Have they got anyone following you?'

'I'm out buying a sodding doughnut to go with my coffee! You've developed galloping paranoia.'

'That's right. Ruth at home?'

'Two kids and seven months gone? What do you think?'

'Call her straight away – and do it so that no one can see you dialling. Like you're continuing this call, all right?'

'What do I say?'

'Doesn't matter. It's her you're phoning, not me. Get it?'

'Look –'

'Just do it. Nigel? Any word of him?'

'What do you mean?'

'He's buggered off. Left me a note. He's on to the same thing I am. He's gone in cold and expects me to be the bloody cavalry if things go sour.'

'What's new?'

'This time I can't just cut and come running. Grant, believe me, these people have *serious* aims. If Nigel was on their road they wouldn't even think about brakes – understand me?'

'I'll bet you a fiver he's back at the house with a bird sleeping off a hard night. You know what the little prat's like. Don't waste your worrying on him, Super – you've got your own problems. If it'll make you feel better I'll drop by the house and if he's not there screwing I'll put the word out he's gone missing. Again. Car gone too?'

'Yes.'

'I know make and number. I'll get it sorted, don't worry.'

'Unofficial.'

'Cost you a pretty large round.'

'I'll buy the pub.'

'The way you're going, we'll have to do a whip-round for your old age.'

'I'm taken care of.'

'Lucky you.'

'Grant, watch yourself – and thanks. Call Ruth *now*.'

'See you when I see you, then.'

Foley pulled himself up and replaced the receiver cursing as he held his head.

Southby held out a large mug of tea. 'Aspirin in the bathroom,' he said. 'Liver salts too.'

'I bet your men love you.'

'The only men I deal with any more are the security staff – the rest are women. Girls really.'

'Then you probably wish they would.'

'Did I catch the name Nesbitt? Was that Sir David Nesbitt by any chance?'

Foley lifted his face from the steaming mug. 'The very one. Why?'

'I met him at Defence. Powerful man. One of those behind-the-scene types the press are always banging on about but who they never quite get into focus. I say "met" but it was hardly social. Got dragged in front of this panel comprised of our top brass and assorted Whitehall mandarins. Nesbitt was there presenting some sort of budget he and his bunch had run up – God alone knows what for because no one offered the information, not precisely. I just had to do a brief totting up, plus and minus, of the case for private security versus the real thing. Us, I mean. The military.'

'Southby, Nesbitt is one of them. Maybe the top man.'

Southby swung himself around into a winged leather armchair. 'I sincerely hope not!'

'I have a contact. You heard me speaking to him last night on the telephone. You may as well hear this. Name's Mayberry: computer genius, bent – both ways – but he's all right. I trust him. I employed him to dig deeper than I could officially, using what information I already had. Illegal hacking, okay? The bottom line after he'd done his work was that something far heavier than my little murder enquiry was going on – run or at least controlled from Whitehall, so he said. He's obviously got a big secret-face-of-government thing going so I didn't take him entirely seriously at the time. Later I called my man Grant who told me that a Sir David Nesbitt was after me and wanted me to return his call immediately. The name Nesbitt had stopped Mayberry dead. Nothing would make him hack into Nesbitt's organization. Marched me out and left me standing on the pavement with only you to go to if I wanted to stay on this tiger I seem to have awakened.'

'From the sound of your phone call just now, the tiger has tuned its head and spotted you.'

'I'm tenacious. I don't let go easily, if at all, when it comes to my job. That fact will be known. It could worry people.'

'I'd say it already has.'

'Why does Nesbitt worry you? Just because he wields power behind the scenes, or something more specific?'

'Because, Superintendent, the programme Nesbitt was seeking major funding for involved land purchases and engineering work costing millions of pounds of taxpayers' money. And – '

'Hold on, I thought you said you didn't know what the expenditure was for?'

'Correct. I did not know what it was for. But, if I was to make an accurate analysis for the purposes of a security breakdown, I had to be told – and the figures they gave me were very broad – approximate size of any given site, the type of terrain and whether construction would be above or below ground. The usual necessary facts. From what I was given I understood that more than one site was involved, that various types of terrain would be encountered and that both above and below ground levels would need to be made secure. Afterwards it didn't take any time at all on a calculator, using the approximate measurements I'd remembered against a mean average of land values, to work out that the capital Nesbitt was seeking involved millions of pounds – and that could be a conservative estimate because I didn't know how many of these sites would be bought and prepared. From examples of terrain I'd been shown, I calculated on the basis of three. And if you're going to ask me why I went to all the trouble of making calculations, the answer is simple: I'm a soldier, and soldiers tend to have this insatiable curiosity regarding the possibility of war. Nesbitt heads up this policy study group – '

'Ecology and Human Resources.'

'Ah, your computer genius? Yes, exactly that. Well, a thick slogger like me tends to want things spelt out precisely, so although everyone and his dog thinks of ecology as being mainly caring about keeping our world green, I thought a moment with a good dictionary might be enlightening. So, ecology, definition of, according to *Chambers*: a study of plants, or of animals. Sounds familiar? Well, we all like to be a bit green these days. Ecology also means the study of peoples and institutions in relation to the environment. Put that interpretation together with "Human Resources" and a soldier tends to start picturing solid, secure installations built and readied for a time when the environment is radically changed, either by nuclear, chemical, or biological warfare or some other, natural, catastrophe. In other words, I began to believe that Nesbitt was proposing some sort of survival post. Or a series of them. Pulling the wagons into a circle, in American parlance.'

'Do you still think that?'

'If what you and Mayberry have guessed is correct, then yes, in a way, that is precisely what he is doing. Pulling the wagons into a circle. He and whoever else is behind all this are making damn sure that the work that has been done is not only protected, it is guaranteed survival and ongoing development no matter what happens to the rest of the world.'

'Wait right there,' said Foley. 'Samuel Hale's original, deep fear – ' He took up the pages of the document still lying on the table from the night before, scanning them quickly. 'Here: "A group of us, research scientists in the field of genetics and equally disturbed members of the team involved in the development of atomic weapons, met to bring our concern for the human race into the open . . ." They took their fears to what I think he terms the barons. Certain members of the House of Lords, all right? Starts again here: "The 'facts' we placed at their disposal were our detailed and deeply researched view of how the world as we knew it would be changed by the power of the atom, as both weapon and tool. The danger of mutation of the species was our greatest fear and therefore our most strident warning. We knew that mutation would occur. Monsters might be created. However, this was not the worst of it. We were convinced that, genetically, man would be changed.

283

Changes would take place on a massive scale and be made irreversible by propagation. 'Normal' man as we knew him would become a minority within two to three centuries. The mutants, baser versions of *homo sapiens*, would have power by numbers. . . . A time would come when the best of what is in us would be removed, wiped out, lost from the blueprint of life we all carry. Our cause, our dream, was to create a strain of man so pure, so strong genetically, that he could withstand anything the future would bring." '

Southby sat back, thoughtful. 'In cold hard daylight – and with the advantage of hindsight, seeing the state the world is in now – I wonder if perhaps he wasn't right?'

'Colonel, what's out there isn't Samuel Hale's dream. It's his nightmare. Remember his warning: "We found the first of the future men in secret bunkers deep in a German forest and we destroyed him. Then we stole the blueprints to start again in England. That is when the nightmare first lifted the edge of the dream." ' Foley stood up. 'All that cold hard daylight has done is make the nightmare even bigger than we imagined.'

'Yet you're not scared off?'

'A drunk in a pub with a straight razor scares the shit out of me; a full scale, brick-throwing, fire-bombing inner city riot terrifies me; anything between that and the Wrath of God is beyond my limited imagination.'

'Anything between a riot and the Wrath of God is war,' Southby smiled.

'Then you can take care of it. What I need to take care of right now is my thick head.'

'As I said: liver salts and aspirin in the bathroom cabinet. Hair of the dog, maybe?'

'I'd rather die.'

'Try a cold shower – works for me.'

'For a hangover?' Foley called from the bathroom. 'Or keeping your mind off all those girls you run?'

The telephone bleeped. Southby reached for it: 'Southby. Oh, hello, Fergal. Saturday golf rained off? No, haven't heard a thing. Just got out of bed. Had a long session last night, I've a friend over to stay. *What!* Say again? At his home? Both of them? Christ! Nobody's bloody safe any more. Hope the police grab the bastards fast and none too gently. I don't envy you your Monday morning, I must say – and there'll be the new broom to put up with. Oh hell, what a sick world we live in.'

Southby replaced the receiver, glanced at his watch and hobbled over to the radio.

'Did I hear you say police?' questioned Foley, wrapped in a towel from the door.

'News on any second.'

'Our problem?'

'No connection I could make. Our Minister for the Armed Forces was butchered last night in bloody Hertfordshire. Wife raped and killed too. Shotgun. Listen.'

The newscaster began with the headlines and moved quickly on to the details; the second lead was the Wardlove story.

'*Christ,*' Southby hissed in anger, knuckles white on his cane.

The newscaster moved on to other news.

'What chance have the police got?' Southby almost demanded.

'Depends. Friend of yours?'

'Not at all. Actually I didn't care for the man particularly. Arrogant type – but hell!'

'*Listen!*' Foley snapped.

'. . . the accusation was made publicly to a crowd of more than two thousand Health Service workers during an anti-privatizastion rally last night on Shepherd's Bush Green. This morning, a spokesman for the Ministry of Defence called the accusation "scandalous" and strongly denied that any organs for transplant were being removed from members of the armed forces except when specific instructions, in writing, were left by a potential donor to be acted upon in the event of their sudden death. It seems certain that the information regarding the internal enquiry into transplant operations carried out on forces personnel was leaked from within the Ministry of Defence, some sources narrowing the leak down to the personal staff of murdered Defence Minister Richard Wardlove. Police investigating the killings have stated firmly that there is no connection

285

between them and the leak. Also near Shepherd's Bush Green last night, a fatal accident – '

Southby switched off, his expression incredulous.

'There's your connection,' said Foley.

'Wardlove *knew*.'

'And he started asking questions.'

'Who told him?'

'Maybe nobody? Could have been something simply passed across his desk. Made him suspicious. They have to launder their expenditure some way or other, right? It's on the cards they do it through the MOD.'

'So why kill both of them? And the rape?'

'You heard the bulletin. Yobs. Sex, drugs and murder: your regular Saturday night entertainment on the box. Who isn't going to believe it? You did – until that just came on. The rape was cosmetic.'

Southby remained still and breathed an obscenity.

'It's real, Colonel. As I told Grant: they've got serious aims. They've just proved how seriously they take them. They killed Eleanor Hale and now the Wardloves. God knows how many other murders are down to them. If they've got my friend his life isn't worth a light.'

'Foley, they've killed a *government minister*.'

'I just told you, they're serious.'

'Don't you see it? Surely now, if we hand in Hale's denouncement of the conspiracy as evidence, the police will dismiss the idea of drug-crazed yobs being responsible and open up their enquiry?'

'I explained last night, all we have are the ramblings of a suicide immediately before he put two barrels of a shotgun into his mouth.'

'Hardly ramblings. It's a perfectly lucid, scientifically explained exposé. It makes very real sense.'

'To us, because we're caught up in it, because we have other, unproven facts to tie to it. But read out in a court of law, cold, with the best Queen's Counsel available acting for the defence, making damn sure the judge warns the jury that what they are hearing is, in fact, a suicide note written when the balance of Samuel Hale's mind was disturbed – the recorded verdict which the judge must reveal?

I know trials and I know juries, Colonel. We'll get flayed alive. All we'll get is tabloid headlines "NEO-NAZI PLOT TO RULE THE WORLD, Uncovered by Crippled Colonel and Superannuated Superintendent." Forget it. Apologies for the brutal reference to your . . .'

'No offence taken. Exactly how they'd describe me. You're probably right. So how do we make them believe us?'

'By giving Samuel Hale's final words credibility. By having *him* believed. By showing that he killed himself not because his mind was disturbed but because it was the final and only recourse left to him and that the method of his suicide – the total destruction of his brain – was in fact testament to their existence and their probable intentions upon his natural death.'

'Which brings us back to Heatheridge.'

'That's right. He was there at the beginning. Waited for Hale at the original meeting in the depths of Whitehall. Saw the horrors in Nazi Germany. The only living witness we know of who – maybe – is not part of the conspiracy.'

'I've found him,' said Southby.

'You've only just woken up.'

'Before I fell asleep I had the idea of calling my club to check if he is a member. We have a good few thousand serving and retired army officers on the list. Night porter confirmed he was.'

'Where's that?'

'The Rag. Army and Navy Club. Pall Mall. Heatheridge dines there on alternate Saturdays. Drives back up to London after dealing with constituency business during the day. Dines alone, eightish – depending on traffic – reads a bit of mail, always occupied, never just sits. Thinks, eats, never known to have had a guest with him. Shuns company, so I'm informed. Sometimes stays overnight after dining. Backstairs gossip has him as a cold fish or an angry man who keeps it corked – but he's generally liked. Straight, they say.'

'Anger? Bottled up since 'forty-five, maybe? Christ, if that's the case why hasn't he *done* something? He's a bloody MP!'

Maybe because he's been silenced? That would account for his anger. We have to be sure where he stands before we commit ourselves.'

'How? If he's Hale's captain we've no choice but to lay it out in front of him. Everything.'

'I did some serious thinking as I tried to get some sleep this morning and I think I've worked something out. I told you, leave Heatheridge to me. You should be worrying about your missing friend in Devon – and the fact that you've probably been posted AWOL.'

Foley moved to the telephone and dialled his Exeter home. He heard the same recorded message begin. 'All right if I leave this number on my answerphone, just in case?'

'Of course.'

Tersely, Foley snapped out a message for Lewin to call the London number.

'You've got your chap on to it? Grant?'

'He'll do his best. Pass the word. Twist a few arms.'

'And your superiors?'

'I need Heatheridge's confirmation, Colonel. I need to go back there with something to show why I've been sticking my nose where it definitely should not be. I'm off my own patch, I've wilfully ignored an official directive informing me MI5 had taken over my enquiry and, as you say, I'm absent without leave. I'm also absent with intent to investigate and interfere with what might possibly turn out by now – because, let's face it, some years have passed since Samuel Hale's suicide – to be a completely legal, top secret government project. And frankly, if it is, I'm not throwing my hand in because giving it legality doesn't make it right. No, I *can't* go back without the truth – or at least enough of the truth to make them listen to me and not to whoever is making them jump right now.'

'What if they still don't listen?'

'They'd leave me no choice but to go to the man who sent Nigel Lewin on to those moors in the first place. Rudolph Moravec.'

Southby grimaced. 'A bit like supping with the devil? You'll get no justice from the trash he churns out. Christ, man! You've just quoted the kind of headline he'd tag this – and us – with.'

'I know. But I'll get a reaction, Colonel, and maybe that's what we need more than anything because otherwise we're all going to sleep right through this and wake up to find Hale's nightmare right there, in place, with *Homo superior* smiling down on us poor bloody *Homo sapiens*.'

FIFTEEN

Jane Haversham had no tears for Adam. She lay waiting
for his creators without trepidation because the drug they
had used lifted her fractionally above fear and kept her
there, floating on a warm waterless sea.

The room was perfect. It might have been designed for
her alone. Pale flesh-tones, pure lines, the complete absence
of ornament, a near art-form. Almost perfect. Nothing lived
or had lived in that room – except herself. On the eighth
day God created synthetics and he saw that this was good.
God, hadn't you thought about the problems with non-
biodegradable material? Or is plastic made in your image,
thus eternal? They don't see the world – their world –
failing in here, do they? Only continuing. Dear God: I
wouldn't mind a flower, just one, as a memory.

'How do you feel, Miss Haversham?'

He was almost perfect too: tanned arms brushed with
gold, tanned face with all the right lines in all the right
places, hair and eyebrows that shade of gold which multi-
nationals spent millions trying to fake and more marketing;
a white smile that promised care and, perhaps, caring too.
Only his eyes failed for her because they saw past her, even
through her, to a future she had not been invited to. Bright
hard eyes focused on a greater cause, a greater ideal than
the Hippocratic Oath made by his lesser brethren. It shone
from him like sunlight – except that the continuous, barely
audible bass hum, the air pressure, and some indefinable
inner knowledge perhaps from early human, troglodyte
memory told her no natural sun touched his body in that
place. Nor, perhaps, his soul.

'Wonderful,' she said, speaking the truth.

'You look wonderful too. Quite radiant.'

'You are a doctor?'

Oh yes.'

She decided his flat vowels were East Coast, Ivy League, and probably Boston. 'Where is this place?'

'Don't you remember being brought here?'

'Flying. I remember flying. That's all.'

'For the moment that's all you need to remember.'

'I killed Adam,' she told him, still without tears. 'And Daniel. All of them.'

He smiled and pulled down her cover as softly as a breath. 'Beautiful,' he said, and she felt his warm hands on her. She closed her eyes, sinking into her waterless sea.

Rudolf Moravec stood on his penthouse balcony, the rain hazing the glass and the outside world.

James Shirer drank the remains of his favourite American beer, his tired eyes ageing him. 'Well then, back to the sun.'

Moravec did not answer, hearing but staying with his thoughts.

Shirer stood. 'So we play the three monkeys. I didn't hear a damn thing last night so I do the ears. You, naturally, have the speaking part but their gag does the job for you. Jane, wherever she's keeping that gorgeous body, just didn't see a damn thing. That how it's going to work? Count on her, can you? I mean, I'm bought, you're fucked – so what sorts her out? Or shouldn't I ask? Will she be another statistic in today's media roll-call of fatal happenings? Christ!'

'Go back to your woman.'

'I will. Oh, I will.'

'And stay sober.'

'I'm not one of your actual talkative drunks, so if you don't mind I'll get blotto when the hell I like.'

'It's up to you.'

'Sure. I don't want my clinic torched.'

Moravec turned, fury – fuelled by guilt – in his eyes.

Shirer stood his ground. 'There's nothing you can do to me any more. Go on, kick back at the bastards – publish even if you get screwed! You can afford it.'

'You don't know a damn thing about my world. You

only stay at the centre of things in this business for as long as you're allowed to. Great or small, you eat mainly what those in power feed you from their table – and sometimes you go around to the back door and sneak a few bits from the backstairs staff, maybe getting away with it, maybe not. But nobody gets away with smashing down the front door with a battering ram and opening the windows and doors for the entire gawping world to see inside. Nobody.'

Shirer shrugged. 'There goes another illusion. I really believed you media giants stood astride the world stomping governments into submission at will.'

'Another time I'll discuss the reality of media power with you. Now leave, and keep your opinions medical and confidential.'

'Moravec, anything that shuts you up turns me to stone.'

Moravec turned away, gave himself a drink from the bar and drank it, staring out at the wire peaks of the Regent's Park aviary but not seeing them, his anger deep, his humiliation complete. They had silenced him, which was bad enough, then they had shown him how well they understood his weakness and had applied pressure directly, the carrot immediately after the big stick, their audacity taking even his breath away:

How difficult it must be for you to establish yourself as being truly British, Mister Moravec. Or perhaps we should say English? The slights, the rejections – sometimes even direct insults? Shameful! You know, nothing in this country opens doors as quickly, or as reverentially, as an honour. A worthwhile honour, of course. Something to place you on a par with your peers? The style you must leave to us, naturally; however, we understand your needs and respect your position – as we're certain you do ours. We do understand each other, Mister Moravec?

'A Detective Superintendent Foley, sir?' his major-domo interrupted, presenting a telephone.

Moravec shook his head sharply, then said: 'Wait! I'll take it.'

The man deposited the instrument on a white marble table and retired.

Moravec stared at it for a long moment, finally lifting

the receiver. 'Foley. I know I haven't been back to you. To tell you the truth I have no word on Lewin. Nothing at all, I'm afraid.'

'He was heading for Dartmoor,' said Foley, almost accusingly.

'Yes.'

'You confirm that?'

'Yes.'

'Did you know that when I spoke to you last night?'

'I was aware of it. However, I explained – '

'You had to keep one step ahead of your competitors.'

'Correct.'

'If I told you I have in my possession from another source the . . . material . . . Nigel Lewin was investigating on your behalf, what would your reaction be?'

Moravec hesitated. 'I'd tell you that the investigation in question is not part of our future planning.'

'Meaning you don't intend to publish.'

'Precisely.'

'But you've received some information from Nigel?'

'I told you. Not a word.'

'Jane Haversham? Where can I find her?'

'An American company offered her an immediate long-term contract.'

' "Immediate" meaning?'

'She's already gone.'

'Goodbye, Mister Moravec,' said Foley, accusation now clear in his voice.

Peter Foley replaced the receiver. 'He's been got at.'

'What made you ask him so directly? I thought you were calling to check on your chap Lewin?' questioned Southby.

'Guilt reduces a man. The arrogance had gone from him. They've made him theirs. How is irrelevant. I knew I'd be wasting my time going to him but I just wanted to hear him say it.' Foley checked his watch. 'Mayberry wanted to see me. I'll see what he's got hold of and meet you back here in good time to catch Heatheridge.' He lifted the telephone again and dialled quickly. 'Mayberry? You still asleep? *What* time? I won't ask you what you were doing.

Today still on? Right. Mayberry, listen to the news – all of it. See you around mid-day.' He put the receiver down and turned to Southby. 'Been up all night working on something – this, I think. About Heatheridge? What'll you do, warn him we're coming?'

'I'm not certain that's the best idea.'

'What then? Gatecrash his table?'

'He generally relaxes in one of the few rooms set apart for men only. I gather he's a bit of a misogynist. We'll eat at the Rag ourselves, I'll call and reserve a table for eight – we know that's his regular time.'

'Clothes? All I brought are a couple of fresh shirts and underwear.'

'You'll do. By the way . . .' Southby hobbled to the door, indicating Foley should follow. In the hallway, he lifted the lid of an ancient officer's campaign trunk. 'Up to you,' he said.

Foley looked in. 'I'm glad I called for an appointment first.'

'Richard and Harriet Wardlove had their heads blown off with a shotgun, I'm reliably informed.'

'I'd hate to have to live with these constantly at hand.'

Southby shrugged. 'Today's world.'

Foley still hesitated.

Southby said: 'Every one is registered. Licensed to be carried off the premises.'

'Not by me they're not.'

'Technically you're already acting outside the law, aren't you? You are defying orders.'

'The "may as well hang for a sheep" argument?'

'I'd call it the self-preservation argument.'

Foley stared at the four weapons glistening dully in the base of the trunk.

'What's your preference?'

'I trained on a Colt .38.'

Southby bent over with a grunt and scooped up a squat revolver encased in a woven leather cutaway belt holster. 'Smith and Wesson .38, Bodyguard Model. Hammer's shrouded so you don't rip the lining of your Armani suit.'

Foley pulled his jacket open.

Southby grinned: 'Well, your real bodyguard doesn't wear Joseph Dorf, Gents Bespoke Tailor, Exeter.'

'Probably earns an Armani-style salary.' Foley accepted the blue-steel revolver, flipping the chamber out. 'Five. Have to remember that.'

'There's a thirteen-round Beretta if you prefer.'

'I've never got on with automatics.'

Southby handed over a small box of ammunition.

Foley pressed five rounds home, returned to the living-room and packed the box of spares in the grip he'd collected earlier from the BMW.

Southby tossed him a key ring. 'You'll need these in case I'm out when you return. Saturdays I usually stock up.'

'An MOD colonel wheeling a trolley around a super-market?'

'We all have to live.' Southby smacked his ruined leg. 'They deliver.'

'Two locks?'

'And both applied. Banham deadlock and Chubb Pipekey.'

'Serious security.'

'Serious world. Even before your arrival.'

Foley fitted the holstered revolver on to his belt over his groin, butt inward for his right hand, then buttoned his jacket over it. 'Right, Mayberry.'

'Take great care,' warned Southby.

'You too, Colonel.'

'I'll use my famed total recall and drag out all I can remember of that meeting with Nesbitt for when you get back.'

Willie's was near Earls Court and on Saturday afternoons had a following which spilled on to the pavement in a well-ordered double-banked line.

Foley drove past the entrance, found a parking space in a side-road and walked back. Ignoring the queue, he held his ID under the nose of one of the doormen. The man shrugged and stood aside, giving his partner a quick nod.

The club was in the basement, reached by a western saloon balustrade. That theme continued, expensively, throughout, with all woodwork carved from the solid: no hardboard, no plywood. No tack, thought Foley, impressed. A large mirror dominated one side of the room. He saw a tall, worn-looking man in creased clothes staring at him as if in shock from finding himself quite suddenly in another, older man's body. He looked away, too quickly, afraid, swearing to take himself to a serious health farm. If his life ever returned to normal.

The music was country, live, loud but bearable with a pedal-steel guitar break scything the humid, beery, smoke-laden air. Foley headed for the bar, pushed his way through the crush and ordered a Bloody Mary.

'Rough night?' asked a pretty red-head wearing a button advising: 'For Safer Sex Keep Hard Men Covered'.

'On the rocks,' said Mayberry, sliding close beside Foley.

'Him or the Bloody Mary?' asked the barmaid.

'Both,' Foley answered, curtly. He glared at Mayberry, almost nose to nose in the crush. 'Can you back off a bit?'

'My! You really are pleased to see me.'

'Very funny.'

'You'd think I'd be able to tell the difference by now, wouldn't you? What's in the plain brown wrapper or shouldn't I ask?'

'All of it. Everything.'

Mayberry's eyes were very steady. 'I doubt that.'

The music stopped. A man with a small cigar mounted the stage, took the microphone and welcomed the crowd. 'I'm in charge,' he shouted, and was immediately assailed by a practised chorus of good-humoured derision from the packed audience.

'I listened to the news,' said Mayberry, forced even closer.

'And?'

'I know why you're carrying that *thing* which is doing me irreparable damage at this moment. It's gratifying to know we're not alone, however.'

'Not alone? I'd say any other interested party is in the morgue.' Foley's eyes were quick and nervous. 'This isn't the place to talk.'

'It's exactly the place to talk.'

The man on the stage shouted the audience down, introduced a new act then pushed his way through to them. 'Did I do well?' he enquired.

'You always do!' exclaimed Mayberry. 'D. D. Hurrell. Owns the place which makes him a star in his own firmament. Officers' Club open, dear boy?'

Hurrell grinned widely and turned tail, swinging an arm exaggeratedly for them to follow.

The Officers' Club was Hurrell's office. A massed photographic record of his encounters with celebrities, effusively signed as proof, filled two walls; a plate glass window penetrated another, looking down on the tightly packed audience below with only the merest hint of noise defeating the soundproofing. Foley realized the window was the reverse of the big mirror he'd seen himself in as he descended into the club. He noted a work-station bearing an IBM personal computer, printer and telephone modem beside a large executive desk and gave Mayberry a studied look.

Hurrell poured heavy measures of Scotch into three thick tumblers without consultation and handed them out, settling himself behind his desk. 'Cheers!'

Mayberry said: 'Time for you to do your walkabout, isn't it?'

'We've only just got here!'

'Your public awaits.'

Hurrell stood and buttoned his checked jacket. 'I can't let them down, can I?'

'The show must go on,' agreed Mayberry. 'Cheers.'

'I'll be back,' warned Hurrell.

Foley sipped whisky, grimacing as the neat alcohol burned his already acid stomach. 'Let's you use it, does he?' he enquired, looking pointedly at the IBM.

Mayberry smiled and flipped through a collection of CDs by a player, selected one and played it. 'I believe it's called ducking and diving.'

'The record or your deviousness?'

Mayberry held out his manicured hand for Samuel Hale's legacy then sat at Hurrell's desk, reading quickly and in silence.

Foley closed his eyes, aching for a few more hours' sleep. Willie Nelson nasally advised him that drink was no antidote to ageing, that beautiful women grew old too, and that he'd no direction to go now but down.

'Are you trying to tell me something?' Foley enquired archly but Mayberry was no longer with him.

Live music seeped through the walls as the track ended. A girl's heartbroken voice sang that somewhere, someone was loved more than she.

Foley thought: country music's the soul of America, bursting with contradictions; the failure behind the winning smile; the quivering upper lip on the stone face of the American Dream. He longed for a cigarette, swallowed a little of the whisky to ease the craving and made it worse. There were cigarettes on the desk: he avoided them. He wished he was back in Exeter. He wished he had never gone to Raethmoor Farm. Had never heard of Eleanor Hale. He did not want the responsibility he was faced with. He did not want to make choices, decisions, plans which were not part of the life he had already set out clearly in his mind. Most of all he did not want the feel of the Smith and Wesson .38 at his groin or the steel of shotgun barrels at his skull. He was not ready to die. He had plans for the rest of his life and dying was on the back-burner.

'Why me? he asks,' said Mayberry, leaning back, arms behind his head. 'It's on your face. Clear as jaundice. But you know very well you're not going to run away from it.'

Foley angrily stripped the Cellophane off a packet of cigarettes on the desk and lit one.

'Better?' Mayberry asked.

'Go to hell.'

'I'm bound to.'

'Why did you want to see me?'

Mayberry pushed a computer floppy disc towards him. 'Once upon a time. Except this is no fairy-tale.'

'Once upon a time?'

'There was fear.' Mayberry tapped Samuel Hale's legacy. 'Fear that drove good men and true to seek protection for what was then a very different Great Britain.'

'I know all that.'

'The fear was proven to be unwarranted. Science and progress dismissed it. Millions did not succumb to radiation poisoning, nuclear power stations did not leak slow death, TV sets didn't poison our bodies – our brains, maybe, but not our bodies. But the fear had created a powerful organization: not exactly a government department nor, quite, a private concern. In fact it does not exist. Oh, it forms part of a department of this government ministry or a section of that conglomerate but it has no beating heart that you can put your hand on and say here, here lives the horror. The problem, Peter Foley, was that the fear had created this – what shall we call it – power structure? And nobody wanted to relinquish that power. For years, decades, these people had been able to get whatever they wanted when they wanted, whatever the cost – and we're talking millions.'

'How?'

'Others made their case for them, others requisitioned for them on whatever pretext. A chain had been formed, each link another loop of power for another official, another department, another research grant to another company in another corporation. The ADAM Project was fed by many Eves and it survived in an Eden over which no God ruled. So ADAM never got evicted. It carried on exactly as it did in the days of the fear. Except they had to find another *raison d'être* they could sell to all those who wanted them to survive. So the fear became the dream and the dream was so good, so convincing, so important for the future of man, for history – which is precisely the kind of music the people we're discussing adore – that they all closed their eyes and let the dream continue, unchecked, uncontrolled and – ' Mayberry laid his palm on the legacy ' – unspeakably evil.'

'You're telling me I can't stop it. It's too big. I know all that. I may not be able to bring their temple down but I can damn well stand outside and denounce what's going on inside.'

'You mean Heatheridge can?'

'If he'll do it.'

'Don't you understand? They don't fear anything. They left Heatheridge alive – and Eleanor Hale – because neither could hurt them. They knew that somewhere along the line a stop would be put on anyone who created a problem.'

'Then they've made their biggest mistake. They've started killing people.'

Mayberry switched on the computer and slotted in the disc, trailing his fingers across the keyboard. A list wound its way slowly up the screen. 'Just to show you what you're up against.'

Foley stared for a moment, disbelievingly. 'All these?'

'That I know of.'

'How did you – '

'I've told you. It's the new world we live in, the nature of the technology, the lateral "thinking" which makes the storing and retrieval of information so effective – and available – to those who know how. I can move laterally on any heading you give me and wring it, and anything remotely connected with it, dry.'

'Where did you start?'

'Where I stopped yesterday.'

'Nesbitt?'

'His policy study group. Ecology and Human Resources. Him personally, I've avoided.'

'So what's the bottom line?'

'You mean top line, don't you? The furthest reaches are dark and murky places: secret departments. The ones the media make a fuss about and those they don't believe exist.' Mayberry touched keys and brought up a single listing. 'Now if you want to know how they talk to our elected rulers, here you are.'

'Joint Study Group? Who the hell are they? Studying what? Joint with who?'

'Whom. They're Anglo-American. Full title: Political and Economic Joint Study Group.' Mayberry touched a key. 'They come under the control of *this* financial trust.'

'Jesus.'

'They deal in information. Their service is entirely free and restricted to those at the highest level of politics and commerce. They're also secretive in the extreme. Their forecasting is uncannily accurate, judging by the results of some extraordinary Eastern European investment decisions taken by companies controlled by the trust in early 'eighty-nine. Almost as if they knew beforehand the dominoes were about to fall. Unfortunately, I've no back door into the Joint Study Group. I hate to be beaten but there it is.'

'How the hell did you track them down?'

Mayberry gave his self-satisfied smile. 'The Civil Service keeps meticulous records of all government expenses. Any item, supposed to be covert but not covered by the Secret Vote, they simply launder through something overt.'

'Covert? Like what?'

'Like regular monthly journeys from Heathrow to Chequers not made in official cars yet charged to Whitehall. It's easy from there: flight arrivals, passenger names, addresses, charge accounts – I could probably tell you the brand of underwear the girl in seat F5 buys.'

'Are you telling me I'm up against Downing Street?'

'I've shown you what you're up against – and that they have access to the Prime Minister at Chequers. That isn't quite the same thing, is it? You're the detective – wouldn't that come under the heading of circumstantial evidence as far as the direct involvement of Downing Street is concerned?'

'Can I take that disc to Heatheridge?'

'Not precisely.' Mayberry casually stole a new, sealed blank disc from Hurrell's desk and handed it to Foley to open. 'You put it in, dearie,' he said.

'Insurance?'

'*Assurance*: confidence, feeling of certainty, subjective certainty of one's salvation.'

'You'll survive.'

Mayberry pushed Samuel Hale's legacy back across the desk, adding an envelope from his pocket. 'Recent news cutting on Heatheridge – profile, with photograph. He's prickly, be warned.'

Hurrell returned. 'I'm going back on stage now,' he announced.

'Wouldn't miss it for the world,' said Mayberry.

It was almost four thirty when Foley parked his BMW in the narrow forecourt outside Southby's flat, avoiding the overhanging trees because of the bird-droppings just as he did outside Divisional Headquarters in Exeter. Momentarily, as he locked the car, he was back in that car park, berating Nigel Lewin for his deviousness after seeing him on his car-phone taking the call from London: the call which had started everything. *Car-phone.* 'Idiot!' he blurted aloud and ran into the four-storey brownstone block, ignoring the lift.

Southby's shopping stood outside his solid front door in cardboard boxes, almost tripping Foley as he turned the corner after the three-flight climb. The two door-keys were already in his hand: he worked the Banham then the Chubb, breathing heavily.

The smell hit him first. It had filled his nostrils more times in his long career than he could count or remember. The stench of faeces, of acrid urine, of blood, sometimes – but not this day – mixed with the more subtle, musky odours of semen and sex. The smell of violent death. Then the man hit him, his colleague doing the holding: a short, hard, piston-like blow, just below the belt, aimed to incapacitate quickly. Within that half-second, Foley knew by their economy of effort, their confidence, their silence, that they were professionals. He knew also that they would kill him. In their own time.

The Smith and Wesson under his jacket saved him. His assailant gasped and doubled over, nursing cracked knuckles. Half-winded but thinking fast, Foley let his knees buckle and the man pinioning him, already thrown by the sudden reversal, stumbled forward and overbalanced.

They will kill you, was the only thought in Foley's mind. They will.

The man sprawled on top of him, fighting for a neck hold. Foley countered by dropping his chin, his hand already closed over the .38 but pinned down. A lethal kick, aimed at his head by the one with the injured hand, ripped his ear before slamming into the arm that gripped him. Foley, half-deafened, barely heard the angered shout but his gun hand was free and elation ran through him: he had a chance to live.

The sound of his first shot was smothered because the

302

.38 was fired directly against the wall of the stomach pressing down on him; the second, immediately afterwards, was covered by the man's agonized scream. Foley heard a snapped '*Fuck!*' from further away and in his mind – which seemed to have slowed time down a hundredfold – saw the wrong hand going for a gun, the other swelling and already useless.

He fired upward twice, uncertain where the bullets would hit, knowing only by the scream that they had hit at all. The gunman slumped to his knees, half of his jaw shot away, blood pumping through a small hole in his shirt just below his sternum, an automatic in his left hand, held weakly, its barrel to the parquet floor, so close to Foley's face he could smell the gun-oil, as his senses, on full alert, rejoiced at being alive. He heard an agonized sob and thick red mucus dripped on to the floor by his face. He saw the automatic lift, achingly slowly.

'I'm sorry,' Foley said, meaning it – now that life was his and the choice to continue it, his also. He heaved at the dead-weight above him, thrust the .38 forward against the gunman's heart and pulled the trigger twice. One choked gunshot sounded as the gunman jerked and fell back, shuddered then stilled. Five only, thought Foley, I had to remember that. Then he vomited.

After a moment, he forced the body off him, sickened by the amount of blood which pooled on the floor and stuck his ruined jacket to his back. He knew one of his shots had somehow severed a major artery and the thought of the man bleeding to death on his back caused him to retch violently again. He ran to the bathroom and kneeled head down over the lavatory bowl but there was nothing left in him except the acid taste of Scotch and bile.

In a frenzy he tore off his clothes and climbed naked under the shower until the water ran clear then leaned against the tiles, head back, letting the hot water sluice over him full blast, knowing he had few choices left now. He expected to hear police sirens but none came. This is the life you gave up – ran away from. London. Or what it has become. Two men killed by gunshots on a Saturday afternoon and no one notices. He wanted to get moving, had decisions to make, urgently, but the warm comfort of the running water would not release him.

Think.

He recalled the car-park had been deserted, except for Southby's automatic Honda with the disabled sticker. The block was off the main road, set in its own limited grounds, surrounded by heavy oaks, several beeches and, going by the droppings under the trees in the car-park, half a million resident birds. Had they heard the shots and risen in one massive flurry, a great cloud, warning all of murder? He knew shock was setting in fast. He was shivering yet felt he was burning up. He left the bathroom, wrapping himself in warm towels from the rail and one of Southby's hanging robes, made himself tea, gave himself a little brandy and stood, trying to decide whether he was prepared to throw away an entire lifetime, whether he had the strength to go on alone – and knowing all the while that at some point he had to go into Southby's bedroom.

He walked to the window, the steaming sweet tea in his hand, too hot to drink yet still he swallowed it. He studied the steel window frames and tapped the armoured glass, knowing even as he did so that they were measures meant to save a life that was already lost – that their installation had served only to stifle the cries of death.

Southby's clothes will never fit me, he thought vaguely, already running in his mind, forgetting momentarily that earlier- fearing the embarrassment of being under-dressed at Southby's club – he had stopped at an outfitter's and purchased a long-fitting ready-made three-piece in pure wool. The sober charcoal-grey suit now lay flat, under polythene, on a hanger in the boot of the BMW next to a new white shirt and a Black Watch tie, which he had decided he would wear defiantly that evening, his former, humble, national service status notwithstanding.

He felt light-headed. He might not have been there at all had it not been for the stench of death. He knew he was close to weeping. The taking of life, even in Korea, had not come easily. Not at first, some darker part of him murmured. He wanted to lie down, sleep, escape. All the things he should be doing – especially calling the police – were matters for another time, another place, where he was altogether another man.

What a time to have a bloody nervous breakdown. On your feet. March.

You are on your feet.

Steady, old son.

Do something!

He sat on the arm of the settee and called Lewin's carphone number as he should have done long before. Idiot.

'Hello?' a nervous, young, male voice enquired, broad Devon, then laughed as someone said something in the background.

'Who the hell's that?'.

'I'm looking at the rad. I answered 'cause you rang.' Laughter again.

'This is the police,' Foley snapped, his nerves raw. 'That car you're in belongs to a missing person. If you can't tell me where the owner is then get me someone who can. Fast.'

'There's only me and one of the girls here!'

'Where?'

'Hire car company. The bloke who owns this Golf, he's got one of ours – hang on. What? She says he took out a four-wheeler. Four-wheel drive that is.'

'Name?'

'Name?' came the repeat, urgently.

A girl's voice answered, unintelligibly.

'Put her on,' Foley ordered, hearing whispering and a shuffling of the receiver.

'Lewis,' said the girl, finally. 'Friend of . . . one of our girls, all right?'

'Nigel Lewin?' asked Foley.

'Yeah, Lewin. Nigel sounds right. Small fella, dark, quick.' A hand closed over the mouthpiece again to more laughter.

'Where are you?'

'In the car of course!'

'Address?' snapped Foley.

She gave it.

'Isn't anyone from your management there?'

305

'You'll be lucky – it's five past five. Only the mechanic and me.'

'Get me the number of the vehicle he took.'

'Office is locked up.'

'Christ! Ask the mechanic.'

'Hang on.'

Foley found himself gripping the telephone hard enough to break it. He relaxed and breathed slowly, bringing himself down.

'Hello? Police? Hello?'

'I'm here.'

'He says Daihatsu Fourtrak.'

'Registration?'

She read it out slowly.

'Any idea where he was going? This is important. Think.'

A hand clamped over the phone. This time there was no whispering.

'Are you there?'

'Yeah, OK. Look, I don't like splitting, OK?'

'You'll be all right.'

'Sure.'

'Just tell me.'

'He was in the staff room with one of the girls. I'm not giving names, right? You can't make me. He was . . . you know.'

'Go on.'

'We were only having a bit of a laugh, me and a couple of the girls. We sort of, you know, listened.'

'What did you hear?'

'What do you think?'

'I'm not interested in that! Did he say what he was up to? Boasting? He does that.'

'Yeah, said he was going to make a packet. Thousands. New car – said he'd give . . . her . . . this one, the Golf. Something to do with TV and newspapers and stuff.'

'Where?'

'In England, where'd you think?'

'I mean did he say where he was going to make this money?'

'Dartmoor. He said he'd maybe start up by the nick.

306

Someone's escaped – maybe from there, maybe from the army – deserted, like. Is he all right then? She'll want to know, see. My friend. I can't just say nothing, can I?'

'You can help. Call Detective Inspector Grant – got that? Grant, Detective Inspector, at Exeter Police Headquarters. Ask for CID and speak to him only. He'll tell you what he knows. Give him the information you just gave me. Don't worry, you're not in trouble. Just tell him the name and number of the vehicle and say it was hired to Nigel Lewin. Lewin, not Lewis, got it? Tell him he's on the moors.'

'All the phones are locked up.'

Foley sighed. 'You're holding one.'

'Oh yeah!' Laughter.

'Call Grant now.'

'Who shall I say called?'

'Just say the police – he'll know who.' Foley put down the receiver. He took a deep breath and went into the bedroom.

Southby was on the fouled bedsheets, sitting upright, naked, his arms pinned to the bedhead by two red rings around his biceps, his splayed legs held the same way to the bottom bedposts. Wire, Foley realized as he drew the curtains back; the red was where it had cut through the flesh. The gag they had used was his underwear – which now spilled from his mouth on to his chest. They seemed to have concentrated on his genitals for that was where the blood lay – amidst other stains.

Why the hell didn't you just tell them? Foley raged. Jesus. Now he wept. Wept for a man he hardly knew. Yet who had been ready to sacrifice everything – and had – out of a sense of . . . of what? Of outrage. He looked directly into Southby's dead, amber eyes: 'I'll tell you what, Colonel, the cost is rising and dear God, I'm going to make them pay.'

He went quickly through Southby's wardrobe and found a loose sweater, socks and a pair of cords that seemed longer than any of his other trousers. They would do to walk down to the car. Next he gathered as many blankets and bedsheets as he could find, took them into the hallway and threw them in layers on the floor to soak up the blood. There was no time to clear up.

Clear up after three murders? What was he thinking of? What was he doing? He must be going mad. Nothing seemed to matter any more.

Except getting to Heatheridge.

And maybe finding Nigel alive – although his hopes of that were fading fast.

He saw the flashing message light on Southby's telephone answering machine.

The voice was quick, almost breathless but not through fatigue. Bewilderment, even fear, rushed the words. 'Super? Grant here. Time's two twenty. Drove over to your house. No Nigel, no GTi and your place has been turned over. And I *mean* turned over. Major redecoration job. Reported it straight away, got told to mind my own business – polite but definite. That's the good news, here's the bad. There's some new faces arrived. Funnies, or some new heavy mob we don't know about? Or maybe you do? Like I said, everyone's nice and polite – Sunday manners so as not to upset us provincial plods – but they smile like they've got ice in their teeth. Your desk is in sections against your office walls. Those nice prints you brought back from that Italian holiday? – frames should make good kindling. Word is that you've been into something really bent since your London days. Still are. They're hinting drugs and big pay-offs. One of the WPCs heard a call being made to your bank and I had a whisper that the Drug Squad took some stuff from bloody Nigel's bedroom. They're tying you two together – really together, know what I mean? They're assassinating you, Super, and you're not here to do anything about it. I can't help you. You have to come back and sort it out yourself. I'll call again later and maybe catch you. And yes, I'll watch my back.'

The machine bleeped and died.

The perfect frame, thought Foley. Discredit both my personal and professional reputation at a stroke. They either kill me or destroy me. Maybe both. One for them, the other for the press. It would be easy. His informers in the London underworld might easily be bribed or otherwise coerced into damning him. And if the bastards wanted to dig really deep for circumstantial dirt they could cite his relationship with a major crime-lord: his former friend and one-time fellow prisoner in Korea with whose wife he had, unwittingly, conducted an adulterous affair, resulting in his discovery of her husband's identity and criminal status and culminating in his own startling request for a transfer and subsequent flight to the Devon and Cornwall Constabulary. How would his then seemingly irrational abandonment of an assured, high-flying future appear under the hard glare of suspicion? Had he been a victim of blackmail, the wife a honeytrap? Or warned off? Threats issued, circumstances banked for the future: get out of town and stay alive and never forget who gave you that choice? Worse: had he been bought – permanently? A thoroughly bent copper who had sorted out his future very nicely, thank you?

His life was falling apart around him. Within a few days everything he had accepted as being, if not for ever, then at least settled, was in grave danger of disintegrating. If it had not already? He wondered if he were dreaming. If this were some new version of his Korea dream. Or if he were actually dead: had been vaporized in the bitter cold of the trenches during an artillery barrage and his lost soul was simply floating through a real or imagined existence which – as now – fell apart. Was the dream therefore true reality and his waking, the dream?

'Bollocks!' he snapped aloud. 'Fuck them!' He stood, fight back in his eyes. Even fire. He dressed in Southby's clothes, quickly. *Nigel*. He had to get on to the moors himself, it was the only way. In the end it was up to him. But Heatheridge first, then Nigel. Heatheridge might have information that could save time – could even save Nigel. He had to meet Heatheridge, he owed Southby that. Heatheridge was the key. He might even prove to be a weapon. And he needed help badly now they'd left him no choice but to fight, sending in their hard boys, expecting PC Plod who didn't carry a gun, who'd lie down, roll over and die. Well they're dead and you're alive. It was you or them. They tortured and killed a crippled soldier and their masters do exactly the same in greater numbers in the name of science and a Brave New World. And maybe our rulers help them do it? And maybe you're the only one who is willing to do anything to stop them? He shut his mind to that.

He went down to the BMW quickly but without haste and returned with his new clothes, meeting no one and seeing no more cars in the car-park.

'Sod 'em,' he said aloud, stepping around the still blanket-covered forms in the hallway, coldly angry and feeling freer than he had in years. School's out. War's ended. Start over – but sort this out first. Once more with feeling. For Eleanor Hale, for Southby – and maybe for Nigel. Nigel, you stupid bugger, why couldn't you have trusted me?

He returned to the bedroom and the dead eyes of his new-found friend.

What did they want, Colonel? Hale's legacy? On present form, it was a certainty they would have known everyone Eleanor Hale kept in contact with. They would have checked everyone she had called the day they killed her. Maybe they simply taped everything said on her telephone? So they homed in on you just as they homed in on me. And your call to me put the two of us in the same coffin. In their minds. Did you tell them I'd been here? Did their executioners finish you off then wait in their still, economical way for Plod to arrive, mud on boots, ready for the heavy questions? I bet you told them to go to hell even when they put the gun to your forehead, close enough for powder burns. It shows in your eyes. Still.

All this he thought, and some of it he might actually have spoken while sifting through the scattered contents from a grey steel box sunk into the floorboards near the bed with sliced flaps of Wilton curling back from it like a surgical wound.

A smile touched his lips and he gave Southby a small careful glance, one pro to another, as he put into two separate piles passport, credit cards, bank deposit and cheque-books, driving licence and vehicle log-books, vehicle keys, and labelled Yale door-keys.

Even cripples run in the shadows, Colonel?

He gazed silently at two lives, complete, whole, and

nothing whatsoever to do with the real man. And of no use to his killers. He had already seen what they wanted, on the soiled sheets – soiled also – between Southby's legs like a death warrant, his true executioner's name written in Southby's own hand: Nesbitt. And below, notated details, the harvest of a spymaster's memory. Foley heard the clipped tones: 'I'll use my famed total recall and drag out all I can remember of that meeting with Nesbitt for when you get back.' I'm back, Colonel, said Foley in silent answer. Your memory killed you.

The passport for one of the false identities was well used, with stamps of entry and exit from Eire abounding. The other was pristine, virgin, a life unborn although a name was given to a face that did not yet exist in the blank box above it: John David Clifton. Businessman. Age, four years younger than Foley's own. Birthdate, coincidentally the same month. August. For a long moment Foley stared at the passport, knowing it was no forgery, no copy, but an up-to-date, genuine, government issue original from a list of blanks passed to those departments who needed them, no questions asked.

You wouldn't dare, he told himself. But he was half-way a different man already.

SIXTEEN

Southby's secret lives included a lock-up garage at the
rear of a block of grubby brick-terraced shops near an
underground station in North London and, Foley suspected, somewhere quite close though not in the terrace
itself, a small, self-contained, anonymous flat with its own
entrance, second-hand furniture and thick curtains. Behind
these his informers would spill, often drunkenly, exaggeratedly and sometimes maliciously fabricated for them by
the IRA, the latest gossip on the Cause heard via the
London Irish club and pub grapevine from which,
occasionally, real gold was drawn by the intelligence ana-
lysts.

Or perhaps there was just one informer, thought Foley,
working the garage lock. One English madman, hero and
actor manqué who had infiltrated the British end of the
IRA underground for Queen, Country, and some other
personal motivation beyond the comprehension of saner,
ordinary human beings. Someone like Daniel Hale,
Colonel? Was Daniel the reason why you lay there, stripped
of dignity, taking it – all of it – until either you could not
take any more or they lost patience? Had you run Daniel?
Then lost him to the Boyos? Their bloody inquisition?
Their meatgrinder? Had you given up all hope for him,
from man or God, then found it was not the Provos who
had him after all – not finally? Was your outrage centred
on one face, one body that didn't die, that should have
died, that *they* breathed their foul breath into? Somehow
now, Colonel, that defiant look in those amber eyes makes
more sense.

The vehicle inside was a Range Rover, neither new nor
old, dark blue and dirty, dried mud coating the heavy-duty
tyres: a hard traveller resting after only God knew what

secret journeys. Foley knew the battery would have life; he turned the ignition and the big V8 roared, idling lumpily before he worked the expected automatic transmission and eased the tall vehicle out of the tight unlit space. He replaced it immediately with his BMW, secured both car and garage and drove back into central London, feeling exposed by the Range Rover's height.

He reached his destination in good time despite growing Saturday-night-revellers' traffic, snapped up the first vacant space he found within walking distance of Pall Mall and strolled easily in the direction of the Army and Navy Club, occasionally halting and turning as if new to the city, checking his back.

He reached the club's entrance fifteen minutes before Heatheridge's established eight o'clock arrival time, walked in with a confidence he did not feel, surprised that the club resembled a large bright London hotel and was not the gloomy, wood-panelled and marble-pillared affair he had expected, introduced himself at reception as a dinner guest of Colonel Charles Southby, and settled himself to wait, positioning himself so that he could see all who entered, familiarizing himself with the face in the news cutting Mayberry had given him.

Heatheridge arrived within ten minutes, being greeted immediately by reception staff with a handful of envelopes and telephone messages. He shuffled through them absently, a tall, lean figure in a green Barbour with wiry, near-white hair tamed by a close cut and a brown outdoors-man's face, deeply lined around the eyes as if he focused into distance for long periods.

Foley recognized him instantly but waited until the MP was almost alongside before rising from his chair. 'Mr Heatheridge? May I speak to you for a few minutes?'

Heatheridge stopped, surveying Foley coldly, his eyes noting the plaster covering his torn ear through which fresh blood had seeped, then glanced quickly, questioningly, towards reception.

'Germany, 1945,' Foley said, urgently. 'A forest deep behind enemy lines, bunkers, a severed head that should not have lived yet did.'

Heatheridge waved away an approaching member of the club staff. His eyes seemed to be struck by fever, his brown face yellowed. *'Who are you?'*

'My name is Peter Foley. I'm a police detective superintendent – although I should imagine that my career is, or soon will be, over. The people who sent you into Germany are at this moment destroying it very efficiently. I need to show you something, I need to tell you what I know and I need your help – badly.'

Heatheridge shifted, seemingly bewildered, yet in his eyes there was a look of resignation – as though something he had long expected finally faced him. There was sadness too – and fear. 'I don't understand,' he said, unconvincingly, and knowing it.

'I believe you do, sir.'

'How did you find me?'

'Colonel Charles Southby is a member here – he was with the Ministry of Defence. He should have been with me now, right here, doing the talking, but he's dead. Tortured first then murdered. This afternoon. Can we go somewhere less public and talk? *Please?'*

'Do you have identification?'

Foley reached for his breast pocket.

'Not here. Follow me.' Heatheridge led the way to one of the rooms set aside for men only, indicated a deserted corner and sat facing Foley, staring intently at him.

Foley held up his warrant card but Heatheridge barely glanced at it. 'I believe you. Who killed Colonel Southby?'

Foley's eyes were fiery. 'The same people who caused Samuel Hale to place shotgun barrels in his mouth and pull both triggers, who a few days ago murdered his widow, who last night blasted your colleague Richard Wardlove's head off, raping and killing his wife to mislead police investigations, and a few hours ago tortured a fine, probably too bright, crippled army intelligence officer to death. Southby. God knows how many other lives they've taken or wrecked besides. You were there at the start – count the years!'

Heatheridge recoiled as though struck, his eyes fixed on Foley, unseeing, washed with tears. And horror.

The head, thought Foley. He's seeing that obscenity as

314

if it were in front of him right now, eyes opened, just as Samuel Hale had described it. 'Was it a woman?' he asked. 'The head?'

Heatheridge blinked. 'Woman, man, girl, boy, all of them. A child one thousand years old. All-seeing. Seeing me now – then. I felt it and it half drove me mad for a dozen years. Perhaps it did. Dear God, I hoped it was all over. Died, naturally, as the years went on just as all the damn good things do.' He held his hand out for the thick buff envelope Foley carried.

'This will take you back there,' Foley warned.

'You don't believe I ever really left, do you? I saw what some might consider worse atrocities commanding one of our advance units into their filthy concentration camps, yet nothing I saw compares with my first sight of the horrors which filled that bunker. Part of me – maybe most of me – still lives in that chilled hell and always will.'

Foley watched him as he began reading, knowing that for him each word was a moment of reality: reality he had barely escaped from with his sanity intact.

Finally, Samuel Hale's legacy was laid to rest on the low table between them and Foley in his precise policeman's way told Heatheridge everything he knew, everything he had learned, even what he had simply guessed at from the moment he had first spoken the name Eleanor Hale to Nigel Lewin in his office until walking through the doors of the Army and Navy Club. Everything, except the fact of two bodies lying in Southby's hallway with blankets by them to soak up their blood. It all seemed a lifetime ago, he thought, wonderingly. And there's no way back.

Heatheridge had smoked a series of cigarettes, most just half-way down, crushing them out absently as he listened, asking hesitant, halting questions as if afraid of the answers. When Foley rested his case and sat back lighting his own first cigarette his throat was dry but his eyes stayed on the man before him, searching for the strength, the courage he knew Heatheridge must once have had and praying a trace remained still.

'Of course I knew, deep down, it wasn't over,' said Heatheridge, too lightly, just in control. 'I knew that they

315

wouldn't have risked such a mission, such certain scandal, if they weren't prepared to use all they gained. *Oh God.*'

Foley pressed harder: 'I have further information which demonstrates the extent of their activities – their power.' He took out Mayberry's computer disc. 'This names names, points towards probable channels for funding their work, shows the depth, and considerable breadth, of their conspiracy. I've also noted down all I can recall of what Southby told me regarding a man called Sir David Nesbitt. Ecology and Human Resources? Government department? Apparently he was the instigator of a massive government-funded land purchase programme for some unstipulated building project. Southby was called in to give a confidential opinion on security. He was convinced after reading Hale's legacy and hearing what I had discovered that that project was part of all this. He made notes after we talked – he'd said he might – of what he remembered of the meetings with Nesbitt regarding the project. Being the kind of man he was he'd placed the notes in his safe, which his killers opened. They were by the body. I have them but I'm afraid they're in dreadful condition – Southby died with little dignity. I believe they killed him because of the notes. Because of his knowledge – or what they thought his knowledge to be. They're striking out in the dark at anyone. Of course, none of this is absolute proof – but I believe there is enough here for the beginnings not of a police investigation but of a parliamentary inquiry if someone with authority, with commitment, could set it in motion.'

Heatheridge looked at the disc but made no move to accept it. 'Surely you can vindicate your actions? Your continuing an investigation you'd been ordered to stop? If you've enough facts – even supposition – to instigate an inquiry . . . ?'

Foley shook his head, despondently. 'I think they've finished me. Even if I fought them every inch of the way some of the muck they're fabricating against me will leave a stain. That's the way of things when your profession is subject to public scrutiny, even whim. You must know that, being a Member of Parliament? I'll never be trusted again. And even if they left me snow-white I don't have what you have: direct access to the top. It *must* be you. You were there. You *saw*. You *know*. Only you can make people believe enough to act.'

Heatheridge touched the pages of Hale's legacy. 'Can you tell me who I should trust? If all that you say is true – and I believe it is – then where do I start? If this involves someone of the stature, the influence behind the scenes, of Sir David Nesbitt – '

'It does. I'm certain it does. Nesbitt made a call to my Divisional Headquarters in Exeter. Wanted me: a grammar-school, no degree, near retirement copper with no social pretensions, little interest in ecology, continually bleating for more human resources, as unaware of his existence as I'm certain he was of mine until I locked on to the name Hale: mother, son, and latterly the father's not-so-holy tortured ghost. Reason for Nesbitt's call not stated but I can guess. Anyway, he simply stepped over me and went straight to the top which I suspect he wanted to avoid doing. As I told you, I was absent without leave doing what I do best, sinking my teeth into something and not letting go – turning an investigation into the murder of an old lady recluse into a personal assault on Nesbitt's secret empire. I imagine that's how he viewed my actions because the next thing I know, my Chief Constable wants my head and my house and office are torn apart by a heavy team intent on doing the same with my career.'

'Then I fear I'm of little use to you. Samuel Hale knew, I knew, that the original orders which began all this came from the very heart of power – real power – in this country. Nesbitt is one of those who causes that heart to beat. Who can I go to now without feeling that if I reveal all of this I too am risking my career – perhaps more?'

'There has to be one person in a position of power or influence you can trust? Trust completely?'

'Someone I'd entrust my life to, you mean?'

'Yes,' Foley said, steadily. 'It would have to be that.'

'How many people do you trust to that extent, Superintendent?'

'At this particular moment? Loyalty is hard to come by

317

when things start looking black but I think I could come up with someone.'

'Only one?'

Foley shrugged.

Heatheridge lit yet another cigarette and drew deeply, straightening his shoulders, as if sucking life back into himself. 'I'm something of a mountaineer,' he said. 'Getting on a bit now but I can still accept the challenge of some of the tougher faces.'

That explains the creases around the eyes, decided Foley. As if in confirmation Heatheridge narrowed his eyes and raised a calloused hand, pointing into some imaginary distance. 'Sometimes you can reach out and almost believe your finger is touching the peak of the next mountain. It's a world I'd like to spend my entire existence in – high above all the dirt, the staleness we create, we foster, down here.'

I've lost him, thought Foley. There's no fight left. He only wants to escape. And who can blame him?

'The thing is, Superintendent, you don't attempt any climb without being entirely sure of the people you're roped to. There's something you haven't told me – and there's no way in the world I'll climb this particular mountain without knowing everything.'

'You should have been a policeman yourself,' observed Foley.

Heatheridge smiled for the first time. 'I spend most of my working life listening to people who see it to be their sworn duty to divulge only half-truths, make omissions and on really important occasions blatantly lie. Civil servants and politicians, Superintendent – two faces of the same coin. Also, I've been a professional soldier who's faced death, killed many times, and commanded too many men who have done the same. There's always a look on their faces, in their eyes, for hours, sometimes days, afterwards. An impossible, conflicting mixture of emotions: shame, surprise, horror, elation. Also, I'm sure you're well aware – painfully, I should think – that your right ear is severely damaged and that side of your face is swollen, quite apart from grazes and minor cuts. I'm surprised you got past the

318

lads at the front door. There again they probably imagine you're with one of our rougher cloak-and-dagger outfits – especially as you're supposed to be dining with an MOD colonel.'

Foley touched his ear and winced. 'Anything else?'

'You've a firearm stretching the stitching of what appears to be a brand-new suit – which leads me to believe whatever you were wearing previously was ruined in the attack which caused your injuries. By the look of you I think you need a stiff drink followed by a decent dinner during which you can fill in the omissions you chose to make in your story. Then I'll tell you who I would trust being roped to on the most terrible mountain face imaginable.'

Heatheridge tossed his serviette on to the table and drank wine, his meal finished. 'I must say you don't appear to be concerned that you could well be charged with a double murder. You haven't mentioned covering up evidence of your presence at Southby's place?'

'I've had time to think about it. The last thing they want is me on public trial. An internal police disciplinary action to discredit me, destroy my career – this could be done with little if any public knowledge. A double murder trial with me giving evidence in my own defence would be unthinkable for them. I'd lay money – everything I own – on a cover-up placing responsibility for the deaths on the IRA. Undoubtedly Southby was running agents and informers against them.'

Heatheridge considered this. 'Yes, I think you're right. A senior police officer, expert in the technique of presenting evidence, could well prove too persuasive – too dangerous to them. Incidentally, what made you think I wasn't one of them?'

Foley took another mouthful of steak, his nerves still too taut to enjoy the food despite his hunger. 'Because you were *there*,' he stated, looking directly at the MP.

'I might have been coerced, bought, threatened. You, better than anyone, should know by now the extent these people will go to to protect their – '

319

'Investment in the future?' offered Foley, sensing deep forces at work inside Heatheridge.

Heatheridge's eyes were far away. 'That's what Hale said, back then, before we went into the bunker. I asked him if what we took out – the results of their experimentation – would be worth the cost of all the human suffering. Dear God, that was before I even saw the horrors. He answered: The future is why we're here. Some future!'

Foley let the silence run, then said: 'We had to trust you, Southby and I. There was no one else.'

'Southby is dead and I pick up his torch? That how you saw it when you decided to go on alone? Marched up Pall Mall to make me an offer I couldn't refuse? Do the right thing? Do what I should have done decades ago? That was it?'

'Yes.'

'Something of a risk. If they'd kept tabs on Eleanor Hale they'd sure as hell have put their watchers, their ears on me.'

'They gagged you with the Official Secrets Act,' said Foley, knowing now.

'Still have,' stated Heatheridge, eyes blazing.

'Only covering the original mission, surely? The work they're doing now – their methods, their victims, for God's sake – must put them outside the law?'

'What do you know of our secret world, Superintendent?'

'Only what I read – or the little extra I glean from this job.'

'Then I'll educate you. Our secret world is in another universe entirely; completely, utterly unconnected with the world you, I, or the man on the Clapham omnibus live in. The law, as you quaintly put it, is for us – not them. They are already true outlaws: burglary, prostitution, drug-dealing, fraud, blackmail, and murder could be described as being part of their charter, except of course they don't have a charter.'

'Because they don't exist,' Foley interrupted. 'I've heard that already. But we're not talking about the secret services, are we? They've a job to do, I accept that and so do most people. But these people are butchers. Highly sophisticated, powerful, well-connected butchers who've kidded too many people for too long with some hare-brained ideological argument that should have died with Adolf Hitler. They're an anachronism that's been allowed to flourish by a bunch of right-wing reactionaries buried in Whitehall and ignored – or worse – by successive governments. We've been hunting reds under Whitehall beds so intently since the war we missed the fascists under the covers.'

A group of crusty, military-looking men seated at a nearby table turned almost as one to Foley's raised voice and across the dining-room the sound of silver on china halted.

'Steady,' murmured Heatheridge.

'Well, *Christ*.'

Heatheridge pushed Foley's wine glass towards him and lifted his own. 'Drink up and I'll order us a cognac. What do you plan to do now? Search for your missing friend? On Dartmoor? Hardly wise. You know from Hale's document that that is where they are. And from what you've said, won't your own people be looking for you? The police?'

Foley finished his wine in one gulp. 'Mr Heatheridge, I don't want to involve you in anything that might be considered illegal. I'm prepared to take my chances but it's unfair, it's stupid, to pull you under with me. That leaves no one to take up the fight. If you don't mind I'll keep how I plan to operate to myself. All I ask of you is that you take Samuel Hale's document, backed up by your own story, to someone who has the power to act. I want – I need – to satisfy myself that Nigel Lewin is either alive or dead. Right now, that's my priority. There's little I can do about the bigger issue. That's your job – your world.'

Heatheridge called a waiter, ordered two cognacs, and waited in silence until they arrived. Then he spoke, his voice low, his eyes hard as steel. 'You have a gun attached to your belt – are you prepared to use it on your friend? That is just the choice you may have to face. They don't waste lives, Foley. Life is their raw material. The concentration camps provided an endless supply for the Nazis and these, their ideological disciples, must have only a limited supply even if they do plunder forces hospitals, damn them.

321

Your friend, if they have him, is in a state, an existence, profoundly worse than death as I imagine its worst concept to be. I *know*, I've seen the eyes of their creatures. Their tortured, lost minds touched mine. I've felt their anguish, their horror. When we incinerated what was in that bunker with the flame-throwers, I swear before God that their silent screams reached my mind. And at the end I felt, too, their release. They were children pushed over known horizons, forced on to a landscape beyond their understanding, their comprehension. I *felt* them, Foley, and it terrified me, changed me for ever. You're not prepared for what you may have to face. For what you may have to do. I am. I'm the only one left – outside their chilled hellish world, that is.' Heatheridge drained his cognac and stood. 'I've waited too long. Run too far from the horror. It's time to stop. To go back.'

At the club's reception desk, Heatheridge took the buff envelope containing Samuel Hale's legacy and Mayberry's computer disc from Foley, wrote a brief, considered letter on a nearby table, then asked for wax, sealing the envelope himself before scrawling a name and address in a bold, strong hand across the face, adding 'By hand'.

'Commons, first thing Monday morning,' he told the duty porter. 'Without fail.'

'As usual, sir,' came the crisp reply.

'Was that safe?' questioned Foley as they walked briskly to the Range Rover, Heatheridge having travelled up from his constituency by train and taxi.

'As a Bank of England vault.'

Foley glanced quickly backward.

'Do you think you were followed?' asked Heatheridge, not copying him.

'I know I wasn't.'

'Me?'

'Why not? They'll be closing ranks right now. They're under threat and they'll think hard about who knows that they exist, who might damage them. Anyone with knowledge and means. They know you have both.'

'So?'

Foley gave a small shrug. 'Won't know until we're on the move. Not for sure.' He glanced quickly at Heatheridge. 'You know, don't you? Where it is on Dartmoor? You've always known.'

'Yes.'

'Is there anything *you* haven't told *me*?'

'I'll take you there,' said Heatheridge. 'First we have to stop at my rooms near Westminster. Something I need.'

'There's the Range Rover,' said Foley, dropping the matter but feeling alienated by Heatheridge's sudden air of finality, as though he had already made a decision he was not going to revoke and certainly not share.

'Know the way?' Heatheridge asked as they moved off.

'I'm a Londoner. Nearly fifteen years with the Met, a lot of it at New Scotland Yard.'

'I wondered about the accent. So why Devon?'

Foley swung the tall vehicle through the traffic. 'We're all running away from something. You're not the only one who's stopped and taken a hard look back. Changes the hell out of you when people are trying to kill you.'

'It's a matter of decisions, looking back. Essentially, you're looking at yourself – what your decisions were, why. Point is, with time, perspective changes, twists.'

Oh yes, thought Foley, his memory presenting uncompromising images of emaciated young men trying to survive cruel captivity and the Korean winter juxtaposed with the same, weightier, older but perhaps less wise men vying, unknown to each other, for the love of the same woman. So what would you do now, given the same circumstances? Run for the hills – and the moors – so that you won't have to choose between duty and friendship? Or be the textbook copper and pass the word along, standing primly aside when the arrest is made, self-satisfaction on face, shoulders anticipating the pat on the back, the light of imminent promotion in the eyes – and sod who gets hurt. Sorry, mate, sorry, my love, it's the job you see.

'One can't judge a decision made at another time – the factors aren't the same,' Foley said, defensively.

'But is the outcome? Whatever decision one makes, the outcome will be what it was always meant to be.'

'Do you really believe that?'

'I don't know. Certainly it would make living easier. Dying too.'

'We won't defeat them by dying,' snapped Foley. 'That was Samuel Hale's mistake.'

'Stop there – on the right, Spenser Street. Parking is tricky at this time but you'll find somewhere fairly close. Should give me time for what I have to do. Come back to the house when you've found somewhere. Number nineteen. Stop here.'

Foley drove off slowly, watching the road behind, seeing Heatheridge's dark form striding purposefully to an unlit porch before hurriedly working the door-lock. He accelerated away, his never-stilled copper's instincts sounding a distorted warning he couldn't quite tune in to. Something was going to happen, something that Heatheridge had decided. Something *wrong*. He parked after driving around for some minutes, locked up, and began walking back, feeling as if he was living on the edge of the world, wary, fearful – yet elated more alive than ever before. Perhaps I'm going to die, he wondered. Everything crammed into the last hours: life zinging like electricity through my veins. He reached the door.

Heatheridge opened it. 'All done,' he said.

Dartmoor was blacker than the night: rolling shapes spiked with sudden, blunt rock-tors like thick nails driven into a soft body. The stars were lost in the vastness above – especially two, flickering brighter, dipping occasionally towards the earth as though searching.

'What are we waiting for?' asked Foley, almost perfunctorily: beyond sleep, beyond exhaustion, even beyond curiosity. Whatever decision one makes, the outcome will be what it was always meant to be. Is that our Bible now?

'Them,' said Heatheridge, resting with the seat-back near flat, his legs stretched out rigidly as if he suffered cramp.

'Who?'

'Look.'

The two lost stars were lights now, pulsing, vibrating as

324

though unstable. Foley rolled down the window. There was no sound.

'Drive closer,' said Heatheridge. 'To the gates. Don't worry, we're perfectly safe, they're not going to risk their cover. They probably know we're here anyway. Our lights would have been seen for miles. They're careful.'

'They're killers,' said Foley, starting forward.

'Yes.'

It took ten minutes over a bad road before the Range Rover's headlights cut through the wire mesh perimeter fence and swept the low roof-lines of prefabricated buildings and, to the west, half-ruined constructions, bullet-scarred walls proclaiming BRITS OUT, SAS BUTCHERS, PROVOS RULE, and obscenities scrawled across murals of Christ. The barrier-pole across the entrance was down, the hut beside it in darkness, seemingly unmanned.

Foley dropped his window and now he could hear, just, miles away, a deep stutter in the night, a beating of the wind. Lights came on inside the guard-hut and two men emerged, armed with stubby assault rifles. One moved to the centre of the barrier, the other towards them. Caught in the lights, neither showed any sign of having been asleep despite their darkened hut.

'This is a restricted area,' said the guard, now at Foley's elbow, his big flashlight moving from him to Heatheridge.

Heatheridge switched on the overhead interior light and leaned over. 'Is it?' He took a small leather case from his breast pocket and held it directly in the beam of the torch. 'Seen one of these before? House of Commons pass. I'm a Member of Parliament, I'm also on an all-party committee currently investigating certain allegations made concerning the armed forces.'

'I've no orders regarding that, sir. This is a survival training establishment for – '

'This is an establishment for the testing of experimental chemical weapons and counter-measure safety devices. I know that and you know that, so let's dispense with your routine fob-off for stray tourists. Bring your commanding officer out here – *now*.'

325

The guard gave a hesitant nod, threw up a salute and moved at the double back into the hut.

Foley looked at Heatheridge. 'Is that true? Chemical weapons testing?'

'They had to have a realistic cover for government, hadn't they? Building deep underground facilities with air-locks, filtration systems – all the things they needed – hardly seems convincing for an army survival course. It's a two-tier cover, perhaps even more, who knows? The public get the survival course, the MOD and the cabinet get chemical weapons and maybe the secret services get something else entirely which makes their heart beat a little faster. That's their secret, Foley: everyone gets what they want.'

The beat was clear now, doubled, with the added whoop-whoop of spinning rotor blades to fill the night.

Foley leaned out at the moment their spotlights came on, pinning him against the blue metal, his hair flying in every direction. He squeezed his eyes closed against the dust and the glare, drawing back inside. 'What's going on, Heatheridge?'

But Heatheridge was already out of the vehicle, standing by the barrier, facing a boyish officer with hard eyes which saw the hovering helicopters but never wavered, not for a moment, from Heatheridge's face and seemingly silent, moving lips – except to look down, once, when the lips stilled, at what seemed to be an old, oblong, velvet-covered necklace case. Except there were no dully glistening silver-white pearls on the ageing silk, just a clouded yellow phial.

Foley saw on the seat beside him, a slit open envelope with a letter inside and, holding it down, a small battery memo cassette-recorder. 'Heatheridge!' he shouted but the helicopters whipped his cry to nothing.

The barrier lifted and Heatheridge started to move off with the officer, holding the opened case before him as if offering it for blessing. The officer walked sideways, stum-bling, almost falling once as he tried to keep turned towards Heatheridge – and the yellow phial.

Foley jumped out of the Range Rover and was brought up short by two raised and cocked assault rifles.

'Back inside!' one man yelled, squinting against the flying dirt thrown up by the blades.

The two helicopters came down close, outside the perimeter fence, wailing through the octaves as their blades slowed. Incredibly bright lights came on inside before spilling out, bobbing wildly as their holders chased the video-camera operators and sound-recordists already sprinting for the barrier.

'*Heatheridge*!' Foley yelled again, his shout a bellow in the sudden silence.

'Stay!' came the reply, half lost because Heatheridge refused to turn, walking stiffly as though his small burden was transforming him slowly into one of the tall rocks on the deep blue horizon.

Foley got quickly into the Range Rover, rolled up the window and locked both doors, the white blast of the television lights blinding him. He ignored the frantic knocking at his window, turned on the tape player and sat back, eyes closed.

'Foley? Heatheridge. The people outside, as you may have guessed, are TV news. Both sides – to ensure maximum coverage. I called them while you were parking. They'll want to interview you when you are ready. Think carefully before making rash statements involving your career. The letter I've left for you – and for them – came with the phial you saw me carrying as I entered the camp. An entry I had planned in advance, as I'm sure you've surmised. The letter is entirely self-explanatory and is from someone you probably feel you know quite well by now. A good man, if once misguided. What I have chosen to do is by far the best thing for all concerned. It will demonstrate to *them* that they are not invincible, they are not supermen, they have no divine right to decide what our future should be – or indeed who our future should be. Your young friend, if he is inside, will either walk out on his own if he is in a fit condition, or I'll have him carried out to you by one of the surface soldiers who I suspect may well be innocent of the evil perpetrated in the cold hell below. If he is not inside, I am truly sorry, for he is probably dead – but perhaps that in itself is a blessing.

327

'You are a courageous man, Foley, one of the most courageous I have ever encountered. You took on an enemy which you soon learned could easily obliterate you and all you've achieved in your life, yet you continued the fight, you brought it to me – where, in truth, it has always rested, sometimes ignored, sometimes crushed down so hard I could never have believed I would take it up, ever. As you wanted, I've taken up the torch from Southby's fallen hand and although this time fire is not the weapon I have to use against them – as I did against their Nazi forebears and mentors – what I have will, I trust, more than suffice. Read the letter now and by the time you have done so, your friend, if they held him here, should have reached the surface. I shall not see you again. Goodbye. God go with you.'

Foley switched off the machine, shutting out the clamour beyond the windows and took up the yellowing letter, already recognizing the hand.

My dear Heatheridge,

Although we have not seen each other for many years now, I know very well that the nightmares I dream are yours too. I don't need to explain. You and I shared an experience that few men would have survived mentally unscathed. If it were only the nightmares then this letter would not have been written, the content included with it never passed to you. I would simply have accepted them, endured them as the price one must pay for attempting to usurp the position of the Creator. I imagine you have surmised that the results of the 'work' we took from Germany have been put to use. I do not say 'good use' because I know now that no good can ever come of it – not when the work is carried out in such complete secrecy, without independent, outside controls, with such utter abandonment of any ethical code of practice. They have gone too far, to fast. Already they are producing substances outside the human body using human genes implanted into cell cultures grown in bio-reac-

328

tors; developing human antibodies outside the body through genetic engineering; developing transgenic animals – animals with human genes implanted into them – as living dispensers of bio-pharmaceuticals; stimulating genes normally active only during human embryonic development; experimenting on live subjects – human victims – attempting to grow new limbs, new organs; worst of all, their brain-cell transplantation programme is achieving results and I fear soon that even our innermost selves will not be safe from them. There is no check on any mistakes they make or wrong turning they take, the result of which they don't always destroy. There is no revelation of disasters in their programme and these have certainly occurred. So who counts the cost? And is the cost too great to bear? It may be that our children's children will curse us to hell – for it is from that place that they may easily believe we originate when they view this fanatical search for 'perfection'. They might only have to view themselves, Heatheridge! Do you see?

Foley closed his eyes, remembering: 'The price we have paid for our children's future may be their lives. When your life's dreams turn to nightmares it is time to die.' Oh, dear God.
He read on:

They no longer trust me, so I have become like you, someone who is within the circle of knowledge, yet stands outside, helpless, neither contributing some good into the growing madness nor spilling their secrets to a world which probably would treat us as fools or scaremongers. People don't want the truth. They want guidance, platitudes, pleasure: waking sleep. You and I, Heatheridge, we dream their nightmares for them. We live them.

I no longer have access to their facility. Soon they will destroy me or I must do so to save myself from them. But I have worked, Heatheridge, quietly, unseen, preparing a weapon to wipe them out as if by a plague. For so long they have tampered with the human immunization system, developing it further, adding more bricks, more mortar, to the walls, and in doing this they have accidentally loosed mutated strains which in decades to come will cause untold loss of life, slowly, terribly. The phial I have passed to you contains my own secret work, developed from the genetic material of their own accident, their own mutation. It will kill their 'future men' in seconds and any normal human within a controlled-environment area such as theirs in the blink of an eye. I pass it to you. Keep it well, entirely secure, and cool. It is deadly. I have no way of knowing its active life because, naturally, it is untested. Only use it where, afterwards, the area may be permanently sealed. In concrete. For all time. You remember, I'm certain, their Dartmoor underground facility? We went there together in more naïve days when science was my religion and 'For the Good of Man' its creed. We both know now that the pursuit of such an ideal can – and has in their hands – become the cross on which man maybe crucified.

Heatheridge, the only way to deliver it is by entering that place yourself. There will come a time – I promise you – perhaps years from now, when you will be prepared to do just that. You might even welcome the opportunity. If you do, you will certainly have the gratitude of millions – although, of course, none will ever know what you have done. Such is the way of things. God give you the strength to make the supreme sacrifice. You would, I know, as a soldier, so perhaps also as a man? A human being, created by God, not by them. Not their future man.

My eternal gratitude will be yours,
Samuel Hale

Foley sat for a few moments, the letter discarded on the seat beside them, considering the documents in the pocket of his raincoat, tossed over the back seat. Southby's posthumous gift to him. If he wanted to take it up. A complete new identity, a new life: no enquiry, no disciplining, reduction in rank, forced resignation, probable sacking, jail. No sudden, fatal accident. As Peter Foley the probability of all these awaited, for he had no illusions as to the extent of their power and influence. As John Clifton, businessman, he'd be free of everything – younger, even on paper, which made him smile. He would be a new man. He would re-exist, entirely legally, with government records to support his background every step of the way because deep cover is no use at all if the facts behind it are shallow. All he had to do was turn the ignition key and drive away, into the night, leaving someone else to sort out the mess. Or cover it up.

He looked over at the letter. The problem is, Foley, you're a copper. Always have been, always will be. No matter what you call yourself that's what you'll always want to be, what you'll always think of yourself as. It's The Job. You don't walk away from it easily. If at all.

Sod it!

He replaced the letter in the envelope, pocketed the small cassette player, and stepped down from the Range Rover, ignoring the blinding camera lights, the thrusting microphones, and the urgent questions. He walked to the barrier, meeting the eyes of the two guards whose assault rifles came up, their faces bewildered, uncertain, lost without orders, simply holding position. Behind them was darkness, except for a single entrance light to one of the low buildings where Heatheridge had entered – and silence.

Foley took out his warrant card and held it before them. 'That the entrance, is it, where the light is? The lifts are in there?'

After a quick glance at his companion, one gave a nod.

Foley moved closer. He spoke quickly, quietly. 'I'm not going down. No one is. You know your Bikini Codes? *Black Alpha*. These people must be kept back. Understand me?'

The soldiers' faces became fixed as they took up position either side of Foley, their guns levelled, relieved that some-one had taken charge, was giving orders.

The news teams fell back, still coiled, ready for anything

331

– instinct warning them that something big was about to break – silent, the soft whirring of video cameras the only sound, their blinding lights eerie and unnatural in the night.

Foley waited, his eyes never leaving the door beneath the lit doorway. Waiting for the small, dark, quick figure which never came. Finally he drew back his hunched shoulders and turned. 'I need a telephone,' he called.

'There's one over there in the guard-post,' said the soldier on his right.

Foley gave a thin smile: 'No thanks.'

A long-haired youth moved forward, warily, eyes fixed on the guns. Foley accepted the bulky portable unit from him, sending him back. 'All of you stay where you are,' he ordered, punching in the number for Exeter Divisional Headquarters. He spoke: 'Who's Duty Chief Superintendent tonight? Right, get him on the line. Detective Superintendent Foley wants him. That's right.' Foley turned again to the lighted doorway, eyes bleak. 'Hello? Chief Superintendent Matthews? Please listen: Bikini Code: Black Alpha. I'll repeat that: Black Alpha. Location: army camp on Dartmoor. The one they use for survival courses and urban warfare training. I'm there now. Yes, I'm certain. Check its rating under the Bikini Codes and you'll have confirmation. You must order the Black Alpha alert *now*. And forget media blackout – both BBC and ITN News are here already.'

He cut the connection, dialled the same number again, and asked to be put through to Detective Inspector Grant. 'Grant? I remembered you'd pulled nights this week. Don't ask questions. Any second now all hell is going to break loose here. Before it does, do one thing – and don't worry about consequences, I'll carry the can – make certain that all evidence gathered in the Eleanor Hale murder inquiry is in your hands, complete and safe. Lock and key job, understand? Take it out of the building if necessary. That's right, we just might have a result. You'll be seeing me soon. Where? Bloody TV news, both channels – if not before on Dartmoor. Anything on Nigel? Didn't think there would be. Grant? Thanks.'

He turned to face the cameras. 'You'll have a statement from me regarding my involvement in this matter and also regarding Mister Heatheridge who, I understand, called you out to this location.'

'He said to meet him here,' one reporter called. 'Where is he?'

'I'm afraid he's dead. As is anyone else in the secret facility directly beneath us. There's been an accident. An accident involving lethal bacteria.'

The entire group reacted as one, shifting back, the lights wobbling unsteadily.

'I've called a Black Alpha alert – you must all know what that means.'

'Is it germ weapons?' called someone.

'You'll get your statement, don't worry.'

'How many deaths?' another shouted.

Foley glanced back at the lighted doorway. 'We may never know.'

'Will they have to seal this place off? For ever? Is it that bad? What about Dartmoor?'

Foley shook his head and walked back towards the Range Rover, enormously tired.

'What about the future?' someone called.

Foley got in and closed his eyes, waiting for everything to happen, drifting into sleep. 'The future's not what it used to be,' he murmured.

The package addressed to the Deputy Prime Minister was placed in his hand a little after he arrived at the House of Commons that stormy Monday morning. He recognized Heatheridge's handwriting instantly and opened it with trepidation, fearing more damage to the government and his party even after the writer had gone, terribly, to his grave, destroying his memory with an irrational, fateful act of terror which would live for ever as one other historical landmark in man's record of insanity. He shook his head sadly as he removed the contents. Even the explanation offered by the senior police officer involved – now suspended pending the inquiry into his refusal to obey a direct order and subsequent dereliction of duty, plus a possible link to a drugs cartel – only made matters worse, offering little in the way of hard fact and adding to the air of madness which surrounded the entire dreadful business.

He placed the computer disc on one side and took up the accompanying letter.

'She's going to make the statement herself,' said the Home Secretary, putting his head around the door. 'Best way, I feel. You agree?'

The Deputy Prime Minister nodded vaguely, his eyes back on the yellowed sheets.

'What've you got there?'

'A letter from a friend.'

'Regarding the press, we're to take Lord Melbourne's advice. Remember it?'

The Deputy Prime Minister looked up. 'Oh yes,' he said steadily. It doesn't matter what we say, as long as we all say the same thing.

'I'll see you in the chamber, then.'

The accompanying letter was on Army and Navy Club notepaper:

My dear friend,

This comes to you for the best and worst of all reasons. The best because I trust you more than any other, and worst because I fear you have been placed outside the mainstream of things in government to neutralize you and strip you of any chance of gaining the leadership of the party. The latter may give you no joy but it serves my purpose well, for you may act without ambition, with a degree of political and personal independence, able to resist the pressures which, I assure you, will be brought to bear if you accept the precarious undertaking I offer.

I beg you to read the enclosed with an open mind, and although I shall not – for reasons which by now are obvious – personally be able to help you cut out the heart of the conspiracy contained therein, should

334

you decide to take up my fallen torch, I shall at least be with you in spirit.

The young commando officer named Heatheridge described in the narrative was of course myself. I was there in that dreadful place. I understand now that I never really left. I must go back, I have no choice. I shared the original responsibility so I must share the consequences. It may be another place, another time, but their inhuman purpose remains the same. This time there will be no explosive, no fire, only their own mistake as retribution.

I realize that what I plan to do will be condemned, just as I will be vilified even in death, but your efforts and, if God does exist, His Will, will ensure that one day my action will be understood, my name restored.

In the aftermath you will hear the name of Detective Superintendent Peter Foley of the Devon and Cornwall Constabulary – trust him as I trust you.

Farewell, good friend.

Richard

The Deputy Prime Minister called in his secretary, asked as a matter of urgency for a printed copy to be made of whatever was stored on the computer disc – made discreetly and brought back to him immediately in time for the Prime Minister's statement in the chamber and allowing no other person to view the contents no matter who they were.

This done, he began reading Samuel Hale's legacy. I am the arbiter of the final words of two men, he soon realized. More: the proxy champion of their cause. Do I need the responsibility? Why me?

The chilling warning from Orwell's Nineteen Eighty Four came to him: 'If you want a picture of the future, imagine a boot stamping on a human face – for ever.'

Now he knew whose boot.

And whose face. His and those who like him walked the easy path, unaware of what lay in the dark shadows of the coming night, thankful for sleep, believing tomorrow would be a brighter day.

If they had their way then it would be a long night indeed. And tomorrow, theirs.

He reached forward for the print-out.

Sir David Nesbitt switched on the big television set in his spacious office suite, already aware that the Prime Minister herself would be making the expected government statement. He watched with admiration as she began speaking, grave-faced but strong, performing a difficult task well – despite extreme pressure from a united parliamentary opposition, outraged disarmament and ecological groups, and a hostile press. Newspapers that morning stood together in their view that the government was facing its greatest threat yet, their concern as to whether it could survive the furore almost overshadowing the fact of the disaster beneath the surface of Dartmoor. The political battle was immediate, they seemed to be saying, out in the open, while the dead were buried under tons of solidifying concrete: no bodies for the front page, no stricken faces and twisted limbs. The only evidence that a terrible catastrophe had occurred was the monstrous concrete blot on the Devon landscape which in time would become a shrine for disarmament groups, if they could fight their way past the already growing hordes of tourists held back behind the wired exclusion zone.

The environmental groups, naturally, were protesting vehemently and in some cases violently, while their tame experts made projections as to long-term damage to local flora and fauna by chemical agents, the massive concrete sealing itself and, in due course, the extra tourists, especially those in destructive four-wheel-drive vehicles. All, however, agreed – because of the extreme danger of total public panic in the area and also because heavy hints were dropped regarding withdrawal of their government grants if their response was not deemed to be responsible – to avoid conjecture on the effectiveness of government emergency action and the possibility of more widespread damage.

Despite the hostility opposite her in the chamber, the Prime Minister completed her statement with few telling interruptions, making clear her intention to appoint an all-party select committee charged with the inquiry and with the sole purpose of ensuring such a catastrophe never occurred again, then sat down amid relative calm.

Nesbitt gave a tight smile and turned down the sound. Excellent performance, especially considering the sparse facts she had been given. Rectifies any damage done by that persistent police superintendent who had come across on television as emotional and somewhat incoherent: the weather on the moors during his interview already worsening, the wind snatching many of his words away. The man was a novice in the art of communication and his choice of a Sunday morning to make his potentially damaging statement showed abysmal timing. He now faced an internal inquiry as to his conduct and perhaps a disciplinary board. Whatever the outcome, his credibility would be damaged. That is the problem with any crusade, Nesbitt decided; people tended to view the crusader as a fanatic no matter how good, how worthy, his cause. Which is why all the truly great causes are never put to the people. They simply don't understand.

The House now was standing in silence, a tribute to all the servicemen and civilian technicians who had died in such a terrible way. Nesbitt doubted if any spared a Christian thought for their late colleague, the Right Honourable Richard Heatheridge, DSO, MP. It was he after all who, uttering threats, had been taken into a restricted, sealed area carrying what amounted to a bomb – and had, without mercy, set it off. His mind had gone, of course. Many were now reviewing his behaviour over the years: never *quite* normal; a loner, somewhat anti-social; if not homosexual then a misogynist who hated looking women straight in the eye, even avoided their company. One said he had once seen horror in Heatheridge's eyes when some earnest Hare Krishna woman with a shaven head had accosted him outside St Stephen's Gate begging a donation. Well, he was dead and would soon be forgotten.

Nesbitt reached for the remote control to switch off as the silence ended and members regained their seats. Then

337

he saw the Deputy Prime Minister stand, holding a large buff envelope from which he withdrew a computer information disc and print-out plus a number of sheets of yellowed paper filled with handwriting. He began speaking.

Nesbitt quickly turned the sound back up.

'. . . was handed to me this morning. I have read and viewed the contents. I feel that considering the tragic circumstances of this weekend my best course is to read what I have here.' He turned to the Prime Minister. 'To read it now.'

Rude voices bawled from the opposition back benches:

'Who sent it?'

'Defence doing a cover-up?'

'Too bloody late!'

'Order!'

He raised his voice: 'The card accompanying the contents bears the name Heatheridge.'

Immediate uproar tore through the chamber.

'*Order!*'

'Read it!' someone called through the noise, his call taken up on all sides.

'Order! *Order!*'

The noise abated.

The Deputy Prime Minister put on spectacles and began.

Stupidity, thought Nesbitt. They'll never believe you. Don't you understand? The only future they care about is now. He switched off the set, ordered in the group of men waiting in his outer office, and turned his mind to the plans which needed urgent attention. Now more than ever.

He took his place at the head of the long boardroom table. 'The future is why we're here,' he told them. None disbelieved him.

EPILOGUE

Peter Foley sat on the veranda, the Cretan sun an ember cooling in the Mediterranean. He had successfully cut himself off, not quite running for the hills, more a calculated step out of the harsh spotlight focused on him. Best if you vanished for a while, was the stern advice from the Police Federation. Somewhere out of the way where they don't know you, and would for a generous back-hander deny your presence if the harder press boys track you down. So he told them: Crete. And a rambling string of beach villas which stayed open out of season. He knew the owner well, enjoyed his company and the food he provided if you were too lazy, or too drunk on local wine and sun, to cook.

So there he was: healing sun, a block of paper, a brand-new electronic typewriter with impressive features bought, shrewdly, from the Heathrow duty-free, and his policeman's memory for detail. 'Insurance' was what he called his self-imposed task, but as the days drifted by, he found himself waking with surprising enthusiasm – even anticipation – for his hours facing the sea, with only the muted click of the typewriter keys and breaking waves invading his silence.

By nightfall he felt disposed to leave his veranda and make his way over sand, rock, and coarse grass to the taverna and give himself dinner and a bottle of something white, chilled, and not too resinous, shared with the proprietor. Afterwards, before bed, he would look, always with surprise, at the growing block of typescript and make half-serious plans as to its future when done.

He avoided feelings, knowing that he had enough problems without those. His strength was in his practicality.

He would survive. He would go back when the time was right. He would defend himself. He would tell his story and even if it were not believed, it would be a warning.

It was more realization of being than awakening. Being, yet without sense of identity; as though he had entered an uncharted mental landscape in which he had fleeting glimpses – not memories, simply an awareness – of some other time. Recognition without recall; moments from another life floating lightly, having meaning only when they touched him.

He might have considered himself dreaming, if to dream had any meaning for him. It had not. There was no subconscious to his world. Or perhaps, all of his world was subconscious and consciousness merely an abstraction. A promise. Heaven.

He tried to stretch the limits of his being and found, at the edges, where the darkness and the shadows gathered, a desolation which made him shrivel and lapse into nothingness – a void – before he found the strength and the courage to creep into his new world again.

There were others who nudged at him, softly, as if knowing their presence could be more than he could take. He felt their being; he felt, too, their pain. He felt, from each one, the terror of the far reaches: of the shadows.

One of these came close to him and a sense of age flowed through him. He felt comfortable with this as though in some other existence he had shared his space, his time, with another whose age was greater than his. But then the concept, the sense, ebbed as if it had never been. What was age? Time? What other existence could there be but this?

Names touched his mind, were his mind, existed with him, were part of him and then in no understandable way he saw them all, stretched out into eternity, probing, seeking, knowing. A great treadmill of thought: reaching out for tomorrow.

He stayed with them, certain that even this was better

than the void which, he knew, once entered he could never return from. At least here, there was tomorrow.

The baby's first cry was strong and fresh. Outside it was spring.

'What perfect blue eyes,' a nurse exclaimed.

'And his mother's perfect blonde hair,' added the doctor. 'In fact rather a perfect birth even if I say so myself.'

'You only delivered the child, Doctor, you're not the father.'

His eyes twinkled above the surgical mask. 'And where is that gentleman, may I ask? Fool he must be to desert such a ravishing creature – especially after spilling his seed into her and gaining an heir.'

'Hush!' the sister scolded. 'She'll hear.'

Jane Haversham moaned.

'You have a beautiful, perfect baby boy,' said the sister, coming close. 'Did you choose a name?'

'Adam,' she said, drowsily, and accepted the child.

Everyone smiled.